This first edition
is personally signed by the author:

TRADE SECRET

✳ **A New** ✳
Liaden Universe®
Novel

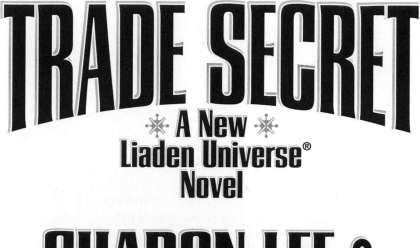

TRADE SECRET

❋ **A New** ❋
Liaden Universe®
Novel

SHARON LEE &
STEVE MILLER

A Baen Books Original

Baen Publishing Enterprises
P.O. Box 1403
Riverdale, NY 10471
www.baen.com

ISBN: 978-1-4516-3929-2
Limited Signed Edition ISBN: 978-1-4516-3930-8

Cover art by Sam Kennedy

First Baen printing, November 2013

Distributed by Simon & Schuster
1230 Avenue of the Americas
New York, NY 10020

Printed in the United States of America

10 9 8 7 6 5 4 3 2 1

TRADE SECRET

✳ A New ✳
Liaden Universe®
Novel

In a Familiar Space-Time Continuum,
Consider the Young Gentlemen

Stateroom Number Two

· · · ·✳· · · ·

Liaden Tradeship *Wynhael*, Outbound from Banth, a Backworld

THE DEBT BOOK WAS OUT and held before him, thirty-one prior pages covered in his cramped and careless hand. Although considered young by most of the society he ventured among, his debt book looked that of an old and garrulous fellow with multiple Balances in play. He'd learned early that Balance against those not properly of the society he walked among need not be counted, else the book might be full three times over, for he was never one to miss nor forgive a slight that might mean advantage for him, now or later. Still, if the book fell into nosy hands to be riffled—or through his untimely demise was passed on to one to complete—the pages already writ held among them the names of some of the cream of Liaden society, some in the person of individuals and others being named in line or clan as owing him. Of the Fifty High Houses of Liad, fully forty-one were directly represented, including, perhaps oddly, his own. This was not a book to be left idly about.

He brought the book to his table with the intent to write in it; then he'd placed it facedown, still sealed to his hand, while he'd allowed the ministrations of his lifelong lackey. Doubtless his man knew what the book was, doubtless he had some minor idea of what was to be written, and why.

He took stock. His nosebleed—acquired quite unexpectedly—had stopped. He'd removed his ruined overshirt. He was, if called upon by unfortunate circumstance, barely presentable to his mother after

1

she'd already seen his bloodied condition once. The damage done his *melant'i* needed urgent remedy, for she'd always had a long memory.

His face hurt, the headache still not gone since he'd refused the pain-saver he'd been offered as well as the wine.

He'd soon enough have wine, as soon as he felt his stomach proof against that surge of adrenal rage and fear and the distant iron of the blood in his mouth. In the moment he shivered in the dim safety of his stateroom, the words of his man reverberating:

"I am not a fully trained warrior, but it appears that if you'll be among the Terrans and the thieves, my lord, it would be best should you wear at least the web armor for the torso, if not also a stranded sleeve jacket and vest, which would have made your stand more feasible. We have packed such, though I dare say they're last year's fashion."

That had been sufficient for him to send the valet off to bring him a complete change of wardrobe, and the wine, asking it for a quarter bell, so he'd have time to write in his debt book.

Yes indeed, debt book. This occasion needed Balance, and more Balance, for not only had . . .

The sight was in his mind again, as were the words. He'd offered the Terran woman the opportunity to buy her beast-brother of a Gobelyn out of the Balance—a tidy profit it would have been at 400 cantra!—and after a hint of consideration she'd snubbed him, *him*, Rinork-to-be! Turned her back with a smirk and some snide words in Trade, and walked away . . .

Bar Jan chel'Gaibin's shiver again threatened to disgorge his meal and more: who'd have thought he'd ever be so close to death at the hands of an alien?

He'd reached to prevent her escape and his hand had barely been on her shoulder when she'd turned impossibly fast and struck him. Not a mere push away, not a shake-off, but a fully realized jaw-snapping strike to the face. He'd been flung off his feet by the force of the blow, vision gone to stars and darkness, not quite senseless but certainly defenseless.

As much as he might deny it, there'd been no way to rise and strike back with his fellows, for by the time his breath allowed sight again, his fellows were held at bay by her knife and the silent approbation of a roomful of Terrans. Animals they all were, and armed, too, with hands eager and draw-ready.

No, there could be no proper Balance there and then. Had he risen then the chance was his throat would have been cut. And the speed!

The woman Gobelyn had been permitted to escape, followed by his ignominious return to *Wynhael*, still leaning on the shoulder of a pilot, nose dripping trail of his disgrace. Then had come his mother's tongue and censure before the co-conspirators.

But the Terran woman . . .

Four hundred cantra! By stars he'd first thought she was going to pay or offer to deal! He could have used the cash—the number *had* twice measured a pressing debt. And then, the violence, so quick and sure. That kind of animal response was a danger. Surely then the plans they were laying were going to make space safer for Liadens. Surely the Terrans would be better off staying around their own uncultured worlds, with most traffic carried to civilized worlds elsewhere by Liadens and only the local traffic carried by Terran shuttles and ferries. Yet that happy result was not enough of a full Balance for one who'd struck him in the face and made him appear a weak fool . . .

Now, yes, he would write the debts owed out of this, Terran and Liaden. To have *Therinfel*'s own captain laugh at him, saying, "My lord, she's a pilot and you're not, and we could all see she's a bar fighter, which Rinork never allowed you. She had speed on you, and experience, and likely the muscle, too!"

There'd been amused agreement by the others as they'd hurried along, and then what he supposed now was actual advice and not a hidden slur:

"The only way for someone like *you* to take a chance like that with a pilot is from behind, and with a gun, and only a sure shot to the head. You pushed in front of other Terrans, and that's stupid—why that's full gravity fail, boy! Did no one ever explain to you that touching a Terran woman in public could cost you your throat? You're lucky she walked away and that no late lover took your kidneys out from behind."

· · · ✳ · · ·

In ordinary times Lord Rinork would have been sitting comfortable on Liad, overseeing the growing empire of ships and merchants amassed by his predecessors and especially by his mother, the delm. He should have been home on Liad, waiting *his turn* as delm, with perhaps the occasional off-world tour to show that he could in fact be a trader, and to enjoy the fruits of being one of the Fifty High Houses.

He'd already found being a lord among the Fifty convenient, for his mother or his *qe'andra* made sure his bills were paid if he happened to forget, and even when his bills were so very personal that they oughtn't be shared with others, he was never pushed or prodded by those he owed, for quartershare time came, and he always paid from the oldest to the newest—or loudest—first, eventually.

But in this time, being of the Fifty was not as convenient as it may have been, for the Terrans were encroaching on Liaden space lanes and trade zones, proving remarkably willing to take smaller profit and the worst of them *proud* to be planet-free. The most ambitious of them, though, were ambitious indeed, gathering together old technologies and hoping to leap far ahead of both Liad's fine ships and the combined might of the growing Combine. For all that their efforts were thought secret, they cost him money, unless of course such ships could be brought first to Rinork's hand.

On other fronts there was Korval, meddling as always, and then the constant bickering and begging of his mother's chosen partners and lackeys. Some were criminals if the news were out, and he supposed in passing that he need correct his man, for clearly when he'd warned of the need for armor among the "Terrans and the thieves" the thieves were the crew of the ships following his mother's plan, and his man Khana vo'Daran was in danger if anyone heard the clarity of his knowledge. His mother's plan, now, that he would not say was criminal, for the Terrans had no recognition among Liaden councils . . .

He sat now, thinking of luck and the fact that *he* was the Rinork heir and not that get of Quiptic . . . of the fact that the mines of Quiptic, which would be his soon enough and maybe sooner, and that he was far too old to be pleased to be called a boy, or have his shortcomings pointed out to him publicly, by anyone, pilot or not.

He had no misunderstanding: he was never, in fact, at his best in a fair fight unless that fight put him with dueling pistol in hand at a length of twenty or thirty paces. He was not fast, but that was not what dueling was about. Dueling took nerves—which he had—and accuracy, which he also had, especially given a chance to work with the house pistols, which would recognize his hand and engage auto-correction and target templating, the while passing for being old-fashioned. At no time would either pistol fire first for one not of proper blood.

This, of course, was not fair.

But he had no qualms about not being a fair fighter—the family history told the futility of "fair fights" as its shame ran through the rabbit's hutch! But who had understood that he'd personally have to right the wrongs foisted on him by an overconfident predecessor?

Obviously, the problems were many, and one of them that had now twice cost him dearly was lack of information. The other problems were proper Balances. So, the information situation could be dealt with by money spread wisely: this Gobelyn thing—the Jethri Gobelyn sucked into the rabbit's den for Balance, his kinswoman willing to slice a Liaden lord for him—this could not be left unsettled. Nor could the laughter of Liaden captains be left unanswered.

Bar Jan chel'Gaibin's debt book had fewer unused pages by the time valet Vo'daran returned with wine and new clothes. Given the views of the other conspirators, his mother the delm refused him another venture to the planet, and Rinork-to-be added plots to plots all night long.

Trade Hall, Cherdyan City, Verstal, on the Flinder-to-Liad Route

TRADER VEN'SAMBRA'S departing bows performed, the squarely turned back was an indication that the session was acknowledged as complete. That worthy continued to pull wares and bundles together, and finally departed, while the properly jeweled and name-badged Jethri ven'Deelin, recently adopted of Clan Ixin, checked files and waited respectfully to place the *returning for trade after break* sign until the visiting trader was actually gone from in front of his booth.

The booth was much like a market stall, the counter having tall wings or walls so that the action and conversation of the next booth were not shared—and so that the sight lines made it difficult for those behind the wait-here line to see or hear as well. Beyond the wing walls traffic might go forth at a steady and crowded pace as it had earlier, or be near nonexistent as it was now, without meaningfully affecting one's ability to trade in quiet confidence.

As for Trader Jethri, the sweat was receding, finally, and he'd deduced that it was not the stress of trade that was at fault, it was the leftover heat of the short walk from their local quarters to the hall, and the hall itself, conditioned as it was for the locals. He'd fiddled with the broad flat ring on his trade finger—sweat was under it and the ring was long enough with him to leave an impression.

On duty, at least, he was to wear the ring, though it was far, far from the Master's trade ring he longed to wear one day. The key around his neck—the Terran trade key—would serve the same purpose on a Terran world, but here, *Elthoria*'s trade budget had bought this modest ring of silver with four simple stone insets. He'd change the insets, one per trade world, until none were the current crystal quartz but were all changed to topaz, and from topaz, he'd move to garnet, and from garnet, to amethyst insets. The big move of course was the boldest: the large amethyst of the tested and confirmed Master Trader, in platinum or better. Today, though, he was the lowly floor trader, and he'd be glad to see the end of this day, and the packing to return to *Elthoria*'s splendid climate.

There'd been a short enough line when he opened for the day, one that had gotten shorter suddenly when the fourth in line, a graying Liaden gentleman of very unquiet demeanor, departed the area hastily after a semisuppressed bout of coughing, which cough had apparently unnerved the third in line, who'd gone off in the opposite direction—leaving a curiosity seeker first and Trader ven'Sambra second.

The curiosity seeker came to exchange cards, and to test Jethri's bows, in effect, for his offer to assist Jethri in learning basic trade concepts fell just short of a Balance-worthy insult. Jethri thanked his visitor, allowed as how he was trading only in tangible real goods for *Elthoria* and Clan Ixin, and looked forward to meeting again on the next voyage, should the trader have such goods to offer at that time.

Trader ven'Sambra's failed attempt at Terran required some soothing, and made Jethri wish he'd been back on *Elthoria*'s trade deck buying and selling bulk items and novelties from multirouted trade-sats and certified world-net screens instead of dealing with a slow man who sought to outwit the must-be-stupid Terran turned Ixin. What a world! He was beginning to hate it.

Sometimes, in truth, he hated being on any world. Despite all his time in the vineyards of Irikwae not a year before, Jethri couldn't admire the atmospherics here, where the water often hung so thick in the air that it obscured the vision, even at ground level. Yes, he'd seen rain and worse at Irikwae, but this morning it had taken him a full half-shift to get physically comfortable in his trading. The lunch chime's quiet vibration gave little joy and he decided that today he would pass on another visit to the famous restaurant row out of doors just two damp streets over in favor of a quiet lunch in the trade hall's own small but properly ventilated feedery.

The desk in front of him had been his for three days now, along with the chair, and at least that was comfortable, once adjusted. He'd gotten to think of the desk as much defense as a counter since this was the pushiest group of people he'd met at one place since he'd joined *Elthoria*'s crew aside those of Rinork.

Wasn't much choice here, though, since the locals all insisted on trading face-to-face and they were all full of formal types who couldn't be bothered to do anything without top-notch bowing and the longest sentences this side of a *melant'i* play, and then they insisted in ways he thought were entirely un-Liaden, being unsubtle at best.

And that wasn't fair. He almost grimaced—*Elthoria*'s comm crew had done him the dubious favor of sending along a copy of several reports on the arrival of *Elthoria* in Verstal's trading orbit, the information shared included the number of pods the ship carried, the recent routings, the names of captains, sub-captains, and traders, and anticipated destinations along with his own name and extremely modest biography among the more interesting tidbits.

He kept the twitch away from his lips: he'd thought perhaps he should send a copy on to Khat and to Miandra—but Khat might not get the Liaden part of it, and Miandra would get it only too well, embroiled as she was with issues of *melant'i* and power in her *dramliz* training. It was just that he was named as the new associate trader on the ship, and it was mentioned he was a newly adopted son of the house with specialties including textiles and trade in Terran regions. That was a kind of gossipy thing traders might need to know—but somewhere along the way the information that he formerly shipped as an apprentice on the Terran trade-certified *Gobelyn's Market* had dropped into the news.

His first two days at trade here had been spent as much dealing with the curious and the tricky as with honest traders—often by himself—since the Master Trader was in heavy talks on a deal that might keep the clan's ships busy for years.

The trade hall was grown somewhat quieter than it had been earlier; and Jethri again caught sight of the gray-haired fellow who'd abandoned line with the coughs. He'd been in and out of sight while Trader ven'Sambra had been the only one in line, sometimes peering at the rotating display screens on the ships-in wall and other times standing back near an exit—and now he approached!

Jethri scooped the TAKING A BREAK sign into place, but he was, just perhaps, too late, as the man actually rushed toward him, urgency unreasonably plain upon his face.

The bow was startling, offering to Jethri as it did honor due to a master of trade with decades of experience, and the undertone of appeasement indicating that one understood he was treading on the goodwill of another by merely appearing in front of him in an untimely way.

Three steps away from the counter he'd stopped; awaiting permission, and it was Jethri's curiosity which drove him to bow at all, using the merest of acknowledgments, thus accepting the honors heaped upon himself!

A good trader might have hesitated to come close to the counter with receipt of such a bow, but this man closed to the trading counter immediately, offering yet another effusive bow, and too, bringing with him the mixed scents of recent alcohol and oily foods, and perhaps of *vya* as well.

"Honored Trader, my certifications, if I may. You will understand that I am largely retired from trade but seeing the news of *Elthoria*'s arrival, and your own, I thought we should both profit greatly from some odds and ends of interest to collectors and specialists, which I have possessed from my own trading years gone by."

They traded names then, Jethri adding Gobelyn with his clan name, and then he dutifully glanced at the material presented, his own *melant'i* being certified by his seat in the hall as well as by his ring and his clan signs.

The trader's *certifications* were worn, and local, and showed a penchant for foods and kitchen goods. The local license typography was awkward to read, and the dates—well, some were older than Jethri. Likely this man, this Trader tel'Linden, had never been off-world, had only dealt in the local markets. His manner was unpolished and . . .

As if reading Jethri's careful study as concern, the man broke rapidly into a locally accented Liaden rush of words.

"I have always been a man of modest means, dealing with modest items, Trader, yet one in my position has been favored over the years to have seen many items of rarity and worth, the small riches of the clans and lines not of the High Houses, and some not of the Mid Houses. These riches I have accumulated as I may, of interest to myself. The research to make use of these, and to find the proper home and buyer, this has been difficult, and it comes time now to reduce my private collections and give back to my clan my investments, as well as give to the universe of buyers goods which are outside the standard trade lines of my clan."

The trader paused then, stood straighter, and bowed his best bow yet, with a reasonable flourish and an understanding that his sleeves were not long enough to give emphasis . . .

"If you will honor me with a gift of time I believe I have trades that will be worth the time we both invest, and yours, star-trader, much more than myself! Understand me, this is not my catalog, but my stock!"

The man raised his large leather-look trade case, withdrew keys from an inner pocket, eyes intent on Jethri's reaction.

"There is a seat you may use," Jethri admitted, "if you would care to join in an exploration of our trading possibilities."

• • • * • • •

The trader's portfolio, lined as it was with sheets of impossibly thin black leather, was itself an item Jethri might like, but the first object revealed, gaudy and antique at once, left him speechless.

He turned his hand over to palm up—a request to hold the item— and wished Paitor was here to see this, or Dyk, who would have wildly differing opinions on the desirability of possessing such a thing. Dyk would love it for incongruity, and Paitor . . . well, what would Paitor actually *say* about such a ring as this?

"Yes," the trader crooned, "this is an object one might wear in many places, secure that it would be noticed and appreciated. The stone, of course, is flawless, and the setting is true multi-banded flash-formed Triluxian!"

The ring was deposited oh-so-gently in Jethri's hand for inspection. After a moment he sighed, looking at it from this way and that—and requested, with a bow, "May I use my handscan for a closer look?"

Triluxian—bonded of microlayered titanium, gold, platinum, with a salting of rhodium—was not something to be ignored. The style of the thing suggested it was a very old ring, and the slight signs of wear suggested it was an artifact someone had actually used—which is to say, displayed on their hand in public—frequently. Thus the scanner, looking for details, and giving back the certifiable purity of the finding. There was value here, but not riches.

As for the stone—he held back a chuckle mightily. Firegem, yes, truly a flawless firegem, but for the worth of it in any state . . . it was a fluted cabochon firegem, which made it odd, but other than that? What it was doing set in—

"Of course," said the trader, though his face tensed enough for Jethri to see it. "You'll find some odd lettering, I believe . . ."

Handscan again. Jethri studied the band of the thing, and indeed, there was odd lettering, which likely appeared even odder to the trader for it being Terran lettering, and very tiny. Perhaps it was someone's name, perhaps there was also a date, Cobol 426 . . . he let the scanner record the thing to look at later. Might as well set blast glass in the thing as a firegem, unless it dated to the original discovery of the things, or was the first . . .

"An extremely unusual item," Jethri admitted, allowing the trader to have the ring back. The ring must be more than it looked . . . else a story worth sharing if it could found.

The trader flipped to the next display page.

There, a simple sheet of metal with rolled edges, almost like one of Dyk's small cooking pans upside down, with diagrammatic instructions inscribed on it, and a few words in oddly stilted Liaden. Instructions for what? Might be of interest to a specialist but didn't touch him very much . . .

A twitch of fingers—within the sheets, for there were two of them interlocking, were fractins.

Fractins. Four of them. Fakes, he thought, just looking and needing no scanner to vet them. The color was—not right. The man's hands shook. As common as these were in Terran space, on this side of the trade line they were deemed Old Tech, and thus contraband, and unmarketable in the bargain. Of course, if they were fakes they might not be illegal—he hadn't got to that section of Liaden trade laws yet, and would have to study,

As noncommittally as possible, he flicked fingers, and there were three more fractins, fitted together, and they were real. They were not only real, they knew he was there, he was sure, knew that they were recognized as real, knew—it was as if they called for him to buy them and take them away.

He blinked. He'd had that reaction several times as a child, the feeling that real fractins looked back at him. He'd *liked* his own fractin, and was always glad it was his lucky piece; he'd been convinced that his fractin *liked* him, too. When Arin, his father, had talked with him about his fractin collections, he'd never doubted Jethri when Jethri could point to his own fractin amidst a score of true-and-fake fractins. Arin hadn't argued, either, when they'd built the fractin frames and Jethri'd insisted that his fractin wasn't comfortable with being put in with the others in this order, but must be in that order or in this position . . .

Jethri realized that he'd taken several seconds too long this time, that he could still feel the fractins calling, even though he knew he shouldn't—no, *couldn't*—be found in possession of them. So he permitted himself a slight grimace, as if disinterested, or perhaps bored by seeing more of the same . . . and flicked his fingers.

And next was another of the curious pans, with a mark he recognized: *this side down.*

Struck by an idea, and still feeling the call of fractins, he could see the outline of the pan in the leather sheet; saw what might be alignment points, judged that if filled with properly aligned fractins . . .

He flicked fingers, to find the next sheet of leather to be pocketed, with nine pockets, and in each pocket showed a portion of similar but not identical . . . things. Devices. Kahjets. They were built on the scale and size of the weather device he'd handled to such strange effect on Irikwae, a device that called an unseasonable wind-twist to the vineyards and indirectly led to Miandra's banishment to Liad. These, too, felt like they were interested, as if they recognized hands that knew . . .

He flicked his glance to the man's face, where there was now sweat.

Jethri realized the trader was at risk and his own *melant'i* as well. He had not, of course, promised to the Scouts he would unmask other owners . . .

"Not these machines, Trader, nor others like them if there are more in your stock; I have clear instructions about such."

The trader's eyes got big and his hands shook. He glanced down, looked up, hopeful.

"Yet these will be treasures, I understand, in Terran markets. These are . . ."

Jethri offered a placating motion and conciliatory bow.

"Alas, as you may not know, given the circumstance of your retirement, my ship aims for no such market in this voyage, Trader, and I am not of an age or *melant'i* to carry devices such as this aboard my ship, nor to secure them, against the hope that sometime I might visit a Terran port. Show me other things, if you have them, since we are here, and you have sought me out."

The trader, crestfallen, flipped past two more sheets, and now there were other oddities, more than a dozen keys in the style used by Terran ships on one of the sheets, and a trade calendar on a flexible sheet, some two hundred standards old, with illustrations of—of star systems.

Practicality and necessity warred—lunch and a rest break called, even more so since he knew that the trader was offering contraband amidst this trade lot.

"Against time we run," Jethri said emulating one of Norn ven'Deelin's phrases. "Let us proceed with pace," he suggested—and there, the next page was shown, a very, very skinny, blade looking perhaps Terran, and *flick*—

A page passed over, and another, and then a small flat guidebook, with real pages, the title, in Liaden: *Dealing with Terrans*. He signaled stop, requested and received the opportunity to look at it. The book was of the age as the trade calendars, and produced by a trade station he'd never heard of, offering hints on language and demeanor, and showing known and anticipated trade routes . . .

"Enough," he said, entranced. "My time presses. Price me this, the two shipping plates and the calendars, as a unit. Also, the firegem ring, which is interesting, but hardly a rarity in these days, if ever it was. Honest price gets honest return."

"Trader, I'd hoped to sell the lot—"

"I hear this from your lips, Trader, but from mine you have heard I will not touch the items from the old machines, nor will I have the squares such as I had as a child for toys."

"Four cantra for the whole I was asking . . ."

Jethri bowed from his seat and stood.

"I'll not have the whole. The partial lot I have outlined only. Only the items, with the firegem—altogether an eighth-cantra, paid now. I cannot use the others and there's no market to test their value or their worth."

There was nothing in the broke-lot that he knew he could sell, but for his own uses, say the information that such concentrations of Old-Tech might exist among the Liadens—that was worth much—and the old trade route information. He'd had the same feeling when he'd discovered the *vya* that had gone to pay for the *Market*'s overhaul. Even the firegem, silly as it was . . .

The man before him began to fold his sales portfolio sadly and ventured, "One half-cantra, Trader, and you break my back at that."

Jethri worked the feeling in his head, remembered Paitor's earnest lessons of give-and-take . . .

"I have the eighth cantra in my pocket for you, and some Terran funds, ten kais. Also, paying cash we need not use the hall's sales registry nor fund transfers. Else, my meeting awaits. Understand, paying cash, I will forget your name."

Jethri handed the trade case back, very concerned. Not about his offer, but about the contents that called to him and made his hands itch to hold them and have them and use them.

The trader's eyes were large. Jerhri'd not meant to threaten, but now he could see the man before him losing composure. Surely, then, he was a desperate man, even more desperate than Jethri.

The man's hands were shaking, but he was already reopening his portfolio. "Done."

As the transaction settled, it turned out that the Terran coins broke to fifteen rather than ten kais, which Jethri allowed without hesitation. Now his urge was to be away from this man and his ragged breathing . . .

The trader gone, Jethri slammed the sign onto the table, tucked his haul into his cloak's storage pockets. He realized he was shivering now, and wondered what he'd done to suddenly feel so cold.

Those kahjets! Not toys, not toys, not toys. Paitor would have perhaps denounced the man, and perhaps Grig would have bought it all . . .

It would not do to dine, even alone, while still so unsettled.

Succor was to hand after a dizzying riot of panic, which he knew he must not succumb to, and then a reminder that some called trade "the quiet war."

With the aid of one of Pen Rel's warrior tricks of centering, he let the hard floor be his base, let the world of breathing be his focus, closed his eyes for a moment to visualize the coming reality of the big ring, firmly on his hand, and he a trader of competence, and hurried for his break. With luck, tomorrow he'd sleep on *Elthoria*!

Chapter One

. . . ·✳· . . .

Clan Ixin's Tradeship *Elthoria*, in Jump

JETHRI SETTLED HIMSELF at his personal desk, breakfast a comfortable fullness. His standard-G weight was easy on him these days, even if that meant his attempted left-side braid tickled his forehead when he moved his head.

As he was no pilot, the longer trader-style hair was something he'd been reaching for ever since his ship-cut, lovingly fashioned by Dyk into Jethri's signature hairsculpt, had been denounced during his first planetside training. Planetdwellers, he was informed, were often put off by the shave-head designs of shipfolk.

He swiped the growing hair back carelessly, the triple topaz of his ring catching light that the crystal let through. He leaned on his left-side armrest despite his best effort to break the habit. Maybe all right-handed loopers did it, but his time at stinks patrol had shown him that his relatives on *Gobelyn's Market* surely had the habit and he'd been busily trying to erase such Terran tendencies in favor of Liaden—or at least Liaden ship-style—balance. Maybe if he could sit straight the lengthening hair wouldn't tickle so much.

Around him the room was both cabin and office, his bed hidden now by the drop down research screen. His chair was a hybrid, an oversized trade-deck extra fitted with the normal connections for a working trader as well as a student's amplified speakers and note takers. All in all, it was the best study spot he'd ever had, though at times he missed the social contact of the library and took sessions there or in the staff room.

Despite the ship dropping out—and then back in—to Jump, yesterday had been one of those social contact days, spent between the library, the staff room, the cafeteria, and the exercise courts where he struggled with the intricacies of *menfri'at*, the Liaden martial arts the arms master worked hard to teach him, as well as with the weight machines and other exercise devices, since he'd been needing to be "world-worthy" as Pen Rel put it—a level of planetary physical readiness many spacers lost over time. He was to be dealing with traders and social necessities and ought not appear—or be!—as weak as an elder if it could be avoided.

Being on rush-learning, there were some ordinary things he did not do on his social days yet—like join in ship committee event planning—which had taken his hoped-for lunch with Gaenor off the schedule since she was, of course, much involved in such. They still copracticed their Liaden and Terran together, but walking the ship at odd moments, throwing words and ideas at each other as they talked was even more a part of that duty than it had been; certainly it would be good to have some quiet time together once in a while.

Yesterday was day three of his five-day regime, and the fact that *Elthoria* had "stopped" at a star they'd barely seen mattered little. Khat would have called what they did a skate-by—the primary was so distant from the pickup point that its light took several Standard Hours to get there—and what they did was all piloting: drop off two pods of supplies and equipment and pick up two pods of compressed and freeze-dried seaweed. None of this had impinged on his duties or schedule other than to inform his current search for the rules of delivery with a little more poignancy since there'd been threat of a glitch that might have delayed them for days.

Some few of *Elthoria*'s crew had taken advantage of the two, brief, late-night orbits around Thringar Six to claim a world by going to the observation deck and eyeballing it through the ports . . . but he never claimed a world he hadn't at least landed on, else he'd have as many as anyone on the ship—captain included—but yes, starting a tour when he was just starting to breathe gave him leverage over folks who'd grown up planet side in good Liaden homes!

Near as he could understand, Thringar Six was a biggish mush of a semihabitable planet with a few thousand workers and a bunch of sea grass and not much else, all around a biggish star that was going to go nova sometime in the next few million years. He hadn't been needed at the trade desk for that, nor in the control room, and he'd slept through the Jump out two hours before his rising time.

So today was a physical rest day, but as busy or busier, on the whole, for today he was his own boss, and a tough one, having waked before the subtle morning shift chime, and been in the breakfast lounge before the tea changed from night-strong to ordinary.

Study and thought, that was the day's job today. The topic was contracts, and he'd been in the same line of study for some while now, since he wouldn't always be able to access the sharp memory of Norn ven'Deelin while he was away from the ship, and he'd be liable for what mistakes he brought back with his name signed in agreement— and both she and the clan—would have to back him up.

Contracts were pretty important. After all it had been a fraudulent contract—in the form of a fake Liaden Master Trader's card vouchsafed as firm commitment on a short-term deal—that had brought Jethri to this Liaden tradeship in the first place.

Contract terminology, now, that was difficult stuff, with the caveat that most of it he was dealing with was Liaden to begin with, and defined over the generations by both force of custom and the sharp eyes and minds of the *qe'andra*.

Words were not to be played idly in the game of trade, and since he was studying to be a specialist like none before him, intensive lessons in Liaden were backed up by heavy reading and study in Terran as well. Who knew there were so many business-essential words that shipfolk never used, never spoke, never even thought?

Birthright.

Jethri'd come across the term most recently in a contract from a Terran world, one allowing heirs and assigns certain rights and duties . . . and now he'd set the search going in the Liaden-centered computer, trying to see what the comparisons were. Being born to a family was enough to guarantee all kinds of things on some worlds—Terran worlds, especially—and aboard some ships, but in Liaden space, it was the delm who ultimately determined what a person owned or could own, down to being denied any part in a clan.

Well, there—he needed to know, as a trader, how often such things might be encountered. He . . . well, as a Terran spacer he'd inherited some stuff from his father and he'd owned some stuff on his own as a kid, things given him by his father.

That must have been birthright, because not even the ship's captain—his mother—would deny it to him now. A couple pieces of jewelry, some fractins all collected now by the Scout, a book—his "logbook" where as a child he'd sat beside his father, Arin Gobelyn, whole shifts at a time, creating routes and manifests for trips he'd make when he was a pilot or Combine trader on the Market.

He sighed, for he was still no pilot, and his mother had stolen the book away when his father died, and hid it, and so pre-told the true tale that he was never to be welcome as full-fledged crew there on *Gobelyn's Market*, name or no, birthright or not.

The family stuff, personal family stuff, he tried to shove that back into the receding mental cubby that was Jethri Gobelyn, since here on *Elthoria* he was Jethri the trader, son of the trader, ven'Deelin the family name, Ixin the clan.

Study and thought, that was the day, and that was fine.

In fact, the day was going well, which was what he'd come to expect when it came to dealing with tradeship *Elthoria*. Very few things caused a stir, very rare was a raised voice or a ruffled demeanor, very unusual indeed was there anything deemed urgent.

Jethri admired this stability in a ship, having come from a ship which aspired to ordinary but whose days had been punctuated by angry outbursts and whimsical orders, and an overdose of what his cousin Dyk had labeled "Jethri do."

There was, of course, quite a difference between the driving forces behind the ship *Elthoria* and the ship *Gobelyn's Market*. On the *Market* the driving force was the captain, who'd also been his mother until bare months before when he'd discovered the awkward truth. On *Elthoria*. the driving force was Norn ven'Deelin, who had been his rescue as a Master Trader and had become his new mother, and behind her was a clan at least as old and as proud as the Gobelyns.

Even granting different base cultures, which Jethri was more than willing to do, the ships were more different than many of his current crew mates would imagine, for they—everyone besides him, that is— had someplace to call home that was not *Elthoria*. Not just a posting or a position or a job or a berth, but a *home*, a planetside building, mostly with roof and windows and a view at least of the underside of a sky.

As for Jethri, he'd grown up on *Gobelyn's Market*—it had been his home until the strange series of events that had brought him to Trader ven'Deelin's office in what was to him, just another port. By then Iza had already given notice that his home ship couldn't house him any longer. He'd become too much an extra hand, too much a reminder of agreements and perhaps even of passion that had passed years before with the death of his father, Arin.

Technically, of course, he had a home now—which would be the distant Clan Ixin clanhouse he'd yet to enter, but inside, in his thoughts, he couldn't call it home anymore than he could call himself Liaden, though his demeanor, his clothes, his title, and his trade-ring all screamed Liaden to unknowing dirtsiders who met him in the rounds of business.

But there, his mother was not his mother, his ship was not his home, his clan was not his family . . . and only some of his family was family by blood and genes.

What had he got from being born? Birthright?

What was that exactly? The blood and genes of his father, and a few odd ends that had belonged to his father, and that in the aftermath of his father's death had, in a roundabout way, been ceded to him.

Oh, the other thing that might be his birthright as Jethri Gobelyn? His father's relatives. They were still relatives as Terrans saw relations, and when thought on properly, they were something strange. What that meant for him, well, that was something Jethri, trader and changeling, would have to decide.

He waved his hands at the keyboard, bringing his research screens to life, and lighting the reminders pad.

He grimaced, then worked to erase that unfortunate expression from his face.

Liadens rarely showed what they thought in their faces if they could avoid it, and he thought it one of the reasons that adult Terrans looked older than adult Liadens. Frown lines, and smile lines, too, were far less obvious on a Liaden face. To Liadens, most expressions were unfortunate, unless shared with a family member or a special, rare intimate.

His manners tutor worked with him diligently on such points, and with a deep breath he relaxed both his face and his shoulders, lifting his elbow from the resting place that would, he knew, have a lasting impression from his time on the ship. He'd seen armrests on the *Market* marked with sweat and wear of decades, and had more than once as a child been accused of shirking his duties because of that Terran habit.

Still, the reason for the grimace was not as easy to disappear from in front of his eyes as his face was to set bland: overdue correspondence, necessary action.

He reviewed the list, knowing he was being hard on himself. Not all of the list was overdue, for many of items were voluntary. It was just that in the flow of his days, he'd not had time to focus on letters to Meicha and Miandra, nor to decide why he felt guilty about having more to say to one than the other, twin empaths that they were. Twins he'd known about before meeting the girls, but empath had been something new. Then there'd been the discovery that, twins or not, the girls were hardly interchangeable. Even with them knowing what he was thinking and knowing what each other was doing, they weren't the same person and had different goals . . .

Letters would be hard—he sometimes wished there was some way he could just hold hands with both of them and let them know that way what he felt.

Nor had he managed to work out what he wanted to say to Khat in a letter to her that might be as well said in a broadcast letter to the whole of the *Market*, but he felt that he had some slight reticence to share some things with the crew entire, as he had some things more personal, more intimate for Khat than the whole of the crew. For all that she'd taken on full adult status and certainly had cares of her own, she'd often been the easiest for him to talk to.

More pressing was the correspondence he owed to his single business partner, and that had been more getting difficult as the distance between them and the time between infoshares had grown. In hopeful theory—if the minute details could be worked out, if the language could be made dense enough and stealthy enough and, face it, Liaden-tricky enough—Tan Sim might soon be employed as an associate trader on *Elthoria*.

It was a bold idea, given the enmity between Ixin and Rinork, and it had been Jethri's innocent question about the propriety of him, an apprentice trader, hiring Tan Sim, a full trader, as an assistant that had begun the entire project. His mother had smiled at the idea at first, seeing it both an amusing and a confounding idea since it would of course be a Balance game of sorts, a winning of *melant'i* for both Jethri and Ixin, if Rinork's best young trader could be willfully brought to serve with Jethri at Jethri's behest.

Ixin's needs were not simple in the situation, though, since a straight buyout from Rinork was unlikely, given the spite that had placed Tan Sim under the contract carrying him away from *Wynhael*, Rinork, and Rinork-to-be.

The point of that contract had been to punish Tan Sim for his insolence, to place him in an isolated position on a ship not of Rinork where Rinork could still publicly claim he'd been given responsibility and opportunity.

The sense Jethri'd made of the contract, and the one taken by Norn ven'Deelin as well, was that the lad was meant to fail miserably. The ship's route was such to make speculative trading difficult at best, and the ship's owner and captain one with little enough capital. Indeed, it appeared that Rinork's part was to sell the contract at an absurdly low price, place Tan Sim on a route with diminishing returns so that one might point to slow genes perhaps and his father's failure, and then to crush him by disallowing his escape from the contract.

To the few Liadens Jethri could discuss it with, it appeared a slow death sentence, the assumption of failure and disgrace meaning that a dutiful child would do away with himself rather than embarrass the clan. To Jethri, that—at first sight—looked like a good reason to jump ship. On consideration, since he'd been reading among the Code and histories, Jethri knew that wasn't likely and so they'd needed another way.

Tan Sim's part in the whole was tricky: in theory he oughtn't be party to contravening his delm's will. If he'd been Terran there might have been cause for him to right the wrong as son of a swindle victim, but as Liaden that was an awkward idea—the *melant'i* of it failing several tests and passing several others. But for Jethri, having been threatened by Bar Jan and falsely accused of assault, there, *there* could be Balance, and with Jethri having—however casually it had been done—put himself in Tan Sim's debt, yes, there could be an exquisite Balance worthy of the playhouse.

Given Norn's own willingness to pursue that Balance, they'd put in motion an enormously complex set of subtle negotiations. What was necessary was to find a third party to transfer Tan Sim's contract away from the ship Rinork had sold him to, and then to transfer the allegiance of the third party and the contract in a way that *Elthoria* and Ixin would have benefit of the trader and his presence without an openly slap-face insult. Subtle insult, now, that was fine and more than fine, and was surely part of the equation.

The thing was that Jethri wasn't permitted to talk about any of that in a letter for security reasons, to explain things, and as a result Tan Sim was feeling left out, worse so since there'd been some issues with more of their salvage cargo being impounded by the Scouts than originally expected, and Tan Sim feeling the blame. When exactly Tan Sim might escape, that had Jethri depressed. Norn had said she was willing to let it go a dozen Standards if need be!

Well, Balance was like that for Liadens, but Jethri didn't need to like it. Easy enough to put off the communication another planetfall or two, or until the end of the route, if need be.

So, next on the list was Terran trade, adjusting a Terran ten-year key to a Liaden ship's data structure wasn't simple and the thing would have to be done, yessir, for he wasn't going to give up his status with them and no one on the worlds he'd been on was willing to press the launch button on his suggestions for how to make it work.

And too, he ought to have been more forward with writing his note to Scout ter'Astin. True, he was still much more than merely peeved with the whole of the Scout organization for their grab for his book and fractins and all the things that had been his by birth . . . and that . . . he sighed, still not having activated a single writing file.

His tutor wanted him to understand Balance, the subtle flow of things like honor and necessity that were the underpinnings of Liaden society, in particular that all-powerful *melant'i*—that concept that had, on the execution of a single bow, led to a simple Terran apprentice trader candidate becoming the appointed son of Clan Ixin.

If he were to be Jethri ven'Deelin in face and action, he must permit the Scouts their madness. The original Jethri Gobelyn, apprentice trader—that young man might have easily died at the hands of offended Liadens several times now.

A collection of breath, a move to research, since clearly he still was not up to correspondence.

In the back of his mind was the knowledge that Balance was still possible. Yes, Balance, both by him, and by those who thought his mere existence an affront worth murder. The Scouts . . . not all the Scouts deserved Balance, but some did. Not all Liadens, but some. He had much to learn.

With a sigh, Jethri brought the comparative contracts part of the day's study live, with the Terran, Trade, and Liaden standard and legal dictionaries tabbed along with *Traders Guild Concise Guidebook of Common Contracts*. He laughed gently—he'd miss-called it the *Guidebook of Common Conflicts* to the librarian . . . who'd known exactly what he'd meant.

Pressing the incoming mail button to hold, he stared straight ahead, and said, "Go."

Taking Delivery was the topic he was starting with today. Lunch, four hours away, was his goal.

Chapter Two

· · · ·❊· · · ·

Clan Ixin's Tradeship *Elthoria*, in Jump

DELIVERY WAS NOT SO MUCH the successful unloading of a ship at a specific place as it was a state of ecstasy achieved when—and if—a signature of acceptance and a signature of release of invoiced goods in good order as agreed (with exceptions noted and countersigned) could be affixed to the same document (in both hardcopy and electronic format, preferably) without reservation.

Jethri pressed on. Some things were not as obvious as they appeared.

The fact that stuff was dumped at a dock was good enough in some places—by deep mud he'd seen it himself with Paitor and Dyk shoving a last lonely plascrate of a make-weight shipment of protein flour into the dust at Marrakesh, the ship's ventilation working so hard it sounded like they had drifted too close to a star instead of landed on a habited world. In some places, it took multiple vid-captures, signatures on five lines of paper and stick-seals, ribbons, stamps, customs clips and . . . and . . .

Ownership of goods changed at different times and different places, too. Sometimes, the book warned, things were sold that weren't owned—and so one needed to have financial recourse available, which varied by trade guild as well as by system, and even by planet and sometimes depending where on a planet . . .

Recourse for goods being mishandled varied. In Liaden-run systems, the Code and its spin-offs were guides, but guides only,

25

dealing with reputable people was especially important with Liadens because *melant'i* was serious stuff with them. In other places . . .

Jethri routed the recourse stuff away to his notes: more of the legal stuff he wasn't exactly keen on. On non-Liaden worlds—which meant Terran mostly—there might be other things to do, other legal remedies and other legal requirements. He read on, skimming, knowing he'd have to come back and knowing that if he ever had his own ship he'd employ himself a law-jaw or an assistant who had that training, at least. Skimming, *Terran basis shipping law special actions . . . See Writ of Completion, Writ of Garnishment, Writ of Safe Passage, Writ of Progression, Writ of Replevin, Writ of Certiorari* . . . and back to normal trade without problems . . .

Right. The proper bow of acknowledgment was the final finish on some ports, while in point of fact, in some delivery situations getting off-port without being fired on seemed to do the trick.

He bowed a bow—a bow of acknowledgment—and the snap of his wrist startled him. He really needed to move more.

Jethri let his mind focus and took delivery of the message that, yes, once again he'd let the words catch him, and the concepts, and he'd gone an extra hour. He, at least, was not on a firm food schedule at the cafeteria this day, but his stomach was growling and he really should see if the rest of the universe existed. His stomach growled again. More than once Paitor had explained to him the difference between proper study and too much study, especially if he forwent stinks duty for it. He knew he really should take a break, get lunch . . .

Pushing away from the desk he stood, immediately dropping into one of the static defense poses he was learning, and followed that with a whirling countermove that left the snapping sounds of stiff muscles bouncing in the air for longer than he liked. The yawn came unbidden, and unwanted. He was, he knew, to exorcise that particular habit from anything but intentional use, just as he was to unship his basic comfortable and agreeable face for the noncommittal and boring trade face of the professional.

He tried that, and felt the jaw muscle give a small complaint. At least it didn't pop as loud as his wrist. He had been trying to use some of the defense moves and relaxes while he worked, at the Master Trader's suggestion, and found that, yes, he was not as tired as he well might be.

Time being what it was, he left the in-mail button off, and jogged toward food.

· · · ⁑ · · ·

Jethri was, as he expected, between shifts, the main-shift tables nearly empty and the premades looking few and far between. *Elthoria* was a large ship, though, especially to someone raised on a family-sized ship like the *Market* and there was almost always something fresh to grab. In his honor there was now a working supply of *'mite* available and he'd from time to time seen others availing themselves of it, if gingerly. He suspected that for some it was a dare—but at least one of the engine room crew seemed genuinely fond of it as a start to his off-day—perhaps he used it as a hangover cure.

Whatever the cause for it being there, Jethri went for the 'mite first, the first gulp or two of the tangy drink quelling the worst of his stomach rumbles before he set off a vibration detector. Then to the covered dishes, where he found two wrapped handwiches and a plate of mixed frosted *chernubia* and headed toward seats while grabbing a large mug of cold tea . . .

One small table was crowded with three maintenance uniforms laughing over something, while at another table there was the back of someone in a head covering he didn't quite place . . .

A hand motion caught his attention, and there was Gaenor making it, a hesitant half-smile on her face as she looked up from beneath a scarf made to look like the head of a bird. She was wearing one of the more formal versions of her uniform, in a brave red that could mislead an untrained Terran shipmate to thinking it emergency crew rigging. He liked the style particularly since the deep square neckline showed off skin as well the necklace she so often wore . . . but this time, that too was not the family seal but another bird.

She bowed a polite invitation, which made the birdface eyes come to him, and he juggled food and drink to take the seat close beside her since there was a pile of stuff on the other seats as well as on the table across from her. In front of her was a comm pad—with an image of birds on it. There was, staring at him from the place setting opposite, some creature with big eyes and facial side-tufts, also on a scarf like she was wearing and . . .

Her smile got wider with his bow of acceptance, which technically he should have given before sitting but he'd been concerned with dropping food unceremoniously to the floor, which impropriety he'd committed several times in the early days of his sojourn on *Elthoria*, always with the largest possible audience. He wasn't a pilot, for all he knew his basic boards, and while his ongoing conversion to Liaden gentleman had helped him learn some measure of grace, he still felt awkward in front of some people, Gaenor—*Elthoria*'s first mate—particularly among them.

The smile got tentative again as she reached for her tea after nodding to his bow.

"And so you have managed to find me here still, my friend. Is this an accident, I wonder?"

His hands were unwrapping the first handwich with alacrity, but he caught an extra note of question, glanced up to see Gaenor's glance go from him to her cup. He followed the glance, to her hands around the cup, and on both of them were also birds—and her clan sigil which was a geometric representation of three cut jewels, red, green, and blue.

Knowing her comfortably enough to enjoy some leeway in his manners, he finished his 'mite while he measured his actions and he fell into the mode they used so often, he speaking Liaden, with Trade to fill in the words he was unsure of, since she'd already spoken in Terran.

"I suppose it is an accident I got hungry and didn't have rations to hand. Have I missed an order or forgotten an occasion, I wonder?"

Learned from him, she shook her head Terran-style, but the tension around her smile relaxed somewhat.

"I think, Jethri, that what you have done is worked without reference to the rest of the universe today."

He felt his face warm, and cup in one hand and handwich in the other he bowed acknowledgment, dipping his head slightly and letting the dip turn into a nod.

"That's true. I am learning the meaning of 'delivery.' It is not as easy as it seems."

Comprehension in her eyes, and a sigh, with a slight grin.

"The trade terms, they are like pilot terms. They mean exactnesses, don't they? I have had the short course on such things, but I am not a trader, nor aspire to be one."

He laughed with a nod. "And I aspire to be one, one day when the rules and laws let me do the job instead of stand in the way . . ."

"So, without the news, you could not see that Vil Tor and I today for the main midday mess gave a . . . a demonstration . . . of some of the ideas for the dressing of us the crew and of the ship's common area for the travel party, the ship's Festival we shall have between Lastovan and Taluda. We together looked for you with interest."

As she spoke Gaenor's face showed an unexpectedly impish expression. She looked at him sidewise as she dipped her head a little, and then she reached up to the scarf, crossing hands to bring the sides together under her chin, and mischievously drew those hands tightly down across the chain and bird of her necklace, stretching the fabric of her blouse downward dangerously, seductively.

By main force Jethri kept his lips together and targeted his eyes relatively safely, the pink of blush slowly rising up the back of his neck and under his chin.

Breaking custom, he fell back into Terran for safety.

"*Elthoria* will have a ship's Festival?" he managed, the while watching as Gaenor's clever hands tied a knot into the end of the scarf, drawing it and her hands somewhat recklessly lower and tighter. The sidewise look, and a touch of tongue between her lips making him draw in his breath slightly he felt the blush fade for something else, for now her eyes were on his, searching, and he wasn't sure he knew the words in Terran, either.

The fabric of her blouse slowly rebounded as her hands pulled the scarf knot down, down to perhaps her waist or belly button, and she stretching her shoulders.

Her eyes were still on him. Jethri knew only one other Liaden woman who'd had shared that look for him, and that woman had been drinking, and openly inviting his company as a bed partner . . .

"Yes, since the ship has no matching Liaden port time soon with a planetary Festival, certainly not in the next Standard, the crew has gotten permission from captain and Master Trader, for a small Festival, of ten shifts. There will be food and singing, a hall parade, perhaps, and . . . and wine and liquor and other inebriants and even all-shift Festival tents or playrooms!

"Since the ship is doing well, Ixin will be sponsor. Each of the department heads will host or co-host a party, and some will gamble and some will music and dancing and contests of . . . accomplishments."

Inebriants and Festival tents? Accomplishments? *All-shift tents*? It sounded like a shivaree to make a Terran gathering proud . . .

"Vil Tor and me," she said, touching herself in that valley between her breasts, "we are of the leaders of the committee with arrangements. The ideas, we wished to discuss with you, and perhaps . . . a party with your stamp upon it."

"I didn't know," he admitted. "I have been . . . busy, I haven't been trying to ignore crew-stuff . . ." He felt the reddening of his face, knowing she must have seen his glances.

She made one of those pilot-style hand motions—meaning *off-alert,* or *stand down,* if he read it right. Something other showed in her eyes, and he realized he was reading tension in a Liaden.

"And yes," she bowed, "I was remiss in not placing the information on the social lists before the start of the ship-day. So, we shall talk of this event again soon, I hope, or perhaps Vil Tor will find the time. If you excuse, my shift begins quickly."

• • • ✳ • • •

The rest of Jethri's meal was heavy on his stomach, the news of the upcoming Festival overwhelming any study thought he might have had. Somewhere there he'd been gifted with clues he hadn't caught, despite his training with Ray Jon tel'Ondor, the ship's practiced protocol master. There were things he needed to know—and he'd purposefully left his trader comm pad in its holster, on his desk, trying to get a time away from study.

Festival—a big party, a big blow-out kind of a party where folks could just let go, where for many the object was to bed a special partner or to share as widely as you could, a shivaree, all for one ship. He'd been too busy to get involved with anyone, really, and too uncomfortable to just plain ask—

He glanced down, both of his cups empty, and the *chernubia* dish as well. He *had* been going over the conversation in his mind, and also thinking on the fleeting smile and wide eyes, and the hints of skin and scarf.

Yah! That's what Dyk would say out loud when confusion reigned, or . . .

"Mud!" That, said out loud in Terran, brought him back to the room, now down to him and a couple staff members doing the 'tween shift cleanups. For good measure, he added "Yah!"

The *chernubia* . . . well he regretted that going by so fast.

"There is no need to stint your meals for others, on this ship, young Jethri," he recalled tel'Ondor telling him, "or indeed, at any entertainment you are invited to. Yes, you should eat gracefully. No, seeing that there is a single item of a treat sitting lonely, there is no need to leave it, for you are worthy, and if it beckons, you should partake."

He knew this, or should have known it, for Stefeli Maarilex, Delm Tarnia herself, had been over these points with him: in polite society, if dinner is served, assume it is sufficient for the invited. His time in Tarnia's clanhouse had shown him the sheer wealth of that clan. Even with Ren Lar being called stingy, he'd hardly been seen as that among the shipfolk Jethri had grown up among, in fact the *economies* he'd seen at Tarnia and on Elthoria were sheer extravagance on-board a Terran ship . . . and now a shivaree, out of foodstuffs and party supplies, and people on hand?

Yes, that was it. The Terrans on their loop ships and family routes were running their lives as *Gobelyn's Market* always had: one bad trip from disaster, one good trip from an upgrade, with enough crew to do the job and no more, enough food on the table at a meal to hit the calorie count, enough 'mite to cover for emergencies. In fact, he'd from time to time mentally lamented not being on the refurbished *Market,* where Dyk had expected new bread machines and ovens, and a new galley layout with the half-century old underfloor replaced and vents, by golly the new grade vents that would have cut the stinks duty in half or more, by all he'd been promised.

But that ship style was not *this* ship's style. Not *his* ship style. He was among Liadens who frankly expected all to go well and frankly expected to be comfortable in ways his ship family could have barely imagined. This ship's lead cooks were chefs, and there were three of them. The ship's protocol master was an attorney as near as Jethri could tell—not Paitor with a half-out-of-date manual!—and he, he— he was no longer just a crew member. He was, by necessity, not just acting like a trader, he *was* a trader. He was not just *acting like* a member of Clan Ixin, he was the son of Ixin's Master Trader.

It was not quite like being a captain, but it was *quite* like having a say and exerting himself and—and it meant hosting Festival parties. Whatever that meant . . .

And that meant he had to learn more, quickly. And put himself forward, soon.

He stretched his way from the table, and glanced toward the food display. Leftovers were rare on the *Market*, but here, if they weren't used, they would likely just get recycled . . .

Well, duty called. Study called. He'd promised Norn ven'Deelin that he would do his best to be a proper son to the house, that he had.

The single dish of *chernubia* remaining he took away with him to study with, and a cup of tea, wondering the while if he had left a dish or two sitting lonely after all.

Chapter Three

· · · ·✳· · · ·

Clan Ixin's Tradeship *Elthoria*, in Jump

BORN AND RAISED ON A SPACESHIP, rarely did the feeling of being pent up fall so heavily upon Jethri as it did now. He strode to his small suite, *chernubia* in hand, his mind full of the promising and confusing vision offered by Gaenor, and perhaps by proxy, by Vil Tor.

It wasn't certainly, that he was *against* the idea of such a personal time with them—either or both—other than the idea that they might not understand exactly what it was they were getting into. Yet he urgently wanted not to disappoint them—either or both—for aside the passing attention he'd been able to pay to Freza DeNobli back on, umm, on . . . not Vincza, but the other one in that system—must have been Chustling—he hadn't had that much experience. There'd been some casual bundling he'd been part of back in that year or so he'd been seen to be closing in on adult size, but that had been pretty tentative all around.

And Freza, on Chustling! By then he'd been dreaming pretty often about her, because they'd been on parallel course there for a while, the *Market* and *Balrog,* and they'd been pretty comfortable with each other, comfortable enough to talk as well as touch. That's where he was still frustrated because not only had they *liked* each other, but they'd agreed that it would be a good time to wander off together while the older folks were drinking and doing their shivaree setups and they'd be able to be out of the wild rudeness some of the older folks clamored for and just have their own time, figuring it *was* time.

Shaking his head, he remembered Dyk rounding the corner where they were standing nose to nose, holding hands, and Dyk saying, "You have to be quicker to disappear than that, Jeth! Captain said if I didn't find you for hatch duty, why, I'd be doing it myself by shift-start. I can see it ain't convenient, maybe, but I found you. Best meet me at the dock for turnover in seven minutes. Seeli's already been calling for her get-out-now."

And Freza had made sounds something very like, "Mud and stinks," and not too quietly, either, before she said, "Six minutes!" and kissed him, hard, like they'd both been thinking about, too, while Dyk ducked his head and said, "Hi, there, Miz Freza . . . sorry!"

Seeli'd seen him come in all grunch-faced, said, "Some ports are like that!" and left him to stare at the boarding screens, Dyk not having bothered to even step aboard.

Freza . . . They hadn't matched shifts again, and ship-to-ship wasn't hardly the same, even when they could at least smile at each other. Not nearly the same when it could be four years before they were on the same route again. Then, of course, he'd shipped with *Elthoria* and it was likely Mac Gold or one of his brothers was all she'd been left with the next portside, and hollow comfort that was!

He sighed, gustily.

· · · ·⸭· · · ·

First things first, he enabled the mail run, and found three other things he ought to have seen earlier, too, *and* the first Festival message from Gaenor, plus a lilting and seductive voice reminder for him to check his mail from Gaenor, that hint from Vil Tor! He shook his head, grim-faced against the missed offer to see the pair of them in their suggested Festival rags . . .

But that had to wait, after all, because if business was on deck, there was a complicated missive and even more complex set of files from Tan Sim, being the record of a dozen or more trades, side financing, short leases, storage and shipping contracts, all executed on the fly between the opening of the jointly bought pod that had begun their partnership and the departure of the Scouts, much of it real catch-as-can of hurry. The worrying part was that a few pieces of this and that had gone missing in the hurry . . .

Literally on the fly this had all happened, as Delm Rinork had created and sold Tan Sim's trader contract and exiled him to a long-route tradeship with little hope of success. Tan Sim parted out the pieces using a contractor and there'd been some assumptions that needed to be tested and worked out, seeing that it might be the partner contract between them wasn't as straight as it ought to be if they were both going to be able to hold their partnership responsible—not that Tan Sim hadn't done them proud, considering the whole of the problems they'd faced.

Then another note, this from Scout ter'Astin, very formal and very curious, and very short, especially compared to whatever it was Tan Sim was on about, admitting that ter'Astin would be happy to make an appointment to see Jethri Gobelyn soonest when *Elthoria* made next port, and that in fact he was applying to the Master Trader as well as Pen Rel for assistance in such a meeting and looking forward to an open discussion . . .

That bothered mightily, for ter'Astin of all people knew the change in Jethri's circumstance from acrobatic Terran apprentice to acknowledged son of the clan. Even the digital wrapper showed the Scout had purposefully aimed it to him as a Gobelyn, which meant . . .

It meant something, and he was darned if he could figure out what. He supposed a careful question to tel'Ondor might give him a clue— a reason to visit Vil Tor!—or perhaps a deep-search of the Liaden Code of Proper Conduct might show an answer.

Was he in trouble? Was Tan Sim? Or had Miandra's training gone wrong—a concern of *his* since he'd been the intermediary in defending her from the overzealous "healing" of a Healer more concerned with order than with people gone awry, with her now loose in space. With her apparent power and known affinity for trouble . . .

That thought had more interest for him than he'd expected, but surely he wouldn't be the first refuge Miandra might seek if—but there, she'd sought him on Irikwae, after all, when friends and family were all about her.

"Clear the board of reds before you move to the first yellow," he said, recounting out loud an ancient dictum Paitor swore was handed down from the days the Gobelyns had first risen into space from a rumored seafaring past.

So, he had to consider Gaenor and Vil Tor's offer and confusion, as recent as it was, to be down in the yellow side of the problems.

Without knowing exactly what it was about, he'd have to figure that ter'Astin's necessity was a flashing yellow, and so not quite red. That was a problem he hadn't thought about too hard before—he was double or triple or worse tangled in the Scout by now, between the weather machine and Miandra, and the save against the ugly Scout and the loan of his childhood "logbook" with cryptic notations from his father and, truth told, who knew what else might have been snuck under those covers? It was clear that he'd missed some kind of training his father was to give, and he wondered if the book held keys to more of that birthright that he'd considered before. A heavier tangle: ter'Astin had seen his father's shattered body—which was more than Jethri had—and recalled him for a brave man, stoutly facing chaos with thoughts for the injured and endangered, a worthy man across any of the races of men.

For all of the tangle, ter'Astin was coming to him. The Scout hadn't said where, but given that *he'd* just got the news from Thringar, and Boltston was up in a bare six-day meant that it was likely they'd be looking at Caverna or even Grammit before he saw the Scout.

So if his board had red lights on it, Tan Sim was wearing them: contract issues, missing objects which tied to money they were owed or expecting, possible conflicts with—

His protocol mentor would be proud of him, he reckoned, if he could see the resolve with which he closed the files and the most pressing thing was Tan Sim, and that was all *his* stuff, not things that ought to tie into his duties with the ship. The stuff with Gaenor and Vil Tor, that was personal stuff, and that could take time from the ship. And whatever ter'Astin was about, if it was for anyone named Gobelyn, that too, wasn't properly ship stuff, but his.

Study screen up, it was time to follow some of the sidetracks he'd come across earlier, looking at definitions. He'd looked at delivery pretty close, but now he'd need to study possession, its relationship to ownership, and legal ramifications of failure to perfect rights of ownership before transfer of possession. And those writs and legal stuff . . . The Master Trader said she was planning to lean on him for better Terran trade results.

Right. Paitor had warned him that trade would look different from the big-ship side, and being a lawyer or word splitter hadn't exactly been what he'd been thinking of. Maybe Jethri *should have* thought that—after all his father had been a trader and had somehow found his way with words and his understanding of what Paitor called trick angles so valuable to traders that he'd been pushed up to commissioner.

Details. He'd have to study the details.

Chapter Four

· · · ·❄· · · ·

Clan Ixin's Tradeship *Elthoria*, in Jump

THE BREEZE BLEW IN HIS FACE, shifting angles from time to time, and the sound of surf crunching into hissing waves and foam near his feet. The hills of the early part of this path gave way to the spot he always chose for the runout—the beach. He'd been looking forward to this since before he sought his bed the night before, this exact concentrated effort, this relief in movement.

He accelerated slowly, his muscles stretching for this familiar challenge automatically, eyes taking in the birds, the people, the boats, his mind dropping away from the recent and problematical protocol lesson he'd had the shift before, a lesson showing him again that casual agreements between partners were among the most dangerous.

His shirt was the last he still wore from the *Market*, all the others having been replaced in the face of grimaces, hints, and outright cajolery. Once outsized, now the shirt pleased him with the way it fit, though it did make him stand out, the large alternate bright red and yellow diagonal stripes proclaiming, in a fancy Terran-style script, *Trundee's Tool and Tow* on the red and *Satisfaction Guaranteed* on the yellow of the black shirt, front and back.

Most of his shipmates wore what they called *gym-sets*; a kind of tabardly wick-shirt over shorts, with wick-socks and light exercise slippers. He'd been advised, early on, to run and work out in a heavier grade of shoe, to promote getting into basic shape for planetary sojourns; he'd also worn weighted wristbands and sometimes a belt.

The belt he'd long since put aside as unwieldy for him, but the other items he'd kept with, and the shirt's schedule rotated, after all, sometimes giving way to a shirt he'd gotten on Irikwae, handed down from a cache of vine-working clothes when he'd had that duty.

His investment in the shirt he wore now had been from returning a defective circulating microsteamer for Dyk—Dyk got a refund and a new pot, while Jethri'd been able to keep the shirt since neither Dyk's careful off-ship wardrobe or his calm on-ship duds had room for something quite so commercially assertive.

He could run the water scene for hours: it reminded him of the calendar he'd been gifted not all that long ago, where lightly clad and even unclad people walked at ease. This was better than the calendar, for if the scene looped, which it must eventually, he'd never consciously caught the repeat, and he'd looked for it.

And, he admitted to himself, it wasn't simply the view of the tanned bodies in the world-sim, though that was good, but the whole experience of moving into the wind and of feeling his new strength.

Iza hadn't been so firm about exercise as perhaps she should have been: maybe he'd not have been so afraid of the open when first he'd met the twins if he'd only been used to moving, or at least used to thinking about moving, in open spaces. And it wasn't only the twins he'd embarrassed himself in front of—there'd been the times he'd flinched at something as ominous as open spaceport roofs and random breezes.

Funny thing was that once he'd survived a wind-twist, many of his fears had been put aside. And it was the cat, of all things, he'd been most concerned about.

The quiet swirl of the breeze changed tune as he picked up pace, and now the ceiling mounts moved to give him a more chaotic mixture as the surf he watched also picked up. The illusion was all the more compelling because of his lack of experience at a real seaside.

He marched on, knowing that much of his new confidence had come from the moment he'd grabbed the cat and made a dash for safety, ignoring the slashing claws for the necessity of shelter for a friend. He'd been out of breath getting to the safe-cellar, but he'd never doubted that he could. And that was because his mother the trader, unlike his mother the captain, had a vision of his success.

Success. Yes, always the goal. Success as a trader was a goal and his own Master Trader's ring the ultimate expression of it. To help him pursue that goal he'd become fit—both as a project that took no obvious study time and to be a hedge against mere local *weather* as he'd experienced when faced with rain and heat and twisted wind. Grig might have faced such, but he doubted that Iza had, for surely she'd have complained . . . and been more exacting in the regime she expected of her shipmates.

Now, between Gaenor's long language lessons, shared striding about *Elthoria*'s public and private passages, and his time working out here, he was probably the fittest member of the Gobelyn family in the last twenty years.

Well . . . he nudged the control up, planning on "catching" the couple running ahead of him on the screen when he heard a cough. Pen Rel's cough. It took a moment, and came again. Or was the second cough actually the third?

He glanced aside, where the arms master's face came into the view field.

"Your workout is impressive, I grant, but I'm asked to accompany you, Jethri, immediately, to the Master Trader's office for a meeting."

Stomach tightening, Jethri reflexively flashed his fingers over the controls to bring his lope to quick halt. Surely if ven'Deelin said immediate, it meant now . . . but—

But this, this was exercise wear, seen only by himself and those of his shipmates by happenstance on the same schedule as he; if there was a place the public dress code was most relaxed, this was it, surely. He doubted it was respectful to be seen above crew quarters in it—

"Immediately I shower and—"

Pen Rel bowed an intricate rebuttal. "Your time is not currently your own, Jethri, for it is both your Master Trader and your mother who have called. I walk with you that you not be delayed, and also that we may continue on to other destinations after, if required."

• • • ⁂ • • •

"Sit, sit, sit, son of my name."

He started an explanation, a concern that he might stain . . .

"If the fabric of this place is not up to honest sweat, I long ago failed at my mission as a trader. And you, too! Sit, my friend! We'll have enough fidgets from Jethri not to deal with yours as well."

Named first by ven'Deelin, Jethri took the seat he preferred, a soft scroll-leather arm seat with firm support; it was the higher of the available seats, and gave him a superior angle to Pen Rel in the conversational triangle established by Norn. If he could find a twin of it he'd have one for his own rooms.

Pen Rel took no time at all getting settled, but it was Norn ven'Deelin who fidgeted at her desk momentarily, answering a half-motion by Pen Rel with a semi-bow and a half-exasperated sigh as well as a wave of her hand that flashed her Master Trader's ring.

"I have called for a nuncheon; let us allow it to be brought before we dive headlong into the unknown. You'll both forgive the press of necessity, I'm sure."

Indeed, the trader calling "necessity" was sufficient to move the ship and crew at her whim, that she knew.

"In the meanwhile, I shall tell you both that we are none of us going to be doing exactly what we expected, come Boltston. To begin, none of us was expecting a Scout to meet us there, but my discussion with the chief navigator tells me that a Scout ship in a hurry—as my missive from ter'Astin indicates his will be—should make the envisioned trip without difficulty within the time frame of our own visit. We must assume he will be there.

"Thus, Jethri, you will wish to shift schedules one shift, starting this evening shift; it will be a double. I have sent already the notes to your files; please read them as you may. I believe you will see some items delivered to you as well; you will pick them up at your service locker on your way back to your rooms."

"I don't understand, ma'am. Must I be on ter'Astin's schedule?"

"No, you must be on Boltston's, for ter'Astin will be, I have no doubt."

She turned with a flutter of hands, which could be read as saying *next topic*, giving her attention fully to the arms master.

"You, Pen Rel, will take the time while we wait to discuss in a more than general way where we stand in Jethri's general preparations. You may include anything you've learned of tel'Ondor in the last days."

Jethri's ears perked up—he wondered if there'd be a change of his direct oversight after all; or if it was simply that trading preparation for Boltston occupied her.

Pen Rel settled, glancing at Jethri speculatively. "I would not send Jethri off to Solcintra proper on a solo mission at this moment, if I may be so bold; yet if it fell to him he would—with the application of common sense—possibly survive it, as long as he was not brought to discuss the matter of main line Balance nor the fitness of Terrans to be on the homeworld.

"For generalities, he is now far more aware of posture, threats, hidden arms, and counters than he was when he first boarded. Perhaps against tel'Ondor's original expectations, he has also continued with reading his bows and is able to read far more than he may perform accurately. He is also picking up more of the hand-talk than I would have expected given how little we on *Elthoria* use it: I gather he has an interest."

A glance at him: Jethri bowed little more than a nod, admitting that last. His heart was racing, which he worked to calm with some of the exercises he'd learned from tel'Ondor for fitting himself to relax for social moments.

A pause them, with ven'Deelin's hands giving permission to continue.

"As much progress as we have, I would not send Jethri to Liad on his own, I would not send him on a mission of assassination, nor set him to rear guard, nor assign him to set security perimeters for this ship, nor in fact to take over my position."

Jethri glanced suspiciously at him—where was the cause for humor, he wondered . . .

The Master Trader laughed lightly and added a bow that even his current level of understanding could not fully unwind—perhaps appreciation, acknowledgment of a hit, an acceptance of the word of an expert . . .

"Yes, yes, no one may replace you properly, this I well know. But if it fell to him to replace *me*? If the situation dictates bold moves, if we discover at our next port that I must be flitting about to elsewhere while *Elthoria* travels its course . . ."

Jethri was so taken aback by this question that he sat, traderlike, without reaction, almost as if he'd been expecting the tack, which he'd of course not been. His hands gave away no tension, nor his expression.

Pen Rel's face briefly showed something like surprise, or even dismay, to Jethri's eye; the man shifted in the seat, leaning forward and then going to a neutral while his shoulders grew guarded, and his tone, when he finally did speak, was more guarded than even his shoulders.

His glance toward Jethri was quick and measuring, as if gauging Jethri's reaction—but then, the pause became pronounced, and finally the arms master sat back, a slight, wry smile on his face. Jethri sat silently, his mind racing, an eerie blandness filling him with a vision of Trader Jethri ordering the ship about.

"Of all the concerns I had anticipated," Pen Rel allowed, " this was not one. Can you not see the levels of difficulty? Has ever—"

"And I have not," she said quickly, "asked you if this might be *easy*. I have asked you if you thought it might be done, if I feel necessity exists."

"Mother," Jethri managed, "but how could I, with ports that deny my license?"

She lifted a hand in his direction, silencing him, as Pen Rel gathered his countenance once more and spoke, this time with more surety.

"If you are of that measure, then yes, it might be done. The pilots know their business as does the ship; so often does the ship run a route that your interventions are no more than having a preference for an evening departure, or a request for a careful inbound or outbound route to permit the planet counters their games. The trade side, that issue is one I cannot answer. If you have no question that Jethri can handle the trade, how might I?"

"How might you indeed," said ven'Deelin, "if I were to say this we would do."

She raised a hand slowly to face, touching her chin as if in worry, then using the same hand, she tapped the ring she wore and turned to Jethri.

"Had we your trade partner to hand, with his license, then I might craft a letter of trust permitting you to direct the ship's trades with his signature holding them on worlds too backward to admit a Terran as a trader. We are not yet so fortunate, I think. But," she said, turning to Pen Rel, "we might at Boltston conjure a trader out of a clan we trade with, one needing the time on point . . ."

She moved her hands, as if lightly throwing something, to Pen Rel. "The question is, will ship and crew take to such a thing, if need be?"

Pen Rel's hands made a motion as if weighing things in each palm, or perhaps of throwing something unseen back and forth between them. Then he closed his hands and dropped the invisible ball or bag, and smiled more fully.

"Yes, Master Trader, it is in my mind that the ship stands well with Jethri. He is seen as young, and perhaps distant, and perhaps odd—but surely he is accepted and there'd be no challenge to his right to direct the trade should it come to that. He is resourceful and asks for assistance; in the case of your absence he need not fear for mutiny nor resistance, unless he becomes arrogant, which I do not expect. It could be better if he were a bit more of the crew—but time is what that takes, and social experience."

For his part Jethri took in the discussion with some amazement— to consider that ven'Deelin would entrust him with the whole of a port's work scared him; that she might entrust much of a trade route's work to him was overwhelming—

"But why, why should you need to leave? Does the scout bring bad news? Does—"

Jethri's questions were cut short when the door chimed low and melodic then and the Master Trader smiled and stood.

"By your leave, I will let the nuncheon arrive, and after, we may continue this."

Perforce Jethri bowed polite agreement with his host, and began setting questions aside for later as the door opened and an elegant cart was rolled in by a smiling crewman, preceded by a very tempting waft of aromatic breeze.

· · · ✳ · · ·

The small foods and two cups of tea finally being disposed of, Jethri dared to cast glances at both of his companions, who'd managed very ably to spin small-talk of amazing variety into a web of interesting but off-topic conversation, much of it informative and with no feel of the artificial or the preplanned about it.

They covered, on account of the tea, which was something called Hightide Stone on Stone, near as it would translate to Terran, times they'd had to refrain from pointing out that the tea they were served was not the tea they were told—in this case not because they had the wrong tea, but because there'd been quite a scandal a few years back where a trader without *melant'i*, and apparently without taste buds, had mixed up a blend of tea and tried to sell it as a singleton rarity, offloading it to an incoming trader as part of a mixed lot. That trader had proudly served it at an open house only to have the first person to have some stop at a sniff and repudiate it as a lie, loudly. There'd been several Balances due, and through the intricacies of that dance of *melant'i* and Balance arrived at a discussion of mislabeled items and thence to ports where such tricks were more frequent and then to worlds where social customs had frozen after a plague, and the common distance for speaking with strangers—even in Trade—might be measured in shouting distance.

"Yes, yes. Jethri, I know," said Master Trader ven'Deelin, surprising him as much with the force of placing her teacup on table as with her words, "elders are slow in moving from one point to the next, and so we are. In this case, it is because we are comfortable and comrades, and can see the possibility of being without each other for some while. And yes, you have a question before us, which, I think, now we can answer."

Now, though, the cups were empty. It took but a motion of her hand and Pen Rel rose in his smooth and silent way, and ushered the cart out of their middle and into the hall before sliding back into his seat.

"The Scout has offered me to understand that he arrives for a discussion which may well require personal attention in support of *melant'i*, and not only personal attention, but personal attendance. I feel he brings a problem of magnitude. He mentions issues of clan and kin, he offers that Balance may well be owed and that he is not the one to measure it.

"What may be the issue he does not tell me, only that he has requested most urgently a meeting at the first opportunity. Miandra and Meicha come to my mind, my son, for they have managed to involve him in their little intrigues, and if that is the case, then surely I should not be taking the ship entire off course again so soon."

She then looked closely at him, and Jethri felt a chill—

"Else, of course, the matter may lie in a different sphere, for you, also, have been taken into the Scout's necessities. Given the connection between the pair of ragamuffins and you—and the Scout— the complexities are many and I dare not be unwilling to deal, for the Scout is a man of extremely meticulous understanding."

This was said as much to Pen Rel as to him, Jethri saw, and in fact the hand motion was emphatically aimed at Pen Rel, who let his face relax slightly, and sighed, outwardly.

"It is so, my friend," Pen Rel said. "I have found it so for several dozen Standards, you know."

There was a silence but for the flick of fingers and the settling of breath, and then the Master Trader sat up and favored both her auditors with a decisive smile.

"And thus, we are all informed that I shall be part of this decision-making, for surely the Scout is spending valuable time in a matter of Balance; and in this case my duty is clear: if I need to part from *Elthoria*'s routine I shall do so, and you, my son, shall be prepared to be seen as trader in fact if not trader-by-signature."

Her hands moved in a motion Jethri thought meant *finished*, but as he shifted she waved him to stay put.

"There are other matters, Pen Rel, which you may be in charge of while clan issues are dealt with here. If Jethri must be thrust forward, he will be, and thus I wish you also to choose for him out of *Elthoria*'s armory a knife, unless he already has one he favors and you condone, and also a small sidearm or pistol."

A pistol? He leaned forward to deny it, yet her hand was already pointing to him, and she was saying, "I insist upon it—it is a matter for *Elthoria*'s crew to consider and know, that Ixin is present in trader, and prepared as Ixin is always prepared!

"Thus, you will have such ready to dress Jethri with come his next full shift. I thank you for your time and for escorting my son to me. We shall be in touch shortly, you and I."

Pen Rel took his dismissal with a bow, and bowed as well to Jethri. This was a new bow; something added there made Jethri's stomach tighten. In review, there was a deeper head tuck, and the hands curving to the intimation of a reach for weapons in support. Yes, the hint of supporting Jethri in need, of acknowledging a leader to be followed.

Jethri stared after the departing minion, knowing that he'd read that right, and that in fact Pen Rel had just placed himself on a different rung. No, he'd placed Jethri on a different rung, higher than he had been by far, with reservations.

· · · ✳ · · ·

"It strikes me, my son, that I hear no rumors among the crew of you, else that you work very hard at aught you do, and that among them you are respectful and quiet."

She was leaning back in her seat, and shifted to face him fully; he shifted also to take that proper position without a third present, respectful and alert.

"Rumors, ma'am?" He wondered if he'd done something worth a rumor, but he was always careful—he'd grown up being last and careful onboard a small ship and such habits were hard to break, indeed.

She smiled very gently, her hand playing a motion he couldn't yet read, other than it was soothing, meant perhaps for her as well as to him.

"Yes, rumors."

She paused, as if choosing words very carefully, and repeated that word. "Rumors."

Now she fluttered her hands and laughed an honest laugh.

"In the course of a route, my son, one often hears rumors, or sees evidence, or understands through the way people stand, or how they schedule themselves, or where they eat, or with whom they eat, or in which activities they take part—one sees or becomes aware of attachments, shall we say, of friendships growing and changing. We—that is you and I as Ixin incarnate—must of course be circumspect, as most of the crew is reasonably circumspect, but one does not carry a ship full of adults from planet to planet for years on end and expect them to be without intimacy, to be celibate as a crew."

"Yes, ma'am," he said, being as he so often reminded himself, not silver-tongued. What else was there to say?

His mother sighed, glanced at her hands which seemed to have said something to her if not to him, leaned toward him lightly.

"The rumors I do hear, my son, are that you amaze those who watch you work at the gym, and interest some of those, but that you work so hard and concentrate so greatly that none dares to disturb your workouts, for all that they admire you. Understand that there is interest . . ."

She fiddled idly with her ring a moment.

"I am Ixin for all purposes here, my son, and it is my duty to see you prepared properly for your life as a trader and as a son of Ixin, served by all that Ixin can bring to bear. Thus, it is important to me that you be a whole person, that you offer more to the ship than an excellent eye for textiles and a facility with a language that is silly, wrongheaded, lack-toned, and—"

His head came up and he leaned forward.

"Ah, you see? Indeed, I must imagine that Terran offers wonders to you as Liaden does to me; surely Terran begins to offer wonders to the first mate, who takes lessons from you."

Jethri was silent, watchful, trying to gather the sense of what he'd not done right, of a reason for rumors . . .

"It is what I can offer the ship when we are in Jump, ma'am. And I learn much from Gaenor, and now from others since I can speak so much better and needn't fall to Trade for simple things and even more . . ."

The Master Trader bowed acknowledgment.

"And so, we come to what the ship can do for you and what a mother can do for you and what needs to be done."

She paused, sighed, laughed to herself.

"Our introduction of you to traders was quite effective as I recall, and in fact, you had the interest there of Parvet sig'Flava."

He remembered—the trader, the astoundingly interesting trader who'd perhaps had a drink too many and a need unmet who'd offered to take him away to her bed. He blushed, nodded.

"I remember her, ma'am," he said.

"I'd be amazed if you did not, my son, indeed I would. I gathered that but for my intervention you would have returned to *Elthoria* in the morning with a stack of first memories of amazing kind and dimension."

His blush grew and she laughed lightly again, her hands making the same soothing motion.

"Jethri, her wiles and her attractions are such that if she offered me a Festival night, I, at my advanced age, might be tempted. I beg you to understand that I am not laughing at anything but irony and situation. You were honored by the offer, and no doubt would have learned much."

He put aside her comment about her age and her own potential interest in the woman, but in her face saw only serious interest in their current conversation, not jokes made at his expense.

"I didn't even know how I could say yes, ma'am," he admitted, "and didn't know how to say no, either. I'm not sure I would have done well either way!"

"Yes, that, that is precisely my point, my son. Should I need to be off on adventure with ter'Astin, or if you do, I must know that I turn loose an Ixin able to deal properly with people in situations of intimacy, so that mistakes are not made. Your partner who we hope to install as a trader here, is an excellent person, and he is the son of a mistake or a treachery or a love match not well carried. Had he been a Festival child and acknowledged as that, all would have been well. Instead we have chel'Gaibin's revenge still at odds with the norms . . ."

She sighed, raised hands, and with open palms, bowed.

"What needs to be done is a matter of care and of comfort, of seeing you confident and aware, of knowing that should you come upon Parvet sig'Flava again in similar spirits you might acquit yourself well whatever your answer."

He must have looked startled, though he felt the blush was gone . . .

"And why not? You will not repeat that I tell you that she is reputed a night's prize of the first water. You are of Ixin, you are of ven'Deelin! Why should you stay your suit if you are interested in such a challenge? Yet you needs must know the rules, and tel'Ondor has been instructed to turn you to the sections of the Code most needed. Yet bookwork and dry study is not enough."

That was said firmly, and her hands were strong with emphasis.

"So, my son, your student of the long walks, she enjoys your company very much. She has brought this to my attention this day, having no one else to turn to on the matter but yourself and finding yourself full of busy eyes and silence."

Now he blushed well and truly—but what else was he to do?

"I had thought," he admitted, "that she might be interested, in maybe bundling or something. I just wasn't sure, and she's an officer and I don't know that I should be bothering officers since it could confuse *melant'i* and, besides, without experience, I'd be a bother!"

Jethri was fiddling with his hand now, seeing that he needed to do something about the hair on the back of it, which was darkening and . . .

There was a genuine laugh then.

"Jethri, a bother? At the risk of breaking confidences, let me tell you that you would be such a bother that Gaenor admits to asking Vil Tor of your inclinations—of your intentions—since he also enjoys your company and hers and he often finds you to hand at the library. I gather, she discovering that you also had no liaison with him, they had hatched a plot to make you theirs for the ship's Festival!"

Despite his best efforts to suppress it, Jethri sighed, a hearty exasperated sigh accompanied by head-shaking and after a moment, a wry grin that he also could not suppress.

"But, well, I like both of them," he admitted. "But I didn't know how to ask for that kind of company, and I'm not experienced and . . ."

It sounded like the trader *snarfed.*

"Jethri, you have *you*. People are interested in you. They, some of them, admire your physical self as well as your personality, and the *melant'i* grows because you are, what is the phrase, low key? And what does a trader ever do? Eh, what does a trader do in moments of doubt?"

He looked at her with wide eyes, feeling dumb.

"You do exactly as Parvet sig'Flava did. You ask for the sale!"

At this there was nothing to do but laugh—indeed, Paitor had told him the same thing how many times in his life?

The trader again looked at her ring, and then slowly stood.

"I have told Gaenor, on being very quietly inquired of, magnificently respectful of *melant'i* that as far as I know there is no physical impediment to your attraction; and also that as far as I know there is neither a spiritual block, nor a love match languishing. If I am wrong—well, you are of *Elthoria* now and will treat crew kindly and demur gently if that is your aim and necessity. You are your own person and I do not now order you to anyone's bed, as this is not a marriage we discuss."

Jethri felt another thrill go through him, for indeed, he'd never considered that line of event. If he *was* a son of the clan as all agreed these days, then Ixin might order him to marry, if he'd read that part right in the rules! What a spot that would be, put down on a planet and left to dangle after a—

"However, it is my thought you have an offer of lesser complexity on the way, my son, and I, at least, wish to be sure of your social graces before ter'Astin leaves my deck."

"But that'll be before the ship Festival!"

"Ah, so you too are counting days?"

She smiled, not unkindly then, and rose with a bow indicating that he should consider himself dismissed.

"Be bold, my son. This should not be difficult for you, as you are so often bold, when necessity is right upon you. Be bold for joy, and we shall all be better for it! You will wish to stop at your mailbox, I am sure."

Chapter Five

· · · · · ✱ · · · · ·

*From a Student's Guide to the Basics of Relationship Balance
as Elucidated by the Liaden Code of Proper Conduct,
Version Seventeen, Amended*

Relationship Balance is an important part of melant'i *at all times and must by necessity change as a person comes halfling and begins to participate more widely in the independent expression of interpersonal dealings ranging from simple friendships through comradeship up to* cha'leket *and contract marriage and even into the esoterica of so-called Lifemate or Wizard Match situations. All in all potentially hundreds of dozens of varying states of relationships may be diagrammed if required, but the bulk of these fall into the simple ranges we will discuss here. The astute student will understand that a multiplicity of relationships may exist simultaneously with . . .*

IMPATIENTLY JETHRI STABBED THE BUTTONS—yes, yes, this much he knew. And he knew that contract marriages were arranged by delms or thodelms for the purpose of producing agreed-on heirs, and that some people had to be contract-wed multiple times if it made a clan good arrangements, but everyone was supposed to be sure there was at least one heir of their own body to replace them in the clan and the delm was responsible for making those arrangements.

He had this letter to figure out, and it was written out formally, and the thing was it was all written in Liaden, because there it was, Gaenor was semiofficially his tutor or mentor in Liaden, and she'd been practicing that . . . and the statement at the top meant something important, because she wrote—"Jethri, I take this time to write to you, both as your friend and your intended *I'gaina Prenada* and would like to have the enjoyment of your company that we might together spend the upcoming off-shift in the guesting suite I have reserved, you and I, in *cher'nuchiada*. This will be great fun, and exercise, and after all, study as well, if you yet need an excellent reason for allowing your brain some respite from trade details and dry words."

He sat back from the task, fiddling idly with the new-to-him chain about his neck, a chain he'd judged to be platinum as soon as he saw it. Linked in back with a fusion clasp of magnetic depleted timonium, the necklet widened in each direction to exactly embrace a twelve-sided cameo—actually not a person's cameo, but a cameo of Ixin's own sigil, the rabbit against full moon. He'd put it on with a touch of trepidation after staring into that full moon for some minutes, still wondering if he was up to this, still wondering if he was going to be tossed for fraud into some Lowport for failing to bow in just the right mode . . .

"My son," had said the note, "in normal circumstances I would have presented this myself, but I had not the measurements from your suit fitting, nor the skill and equipment to adjust the clasp to your own neck. Between them the armorer and our machinist mate have done these things; I hope you will be able to proudly wear this for your interlude as it has graced male necks in our clan for several hundred Standards or more. The full story of it will be yours as time permits, but for now, for the clan, wear it, and be amused as well as entranced this night. One should, at all times, wear the moon-and-hare, and if it lights the way, do not be surprised!"

If nothing else were done, the moon-and-hare was on.

The thing is there were other situations, like a *cha'leket* and that was like being best friend and brother or sister in heart all at once, maybe *heartkin* was the right word there, and there were formal things that needed to be done if someone was insulted, or killed, and there were other arrangements—the long term relationships, almost married, what the heck were they called?

Nubandaria was what it was—it was like being promised lovers, an official pleasure love who family and friends could expect one to admit to, and one could agree to it and it was almost a legal thing, but then one could get over it without a delm doing a thing, all one had to do was—he'd seen that, there it was, give a *nubiath'a* and that was a parting gift, but there were back-rules to that, that if one gave a *nubiath'a* one wasn't ever expected to go back with that person again. Somehow that seemed rude to him—to just sort of pay a sex-friend off when one had not started out on a cash basis, but then it also said they were appreciated and—

But this word here was related but choppy, as he thought about trying to translate the pieces, since ally or joint effort was implied and so was joy and so was passing, as in short term and—*cher'nuchiada*.

He didn't want to agree to something that was going to make him stay away from Gaenor just because they messed around of a night, but no, *cher'nuchiada* was just a fun thing, like Dyk might call a flash-fling, well, except *they* were usually with someone one faunched for at first sight portside, as he had it, so not a flash-fling but still—

"And for our assignation you must but needs arrive. We shall consider it Festival and thus we shall meet as if at a Festival pavilion; directions follow to a room which is reserved to me, that none other need know—or should know—who it is shared with. Do not be concerned of food or drink, for I shall provide a meal and delicacies for us. Arrive on time and I shall be but a few moments behind you."

• • • ✦ • • •

Be bold for joy, his mother had told him. Be bold indeed! Who expected mysterious travel instructions on one's own ship, in halls he'd thought well known to him? Who expected that the woman he'd been faunching after for many days would offer to be *I'gaina Prenada*—his body mentor?

He passed other crew members, wondering if his face was yet as flushed as he'd felt it before leaving his room, for the excitement was in him now, anticipation. He recalled the blouse Gaenor was wearing the last time he'd seen her, and hurried up the 'tween deck-ladder rather than waiting for a lift.

He carried in one hand the flimsy swipe-key and his brief letter that had enclosed it—as found at the mail drop, the Master Trader having been more informed than prescient, was his guess. The letter had inspired his research, as well as his shower, his careful inspection to be sure that his mustache and beard were yet under control, Liadens being odd about face hair, he knew.

The directions, he realized, were part of the game of this, and they reflected Gaenor's quiet idea of fun. She enjoyed puzzles and enlivened their walking language lessons with word games and trivia; at times she gave him jokes that were double or triple deep—well worth the time of a trader. But the fun she was promising this time . . . He hurried, knowing that no spot in the ship should be very far from any other, and that certainly ten minutes would be more than he'd need, but if the goal was to tease and excite, her instructions were managing that.

· · · ✢ · · ·

Jethri stood in the back corridor on *Elthoria*'s second level. In his mind he traced the ship's plan as far as he knew it and saw that he was in the section occupied largely by pilots and technical crew—but in the long corridor with a short jogging turn giving good access to the onboard trade deck and conference rooms and perhaps, but yes, the guest suites; ahead was a corner, giving way to a short connecting corridor to an access walk to the outer rim. There was a suite entrance there, too, he knew, but the numbers escaped him momentarily.

Coincidentally the room was next to one of the combined lift and stair shafts, an excellent location for quick and quiet access.

And there, GS 3A it was—he recognized it now—for like the three other guest suites there was a multitoned occupancy marker as well as the key swipe at the door. It seemed a silly thing to do on a ship that otherwise read his hands or eyes for admittance anywhere, but he swiped the key and entered, curiosity not the only thing behind the advanced beating of his heart, for if Gaenor waited . . .

The suite opened almost silently, and he entered, to discover a room like none other he'd seen on *Elthoria*, hearing the door seal behind him. While the low lighting might be simple energy conservation the rest of the room was rich-looking; there was a small couch of fine leather, and a meal table of carved wood, and a bunk—well, no, a bed!

The bed was triple or more the size of a bunk, he thought, with pillows piled high and piled about, and both headboard and footboard of wood that matched the table and—well, the whole room. There were low-lit alcoves, and viewing screens on several sides of the bed, and a well-equipped work area with multiple chairs and a desk and work screens.

The walls were covered in a finely decorated cloth, and there were vents, and more vents, shades of a workroom, high and low—his time with stinks runs on the *Market* left him no doubt that he could dump a half tub of beer and not one bit of the odor would go beyond the room, unless he spilled it on himself.

The colors of the room were hard to define since the lighting varied from spot to spot, with some areas shading green and some blue, though it was clear that the bed itself was more lit than the couch or the table, though the pillowed top was near as dark as any portion of the room. He blinked: the light *was* slowly changing in the room, cycling in a way he couldn't measure, the colors and intensities from each source altering moment to moment. Those changes changed the shadows—now the pillows at the top of the bed were in more light, and the center was mellowed . . .

Too, there was an undersound, not of a regular ventilation but something else he couldn't quite place. It rose quietly, then swelled to a hiss that almost became a slap, and then receded; in its midst were other sounds he couldn't place, not unpleasant, but not ship sounds, and not music of a kind that he knew. Certainly the rising and falling of the swelling sounds were orderly and cyclical while the others were not, but sounded purposeful nonetheless, and sounded familiar.

He wondered if the lights and the sound were coordinated, but his eyes were drawn to a portion of the room with steady illumination, and his name writ large.

Standing on the small bar were several fancy cases as well as a tea set, glasses of a number of sizes, and a box, all fancied up with glowing striped ribbons, and a sign on top that with hand-drawn letters that were hand tall spelling out JETHRI.

Drawn there, he saw the note under the sign, and opening the fragrant sheet tied to the package he discovered, handwritten in Terran—

To Be Opened on Sight by Jethri! Wear if you dare! Wear for joy!

The seal was the ribbon itself, a single ribbon which was a knotted puzzle, too, and he studied the knot before working it, wishing to keep the ribbon intact if he might. There was a way to do a quick pull, but he'd felt that would be cheating if he could . . . yes! His fingers fumbled now that this goal was in sight, and he wondered if he really was vibrating or not. There was a slip, there, a small spot where he'd relieve all the tension and still be able to free the box, and he did that, an inordinate sense of accomplishment making him smile.

"For Jethri for our own first Festival, a gift, for this trip or for lift. Wear and share with joy."

Out of the mysterious box, then, from within a fine and worthy keepsake silky sack, came layers of a soft and wonderful cloth, all in shades of blue. He'd hardly touched such, for it was meant to be a personal kind of a thing, the like of which he'd seen before on specialty tables, and once, heart-stoppingly, on Khat as she'd left the *Market* for an assignation, her unsealed overcloak revealing the shimmer and cut of it, though thankfully not the full measure of the things.

It was what he could only think of as "an outfit" or a "getup"— both labels used among the traders he knew to mean clothes for quiet get-togethers or rowdy parties where the parties were meant to end up in bed or other handy place with the object being to be spend as much time twisted up in each other as they could, with the clothes being a transition phase not meant to last on a person much beyond getting to and from the athletics.

And there—he'd dressed himself up in what were quality onboard clothes, thinking of the admonition that this was a private party, and that none need know—and now she'd provided these clothes, recalling her promise to be with him shortly after he arrived.

He felt an adrenal, hormonal surge, wondering just what clothes Gaenor might bring . . .

"Wear if you dare"was certainly a challenge; he retired immediately to the sanitary facilities and dressing areas on the left— seeing one on the right as well—and closed himself quietly into the well-mirrored room.

· · · ✳ · · ·

The clothes were amazing: a brief lower undergarment of a fine foggy blue, silky smooth, shimmering and near transparent, and slightly stretchy. There was a shirt, of the same color and fineness, and there were trousers of a sort, with a drawstring, and then an overrobe of the same foggy blue . . .

He laid them out on the slick counter top, looking at himself in the mirror.

His thoughts were all a-tumble, visions of Gaenor running into odd thoughts of distant Khat and then the twins Miandra and Meicha and—

He wasn't any of those other places, he was here, on this ship. He'd willfully left *Gobelyn's Market* to come here; he willfully told his mother, Captain Iza, "I've found my ship!"

The choice now was straightforward, and he stripped, the straight-white light from the mirror making his skin even paler against the small tangles of dark underarm and pubic hair. He thought he heard a sound on the other side of the door, and moved quickly now, with ever more confidence, pulling on the wonderfully soft and caressing underdrawers, marveling at their touch and their fit, the way they showed his shape, both supporting and bringing him forward. He blushed briefly, seeing himself thus in the mirror, and said under his breath, "Be bold, Jeth!"

The rest of the clothes slid over his skin gently, like the touch of a loving lady, and when he peered into the mirror again, gently brushing his unruly head of hair into what perfection he might, he could see through the outer layers to the smoky shadowy transparency of the inner clothes, his pale skin giving an extra radiance to the blue.

The footlets he also pulled on: clearly they were part of the package and were effective against the cool floor—they stretched too, so like the other clothes needed only be approximately his size. The choker he wore fit very nicely and rode comfortably for all that he was unused to wearing much around his neck. It was almost as if the moon glowed blue in the bright light of the little room.

He turned one more time, to see from the side, and then to half see his back, and then retreated a half step.

Looking back at him was a man he'd hardly met. Time to find out then, what this man could do.

• • • ✳ • • •

Gaenor alas, was not obviously present in the suite, though the catering cart she'd brought with her was parked near the wooden table, fine aromas spilling into the air . . . and yes, the rushing noise was louder now, and the airflow heavier—perhaps Gaenor had adjusted something.

The door to the other dressing room was closed and he imagined he could hear her movements; he tried to remember what the Code portions had said about meeting with a to-be lover. Was he to stand? Should he sit? What distance then—for they carried themselves as comrades properly when they walked the halls trading languages, much closer than the distance for trade but not yet the casual touching passes such as crew members on the *Market* shared in those slender passageways.

He wondered then, seeing several beverage containers, should he be pouring yet? If so, which first?

He studied the cart, went to it, dared to lift lids from covered foods to sniff and wonder at them. It was a plague, knowing more than he used to, for now that he wasn't an entirely ignorant Terran, simple social missteps showed not carelessness, but impertinence, or—

Ah, what was this? In a flat container to be taken out there was a sealed storage bin with something that looked very much like a dark Terran double-fed cake, and beside it was what looked very like whizzywhite topping. Now that would be good—he wondered if Gaenor could have recalled him talking about it in one of their trades—tell me your favorite color, and he'd said blue and then she'd said *tra'haina* . . . but no, that was a food of hers, maybe a soup, yes, a soup local to Liad.

The color she'd called then was *drai'vaina*, and he got that it was a kind of bright red—she'd promised to show him one day the exact shade—and then they'd talked nuances and off-shades and tints, since he needed to know such things for the trading, and they'd got into favorite dessert and she'd talked of a frosty cold *chernubia*—he had it in notes, he'd have to look it up when he could.

He leaned on the cart with both hands and peeked closer at the cake and suddenly, with the rush of the background sounds falling and fading to a snap and then a swish, he knew he was not alone, and looked up.

He also knew then exactly what color *drai'vaina* was, and when he remembered to breathe, was never happier to see red.

* * * ❋ * * *

Jethri had to twist his head slightly, to look up into Gaenor's face as she moved toward him from somewhat behind and to the left, catching her wide smile getting wider as she looked at him standing there, and then their eyes met and the smile was there too, without reservation.

Her voice went all husky and musical on him: "Ah, Jethri, my friend, I am so pleased to find you here, and party-clad. I hope I find you with as much appetite as I have."

She'd caught him leaning and was taking him in with evident delight, as he was her.

He stood up to execute a proper bow of welcome, but her bow came before his as she moved forward. Her red top blazed for a moment in the light, and for another moment nearly disappeared, her breasts tantalizing and then shimmering into an opulent translucence . . .

He managed to complete his bow then, and in rising from it saw his own leg and thigh as if nude and then only slightly more hidden as he finished—

Gaenor's laugh was magical with delight, and she reached out to gently touch his wrist and then moved close to smile again, releasing his hand and raising hers to encompass himself as well as the room, the fabric of her top playing magical games with his eyes in the dimness.

"It is so good to see you this way, after all this time, my friend. Also, I should have warned you of the lighting. It is a wonderful effect, is it not?"

He was at once trying not to stare and to see her as he'd never seen her before. She wore some hair cosmetics which glittered gently in the overhead light, her lips glistened and she laughed again . . .

He wasn't sure what to say but she raised her fingers to her lips in the sign for silence, and bowed, quite close to him, a bow requesting forgiveness of a comrade.

"Jethri," she said very quietly, "this evening will be excellent. We shall enjoy ourselves immensely, and we shall both learn. I am informed that you have need of someone to be your *I'gaina Prenada*. This must be clear before we begin, and also that as *Prenada*, I will set limits and you will follow."

Jethri began to bow, but Gaenor continued, raising her hands yet again, drawing his eyes, and he understood then this was one of the Liaden set pieces, the things that must be said . . .

"In this place then, we are, you and I, without immediate call by the ship if we wish; only an emergency will penetrate the comm system without our will. I have taken the liberty of making sure that is so; our calls and mail do not follow us here. Assure me that this pleases you."

He nodded, and turned it into as elegant a bow as he could manage, with honor to the teacher flowing into an acceptance of joint necessity and that flowing into a declaration of absolute dedication to the project at hand. Indeed he could think of nothing that pleased him more, for his eyes were filled with Gaenor who was every bit as beautiful at this moment as any women he'd ever seen.

Her face showed smile lines at the corners of her mouth and the corners of her eyes; and her eyes were intent on his, while his searched her face and allowed his vision to see the unexpected glint of finely netted and sparkling jewelry which encircled her ears and depended from them, leaving the folds of the ears and the enticing lobes bare, available, and the sweep of the gossamer collar making him sigh.

"I am pleased to be without interruption from the ordinary, and honored to accept your guidance this night. In all things, it shall be as you say."

Her eyes brightened as did her smile, and the graceful bow of acknowledgment she performed added interest to his view.

· · · ✦ · · ·

"*Fa'vya*?" Gaenor offered the glass to him, not to drink but to sniff in emulation of her motions. "This is true *fa'*vya, properly vinted and stored, I promise you, not the powder stirred into a random year in the hopes for a quick-wall rush-a-bed."

Jethri accepted, and sniffed politely, his nose not yet fully trained to the mysteries of wine as much as tel'Ondor and ven'Deelin tried.

"... and are you familiar with *fa'*vya, after all?" she went on, holding her glass politely rather than rushing into a sip before he reacted or replied.

As for the sniff itself, it was a wonder: he could identify several of the notes he knew he was to look for, and glanced toward the bottle—

"It is a landmark vintage," Gaenor purred, sniffing at hers again.

He stared hard at the glass, the lights having shifted and turned the left side of Gaenor's blouse transparent again. She noticed and smiled, pleased that his eyes drifted toward her.

"I know of it," he bowed in her direction, and admired, "but I have never had *vya* in any form—candy, cracker, or drink." Jethri named the ways he'd heard it offered—though often enough he gathered it was in fact dropped as a powder into glasses to power glasses of portside beer rather than made part of a fine wine like this . . . The *vya* responsible for him being here, now, that *vya* had been a powder concentrate he'd discovered in a poorly constructed warehouse catalog and pointed out to Paitor, who'd marketed the load of it at a Liaden port and seen enough profit to refit the *Market,* with all the crew changes that had entailed . . . including the attempt by his mother to trade him off to work a cramped, all-male ore boat.

Now . . .

"Then you are starting with the right way, my friend, for wine is a good way to become familiar with herb. We shall have this glass and begin dinner comfortably, with more available at our whim."

The lights shifted again and with it the view, with Gaenor's earrings giving off rainbows and her face a-glitter.

After their salute he sipped willfully, as did she, and then had another sip, permitting the notes and angles of the stuff to fill his mouth. He shifted himself slightly in the seat, the stretch of his fancy underwear suddenly noticeable to him as Gaenor's closed eyes and her tongue tasting the flavors on her lips became his focus. Then her eyes were on him, quizzically.

"It is very good," he allowed. "Thank you for sharing."

Pointedly he had another sip, and then relaxed, for if this was a test, he knew it was one he would pass.

• • • ✳ • • •

The several courses of the meal passed their lips as did a second glass of wine and they stood now close by each other at the catering cart, debating the size of the dessert they should cut, it being a new dish for her and a favorite of his. In the midst Gaenor leaned against him and he looked down and through her again see-through top and said without preamble—"I'm not sure I had need of *fa'vya*, you know. I am . . ."

Gaenor leaned closer against him, looking down rather than up as well, as the lights turned his clothes transparent now, her arm going around his waist and then her hand was on his hip and stroking his hip and buttocks as his interest became more and more evident.

"I've known that for some time, Jethri, and believe the same of myself." Her hand teased briefly toward the front of his hip and she looked up then, quite seriously, drawing away with a decided air of control. "Yet you'll need to know something of the drug, and what we shall do is have this dessert with a glass, and then recline ourselves on the bed where we shall have proper lessons and proper lust. After that, we shall see, my friend. But here, point our way to the table and let us have the first course of our dessert."

"Must we do dessert?" he asked, and she laughed, leaning hard into him now, her hip finding his willing crotch teasingly for a moment before she drew away.

"Ah, yes, for my duty is plain. We must have dessert, for while I can understand something of the urgency, I am, like you, now a spacer, and my understanding therefore clouded, according to those who stay planetside. We must train you for the necessities of traders and formal places, wherein leaving out a course or faulting a food might be enough to lose a trade and have an entire port visit fail! Dessert first! We are in training!"

• • • ✳ • • •

Dessert was eaten side by side on the couch, obedient side tables holding their portions while Gaenor's demeanor only fed his growing necessity to—do something. To touch her, to see all of her, to . . .

But she'd put her portions on his side and had him put his on hers, and then set them down as the roll of the sound in the room cycled again.

"I love the sound of the sea, don't you? Vil Tor tells me you exercise to a sea scene, and it is one more joy we share!"

She pressed against his left side, ankle to thigh, leaning so that she looked up into his face, and said, "Here, my friend, let me feed you, and you feed me,"

It was silly, he knew, but it was perfect.

Her careful left-handed sporkful brought her close, while her right hand drifted from his hip to thigh and back again, and the lights collaborated yet again with the sudden transparent red of her top, masking and unmasking her as she moved close.

If ever cake tasted so good he could not recall it, and his eyes found hers, full of joy, inches from his face before she turned to bring him his glass, offering perhaps more wine than he'd normally have for such a bite of cake, but . . . he drank and she held it near still, using her right hand for leverage to keep her far arm steady.

His mind reached for words that would unbedazzle him, leaving him with the confession . . . "I've never been to the sea. I've only seen the pictures and the vids. I didn't even connect the sounds. . ."

She laughed, threatening them both with spilling the bouncing wine—

"What, never? Not ever? And here I was being subtle for you!"

"More, and some for me!"

He took the "more" of the proffered wine, and then he turned to his uncertain duty—he thought he'd never fed anyone before, not anything. He hadn't thought of it but she leaned back against the cushions, and as he turned toward her, offering, her right hand swept from his thigh to his knee and back, nearly breaking his careful concentration, the swell and crash of the waves picking up meaning, the eager reach and lick of her lips as they accepted the cake sharing his attention with her eyes, her dark eyes, her knowing eyes.

She held the spork with her mouth, sucking the contents off, while the squeeze of her right hand was almost a knead on his thigh.

Recalling himself, he withdrew the spork finally, bringing to her lips now the wine, which she sipped, using her tongue to wet the edge of the glass as he withdrew it at her nod.

"Very good, this cake of yours, my Jethri," she said. "It goes well with our red. Another taste?"

They traded small bites of cake until there was no more, and she showed him then how to wrap their hands in such a way as to each offer the other wine at the same time. He'd been surprised to find his hand on the fine textured silkiness of Gaenor's leggings, to stroke her hip and knead her leg as she pressed even more against him. Face-to-face they were, and nearly lip to lip when she whispered in his ear, "Jethri, Jethri, Jethri . . ." as she moved her hand to stroke his hip and then his knee and then to stroke him where he was already stretching against the bounds of the cloth, where the light made the blue transparent and made her smile.

He caught his breath.

"Now, my friend, we move our Festival to the bedside and bring you to me."

Releasing him with firm reluctance, she stood with dancer's

grace, and temptingly removed her overtop. Then she reached for his hand as he rose, and they gathered their bottle and themselves to the bed.

. . . ⟊ . . .

"I am very thirsty, my friend, and the bottle is on your side."

He was now waking from a drowse of such excellence, of such satiation and satisfaction, that he almost didn't hear the quiet voice, but then his mind processed it and the hand that had been on his knee stroked upward and Gaenor said then— "Let us finish this last glass between us, and see what else it is you might learn."

He poured into the closest glass, nearly filling it, and Gaenor raised her head and then stretched, arching herself with provocative intent.

"Have your sip," she said. "There's still work to do, but give me mine, too . . ."

While he sipped she began teasing and he sipped the glass half empty before he handed the glass to her. Her two-hand hold permitting him range, he bent to kiss her ear, and then as she giggled and finished the glass, reaching to the bedside he put his hands on either side of her waist and drew her to him, hands now under her arms and caressing, pulling his willing mentor toward him in a hug fraught with possibilities . . .

Then she said, "One more thing I must tell you, that you must know before you are pressed upon the worlds, my friend."

She twisted within his arms, nearly a move from his self-defense classes, and she pushed him back to the bed.

"Still," she said, "be still."

He laid flat, or as flat and still as he could, for her hands were just below his navel, pressing . . .

"Your fur," she told him, "is much to be admired, and I hope to brush it for you many times and curl my hands in it, for it is not what I have known before now. Liadens are not equipped with so much luxury! But I must correct you . . . for myself being incorrect."

He started. Everything they had done had been perfect! What correction? He tried to sit up. but her hand was still flat and firm below his navel . . .

"I think," she said seriously, "that you were following my hair and then my earrings and—as we were both involved elsewise as well, I didn't realize what you would do, and so you . . ." Here she sighed, and he strove to think: what error might he have committed, how could he have hurt her?

Her breasts were close and he thought of reaching out and tasting them again but . . .

She laughed, husky, for no doubt she'd seen his reaction to that passion!

"Just moments and we shall, yes we shall."

Awkwardly then, she put her hand to his lips, and he kissed her finger. She bowed where she was, which was very nice and now she giggled . . .

"Nearly hopeless. Next time we'll schedule one hundred hours and be sure I have backup for when I rest . . ."

He started to speak but now she pressed her finger harder to his lips and sighed.

"We were enthralled in the moment and lost to sense; I trust you will share this with none of your future lovers—at least none Liaden—unless you bring them to bed as your all-time love. For this thing you did—and which I did to you in return" . . . Now her hand left his lips and began stroking his face, not only under his chin and on his lip, but his cheeks and forehead, touching the side of his nose and his eyebrows before leaning low and kissing each eyelid.

"This touching of the face, which you admire and which I find I admire . . . this is a touch that is reserved for family, for the brushing away of tears of the young or the old, and for showing where too much tension or decision or emotion is displayed in a face. Yes, I may do this," she said, and leaned suddenly, bringing breast to tease his lips and his mouth, but she withdrew, and then she saw him bounce and leaned her face, laughing, touching her cheek to the side of his erection, her lips touching his eager head for one sweet second.

"That we can do," she said, turning to him and showing hands fluttering. "But the hands and fingers are not to touch the face of any but family and life-loves. It is as forbidden as the inking of words or letters or arts upon a body; it is as forbidden as piercing the body with permanently installed devices or jewels. It may be that upon a drunken night on a port where you are unknown or in a Festival on a world where you'll not return, that one might as a dare or a thrill do such a thing. But else, my good friend, doing such a touch might marry you on the spot, or name you pervert and have you hunted down and hounded by Balance for *melant'i* errors."

"But why?" he blurted, trying to recall the rulebooks, the Code that covered such things, knowing that he'd not pursued all the studies he should have . . .

She continued. "Kissing is a gray area; for families may kiss, and lovers, but one may not purposefully stroke the face . . ."

"But you're beautiful!"

She sighed, perplexed. "Am I so? Beautiful? Well, my friend, you make me feel thus. Your eyes and your hands and your touch and your enthusiasms, yes, you make me feel beautiful."

She sat up somewhat then, holding him down with one hand and leaning over him, using the other hand to tease his ear with a sigh . . .

"I should not, you know," she allowed, but then, despite her admonition, she let the hand trace his ear to the side of his face, and put the whole of her hand on his cheek.

Her hand and her glance moved down his chin, playfully traced the choker—spanning it with her finger and thumb before pressing very gently on the rampant rabbit where it echoed his pulse—and then drifted downward, across one nipple and then the other, now down across his navel and teasing lower.

"Dance for me," she offered with a tempting smile, "and you may rub my cheek!"

But his hips were moving already as her cheek flattered his belly, and there was another lesson or maybe two, before morning.

· · · ✳ · · ·

Morning brought its own delights, with one of them the scandalous way Gaenor risked the door to tug in the breakfast cart, dressed as she was in only her flimsy overtop. That top had been put on to explain the names of clothes he'd never seen before, and the names of seams, inner workings, and to explain something of the disappearing. Perhaps he should have gone for the cart, had he known her intentions, but there, though he might be somewhat dressed in the see-through bottoms she'd had him put on again for this technical discussion, there was no doubting that an accidentally passing crew member might be surer of what he'd been up to than her.

In any case, her laughing countenance assured him there'd been no major exposure, and the breakfast she brought to the bedside, and the dessert she offered, was just what the famished trader needed.

Chapter Six

· · ·✳· · · ·

Clan Ixin's Tradeship *Elthoria*, Boltston Arrival

HE'D HAD FIVE MINUTES, from the time the emergency wake-up did its job until the door sounded Norn ven'Deelin's tone. Jethri had managed, in those five minutes, to dress, though he had not, he feared, dressed *well*.

Worse, he had been late at his books, and short sleep had likewise shortened his temper.

"Ma'am, I'm in no case for a meeting," he told his mother as he opened the door.

"Scout necessity," was her answer. "Be at ease if you will! And come with me!"

"Ma'am, I'm hardly on the shift schedule—" It was hard not to sound annoyed, and he didn't hide it well, with a sharp edge he rarely used for anyone, much less Norn ven'Deelin.

His blush was minor: there were none to have heard it but him; he was fully deserving of her increased speed and more. But she relented as she hand-signed him toward the passage leading toward the small break room.

"None of us are, twenty breaths out of Jump and ten out of sleep, child."

He took the hint. More complaints would be really bad form, despite the provocation.

Well, and that was the problem: he'd been half-muffled in his bedclothes when the annunciator went off, and barely dressed when

Norn herself appeared at his door on her way to their sudden breakfast. All this after he'd spent a late night writing notes. The easy part was one each to the twins, promising an excellent update when he was not so pressed for time—that task made more difficult by having to say some of the same thing in different words, in case they shared his message—he'd not be so gauche as to be sending ladies cut-and-paste correspondence!

The hard part—he'd hoped he'd reassured Tan Sim of his trust and continued goodwill, while admitting that the missing items might be a difficulty. That Tan Sim was well aware of the intricacies of both the delivery and ownership portions of this problem he didn't doubt.

A muffled sniff brought him back to Norn and her ironic smile.

"My son, I am required for this, for all that it may be your business. Forgive me: the information came in cipher and tagged for myself; there'd be no use having the mate refuse you despite the news is yours more than mine."

"She can't tell me, then?"

"It would only pain you both and that, my son, is something you'll need to recall and refine as time goes on: the duty of a superior is to increase and protect the ship's interest as the clan's interest. Rarely is such an increase favored by the breaking of regulations or the reliance on friendship."

He nodded, which the trader didn't notice, having a half-step lead on him. *Melant'i* was all about stuff like that—that just because they'd chewed each other's ears, he had no right to ask or expect Gaenor to be spilling secrets. Same thing traders knew anywhere, anytime, he guessed. "There are secrets in all families," as he had it from Grig, and this was no different.

The small break room merged into the two larger ones at the touch of a button but Norn left the button alone, dropping from fast walk to still as she touched the fingerpad, letting the ship—or at least the command center—know where she was.

Perforce, Jethri stopped, watching for a signal. It came from her hand, and he hurriedly stepped into the unoccupied meal line, pulling for himself tea and breakfast and 'mite. Before he was done Norn passed him, hurrying, and stopped and took motion again, this time toward the outer door, where Gaenor's voice brought him round suddenly—along with the familiar voice of ter'Astin.

Norn ven'Deelin's signal was solid enough, so he went, his fleeting catch of Gaenor's glance an elation and then a sense of dread—for while she permitted the briefest of smiles her eyes held not a smile, but wary concern.

Jethri went by the green "reserved" light, on to the small break room, passed the head chair at the small table and was angling for a safe middle spot when from behind came the Master Trader's voice, with perhaps a tinge of amusement.

"You will grace me at my left hand, if you please, and the Scout will sit at my right."

He blinked: he on the left, she to the right, offering him the first voice. He bowed, seeking the proper phrase of thanks and acknowledgment.

The Master Trader sniffed dourly.

"Yes, of course. But it signifies very little when one deals with a Scout in a hurry, I assure you. We might as well meet in zero-G with you upside down on the ceiling for as much attention as he will pay!"

· · · ✳ · · ·

It seemed to Jethri that Norn was wrong, for the scout arrived with a small meal to hand and made all the proper bows, exact in degree to Norn, and then a move full of nuance and complexities to him, with overtones of an admission of failure and error of judgment, even a request for forgiveness—there was little in Liaden that allowed of anything nearly as simple as an "I'm sorry!"

There were just the three of them, and from the exultant formal they moved instantly into a mode Grig would have called war-room.

"Eat," the Scout advised as he sat, "for one of you will be departing with me, and *Keravath* has already filed a tentative outbound, with a departure within the local twelfth day, if you please."

Before they could reply he expanded the statement of his bow, addressing the pair while favoring Norn with a particular nod and wry expression.

"Almost I begin to think that my errors should include my failure to refuse a summons from one surely not so well versed yet in *melant'i* as to include a life path for me . . ."

Then looking directly at Jethri, who'd managed to bite off half of a breakfast dumpling before being addressed:

"You, sir, entrusted me with a notebook, in order that I might have it studied and copies made. I am of no doubt that the notebook is your own, and I promised to return it to you safely. That notebook and some related material have been appropriated—or perhaps misappropriated—by an internal agency allied with our organization. They've removed it from our facilities and taken it, we believe, in order to take control of several other pieces of property which may be forbidden technology, or which may simply be property of your own which you have yet to be made aware of."

"Property? What kind of property? Why would they take my journal?"

Internally, Jethri grimaced—he hadn't meant to just start in like this. But unless there *were* secret pages most of what was in that book was silly kid stuff—like his count on the fractins he'd bought at different places, and how many were "good ones, real ones" and where were the best places to look, and like the trade routes he'd outlined with his father for when he would have a ship to fly or trade with, and . . .

The Scout sighed, holding his hands in a gesture Jethri took to mean *slow down . . .*

"Some of these questions may be best answered by those associated with the removal of the items from a supposedly secure area within a Scout facility. The question of the property itself cannot be answered without the book—it was removed after I wrote a study approach for the experts who were to do the evaluation for me, since there are subtleties which I know of but am not expert at. They performed only the first of these before the material was removed."

"Can't you just tell them to bring it back? They're Liaden, they're *your* associates—can't your bosses just order them?"

"That would be the case normally, yes. However, my superiors . . ."

Jethri caught an expression on the Scout's face, saw his glance toward Norn ven'Deelin.

He bowed a bow requesting assurance of the Master Trader.

"To reply properly I shall need to discuss information of a confidential nature."

Norn's face had gone bland, and her hands made the little go-ahead common among traders, the left hand palm up and open, a two-fingered fist orbiting beyond the open palm and then sweeping toward the requester . . . that would be "offer the deal."

"The problem I have," he said quickly, then, "is that some of the permissions given to make this happen came from levels well up within my organization. There is a debate going on, a stressing of boundaries, perhaps even a disaffection. Additionally, there is a jurisdictional difficulty. With the action being removed from Scout headquarters and common Liaden space in pursuit of items known or suspected to be in Terran areas, the possibility of *jedante*—the setting of precedent—becomes a difficulty."

The Scout paused, his face intent as he sought another point.

Jethri's frustration grew and he fell into Terran, interrupting. "So you're saying that the bosses don't care that you promised me I'd have it back and they're going to ignore you and your promise and take what's mine, while they mess around with my notebook—and who knows, maybe using my name!"

With a voice slightly raised now, and eyes seeking to dominate the conversation, the Scout used a bow indicating "I understand your concern." The Scout replied in Terran, not too badly accented.

"The matter allows of multiple interpretations. Let me say this: the division in intent extends both up and down in the organization, yes.

"*Some* of the bosses are in favor of the action that's been undertaken. Others, such as those closest to my own areas of operation, feel that the *melant'i* of the Scouts suffers greatly if the word of a field agent may be ignored or disarranged so fully."

He paused, then went on, his face going blander, bringing Jethri's already strained attention up a notch.

"I feel I must insist, with no disrespect meant or offered, that at least one part of your statement is wrong. I promise you that, *no*, they will not just ignore me and take from you. That would be outside the bounds of proper behavior in several of our shared cultures."

He rose, smoothly unwinding to his modest height, and bowed to Jethri again.

"On my name and my House, as witnessed by one not of my clan, they will not just ignore me on this. Again, I promise you, Jethri Gobelyn, I will do my utmost to bring you face-to-face with these miscreants, that we may together return to you what is yours."

• • • ✳ • • •

Apparently the "witness" part was even more formal than he'd gotten from tel'Ondor's training since it required a solemn stand-up bow from *both* the Scout and his mother; and the insistence on "Gobelyn" in this had some depth he didn't at first fathom.

"It occurs to me that I may have my own backups stand down," Norn offered judiciously as they sat again. She had her hands spread on the table then. Jethri saw her staring hard at her Master's ring before she looked at him, her mouth going straight, and perhaps grim, before she turned her attention to the waiting Scout, her look giving him permission to speak.

"Yes, that would be the case," he said. "If we are to move among Terran boundaries—you understand that we have no time frame for this, except as soon as possible? They have to pull together a team and the pair of us shall move with more speed, and perhaps have more access, as well as less likelihood of a crossing of my Balance with your own."

Norn bowed acknowledgment and looked at both of them.

"You, Scout, for yourself and for your organization, have brought this to us for solving, and the solving requires great trust. This I accept. My son has necessity and must be gone from the ship for the purpose of Balance both ethical and physical, a purpose he agrees with, and which may have cultural subtlety beyond my comprehension. Is this agreed by all?"

There were bows from both Jethri and the Scout.

"In that case, you will know your business better than I," she said, a hand motion indicating them both. Then to Jethri: "My son, never forget that you may call upon the clan as you need. You will take and wear your collar pin, and use Ixin's name among any of our allies as needed. Take the choker, it is yours, if luck so follows. Dress as trader, and take at least one of the good suits."

She glanced toward ter'Astin's bland face and saw something there Jethri must have missed, continuing with an emphatic slap on the table.

"In fact, take the very best suit, for you will be a diplomat for yourself. *Jedante* will be properly served if necessary. This is a matter of necessity on several fronts, this venture. Do us proud, for I expect to be by your side when you tell your tales to my foster mother!"

She stood, bowed. "Safe lift, my son. Move as quickly as you can, that you may return to me as soon as may be, to make yourself, Ixin, and *Elthoria* whole again."

Chapter Seven

· · · ·✳· · · ·

Control Deck, *Keravath*, Outbound from Boltston

DIM ALMOST TO THE POINT OF TOO DARK, the board colors were close if not exact, and ter'Astin's toss was good, and into the right-hand seat.

"I'll sit pilot, of course, you'll sit left seat, and since you'll be at the board, we'll log you in as sitting second."

It was, Jethri knew, some kind of a sop to his honor, but he could feel his shoulders clenching. If there was one thing his mother the captain had made sure he knew was that he wasn't any pilot and wasn't worth teaching: on the *Market* he daren't ever *sit* in a command seat, not even while doing stinks on port. He shuffled the largest of his bags toward the bin to the back.

"Not a seat for me, I think. There are two more and I'll just . . ."

The Scout's tone firmed. "If you please, *do* take the left seat. I appreciate your understanding of etiquette but I dislike having to talk over my shoulder. You'll sit second and earn some keep."

Jethri looked up, the pilot's hand motion designating Jethri's spot with emphasis. "Bully and fool," he said with a touch of asperity, tucking his day pack into the indicated cubby and testing the catch web with a stronger tug than it deserved.

"Forgive me, young sir; this trip is not likely to be an easy one, and if you think the pilot's a fool, we can cancel it and let your . . ."

Jethri snickered. "Just naming the seats the way I was taught, sir."

"I find it hard to believe that the Gobelyns traveled on a ship where they allowed the captain and first board to be called a fool."

Jethri turned to him, realizing that Pen Rel's excellent teaching had the pair of them playing Balance games; the more his mood was uncertain, the more the Scout would automatically react and . . .

"Good," ter'Astin bowed to him. "Let us not waste adrenaline in such a fashion. I am still at a loss for the words . . ."

Jethri stared into a corner—there were lots of them, and they were dim, because measuring one's space was a good plan for anyone on a ship's flight deck, in any case and at any time—and he didn't have to look at the Scout.

Gathering energy he finally relented of his silence.

"There's a saying a family saying, maybe, or a Terran one. I heard it enough though, and maybe it was just my ship . . ." He paused, considering *melant'i* and knowing that any time a Terran-born tried to play with that delicate balance there was a chance of error. So he looked directly at the Scout, who was by now in his seat, and testing straps for the away phase . . .

"So it was said, sometimes, that 'When the first board's a bully, second board's a fool? That means *I* sit fool.'"

The Scout allowed a slight grunt to acknowledge his hearing of the phrase; but his hands were already talking to his ship with the same kind of surety Jethri'd seen Iza display, or Khat. Jethri'd longed for that kind of surety when his father had been at the boards, and when he's assumed that one day he would . . .

"Your father," said the Scout accusingly, "was a pilot. His father was a pilot, and his before. Your captain-mother Iza was a pilot. Is it odd that you are not?"

Jethri settled back, hands already reaching to the slightly wrong spots for the belts, and then, with a glance, discovering the right spots on this ship and tugging them into place, checking the lock/unlock sequence, sitting tight against it for sizing. This was also a useful way to hide his perplexity—was the Scout testing him, aware that Iza was not truly his mother? The mention of Arin's predecessors . . . made him nervous.

The seat was a remarkably good fit to start with and he could feel it adjusting itself as he reached his hands to the board as he'd seen others do too many times to count.

He wet his lips, finding there was no retort there when he expected something, though resentment was a fringe aura to all his thoughts still.

"Dunno 'bout odd," he said in Terran, this being a discussion he'd prefer not to have, in any language. "Just know that them on the *Market* made it plain that I wasn't ready yet, and the captain, she made it plain that pilot's not in me. The others could see it too, I'm guessing."

The Scout didn't reply to this intelligence, rather used his chin to gesture toward Jethri's side of the board.

"You'll want to push the bottommost button on the right once, and then flip the secure switch to the right, and lock it. That tells the ship what it knows: not only that someone's in the seat, but that person is alert. More than this we won't do on exit."

Jethri followed the instruction, and several more, found the arming handle for the abandon ship capsule and understood those instructions, which basically said that if something went wrong and there was absolutely no way they could survive after the pilot declared an emergency *and* declared abandon ship, he was to pull that handle and take whatever more time the capsule gave him to breathe to transmit and record what had gone wrong so that someone else might be able to achieve Balance for the dead.

He wore the earpiece for comm, listening in; he activated, on order, enough of the board to be able to see that the front and rear hatches were secure, that the docking strut was engaged but not locked, that—well, he'd had been listening to these kinds of things since he was born, and though more than half of the traffic was in Liaden there really wasn't that much difference from a run out from a trade stop on *Gobelyn's Market*. Nor was the board much different, and that was likely not Liaden difference but the difference between a family freight ship and a Scout's light duty.

Jethri listened now: voices from *Elthoria*'s flight deck reached out to the pilot, ignoring him, assigning, agreeing, confirming. Gaenor's voice now: this would be the official—but no, it must not be, for ter'Astin was talking, naming Jethri Gobelyn ven'Deelin Clan Ixin as second board on *Keravath*, while in his ear Gaenor was saying, "Communications check in process, on comm *Elthoria*, Gaenor tel'Dorbit, checking *Keravath* Second Board Jethri Gobelyn ven'Deelin."

Ship habit more than thought: "Second Board, signal caught," he said, "open line."

"Jethri, I'm sending secure relink now, please test."

He looked over the controls, close enough to Terran after all, found the symbols needed, punched the button as around him *Keravath*'s familiar-enough preparations went on.

The two central screens were live, one with technical scan showing radar and a radio-source overlay, and one with a forward video. He guessed when the *Market* came out of rehab she might have setups only one or two generations behind these, but there, he'd been reading up on the Scouts and knew they often were ahead of commercial installations by a dozen Standards.

The link showed live; Jethri spoke.

"*Keravath* Second, testing secure link, *Keravath* Second testing link . . ."

"Shield ratio?" Gaenor's voice had changed—maybe it was the secure line's special harmonics, or maybe it was her playing on a sudden sense of privacy, but—ah, darn!

Jethri was stonkered: he'd never tested a secure link beyond touching a button—and that just once, with Iza off-ship.

Apparently it was a secure link: the Scout was carrying on so rapid a conversation in jargon-laden Liaden that it took Jethri's frantic hand-signal to gain his eyes.

"Shield ratio?" he asked doubtfully of the serious face, fearing that he'd interrupted . . .

Ter'Astin gave a sharp bow that was almost a nod, pointed to one of the small sub-screens down on Jethri's right side, hand underlying the duplicate on the Scout's board.

There: a clear-reading color bar, with the red side showing a reading of three digits, the blue . . .

"*Elthoria,* that would be, 937 over 063."

Almost without pause came the rejoinder, in a quiet purr of a voice . . .

"Jethri, that is very fine," she said in Terran, which words he'd heard next to his ear not all that long ago, and which reminder was distracting at best and . . . "and so, since you shall miss the Festival here and I gather also Festivals where you travel, I am to relay to you Vil Tor's hope that we three may, as he says in his best Terran, be 'festive as all get-out' on your return . . . and that you return soon. In the meantime, he points out that we shall party in your honor, shall we not?"

Jethri wanted to frame a good reply in Liaden, but the modes crashed his thoughts for a moment, and then the ship around him shook with the preliminary cast-offs, going to internal power entirely, and the gravity shifting oddly, a reminder that *Elthoria* was easily a hundred times more massive than *Keravath*.

"Gaenor," he managed finally, "yes, I would very much like that, but you must tell him I am unpracticed . . ."

She laughed gently in his ear.

"Jethri, believe me, you'll find him just as pleased as I to help rectify that situation."

"Second," came ter'Astin's voice, amused, "we'll be needing some concentration here in sixty seconds, if you please . . ."

"I—" he began, but Gaenor's voice in his ear came quickly.

"I heard the pilot's voice, my friend. Quickly then, Vil Tor and I offer a commission to Jethri the trader, to acquire for all of us, if you can, such scarves or scarf clothes to make our festives better. You have a measure of the cloth and the wavelengths; if necessary Vil Tor can tailor from base cloth. We shall make it worth your while, indeed . . . *Elthoria* secure out."

That was said just as *Keravath* shifted slightly, announced by the shifting center of gravity . . . and Jethri heard the Scout say, "Control jets test good, we're set now," this unlikely sentence in Terran as the Scout looked at him meaningfully from little more that an arm's length.

"You don't understand—the connection is broken . . ."

Jethri hoped he wasn't blushing bright enough to light the ship; ter'Astin laughed very lightly, and went on in a gentle voice, and a mode of comrade.

"Acquit me of such, Second. I have been flying solo courier long enough to understand very well the sigh of departure and the problems of connections being broken. And for you, so early in your career, and so badly used by my timing, I owe another Balance yet.

"Now, then, practical piloting lessons—pay attention! I shall expect you to retain much of what I tell you."

· · · ✵ · · ·

There was a phrase known among Liadens and Terrans alike, and Jethri began to appreciate its nuance quickly under ter'Astin's tutelage. That phrase was "to fly like a scout . . ." and it meant to move a ship faster, more accurately, with less fuss, and with more elegance than most ships moved—and the Scout had begun it before *Elthoria*'s call of "well-away" was fully voiced.

The little ship was nothing so gaumy as a shuttle nor as laggard as a trader's family freighter; spinning on axis as neatly and carefree as Jethri might have in a stinks-run zero-G leap; the press of correction jets exact and efficient, with none of the overburn Khat deplored in Iza, nor none yet of the prissiness that Iza accused Cris of when he filled the chair.

Jethri croggled at the front video as the Scout skimmed *Elthoria*'s main pod-deck as if he were lifting from a planetary airport, the pressure growing as the little ship accelerated toward the line superimposed on the radar screen, a line reaching well out from *Elthoria* toward a Jump point that looked far too close to the world they were leaving for a safe system exit. The image almost brought on the kind of open-space fear he'd felt on planets—and that, of course, was absurd. He held on, saying nothing . . .

"We of the Scouts are like pilots everywhere," came the nonchalant voice as Jethri maintained his grip on the armrests, "we offer and expect assistance of other pilots. There, we have taken a look at several pods from a less static location, giving images available to *Elthoria* without the launch of a remote—and in turn *Elthoria*'s eyes can be sure that in my haste I've not forgotten to uncap a jet nor left a cable dangling."

"Left a cable dangling?" Jethri managed.

The Scout looked across at him, serious.

"Oh, indeed, Second. Couriers and small ships are prone to such, since we often don't fit the usual attachment points and must use secondary points or transient attachments. I have myself, once only— and I tell you in strictest confidence—while I repeat *once only!*—managed to part from a station with technician's cleaning cart still attached by umbilical, station to cart to ship. It was not *this* ship, I assure you, and in the end the fault was multiples of faults, for things were powered down that ought not have been, and others powered up that ought not, and . . . in the end there were mutual fines, and I'm sorry to say I lost five good days of personal leave to the fixing of things. Ugly, very ugly indeed, I was for a *relumma* or more . . ."

Here he paused in recounting the story, making sure Jethri was looking at him as well as the screen where the ship was nearing the long dotted line to the Jump point . . .

"Yes, ugly I was, for I therefore missed a Festival rendezvous with a favorite. I will expect you to be careful indeed, Second, that we not fall into such a situation on this trip!"

Before Jethri could reply other than shake his head at the unlikely need for his aid in such things, the pilot did something complex on his board and visibly relaxed—

"There. The course is set. And so, the course we have set is for Balfour, and I would like you to check my course, if you would, check my math—"

Jethri stared across at his companion starkly. Balfour was on a route *Gobelyn's Market* had run several time within his memory, with barely even a sub-crew. Balfour shouldn't be named by itself, of course, that was silly. There was another place that ought to be part of that run . . .

But there was so much he didn't know, and he had no training at all, just—sense came to the fore.

"I am not a pilot! I don't even know where to find the course—"

The flight deck had darkened as they traveled, but Jethri could see the pilot's eyes tighten, and heard the slow *duff* of someone not fully reining in frustration.

"This is true, Jethri Gobelyn, and not merely the handy excuse given for security reasons? It is true that you have not learned to pilot, nor to navigate, nor to plot courses?"

Jethri froze in his seat, feeling the eyes pin him where he was, reviewing his life to be sure that in none of these days had he accidentally done those things and forgotten, that he—

"None of it, Pilot," he managed. "I was last on the list for flight deck training. If I would have stayed on the *Market*, I suppose they would have broken down soon and got me my time on the lifeboat boards, but not even . . ."

"That's criminal! Surely you must know your homeworld's coords at least . . ."

Jethri heard the Scout's error and shook his head, several times, suppressing the urge to raise his voice. The Scout's choice of words became "birth home" in Terran.

"My birth home's a ship," the trader said blandly. "Now and always. The only coords I know is what I played with on the toy board my father gave me, and what I learned from playing Trade N Traipse, on the off-line spare board. You probably don't know the game . . ."

The pilot lifted hand to face, eyes closed. Finally, he removed his hand and glanced forthrightly at his supposed student.

"Coords from a game and a child's toy? Well then, your father was a pilot, so I assume you at least got an accurate toy. You do know, then, where the controls are and what they are supposed to do?"

Jethri lifted his hands and held his face as steady as he might. The truth was that he'd heard Khat say something like it, and Paitor, and Cris. Seeli once or twice had even hinted that some rules "needed to be modified or the boy allowed to follow them . . ."

"Observation only, and from the 'prentice board my father . . ."

"Hold! Less and less I esteem your former captain. And you?"

Words didn't come: what was there to say? Iza's long plans had never included him—never!

"Tell me then, as we have some time, what would you do if I were stricken with some accident or poison, paralyzed here in my chair. How would you get on, how would you save us both?"

Jethri shook his head. "I couldn't!" he blurted, feeling the flush of frustration. "I told you I'm not a pilot, and I told you I've been pushed away from the true board my whole life! Pilots do secret stuff!"

"Halt!"

The word was said so quietly it barely reached between them, but with such anger and loathing that Jethri froze again.

There was silence but for the proper sound of a ship prepping for transit, some blowers, some slight buzzing, a hum . . . perhaps even the creak of leather seats as the two men stared at each other.

Then, unexpectedly, a bow, surprisingly low from one already seated, and the words in Liaden, and then following in Trade equivalent, and then following again in more than passable Terran.

"Forgive me, forgive me, forgive me. I still feel that there has been something criminal in your education, and I see that my assumption has colored my approach in this. I am a Scout, and therefore, I assume too much in this case, from having only partial knowledge. I know of your father, and more now than when first you and I met; I know of your uncle, and more now than when first you and I met, and what I did not know until now was the depth of your captain's error.

"If you will permit, let me speak with Jethri Gobelyn, with Jethri Gobelyn ven'Deelin's permission, and we will work with this in Terran, where you may correct my language if need be. You see, I understand these things: Jethri Gobelyn is not a fool, nor is Jethri Gobelyn a coward, nor is Jethri Gobelyn a child."

Again a pause, this time as a small two-tone signal disturbed the room, and then another. The Scout's knowing eyes sought something on the boards, his finger touched a control, and he leaned back, staring straight ahead.

"Let us play a game of sorts, Jethri. I will rephrase my question and will offer replies—and there are no wrong answers. The fact that you do not know does not mean you wish not to know—I can see that from your learning since I saw you first all out of breath and taking on a space station if you must. No fool, and no coward, that I know. This game, we shall both learn from it."

• • • ✳ • • •

The game was survival; the questions started over, without rage this time: what would and what should he do were he left in the ship, this ship, alone in space?

"I need to explore and understand the escape pod—one that will take me to safety if the ship is damaged. I know there's an abandon ship control, but I don't know what it does other than bring down an emergency suit."

"With myself suffering from a stroke, how would you start?"

"That would depend on where. In Jump, I'd have to try to help you, and otherwise wait until Jump is over. That's automatic. Then I'd call for help."

"And if we arrived and suffered an instant debris strike, disabling the vessel?"

"I know the symbols, but this ship doesn't show the Guild signs I know. There should be a fast passage from here to a hatch or a release."

"And so if we were on port, or in an inhabited planetary orbit, already you know enough to survive: call abandon ship and the suit comes when you push, unfolds from the overhead; in abandon ship the luggage bins fold out and the hatch behind on either side can be used."

Jethri looked at him bleakly.

"There's luck and there's luck—how many accidents happen in . . ."

The Scout held up his hand and began pulling up info screens, dropping them one after another onto Jethri's backup screen.

"How many accidents happen in an inhabited system? Why, most of them." The Scout, moving quite expansively for someone strapped into an acceleration couch, pointed to the top screen where there were several lists of incidents.

"At least the ones we know of . . . most of those happen in crowded space, orbital space, gravity circuits. This is where ships hit ships, where satellites hit ships, where basic valve failures from overpressure and sloppy loading are exposed, where 'loose objects' like lost hatches and mislaid tools and parts of ancient space probes manage to find a way past low-grade shields or sleepy watch crew.

"Stupidity happens more often in crowds: runaway pods, ejected crew members, accidental weapons tests, I can't tell you how many such things I've attended myself—But yes, that's wrong. I *can* tell you even if I can't recall them all instantly to mind. I should not so misspeak, since my records are available to us. You will, of course, regard anything I may show you from such files as confidential between pilots—and in particular you shall not discuss the cables I unleashed, but there, a pilot will not . . ."

"But I am not a pilot!"

The Scout laughed lightly.

"You *must* be a pilot, my friend, at least a basic pilot, and by the end of our trip you shall at least be able to find your way home—or to a safe port since you claim no home, which statement would pain dear Ixin no end, I'm sure. Even if in a most basic manner, you must. I am not looking to make you a Scout nor a liner captain, but your education as a trader will not be complete—no matter what our good Pen Rel might say—until you can from the inside understand something of the desperations pilots go through on behalf of trade, and on the behalf of uninformed traders."

· · · ✳ · · ·

The lesson went on as the ship moved toward the Jump point,

with Jethri wringing what patience he could from his already fraught psyche.

"Yes," he admitted, "I can see that you trap the previous Jump coordinates, but I thought they vary considerably for going *to* instead of *from*, that—"

"Ah, well. Yes, coordinates are not perfectly static, and the likelihood that a ship needing to Jump precipitously would find exactly the same orbital slot to fall into that it left is . . . unlikely. So, we will assume certain things to start, and then while we are in Jump we will discuss more problematical situations. But first, some basic maneuvers.

"I am bringing your board live, in training mode. This means that it will function entirely as it should . . ."

Here Jethri felt his stomach drop for all that they were flying a perfectly normal course. Surely his face showed concern, for the Scout showed a patient and calming palm.

"Good, and thank you. I shall now finish the sentence! The board will function entirely as it should in principle, but each step will need confirmation from my board before the ship hears. This method of instruction may be one step up from the method wherein one leaps from the edge of a gravity-bound station section into zero-G, trusting . . ."

Jethri sighed, staring across at the Scout. Yes, in some places he was known as Jethri the Leaper, and there were drinks named for him, and on one station, at least, several medical terms: leaper's lag, transit bruise, and gravity burn among them. It was not so long ago that he'd escaped from hounding Liadens from a low-class ship by doing that very thing—and, in its way then, it was part of his *melant'i* as a trader and . . .

"Is that more than sufficient reminder of past error, do you think," he muttered, "for a trader you wish to bring under your tutelage? One presumes that it is necessary that I learn this task not only for my sake, but also for yours, as well as ven'Deelin and indeed, for Ixin. If that is the case, then I shall do my best. Is it true that I am not to be remade in your image, Scout, but to be made secure in mine?"

The question was asked in mode of equal to equal, which, of course, was only outside the bounds of reality if one considered their respective ages, their respective experience within their specialties, their actual rank within their particular professions, their—but no, he, Jethri, was here as one owed a debt. It might be sufficient.

The scout was very quiet for a long moment, and then his hands fluttered one of those nearly too quick motions, and his mouth hinted at the smile that hovered behind the eyes.

"And so you have a point, my trainee. I will admit you to be the least avid, the very least eager piloting student I have ever offered my tutelage. I am a pilot of some renown—which is of small moment to one who would rather be perusing opportunity lists, I suppose. I am, you must understand, properly placed!"

Jethri failed to be flattered, or even satisfied, but he did feel the tension go out of the deck.

A burst of noise on the audio, a quick counted warn-away from light-hours away as a ship Jumped in-system on the far side of the system and well up the ecliptic. Likely wasn't another ship within a light-hour of it, but the warn-aways, the warn-aways had to be observed, Khat had said when she'd told him of her basic training . . .

Jethri stared down at his board. *His board.* Gingerly he brought visuals on screen four live, and selected a feed from the ship's computer. He'd seen this happen from time to time on the *Market*, despite Iza's lazy enmity; he'd seen it as a child back when his father had thought to bring him fully into the command line back when he'd has his own Jatze Junior board to play with. He'd set a course for Balfour as a child; it was one of the destinations his father had been to several times as commissioner. Now though . . .

"Balfour," he said, "is a Terran planet orbiting a star of the same name. The general coordinates are on my screen now, backdated but marked as acceptable." Here he swallowed, seeing a date close to a dozen Standards old. "How do I proceed without going first to Waymart?"

"Waymart? And why should we first go to Waymart, Second?"

Jethri flushed.

"Are we north of center, then? In most directions Waymart comes first, just from north . . . Ah, Terran trade routes, these you remember?"

Jethri shrugged noncommittally. It was one of the things he did know—he'd remembered that, since he'd won games going first to Waymart, then to Balfour. There'd been a reason, if he could remember it. That's right, it was one of the downall routes he'd taught himself.

"My ship, that's how it usually went to Balfour—first to Waymart. I mean *Gobelyn's Market* when I say that—*Elthoria's* never been to either of them, I think."

The Scout waved a hand for attention. "Our business is not ordinary trade, and it takes us to Balfour. Please observe."

The Scout moved on his acceleration couch, and the coordinates changed color. "You begin by telling the ship to update and project the coords to a time approximating our reaching a safe Jump distance— you'll see what I have set—and then use the ship's computer to project time in transit assuming a neutral, spinless, and massless shift. Once you have *that*, you'll add the ship's mass into the basic equation—for our purposes now and for emergency purposes on a vessel like ours, you can usually trust the ship's understandings, but *do* check the most recent arrival mass against known major additions or subtractions— and then do add the corrections using our acceleration against our current reference frame."

Jethri shivered with concentration, finding the reference frame numbers changing, the variations in acceleration flashing red notes at him, the—

"Also make sure you're adding in the ambient and gradient energy fields, which will help take into account the drifts caused by the local stellar winds, coronal outflows, and magnetic bubbles, as well as the effects of outer rim planetoids or comet clouds."

Jethri closed his eyes, pulling a deep breath into his chest as the additional information meant more screens needed to be added, more—

"We have hours until basic Jump point, so do not thrill yourself with an unnecessary rush. Scouts and pilots prize efficiency and misuse of adrenaline is not efficient. Here, here the triple green line you see on this screen is the boundary. I know Terrans use a single blue line, but learn with ours—and see that as you change these little things the triple line changes. We have a very precise system. Under no account are you to attempt a Jump inside these lines—such Jumps are fatal!"

"But I've heard that if you've got a—"

The Scout laughed, very softly.

"You've heard that sometimes one can do wishful things with the spaceship, and all is well. Understand that this ship is not as . . . as approximate, let us say, as certain other ships are. Ships that must carry bulky freight and such, driven by Terran engines, such ships are very powerful but are not as finely scaled as this."

Jethri was still adding numbers in, trying to backup calculate in his head what the computers did so effortlessly. He nodded, saw numbers stabilize, knew there was something else he had to do—oh!

"But what's the energy density of the coils and—"

"Ah, so you *have* been on a flight deck before? It is not as though you know nothing . . ."

The numbers had slowed their change even more . . . .

"I know that energy density is one of the things pilots talk about; they make jokes about it, and what it means to forget about it . . . but I was never allowed to study it! It was in the game, and in the toy—but I couldn't reach the files. Just the toy board, and what I could read and see in the game editions, that's what I knew."

Silence for a moment, and then interruptions as another burst of radiation, Jump glare from an outgoing ship, hit the audio.

"Not even *permitted* to study on your own? Locked out? Yes, *criminal*. But for the moment, we will not be concerned with energy density of coils: there may be a time just before Jump when that information is important. But consider it a last moment correction: the basics of the Jump may be calculated without that, it is like knowing wind speed or ambient air pressure on a planetary landing . . . but again, that comes later."

Chapter Eight

* * * *❋* * * *

Flight Deck, *Gobelyn's Market,* Local Day Graceful 23 on Kinaveral

CAPTAIN IZA and Acting Second Pilot Khat had been over the ship a dozen hours today, walking and sitting, and a dozen yesterday, with multiple tests of computers and signal systems, with lock section tests and signal ablation tests—sometimes nearly full crews sitting station and all but live and others just the pair of them on lines.

"Won't be happy until there's no wire through the hull," she'd told Paitor three times within Khat's hearing, and Grig had mentioned that phrase too, which was "no good sign" as Seeli told Khat, Seeli having heard it too, "Twicet or moren that, if I think hard on it."

Seeli had an infant child on board so Khat could see her concern, and now, Seeli had that infant's Da on board again, which was well, as Grig had returned to her from a jaunt which ought never have happened, except that Grig was in some ways Jethri's closest kin now that it was out and open that calling Iza "Ma" when it came to Jeth was about as far as could be from true . . .

Khat's knowledge of the rebuilt ship was still fresher and deeper than Iza's, and that was just one more jagged edge in a ship that was supposed to be a fine-running team machine any day now, up to running orbits out of habit like they believed 'em, with Iza fully in charge because she was better, not because she used to be better.

Iza sat at the board, eyes closed, adjusting her brand new seat. This was practical work for a pilot, necessary work. Her hands reached out to the right and left, tapping . . .

With words that might have been "mud and muck" said between clenched teeth, Iza touched the *lean left,* on the adjustment stud, stood up, eyes still closed, turned twice, dropped into the seat and pounded on the main system engine's full thrust button like to drive it through the hull . . .

"Works," she said to space, since everyone else was studiously trying not to watch or listen to her.

The button hadn't worked the engine, of course, since the board was still in training mode; but what had worked was that Iza had the seat set for her, and if she came in blind or bloody, that reach would put the ship in her control exactly as it ought, almost like the *Market* hadn't been refitted with as much all-new as they could afford, and a bit more, too.

That being done, Iza punched a live button and got her scores out of the trainer, hissing under her breath and glancing at Khat with a straight-lipped seriousness that might have scared a lesser person. Khat, however, had hand-carried Iza back to the ship deadweight and fighting mad from the cop drugs and she sat second board with authority, just like she could sit first on more ships than ever she'd thought in her life. Khat nodded and waited for the captain, who went on as expected.

"You had a second on me in the run-in drill and two-thirds on the close down, before I adjusted; I'm thinking we're right close to even on it now."

"Imagine so. You were never sharpest in a drill anyway."

That last was true, if pushing it; when Iza had last been on the boards live there wasn't anyone else who'd been able to match her across the moves. Now . . . well, now, Iza'd been off running someone else's ship and using their settings and so she'd learned those habits and would have to unlearn them. That was true. Also true—that Khat had been trading and flying ships as often as every other quickflit; they'd throw her something new as long as she'd flown something close and by the end of the refit she'd got fifty-seven new ships or varieties and that hadn't been mentioned, and oughtn't. Captain being captain . . .

"Got stuff we don't need to share portside, I'm thinking, so if we can just go to standing order, say me and then you and Paitor to get us off this muck, we'll do. We have some calibration to do, and some staff talk, seeing as how there's a child on board, and we'll need to be clear as to who does what. We'll just set into a long orbit when we get off of this place and have some time for planning."

Khat closed her eyes against the reality of the screen, now that the long orbit was mentioned. She hoped there wasn't going to be an argument now about Paitor's careful plans, made as well as could be when Iza was off-ship and safely tucked away on a long-haul so she couldn't run riot at the shipyard.

"Shall we," Khat suggested, "do some random route checks in the morning, maybe drop a couple of new safe-runs into the computers so there's nothing that might be obvious left from the old runs?"

And that, of course, was necessary and Iza would snap it up as quick as she could. As sure as her name was Khatelane Gobelyn Acting Second, she knew that first board would have to go for that . . .

"Old safe's are still set, right?" Iza said, hands punching a couple more things live and drawing out some things that weren't usually touched within a quick scan of port much less still wired to the dock.

"All of them are still set," Khat acknowledged, nodding and touching a button on her board to illustrate the first half-dozen of the secret presets, including Connerville.

That was a challenge right out, since Connerville'd been one of Iza's favorite girlhood ports, and the one she'd snagged her original backup—who'd become second officer and husband . . .

Iza didn't flinch. A lot had changed with Jethri finding his own way out of a bad bind, and the captain looked over the list, nodding carefully as she looked it over.

"Don't see one we can't do without, and most we ought to have been gone from a dozen years or more. Lift with these and the ones in my head, but we'll clear the lot as soon as we're able. Can't figure but what someone looked 'em all over in dry dock." She paused and even smiled, lifting a finger and shaking it in emphasis as something got decided in her head.

"You know what? We'll have a paper pull—I get six to put in, Cris being gone you get four, Paitor'll get four, and everyone else can throw in a pair. We'll do it for first clear dinner once we're away. How's that to choose the first?"

That was actually pretty good; it would let them do some work as a whole crew—

Khat lifted an eyebrow. "Everyone? Even Dyk?"

"Sure," Iza allowed, "even Dyk. None of us have to know who puts what in, but if we end up with Vertville I'll just put it last on the list."

Khat laughed softly. "If we end up with two Vertvilles, what then?"

Iza laughed now too.

"Dunno if he's that much of a gambler, but I'd think not." And, she said with a wave of her hand, "I doubt anyone owes him that much of a debt to fling away one of theirs."

"Hadn't thought of that," Khat admitted. Not that it was likely, after all.

The point was that each of the worlds chosen ought to have an element of safety about it for serious problems—like a run-in with a pirate or a trade commission attempt to confiscate major cargo, or to save a crewman's life, or the ship itself—and someone on the ship ought to have a special connection there, something that might provide an edge. A lot of the loopers depended on family links, or birth registrations, or membership in a trade organization . . . but it was hard to look to a planet when the whole of ship life argued for staying off the things since each lift from surface was a lot more costly than a swing-by at a trade station.

Still not quite returned from his run as a co-chef on a small tour liner, Dyk now, he'd see Vertville, with its twenty-seven-hour-a-day non-stop casino show-bar theater, food-food-food all-tourist-all-the-time atmosphere as the perfect place to run to; always were job openings, always has lots of ship movements, always . . .

Well, that was for crew to decide once the trip was going. Dyk was due back in seventy-two hours, with Cris due in well before that, and that was good as far as Khat was concerned, not only for her personal comfort but for the ship's good: Iza needed to have someone to go over the changes with, and Paitor wasn't doing very well at it, being not in the immediate flight chain of command and especially since his stock with his big sister had dropped considerably since he'd voted with everyone else about Iza off-shipping during the rebuild.

On top of that, Paitor's concentration needed to be on getting out the news that *Gobelyn's Market* was soon back to space and searching new cargo and routes starting at Franticle. There was a trade center there, and a good-size port and—

Khat could do that kind of stuff, but Paitor was much better at it:

already on land links to portside outgoing ships that could carry the news, and twice a shift he'd check the orbiting ships and squirt the news to any that were receiving news to spread, and sorting news they might have. Traders lived by that kind of network, after all, and so did the ship.

· · · ✦ · · ·

The ship felt crowded suddenly, so crowded that Khat let Cris go with a hug and a "Hi, brother" though they'd been parted for months. Zam and Mel were loud in the passage—perhaps against just such a need—and Grig had shown up and his happy voice had reached even this far, so he was projecting as well. Maybe they were being noisy against bothering Seeli and him. On the other hand, maybe they were just plain glad to be back on the ship they'd grown up on.

Khat walked behind Cris as they hit the control room, the sounds there more subdued, as always, as was the lighting. Cris took second, Iza was already in first, Khat picked up the so-called nav seat and its boards; and now, downship, working from the office, Seeli was using the all-call compartment by compartment, testing call tones and voice, testing code response and video—so that's where *she* was.

"Mel," Seeli's voice drifted through the ship, "your new warehouse keys are still here in the office, need you to sign them out before lift. Grig, those supplies are in for the med cabinets if you'll check by, and there's more notes on those replacement actuators. Zam, Dyk's still not in yet—you're free to make lunch starting anytime now . . ."

Khat's boards were live and sharp; the view of the outside of the *Market* an odd blend of the familiar and the new. She blinked at the screen, realized that part of the problem was that they had no pods attached but the refit had changed several of the video and sensor angles on her . . .

"Iza," she said, "we've got new views on topvids . . ."

"Was noticing that, and Cris tells me the wide angle's not as wide on the deck monitors at hatch one and two. They look bigger to me, if you'll check . . ."

From downship came Zam explaining why supplies came first and then lunch, and if crew was hungry they'd have to ask . . .

That idea got caught in the midst and changed—being back on the ship together, it did feel like they ought to be able to just call on Jethri to pick up whatever slack there was at the low end . . .

Seeli cut off a couple seconds and so did Zam, and then something was settled and the all-call carried again.

"Zam, stick with supplies then; Grig'll do handwiches all around and cater 'em too—and by my clock we have a rough count of four hours and fifteen minutes to lift. Has anyone heard any more from Dyk?"

Khat settled back, glanced at the dock monitors—

"Seeli, Dyk's closing fast with a motocart. Grig, hold up, looks like he's got carry-on for us all."

The captain's tone went out then, and Iza spoke to the ship:

"All hands! When Dyk boards I want that hatch locked and set; someone help him get in and away from the lock so I've got a confirm on how that video view looks for us up here. We'll seal and go to full ship air and pressure, and I want any remaining external lines dropped and confirmed. That's the 'genda.

"Seeli, I'm after port to get us out quick as we can; I need your confirms on crew and contents once I get confirms on seal. Cris will take reports of all outside lines and buses still attached, starting now. Soonest we get that move to hotpad, the sooner we'll be sitting to dinner!"

There was extra busyness for a while then and the latch-on to swipe them out of the dry dock and over to hotpad fourteen took them through the lunch Dyk provided. He was still all gussied up in his Legot Lines purple smock but he'd reversed the hat and wore a multidozen-years-old *Gobelyn's Market* tradeship show pin as jaunty as could be on the left side of that hat to show he knew where he was. He was Dyk, which meant he was fussing and whistling all the while, and he delivered. He mentioned he had an extra of this and an extra of that and an extra of the other as he went around but he didn't mention nothing about extras to Iza, and Khat realized he'd fallen back to old-time normal and ordered something too, for the absent Jethri.

The dry dock folks were glad enough to get Iza out of their space; Cris and Khat traded off comms and they only mentioned Iza's name once, because of the legal they had to say, else Paitor and Khat, and twice Seeli, had already signed and posted and acted for the ship on the legal.

The clunk of the release to the hotpad might have been extra strong or might have been just the way things got done on Kinaveral; the hotpad, as Zam was telling everyone later, just took 'em and tossed 'em, and that was right enough—if Khat hadn't been all over the ship with Seeli and Paitor while Iza slept she'd have thought the yardmaster was trying to put something more over on them.

Cris looked over to her with a relaxed smile more than once, which helped make Khat's time in the nav seat sit something better since he'd looked serious and even distant when he came in, and then Paitor called up from the trade board, with news that he had a pickup of three light transship pods, two of them empties, bound for Clawswitts, which was the agreed-on third bounce of the strategic Jump and long range loop plan he'd pored over for a Standard Year.

The key was to carry something paying into the next port, and that's what they were doing; the risk was that they'd only spec cargo lined up there so far, much of it coming in lined up for Trader Jethri Gobelyn, on account of the news of his last co-trade for the *Market* having gotten around. The outgoing from here—one of them was dustfall from that, too, and Paitor glad to be carrying anything since they'd been so unsure of ship-outs 'cause Iza hadn't been much in the way of answering her mail when she'd been out doing her exile.

For her part Iza ran numbers and got ahead of folks as she usually liked to do: the pod pickups were in a mid-orbit and they already trailed *one two three* pretty much on the way to the Jump point so if Iza and Cris were good—they'd be doing the work on this shift anyhow—ship's dinner tonight ought to still be an all-hands affair.

The call for lift-off places made it all seem real—*Gobelyn's Market*, better than ever, back to trade; Iza's call around went quick and she even remembered to call Travit, Grig, and Seeli in one call, which was a clean way to do it.

Seeli, this time at least, got to trade away the admin office for the nursery—Travit had been sitting in with her but for his first lift-off he'd be in Nursery A—that being what Jethri's old room had always been listed in the ship roster, anyway—in what traders usually called a bash-tank. A bash-tank could help hold someone in bad shape together through high-G if need be. When it had the cradle insert in it the bash-tank could lift a near newborn at four Gs but they weren't planning on hotfooting it and any of the usual routes out of the dab-smack if the equator launch point didn't call for anything higher than two-point-six Gs. Still, Grig as medico, would be standing by.

"Set numbers, boards check in!"

Three quick breaths, and boards all showing they were talking to each other, and pilots doing the same, and Khat found she needed a half-cent more of foot room and kicked the seat for that . . .

And then things got really busy, and the dust, dirt, and mud of Kinaveral fell away.

• • • ✳ • • •

They'd worked longer in the day than usual, but the crew was still bright with the return of proper routine and familiar faces. Orbit gained and rendezvous performed *one two three* pretty as could be, they locked in the transship pods while Dyk hijacked assorted bits of the crew's free time as he got together a big meal.

Khat was looking forward to her stint at the board while the first mate and the rest of the ship got the start of dinner; then Grig would come by and relieve her while she got dinner, and then the meeting, after all.

• • • ✳ • • •

They went around then, starting formally at the top, making sure that the crew order was confirmed, one after another, each knowing who was one step up and one step down—and one step sidewise, if that was the case. Iza'd pointed people to places after they came in, but that was just Iza; 'course being captain, they'd moved . . .

"Iza Gobelyn, Captain-Owner and Pilot." Iza said, sounding as even as a pod rail, and just a bit bored. The last time she'd been around crew for something formal it had been the Crew Having a Word; that had been a lot less pleasant for all of those present, and it echoed here, for all that Iza was as pure and clean, drink-or drugwise, as the best hydroponics water. She looked at each of them though, a sweeping look with no fidgeting, giving each one a nod.

"Paitor Gobelyn." Paitor paused, like he had to refigure the talking order. "Co-owner. Trader and Reserve Warehouse. Reserve Docking Pilot," he said.

Khat blinked in the silence between. She'd forgot that last, since it wasn't like him to claim pilot usually, even if they all knew he could. On the other hand, he'd called co-owner first, too, so he hadn't forgot the to-do when Iza'd been given leave to take an outship for the duration of the refit. She guessed she ought to ask if he'd got more time in . . . if he didn't tell the ship credits before they hit Jump.

Sitting next, up against the wall and on the backup board so that someone was on duty, it looked that Cris was caught by Paitor's presentation, too. He hurried, head bobbing, tongue making the words sound short-snapped.

"Cris Gobelyn. First Mate and Pilot. Technical Officer and Maintenance Director, Reserve Admin. Reserve Engineer."

He hand-signed *go* at her, flat-handed and clipped as much as his words. This worried her. Was she out of the circuit? Was he watching a problem?

Her lips worked for her and she nodded up and down once, each time giving little pause, running things together. As she spoke she thought that there was a little oddity—maybe Seeli ought to be in her spot. But Seeli had no claim to pilot, and if that's what Paitor had been on about . . .

"Khatelane Gobelyn. Second Mate. Pilot and Engineer and Reserve Technical Officer."

Done and nodding on, seeing where folks were set now, she saw Seeli, serene, who should have been one up the ladder, at least.

"Seeli Gobelyn, Admin and Reserve Chef."

Hesitant, then came, "Dyk Gobelyn, Chef, 'ponics and Supplies," who knew of all things that Iza'd sat him too high, with only the kids properly belonging below him. For his goodness, Dyk did mutter low on the ears when he nodded at Grig, saying "'Serve, next."

Well, that was clear. Someone had given Dyk an order he didn't like, but he'd come back to the ship when, like any of them 'cept the two youngest, he might have had honest work anywhere in good space, long as he didn't need Liaden tickets. After all, he had his investment, and then Grig began and had everyone's attention, not just hers.

Cold. Accurate. Sounding so much like an Arin it had to be on purpose, the first part, and then nodding expansive and calm to Dyk, relaxing maybe, but sounding then amazingly like Arin's Jethri, whose voice was yet too young to be Arin's, and maybe never would be.

"Grig Tomas. Chief Medico. Chief System Engineer. Reserve Pilot. Warehouse and Reserve Chef."

The first part, the "Chief Medico" and "Chief Systems Engineer," that had been said, spiteless, but right to Iza. "Reserve Pilot," that had been said to Cris mostly, and to Paitor, and then to her, for all that it ought to be a lie. Grig Tomas had been Arin's pilot besides being his cousin, and Arin, who had been a damn fine pilot, put Grig above him in a pinch. Warehouse and Reserve Chef, that had been to Dyk alright. And Dyk knew like Grig did that half of his skill was learned from Grig.

That was the thing about Grig. He knew things. Lots of things. Grig was older'n he looked, had small-ship flying time and he'd been a board pilot for a couple of middling cruise ships, too. That older-than-he-looked stuff—the man was always busy with something, getting certified, accredited, studying, reading, collecting, knowing. He'd been part of Jethri's orbit when the boy'd needed steadying, and it was hard to know what he knew because he stayed busy, and knew what he knew because he'd flown the route. Thing is that Grig could probably run the whole darn ship by himself if he needed to, and ought to be something up the ladder on the pay scale and on the crew call.

Mel was patient for a change, like he'd just learned something. When he did speak, it was low and respectful, like he'd learned something too when he'd been off-ship working the yards and such.

"Mel Gobelyn, Technical Mate, Reserve Medico and Reserve Warehouse." Mel nodded to everyone, and so did Zam, right behind:

"Zam Gobelyn, Assistant Admin and Reserve Supplies."

Seeli spoke up then, reminding the whole crew, and Iza too:

"There's also my son, Travit; he's a general trainee with ten week's experience, trip-berthed in Seven A when he's not with me."

Khat almost hurt her neck when she stopped herself from searching everyone on that. Seeli'd made no secret of her and Grig's being a pair for the long run, nor of her and Grig sticking with the ship. What was missing here was that last name: would be Tomas if Seeli was willing to travel off-ship with him if need be and Gobelyn if she was staying no matter what—or if Iza, lacking a vote of the crew, had formed a major opinion. Not having that name yet, that was a sign that deciding hadn't been finished, which Khat couldn't measure as a good thing.

Ship's airflow became suddenly loud, along with the sound of breathing and the little sounds people just sitting make. Cris in particular was making sounds as he sat the reserve board—that in part because he had to check it in sequence, chording the nonessentials, and in part because he was nibbling on the edge of saying something that wouldn't quite come out.

"Proposal on Precedence," he finally managed, which turned all the heads at once—it was one of the few things that had to be dealt with immediately since ship's command structure needed always to be clear, and if he was challenging Iza's rating of Grig—

Iza sat straighter, smiling countenance gone all gamble-face. Around the room others sat taut and quiet as well, but no one called the point. Grig sighed, very gently, since *someone* needed to recognize the call, and did so just before Khat could open her mouth to accept it.

"Captain, crew has need to discuss a Proposal on Precedence. First Mate begs attention."

Khat remembered to breathe, wondering if she'd been left out of a premeeting discussion somehow, and watching the hands of those who had them above the table, and the faces of others: some nerves here, of a sudden.

Properly, if with an edge, came Iza's return: "Are you acting as joint ref on this, Grig Tomas?"

Grig shook his head side to side, showed palms up.

"Not unless needed, Captain, just getting the move on. Crew ought to be set before Jump if there's something to change."

Iza nodded, made an *open channel* hand-sign, and said, "Station's yours, Cris Gobelyn."

Cris nodded, to each of them, and motioned *sorry on delay* as he stood away from the monitors so everyone could see him clearly.

"Captain," he said with a nod, and then, "family." He looked down at his hands as if surprised to see them still forming *delay* and *sorry,* and laughed, letting the smile fade into a wry grin.

"If we hadn't been quite so pressed for time," he offered diffidently, "I'd have had time to do this with some discussion so no one would be surprised. Couldn't happen that way, so here's the thing."

He made a quick motion encompassing the room and the people.

"We're all here, and that's great, and we're all able to do our jobs. That's really good—we've all got confidence there. Might be some got a little more on their day sheet than others, but that's always the way. There's changes—looks like stinks run is spread out some but it's a chore that's sixty percent easier now than it used to be, I think."

He paused, looked to Iza, and then to Khat. His grin got obvious for a moment, then flitted away.

"Ship's changed, though, that's my point. I figure that it's not quite the ship we know yet, and we're not the same crew as was doing things together as we were before."

Cris looked to Seeli, made a *see you* motion and went on.

"So, Admin, it'll be hard to schedule everyone until we know how *this* crew flies *this* ship. Captain, it'll be hard to be sure of where's the blind spots for local, just like we got to make sure the clean sheets we have will go as far as the catalog tells us. A lot of the changes here go across all my jobs."

Finish said his hands, and he summed up quickly, touching left hand to right palm with each point.

"Red—change to the ship systems, from controls to vid sensors to locks."

"Orange—change to maintenance specs and expectations."

"Yellow—change to trade hardware, podlocks, stasis systems."

"Green—restructuring of crew-missions."

"Blue—change in personnel experience levels, training, and competencies."

He paused, and hit the final point with an audible slap to the palm:

"Violet—as my time off-ship was spent as a backup and reserve officer on a large vessel and my actual board time was minimal, I suggest Khat—with numerous recent high-grade commands to her credit—take over first mate duties at least until our shakedown is complete. I should assume my primary role as technical officer and maintenance director and be placed in reserve pilot mode as well as retain my other reserve roles. I can best serve the ship and crew by helping us know the ship as well as we can."

Khat closed her mouth firmly, seeing the truth of it. She was not going to shout out for her own promotion, though. Even a temporary one . . .

The sharp laugh was from Iza, and it was followed by a thin smile and a small shake of her head, as if she'd not quite expected this bit of a proposal when there'd been so many other possibles.

"Pilot math there, son. I appreciate it and wouldn't have suggested it if you hadn't—but there, I'm for it. Show of thumbs and we can declare it done!"

Thumbs up all the way around, and there it was: Khat Gobelyn was first mate on the ship she'd grown up on.

Iza waved them up and about, charging the lot of them with their duty:

"Let's get us away from this smelly mudball and get Paitor his new run. But one thing you all have to remember: as good as this ship is, we're owed from a promise and a payout to get in line for something better."

Here she stared at Grig, and then at Seeli.

"You'll be in the chair rotation more regular than I thought, Grig Tomas. You and Seeli are gonna work, we're fine with that. But Travit Tomas now, Travit's call on this ship is ship-born passenger. My chair ain't his, and that stands until he's on his own way! Too much of Arin's nonsense about you still, unless Uncle's shipyard ain't a myth, after all. You hear from that side, I need to know it."

* * * * * * *

There'd been one last bit of business at Kinaveral, and that was setting up that Jump list, and it looked like a bunch of someones had decided at the same time to flex just a little bit of energy, because there on the emergency where-to list was Vertville. Everyone but Iza . . .

"I see some jokes just don't get old, do they? I have to say, from technical viewpoints, from security viewpoints, Vertville makes some sense. Lots of ships go in there and some of the regs are kinda fuzzy. Not so hard to find a berth; not too hard to find a meal. And . . ."

"Fourth best connectivity point in this quadrant, Iza," Paitor said patiently, "and the three better are Liaden controlled. Really isn't a joke even if . . ."

"Oh, no, Paitor, still a joke. Arin's joke on us, and on me, letting the kid play with make-believe routes and then having us run it. Commissioner has a lot of say, you know, and we'd needed a break, he said, so we did it—just like it was an accident. Damn fine joke the way he convinced all of you the place had some special sentiment for me, damn fine joke that he'd set up a commissioner's meeting without letting hardly anyone know, and good, good joke that he happened to have lotsa old contacts there."

Then she'd turned colder than ever, and pitched it: "So we'll go with the damn fine joke, so long as I ain't sitting in the seat. Something makes us rush out, the seat decides to accept or reject the first punch. That one's not mine."

• • • ✳ • • •

Khat sat second with Grig on the extra nav and Iza first. No one sat First on Iza's board except Iza, and no one sat second there, either, in case her duty was elsewhere. Just ship's rules—each ship and each captain had 'em. Khat had gotten used to sizing up a board in quick order and adjusting only enough to make her hands and feet sure— but Iza, Iza was getting firmly set in her ways and must have been a pretty problem on her out-shifts, fussing and . . .

Khat cut that line of thought, which was not the way a first mate— acting or solid—should be thinking. Ship's rules were ship's rules.

Too much time to think in the short holes between stuff: she couldn't study something new, couldn't just up and talk about what she or Grig'd been up to because Iza was never one for small talk on the working bridge. She did recalcs in her head, traded the least amount of text about meal shifts with Dyk now that they had Franticle dialed in for the second Jump.

So, they'd hit Serconia as a waypoint, not really even having to talk to folks there, but it didn't make sense to go for an uninhabited or frontier world on their first run of the new systems, after all. Serconia would mean an eightday Jump, and a layover for retests and checks, a few days orbiting there, and then Franticle. With the new approximate ingress and egress time on the Jump known, he could schedule his breakfasts per and get them a light lunch just before breakout. He pointed out a short-spot on her suggestions, and she nodded to herself and sent a query to Grig, who'd apparently been following along and had a whole grid of suggestions . . .

Right, food schedules were never a problem for him—seemed like he could eat whenever there was food, but wasn't much concerned about what it was if it wasn't much—but now he was keeping an eye out for Seeli and the babe as well.

Clock running numbers she saw, time to get to work.

"The mark's coming up on seventeen-point-five minutes, Captain. Protocol and checks will take us to three minutes even if we start at the point."

"Lead the way, First. You and Grig run it to the two minutes and then I'll take Jump."

Chapter Nine

• • • •❖• • • •

Flight Deck, *Gobelyn's Market*, Raising Serconia Three

SERCONIA THREE had not been quite where they'd all expected it when Jump broke, and the thing was, the numbers were good. It should have been Khat's own shift by two hours but Iza'd allowed how she'd not been getting the right sleep on account of the new blowers were too damn quiet for a body to be sure they were running proper and so she might as well just sit right here anyhow and bring the *Market* in-system . . .

And they all knew where Serconia ought to be: ships had rhythm and personality and the *Market* had always favored a little wide to port, high about a quarter sec, and with a proper motion bonus of about 20 percent over whatever it had been on Jump. Shouldn't been that way, was what theory said, but they'd got so used to it that they always allowed for it right in the calculations and—

"Well, frozen mud, will you look at that! Ain't no wonder . . ."

Iza was smooth enough, and there weren't no alarms, but—

"Grig Tomas have you ever seen the like—"

They were looking at it, and Khat had already started calling out the numbers they could all see clear enough, with Grig doing a confirm on her numbers and watching the warn-aways, all of them checking their particular instruments to be sure they had clearances and the ship reporting all-clears over comm while the flight crew started screenwise.

"Far as I can tell, Captain, we've arrived within a few percentage points of the set course; with a slow tumble."

"Yeah, we did, didn't we?" the captain allowed. Then, "Kill the tumble, Khat, while we check the rest of these numbers—I'm going to have to start shooting straighter if this is what we get now!"

The tumble was a bother, but not too bad since Iza'd allowed the gravity up a few points because of a kid on board. Without that they'd all be leaning into the back right wall of the ship by now, or tending toward it. But that shooting straighter and getting it right made Khat sigh.

That would take practice and Jumps, Khat knew—the tumble might just have been an ambient flux they hadn't caught on the way out, or one they'd caught on the way in, or a calibration they could adjust or a calibration they couldn't. But Iza'd aimed them for clear space on the ecliptic, assuming a proper motion about right for a local asteroid, and instead they'd come up on the wrong side of the damn primary, giving them a retrograde orbit and more than trebling their chance of hitting nasty dust or grit or even boulders at speed. Didn't really help that they were a quarter sec or more low, Serconia having a double cloud that would pump iceballs and gas clusters in at all angles.

About then, the equipment started sorting out frequencies and getting radar returns and they were busy for a while, including a flurry of trade queries. Trade queries weren't all that unusual for a ship just Jumping in, but Khat's back brain was making notes, with some of them getting voiced and recorded and the others saved for her own recollection in quiet.

· · · ✳ · · ·

Khat's notes took her striding towards Paitor's trade office on break because it was no good bringing up the kid—that was Jethri's, not Grig's git—anywhere Iza could hear of it. They'd all got the security bulletin she'd drafted about the run-in with the Liaden punk claiming Jethri'd stole his kin—Iza couldn't hide from that because Gobelyn's name was in it.

Khat couldn't hide from it nor anyone else from the ship because Liadens were tricky, and it had been pure unplanned Gobelyn muscle twitch that she'd knocked the guidestars out of the lead pirate's eyes by knocking him down thorough. She was sorry for the hangover on it, but it had been the right thing: roomful of Terrans with guns weren't likely to let a couple Liadens get too overstrong in their attentions that far in the fringe. One wrong move could have left them licking vacuum from their shoes while word got out of an unfortunate collision of pilots unfamiliar with Terran routing orders . . .

Khat shook that from her head. She didn't want blood on her hands, no more than Jethri'd want it, and she knew he'd taken that suicide that happened on the ship's apron as his fault, though damned if she could see it. So there: Jeth didn't need any more blood on his hands and she oughtn't be thinking about—

Paitor stood in the sliding door, looking downpassage like *he'd* been thinking about something far away, or else avoiding the data screens hung all over his work room. He nodded, moved himself, and pointed toward the several seats, giving her a choice. The ship-to-shores were carrying on local talk and he'd got them tuned down, though a couple of the lines were open enough she could hear words she knew.

"Hey, Khat, come on in and break in a chair, why not? I got a green one and a blue one that haven't been sat on by crew yet; or you can help even out the red one or that yellow . . ."

His mouth quirked into a smile: "Dyk tells me the yard did the same kind of mix anywhere they worked—him and Cris are thinking we ought to have all the same color seats in the same places if we can."

Khat harrumphed and shook her head, pulling herself into the back corner and taking up the blue with her back to the wall, "I dunno that seat-changing's a problem, but if Cris is on it, then he'll decide."

She shook her head silently, waving her hand at the new stuff: "Iza annoyed them like a wonder and a marvel both, she did, so we'll hope it's only stuff like seats that got randomized."

He settled into the red—by the pile of flimsies, data chips, and note-knockers right there, he'd already warmed that one up.

"Come to talk about my sister, the captain?"

She looked him in the eye and sighed. He looked back, so she went on.

"Not exactly about her," she admitted slowly. "I'm in the spot, though, and the job means I gotta think ahead in case the call's mine. Not an order, but I'd appreciate it if you can give me some stats from our last fifty or a hundred Jumps. Didn't want be setting up the search with Iza right there, since it wasn't immediate need stuff, and besides, not sure I have that in a searchable base. Trade stats, kind of, but might have a bearing on security, too. And you'll have to give me a better lecture on what Arin was doing with his theory and his connections, if you can."

"We have time," he said, finally letting their shared eye contact go in favor of looking at the one screen that showed local space with course and shipping overlays rather than contacts, trade offers, and search lists.

· · · ✳ · · ·

Whatever he saw in that screen, it mostly kept his attention while he talked in a quiet monotone with the occasional flicker of a glance in her direction to make sure she wasn't asleep. Since she'd asked, Khat just listened.

"Pretty basic really, once you remember two things. First is that Arin and his kin, they'd been around a long time. A long time. And chances are that Arin'd been around longer than I knew—he was older than me and never quite looked it, but they come from a long-lived bunch"—here he took a look in her direction before talking at the wall again, quieter, like he didn't want his voice to carry down the passageway.

"So I figure Grig and Arin both got long view on us; if Grig claims forty-five Standards I'm guessing he's got twice that and more, same as Arin had that many and some more, too. Understand me—this is not entirely a guess: Iza did a bunch of research a little late, just after Arin come back from a long run of commissioner business with a barely born kid he claimed as his. Not the kind of thing someone who married partly for love wants to hear, I'm guessing—well, it didn't take a lot of research then to see that Arin been married twice before, and the first time he'd been married they called him thirty Standards old and she'd thought she'd met him when he was thirty-three—'cept there was at least three of his claimed git out there working as pilots already . . ."

Khat nodded at his glance—some of this had seeped in over the years, but—

"So that's aside your point, but astride mine: these Tomas brothers and their cousins, they'd been right slick traders and dealers and spaceship types for a lot of years, but never what I'd call family of our likes—us being Gobelyn and Karter and Turnavitch and well, you know the names, because we've been loopers for a few hundred years, and so have they.

"The thing is that these Tomas folks been there at the fringes, being a little too ahead of things sometimes, and a little too knowing, and always did have a yen—including when Arin come along—to deal in just about any old-time or Before thing what was come across.

"What you'll want to do, in part, 'cause now you're officially in the line, is to look at at the logs and the Gobelyn bloodlines as way back as you don't get bored by it. I've got a database of every place this ship set down and most of the contact info . . ."

Khat sat up a little straighter. "Then you already *have* the analysis of how often we deal at mostly Liaden ports, and how often we come into Liaden space and . . ."

"I do. Arin made a study of that, like he made a study of a lot of stuff. That's why he was rousing the loopers to set things good, because he could see the Liadens coming in and he could see—and predict somewhat—about another problem, one that was face front and nobody wanted to talk about it."

"Good," she said, "so we have Arin's plan on competing and I . . ."

"Let's not get there yet, lass," Paitor said, "because there's a lot of philosophy between here and there, and some history, too. I don't have a full copy of that plan, and if Grig does he's got it against Iza's orders. Why not tell me in detail about the charts and numbers you need, and I'll trim 'em out and get 'em in your direction."

She nodded. "Right, then. I need that history that shows every time in the last half century the *Market* has come into a Terran port where there was a Liaden ship on port. I'm guessing there must be a way of doing that. If that takes going into the logs or something, I can do that part. I want how often, where, and if there was more than one Liaden Ship at the same time. If we can pull some larger database that'll show our regular routes and when Liaden—"

Paitor raised his hand for *stop*.

"Khat—I told you. Arin did that. You were too young probably to listen, but he did that and I have some of it. What I don't have, I guess Grig's got anyhow, or can tell us who still does. If he won't tell, *Wilde Toad* had some of it before they went down, and I so expect their cousins on *Nubella*, *Nubella Run*, and *Balrog* have some. We're not alone in this, you know."

She looked at him with a sudden dread.

"Iza don't put that information on her boards. I mean, maybe we ought to be running with notifications, and charting these things. There's got to be something here that . . ."

Paitor sighed, and stood up.

"Here's where there's a problem, Khat. There's a couple ways of looking at this, and we're flying on a ship with captain and mission that says our job's pretty clear. We fly our loop and we take what comes our way and we live on it. How it is, how it's been, how it will be."

She nodded.

"Iza's set that way, I know."

He looked away, letting his eyes wander the screen, letting them catch the changing infostreams offered and available, seeing the ships he knew from experience were dropping into a queue for one of the stations, seeing others that were off to do private transactions away from the eyes and probes of the planet-bound. Gathering himself, he made the hand-sign of apology, and faced her squarely.

"What's happening is that there are changes, though, and Iza's pretty plans aren't going to work. There's some that see what's coming, and some that won't see, and a dozen sides to each and a couple of major philosophies."

He paused again, let the phrases find themselves.

"Cris, he's been on the side of sister Iza, mostly. He did a brave thing to give that chair up to you, and I honor him for it. Else I pity him."

Khat stiffened involuntarily, preparing to defend her elder—

"Can't do it that way, Khat. This isn't just about your comfort. See, the Tomas contingent and their uncle, they got ideas that they see what's coming—and Iza wouldn't hear it, wouldn't see it was a problem for us, seeing that it's a problem fourteen years out or forty years out or a hundred and forty or five hundred and forty.

"What Arin said all along, was that the Commission could do this proper, and keep the looper ship's running their courses—and us loopers staying in trade with a few changes here and there, and maybe, just maybe, get a leg up on the Liadens and whoever else. Me, I'm on the 'here and there' side, myself. But then the Befores started being trouble, and Arin's uncle said they had to be picked up and studied and collected before something bad happened. Really bad.

"Me, I didn't see that. Damn fractins didn't seem to hurt no one, and the other stuff—the handholds and minipods—it was mostly one-offs, as far as I could see. I heard that if you wanted it bad enough there was timonium in those things, but it wasn't hardly recoverable and it was mostly at end of usable half-life."

He fluttered his hands then, the *is as is* sign, fact are facts.

"So the thing is that Cris has always lined up with Iza, thinking this scheme of changing how we do business—of changing how *everyone* does business—that it don't make sense. She does think we can maybe do better in the way of ships, and she and Arin, they threw their marriage portions together on a project some of the other loopers went in on. The *Wilde*'s did, and we did, and all the branches of DeNobli . . . supposed to be a small shipyard doing research. The Commission was with the deal for a while, too, but then it turned out there were a lot of politics going on, a lot of sneak, and people trying to take the project over, take it back to some idea of building really big ships to just rival the Liadens lock to lock."

Paitor shook his head. "So everything fell back to this research shipyard and then Iza had Jethri to deal with, and found out about the age discrepancies. And found out that Arin wasn't talking about exactly where the shipyard was, either.

"Arin's Uncle, he never came out and made full-scale pitches—he just allowed things to be known. Saw him once, but he wasn't one to be seen except when he wanted to be. Hard to find images, hard to find descriptions. Never was quite the person to come out with what he wanted.

"One thing Iza's research did was confirm that however old Arin and Grig are, there's been an Uncle, someone everybody called Uncle, anyhow, in that line since before records got coordinated. Always an Uncle. Always had his own ship or two. *Always.*"

Paitor turned and fixed her gaze with his. "Centuries, we're talking, and not just a couple of them either, looks like. Family resemblance between Arin and the Uncle, I say, and Jethri a twin of his dad."

Paitor nodded at her hand motion, which was a simple *confirm*.

"Oh yes, a twin as much as a son. Iza saw it, finally, and we saw it. Cris knows it. Got to be damn plain, actually!

"Iza—well, you heard her, and you saw her: don't want nothing to do with Jethri and threw him off the ship because he was looking and sounding more like Arin every single shift. Hearing him on the all-call was enough to make me shiver, he sounded so much alike. She's not taking *any* chances with who Grig's kid's gonna be."

Khat nodded, managed to interject: "But all these records—what's being ignored? Facts is facts!"

Paitor agreed with a nod: "Facts is. Like Jethri is a fact. And the fact is that Arin did some computing. He wanted to disagree with that Uncle of his and he put together a little computing engine—using some of those fractins and racks he was collecting—and he and Jethri talked it all over . . . well, that might not be to the point. What are you after, Khat?"

She pushed herself flat against the chairback, finding the local traffic screen just as interesting as Paitor had moments before, seeing that the chair was more comfortable and more secure than the ones they replaced, no matter the color . . .

"I'm just seeing how much we know about these Liaden—let's call it incursions—into our trade space. Are they coming in groups, or just one or two? Is it like the Combine, is their trade guild pushing it, or is that they've got such competition that the short-on-fuels have got to share orbits with us?"

Paitor shook his head. "Too much to get from one set of figures, do you think? But I think Jethri's new trader has the right of it: we're all doing more trading and we're sort of equalizing what we want and what we need. It was one thing when everyone was working just to get ships in space and just to get the stations up, trying to set defense— and it's something else now that some of that's maturing. And you're right—there are going to be areas where we're going to be seeing more of the Liadens. We're reaching for more of the same resources, and we're smart to see where there's already signs of overlapped interest."

He looked this time at the ceiling, where there was a vent, and around it a few odds and ends of a child's artwork. Jethri's artwork, a ring around the vent, with a design of fractins he'd traced around and then colored in, with connections showing here and there, and a pile of fractins with cracks and bad edges sketched off to the sides. The refurb crew must've left it for wanted decoration, Khat thought; and then thought that she'd've missed it, if it'd been painted over.

Pointing to it he went on: "See, the other thing is we probably had a lot more of that information available. Heck, we just shipped a bunch of it off, I'm thinking. You know, Arin talked to Jethri as hard as he could on account of Iza ignoring the kid; talked to him like he was an adult from right young. He had Jethri with a kid's board, had him running those trade routes Iza's so peeved about, talked to him about technical stuff—the boy has a grounding in value versus worth versus cost versus utility. He knows stuff he doesn't even know he knows!"

Paitor fiddled with his chair controls a moment, using the short break to say Jethri's name a couple of times with a shake of the head before turning his full attention back to her.

"Me, I was ready to let him loose, call him second trader and give him a real podshare for himself—but then Iza's spooked about all of it, and she wouldn't open the books, wouldn't open Arin's stuff, didn't want to see what was in there, just wanted it away. Not sure what she spaced—I gotta think there was stuff he only shared with her! So what you shipped to Jethri could be a treasure, for all I know, but Iza didn't want to know! And the boy would've been as good as Arin, likely, if he'd had his training. As is, I'd be having us run Jethri's route next time around, Khat—that's why Iza was pushing so hard to let him go. Just luck he got himself out of doing stinks and hauling rocks."

A ship bell sounded Dyk's attention call for the kitchen, and Khat rose, touching wrist to show that was her reminder call.

Paitor went on for a moment: "When you get a shot, we'll try to close in on all this. I'll pull what I have together and see if I can't include it in an upgrade to the trade-side charts you get. May have to run it in over a few sessions so Iza won't feel pushed . . ."

Khat nodded and gave a wry smile.

"Thanks Paitor. I'm not trying to make a run around Iza but . . ."

Paitor stood and waved her out the door.

"Looks to me like your brother Cris has an idea we need change, and knows he can't quite stand the blast pressure himself. The ship's been upgraded so we've got to upgrade the information side. I'm willing to see the work done, seeing I didn't get enough of it done to keep Jethri onboard. And it seems to me staying in touch with Jeth—and maybe talking one to one sometime, seems to me that might get us some answers, too."

Khat sighed as she nodded and took her exit cue. Thing was she'd long realized that Jethri was going to be a key; the boy'd been faunching after her something fierce there the last trip around—likely just hormones, but something she'd rather be sure was cured before she got too many messages off in his direction. Cris had been a trifle put out by the fact that she genuinely liked Jethri—and that she'd made a big effort to keep up commlinks with him when Iza'd been trying her best to split the kid from the ship.

"Will do what I can there, Trade side, do what I can. Thanks for the 'view."

Chapter Ten

• • • • • ✳ • • • • •

***Keravath*'s Second Cabin, in Jump**

JETHRI STRETCHED AND YAWNED, his hand just touching the sliding storage on either side, and if he reached he could tangle his hands in the shock-webbed sleep net that kept sleepers in place against sudden sidewise accelerations. Under way, with gravity, it rolled down from the ceiling. He'd gotten the quick tour, knew what the lights meant and which ones he might want on or off, played with the airflow, looked at the instruments . . .

The Scout had apologized for the size of the bunk, but it was a private bunk and space, and very nearly qualified as a room—he could actually undress and change without laying clothes on top each other—and for all that, it was a working ship, everything was newer looking than he was used to on the *Market*, even if the measures were a little closer, being sized for Liadens.

There were a couple dials and measures he'd need to figure out . . . but there, the *Market* had local gauges all over the place and most meant nothing anymore—or might now that the ship was refitted—because other than O_2 and overpressure, Iza hadn't thought most of it needed much more than autochecking, nor had her mother before her. The problem wasn't guessing if they were working, but what they meant, since not only were they marked in Liaden, they were Scout-abbreviated as well.

The fixtures were clean and smooth, the walls had just enough padding to be useful in a problem. He wasn't expecting to be treated like a guest, anyhow. *Elthoria*'s luxury was just that—luxury—and he knew it.

He'd spent the run up to Jump learning, and then they'd sat and done a recheck on the emergency procedures and snacked, with the Scout surprising him by sharing a robust cup of 'mite with him—and then the Scout had left him alone on the bridge and taken a short nap to try to catch up on his rest, leaving Jethri on proper shipwatch for the first time in his life.

The external screens showed a dull green, not because they were off, but because that's how the sensors showed the confusion that was Jump. That was adjustable, of course. Iza tuned her screens on the *Market* to black; apparently Grig and Arin had flown with a foggy blue, and *Elthoria*'s choice was to overlay the view with a cycling imitation starfield that was supposedly the view from above Liad's Solcintra Port. On that ship they gave extra points—that'd be *melant'i*—for having extra knowledge, so this run could do bonus for him if he'd get out of his own way.

· · · ·✢· · · ·

Shipwatch. He'd never been in the crew order for it on the *Market*, and on *Elthoria* shipwatch was a crew of expert pilots and crew. In theory he'd draw a backup watch every hundred days or so—but that theory hadn't come to pass since his training took precedence.

Most of shipwatch was automatics—the Scout had been clear on that. His board, such as it was, was basically set to sound alarms, and those—while in Jump—all dealing with internal conditions. Jump being in progress there was nothing he could do to unJump them or to bring them out ahead of time—the Jump would proceed.

What he was to be watching for were any of the numerous failures that could happen while in Jump, but rarely did. Too much or too little oxygen, for example, or an explosion in some onboard storage tank. Jethri winced at that—there'd been two children close to his age, kids he'd met, who died on a looper ship when the refrigeration system messed up and froze them into a compartment they were cleaning while the adults were all partying during a long Jump.

Well, that wasn't an issue now—as far as he knew there was no major refrigeration system on this ship, and certainly no pod supports to watch. So mostly what he did was pay attention to the cycle, and study, practicing the what-if of arriving somewhere with no other pilot on board, and then drifting into a bigger what-if of traveling wherever in the universe he wanted, with no one else in charge of his destinations.

From distant memory he pulled the names of waystops he and his father had talked about, and what he recalled from Trade N Traipse; he set up a trade loop on one of the mapping screens. He'd designed a loop for himself while very young; that'd amused his father and Grig—heck, they encouraged him to do it!

Some of the stops were selected for his own interests—like a place that had an annual King of the Cakes Festival, and another that was supposed to be the Fractin Capital of the Quadrant. Dyk had added one or two. That all said, Dyk was a food-dreamer and he'd go anyplace where there was a lot of food choice, and Seeli'd played along, adding one world where each town made its own beer—no one was allowed to transport it across borders! That had hit his funny bones as a kid—he usually shopped beer sips from person to person as a kid, and had turned out to be a good judge between good beer and barely acceptable before he was half-tall. It was an ability he had to keep close on some ports, where kids weren't permitted, but he could tell one from another, even from sniffing.

Balfour'd been on his Loop, and it thrilled him in an odd way that the four backup Jumps on his "try to calculate this ahead of time" project were all from that list. The Scout likely knew that the ship's measure on all of them were half-dozen or more Standards dated, so that meant that his recalculates were to help there . . .

That gave him something better to do than staring at screens that refreshed and told him the same thing every thirty-six seconds, the only change so far the calendar updates and arrival countdown. The pressure fluctuations that showed, he knew now, was the ship tracking his breathing, and he'd have to ask then where the medical tracking was. Likely as all get-out that the ship was catching itself a base of his heart rate, blood pressure, perspiration rates and temperature flux—he'd listened long and hard and perhaps harder than his father and Grig knew, about how the small ships and single ships had backup and warning and such that the *Market* ought to consider putting in . . .

He thought back, recognized some writing from the room gauges. Indeed! His personal oxygen history was available here, and so was the Scout's. Board One and Board Two signals were clear—and there was room on the charts for a couple more. Likewise, the ship had him read in as a temp Board Two, so unless he declared emergency there was a lot of ship stuff he couldn't run, though the Scout had made it clear he could get at any of the piloting manuals and star charts he wanted to.

The Scout, Jethri noted, looked to use less oxygen and run at a lower pulse rate than he did—but of course the Scout was sleeping. That other—ah, that chart was likely blood oxygenation levels and there they seemed to be pegged, and—

He laughed gently and out loud, and the rates shifted with him. He wondered if the Scout would be able to tell when *he* was dreaming, just from such stuff and recognized a related gauge that also was marked to Board Two, and another. The last was all zeros but for the skinniest touch of pink, while the corresponding gauge for Board One looked to be blocked into segments of different colors. He tried breathing fast, and stood, jumped into a run in place and set other numbers on his side moving . . .

The one with the pink sliver moved not at all, but he exercised for awhile anyway, at first missing the running machine on *Elthoria*, and the views, and Gaenor and . . . several of his numbers rose, but he ran in place for a while more, counting steps. He'd never been the only one awake on a starship before, and he wondered how long it would be before he'd sleep with someone else, anyway.

Eventually, his exercises and his reminiscences through, he opened the files, checked to be sure his board was as neutral as could be, and read up on piloting until he was relieved for breakfast.

Chapter Eleven

• • • • ✳ • • • •

Wynhael, Sater System, Orbit

WYNHAEL'S JOURNEY around the Sater System had been very quiet so far and Bar Jan chel'Gaibin was just as pleased as could be, the histrionics of their last frontier planetfall still close to mind. The other ships of their band were scattered for the nonce, with *Wynhael's* play in this system a meeting in person with one of his mother's contacts.

His mother was settled into her travel routine of sleeping according to Liad's time, claiming it was far more natural than ship-time. He didn't gainsay it since it also gave him free time in the trade office and among the databanks. He'd found the keylogger and fed it a substitute made up from some of his recent trade days; he'd also made sure his shadow of her secret file was being triple-saved.

This morning—ship-time—he'd roused himself for a good solo breakfast and dressed with care, unsure of the day's schedule and unwilling to appear less than fully aware of his proper High House *melant'i*. His mother pushed at his readiness to have his own trade vessel and if he could not move her out of the way, he must be prepared to take charge of his own affairs until he could.

Also on the schedule was an early examination of some odd message files he'd stumbled over. They could be mere technical reportage and if so his lack of depth in that area of files wouldn't matter, else he might have to bring yet one more staffer under his sway, and he knew he was approaching a maximum in that

121

regard—a dangerous maximum. If Rinork became concerned, she could have him bond-contracted as well as Tan Sim, showing a fair face to the Council of Clans and none to either of her trader children.

On ship he was not wearing the heavier duty safety vest, but he and his man knew where it was at all times, just as they both knew it wasn't a mere safety vest but high-grade armor.

His man's man also kept after him on his exercises, and on his daily weapons and defense training—a happenstance he wasn't sharing with the coconspirators when they met on port. Khana vo'Daran knew well where his loyalty sat, since Lord chel'Gaibin's firm plan would catapult him and his clan to first servers sooner and faster than hoping he caught the eye and interest of Rinork-in-place. Vo'Daran had grown up with him, being a mere fifteen years his elder, and his *melant'i* was set.

The movement on the trade screen showed him soundless points of light entering and exiting—he had no interest in the casual chatter of spacers, be they Liaden or Terran—and it was live, to have something to look at from time to time that was not just painted wall. The screen showed what he knew to be true: the bulk of the travel here was Terran.

The sound of the door slide operating had him touch his near screen to a text screen dealing with the shipping cost of multipod quantities of locally processed, compressed, freeze-dried, powdered, dehydrated onion juices—a happy specialty of the Sater System!—but rather than his man, with a tray of morning tea, it was Rinork herself, his mother, quick-dressed and not yet fully combed or jeweled.

He rose and bowed to the delm, as he did every day on the first sighting of his mother—it was all that was proper, after all. She acknowledged it briefly, careless steps placing her in a spot to look over the text he'd been looking at.

"Bah. Imagine that I find you at work with real things instead of your precious decanter collecting—or have you already bought the auction lots offered at Curnby House?"

"Here? Actual Liaden decanters?"

Rinork's heir chel'Gaibin wasn't sure which was more surprising, his mother's arrival or the news that he might have missed an auction . . .

She laughed at him. "Yes, there's a listing. One would have to see it in person, I gather—an expert like yourself—and we may not have time for it. If you like I'll send the details, I forget me why I have not yet already."

He fumed to have her in his work area, pleased to have reacted promptly and unpleased that he'd not thought to do such a search himself. It would not, after all, have been the first time Liaden rarities had made their way to the Terran side of things, some Terrans were willing to spend absurd amounts to be seen as sophisticated. As for him, he'd gotten himself interested in decanters while researching containers he might use to smuggle bellaquesa. Addicted to the drug? No, nor interested in becoming that way. Addicted to the decanters from fourth century? Yes, of course. Decanters!

"While you work so diligently, I have been called from my sleep; our courier ship is lately arrived. Perhaps you were not expecting it?"

The heir acknowledged the truth of that, dread building. He'd seen her work before and heard amusement there. He let his hands add secure layers over his work, the while watching his mother's eyes, avidly scanning the large screen.

"There!"

She pointed to the name tag just recently formed on a ship dot well distant. The clear and sensible readability of *Tyrka* amid the alien lettering of the Terran ships made it welcome.

He had no sense of the actual distance from the plotted points, but it appeared on the very edge of the local screen, which meant a day or even three or four, before the ship could do more than beam or radio information to them.

"That's some time away, my delm," he said, having little practical idea of how far it was but knowing that it was far from the coplanetary orbit they shared with a dozen other tradeships around the paired planets. "Have you more information?"

"Yes," she said, "I do. There's movement on several fronts, including that of my other son. As for the most important news, the arrival of the courier here tells me that we shall be taking action soon on the ship side of this—but which action? I cannot say until the information is in hand—indeed we shall wait until we have a direct report. That may be tomorrow, even if we bribe control.

"In the meanwhile, I shall breakfast, and you will tell me if we shall be shipping pods of"—here she sniffed exaggeratedly—"*onion powder* to our next port! So, walk with me, and please, close all the files when you go rooting about, if you would. I'll wait."

The dread in his gut was only mildly relieved that the delm moved closer to the scan board, as if seeing in reality the distant courier, while he did as ordered.

* * * ⁘ * * *

The courier stood before them, her bow exquisite almost to the point of irony. Bar Jan knew the courier's background but wasn't cowed by it—there were enough former Scouts in the wild that meeting one was not entirely rare. That this one, Rand yos'Belin, was a private courier and not a Scout any longer was due to her voluntary resignation in the face of multiple investigations over her continued flouting of rules and regulations.

This amused Bar Jan, having heard from vo'Daran since childhood that the strength in the Scout was sometimes thought to be their extreme flexibility in interpreting rules in their own behalf.

The comely Courier yos'Belin was yet loose upon the star lanes because she'd retained both her Scout pilot rating and her independent ways upon release from the Scouts. Her marriageability was less important than her pilot's income to her clan's increase, and her unwillingness to bend to Liad's ordinary social codes was considered "Scoutish," though few who met her would hesitate to call her rude—just not to her face.

All was smoothness at the moment.

"The dispatch from our friends on the Council of Clans shows the Council disinclined to study the trade situation as a group. Indeed, there is a reluctance to encourage any joint study which might permit our overwhelming trade and technical superiority to confront Terran trade plans directly. Ixin's approach is flamboyant—just treat them as equal! Korval, meanwhile, has enough equipment and builds yet another shipyard, so that the trading interests in the Council fear banding together against this rumored Terran strategy lest Korval subsume the effort and own all the trade!"

The courier divested herself of various infokeys and file cubes as she spoke, and added several folded pieces of hardcopy printouts from inner pockets as well. These items, of course, went to Rinork, and while she was perusing them, Bar Jan realized that the courier was perhaps studying him as carefully as he was studying her. He bowed very slightly in acknowledgment, as she did in return, smiling primly.

Well then! His mother's travels and the required secrecy had kept him rather chaste other than an occasional therapeutic rubdown, but if the courier might be about for a while he was sure she would be within the ambit of security.

"Here, Bar Jan, you will look these over and return them to me. Korval runs ships or proxies on many of the routes that we do, and the names you see here, afraid of losing ground to Korval, may help us with our goal, if we can but offer them slivers and shares from what we shall control. By the time you are making marriages for the clan—within forty years—Korval will be as much in our hand as the rest of these, and pleased to pay well to marry to Rinork!"

Bar Jan bowed to this as he received the sheets, hoping that in fact his marriage-planning days would arrive much sooner than that. Once his mother was out of his way he would take a much firmer control of these matters. *Much* firmer!

The notes were copies of notes taken in hand at committee meeting, and the names were all of them known to him, and oddly, all of them in his debt book for one or another offenses. Most were there for their lack of consideration of his proper *melant'i*—but, that too could be solved faster once his mother was . . . elsewhere.

His mother moved on to the reader, and yet Bar Jan felt looked upon—and indeed, the courier was watching still, he saw, and he was glad he'd dressed well this morning. He often preferred his women to have longer hair, but the courier's hair was neat and tidy, and she had none of the barbarous slashes and designs the Terran ship people carved into their heads.

Her eyes, he noted, were a very deep blue.

Yes, he must be prepared to take charge of his own affairs!

· · · ✦ · · ·

The courier, it became obvious, was far more than courier. His mother's previous description of her duties was perhaps incomplete. He wondered, hearing the phrasing carefully, if in fact she knew as much and maybe more than the ship captains his mother'd inveigled into the scheme. It almost seemed as if she guided the plan more than the other captains, and her assumptions of familiarity—she'd somehow become "Rand" in conversation rather than "Pilot"—showed his mother's willingness to grant her such terms.

Rinork moved them through tea and then to a longer session where Rinork shared strategy and tactics over their next step with the pilot, allowing Bar Jan to ask questions and give opinions. Yet, as the *melant'i* of discussion showed, it was yos'Belin who was aiming discussion toward the end of the meeting, and it seemed it was she, rather than Rinork, who was expanding his entry into planning.

The courier's biggest concern: "*Therinfel*'s understanding of urgency is not firm. More, the information flow when information is present is more circular than it ought to be, which is to say that the application of talk and thought to raw information is time-consuming while the filter of consideration adjusts and even consumes facts. Scouts train against such habits. The captains in your association perhaps have not the same training.

"In particular this has been costly in two arenas. In one, your heir"—here the bow to Bar Jan was particularly fine—"was underinformed of the risk of personal attack and the difficulties of recovering *melant'i* in the case of such an attack—just as he was undersupported. The result is a world where your influence will require bribes and time to be brought to the proper level. These are recoverable, but the delay might convince *Therinfel*'s party that they have more influence than they ought."

Bar Jan bowed in agreement to this, ruefully seeing that, yes, this was easily both a personal affront to him and one to his mother, and thus a danger to all of them. His debt book was not lacking in that regard . . .

Here the courier faced Rinork herself more than Bar Jan, speaking in a quieter voice as if there were any concern of being overheard, here in Rinork's own sanctum.

"The other arena is that of obtaining the plan we are assured exists, of which we have overheard discussions. No less than eleven Terran ships, comprising portions of four family groups, are known to have copies of this plan, while potentially dozens more have been treated to discussions of it. That the material has been successfully eradicated from the files of the Commission's archives indicates a cabal of some potency. This plan, as we have heard it described, this manifesto, was presented to several dozen commissioners and their aides Standards ago.

"That I know of it was a matter of timing and placement, and indeed, I shall admit, the failure of my supervisors to pursue, it increased the speed with which I parted from the organization. Liad must not permit Terrans the opportunity to expand so easily, nor permit them to keep our natural advantages minimized through secrecy.

"But here, we have—"

She stopped, an insistent tone bringing Rinork to her feet. Then the delm touched buttons in reply, holding hand to ward, and turning away, not only from the courier, but from Bar Jan. She spoke in hushed tones, then turned to the courier with a bow of request.

"Incoming is a ship bearing a person I must, quite like yourself, speak to directly and confidentially. Alas, they profess most acute timing issues and I assure you that it is through no disrespect to yourself that I feel they must not be put off. Might I offer you the full courtesies of our ship, just as if we were comfortably at home, that I may spend several hours . . . no, better in fact, let me call this our evening, offer you dinner and a room. The three of us can continue our current meeting in the morning, likely more informed than we are even now."

The formal Scout bowed a pretty bow of thanks, and of acceptance.

Rinork briefly returned to her confidential message, and then turned away, offering to Bar Jan, "My son, please allow housekeeping to know of this change of plans, and also, procure for yourself and our guest a fine dinner—surely our work today deserves it—while I prepare for this conference. You shall host dinner, and on the morning shift I will do the same for breakfast. It is fortuitous indeed that we can be so flexible! You may draw from the deepest cellar, my son!"

· · · ✳ · · ·

The deepest cellar was an honor indeed—those were rare bottles of Rinork's favorites, not the best they owned, but certainly the best they cared to travel with. And though technically her son might draw on any of them at will, it was not really the case, as they both knew.

He sighed, taking rein on his impulse and managing not to order of the cha'Ravia with its reputation as spirited wine fit for extremely quiet dinners. That it was said to be an aphrodisiac, well, he knew very well the times his mother ordered it. But the yos'Postal, that was also a fine wine for quiet moments, and of subtle palate as well. Being somewhat rarer, it might well have convincing qualities of its own.

· · · ✧ · · ·

They Jumped, did *Wynhael,* almost two Standard days later, after pushing the ship's meteor shields as they rose through the wide rocky belt to achieve an outgoing orbit above the ecliptic to arrive at the shortest runout possible. Rinork's second confidential visitor, taxied in from the local trade guild, was gone by the time breakfast was served. Courier Pilot Rand yos'Belin, however, remained with the ship until the final runout was laid in, dropping her vessel away and out of the Jump-effect range with a bone-breaking acceleration to permit the trader's final numbers verified and safe.

The exhilarated Bar Jan stood on bridge in the aftermath of the Jump, his mother long retired to her stateroom. Screen seven still held the frozen image of the courier ship at cast-off, an image he'd requested be taken. It was, truly, a beautiful ship for a spacer, with no offsetting pods or pyloned add-ons to mar the symmetry of the thing. Most spaceships lacked the look of speed that her ship had, the look of purpose—

No matter if the crew felt he was exhibiting unusual tenderness for the moment, for surely there was an understanding that he'd spent several shifts with the pilot, his man called to deliver meals and wine for two and nothing more.

"Our destination—how long before we broach optical space there?"

The navigator being closest, the response was rapid. "Nearly eight Standard days, lord."

"And a courier, would it take so long?"

There was some confusion as to who should answer, but again the navigator was closest.

"Much depends upon the willingness of a pilot to take pressure and discomfort, lord. It is what courier ships do, after all. An ordinary courier ship and a tradeship ought to *arrive* within a few percent of each other for the transfer stage, but courier acceleration and deceleration are superior to trade ships. Departing from the same rest orbit at the same time, aiming at the same rest orbit in another system, one might assume a courier to have a half-day to a day advantage based on in-system traversal."

Bar Jan considered the statement, feeling several layers of stealthy evasion . . . and what issues might require such?

"Am I to believe then that the ship in the viewscreen is *not* an ordinary courier?"

Among the bridge crew, a hush as they realized their subtleties had failed them.

"Captain?" Bar Jan dared challenge the seated senior pilot. "Is the ship that was docked with us not an ordinary courier?"

The captain rose from his command couch after handing several duties to his minions, and moved to stand beside Bar Jan, the while staring at the ship.

"My lord, that is the case. To begin with, an 'ordinary' courier would have to be available to be bought from a standard shipyard or ship line, to any with the cash. The ship on view here is not so usual as that. The ship on view here—I would suggest that the major difference between this ship and a top-of-the-line Scout courier are the markings, my lord."

Still levels.

"So Scout couriers are as divided as regular ships into ordinary and extraordinary?"

"Yes, they are. Any high quality pilot might fly a Scout courier, this I know from the Scout pilots I know. The top of the line—those I gather are matched very closely to the pilot . . ."

"I see. Extraordinary Scout pilots are given extraordinary ships to fly."

"Yes, that is close to the case, as I can see it. Certainly a pilot of proper *melant'i* will be well aware of the 'too much ship' problem when it comes to accepting captaincy. One must be comfortable with the capabilities of the vessel, and of their own understandings of those capabilities."

They stared together at the ship on-screen, Bar Jan struggling to recall what ships he might have noticed as Scout ships over time. He'd never felt the piloting urge, nor wanted to be more than Rinork Himself, nor had much beyond pod-carrying capacity and the *melant'i* of a ship's principal trader. Traders were what marked a ship, and a firm; it was traders who had rank to him, and some even outranked him, either by clanhouse or ring. Since his own needs were sometimes flexible, being aware of the *melant'i* of a trader was far more important than purity.

Pilots, now, pilots he'd always considered as employees, bought and paid for, employed at will, dismissed at will, and though sometimes entrusted with confidential information, replaceable.

Yet his recent investigations had shown him that he'd perhaps undervalued pilots, that in fact it could be that pilots could move events if given the opportunity.

"And the scouts? Do they publish ratings of their pilots as insurance pools or shipping cartels might?"

The captain laughed, short and sharp.

"The Scouts do not publish such a list, to my knowledge, but piloting is as much an art as a trade, with the artists showing most at the edges of size and at the top edge of ship value.

"Thus the principal pilot of a major tradeship or cruising passenger vessel will be resourceful, capable, alert, pragmatic. The same will be true of courier vessels in general and Scout couriers in particular. The newest ships—which the vessel shown here approximates exceedingly well, by our image matching—why, who would put any but the best pilot in a courier ship that costs as much as a major cruise liner?"

Bar Jan froze his face as best he could, but felt the captain had missed his slip, in any case.

"I see. I have never flown with a courier pilot, Captain. Have you?"

The captain laughed, this time with more of joy than of irony.

"Indeed, sir, I was a courier for Ixin for some few years in my youth, and thus you may say you've flown with one. It is a style of flying suited to the young and the restless. But the demands of courier are many, and when I was offered the opportunity to regularize my schedule and my comfort by taking up the administrative lifestyle, I was easily persuaded."

"As both my delm and myself value your service, it is good that you have," Bar Jan said, offering an appropriate bow and accepting the proper response, and also seeing the next question rising easily, and seeing too that he'd been in some ways more honored than he'd known by the attentions that Pilot yos'Belin had persuaded him to pursue at some length, as well as by her sharing of her special and intoxicating blend of *vya*.

"What drives a courier pilot, if I may ask, and what special qualities does one need to continue long in the profession?"

The captain mused, his hum accompanied by the hand motions so often loved by the pilots. Bar Jan wasn't conversant with the hand-talk, never having a desire to do deep trade with non-Liadens. But pilots, he'd been shown just recently, used such motions in situations where noise might obstruct conversation, or give it away. So yes, he now knew the signs for *more, again, continue, pause, enough, stop,* and, *capitulate.*

"Pride, necessity, money—they flow together, lord, but in the end it is the challenge that is all-absorbing, which is the drive, for the time between the action is often long and one must be focused very much on a goal, and have study, strength, and stamina. If you have that drive, why then the rewards are very great. I suppose there's one more thing, in truth, in case you have a sudden urge to become a courier pilot of an exceptional ship, sir.

"To be exceptional, one must know to an exactitude how much pain one is capable of bearing, and then be willing and able to perform beyond that. Pain is the most difficult thing, if I may say so, sir. Pain of exertion. Pain of acceleration and deceleration. The pain of heat or cold, the pain of exhaustion, privation, thirst. It is essential that one does not become intoxicated in it, and believe it the goal. It is essential that one not become addicted to it, and thus push past that point of no return."

Bar Jan bowed the acknowledgment of truth received.

"Clear this screen," he said finally. "Do we have a trader's image, or a tactical image, of Franticle? I should like to study the relationship between the trading zones and the Jump zones there!"

The captain gave orders to make it so, while Bar Jan recalled Pilot yos'Belin with extreme clarity.

Indeed, pain could be intoxicating, getting and giving. Yes, it could. He'd made promises, he'd accepted and offered, and how much of it was *vya* and how much his own desire he was no longer sure, if he'd ever been. Moments of frenzy, stretching for hours, and among it the sharing of his personal necessities, his Balance against this upstart Jethri ven'Deelin, and his glad assumption of Rand's immediate needs. She'd been so strong, and so insistent—he thrilled even now thinking of the pain raised to joy in her.

He'd heard her advice and knew it good. Challenge the Terrans, and never trust those allied with Terrans. Be strong—soon would come a meeting with this Ixin upstart.

He would rise to Rinork. And she would be sure to be there when he did rise, to help guide him and to introduce him to the powers beyond the Council of Clans, where he could reach his full potential. He would be worthy of her, and all Liad would know it!

Chapter Twelve

• • • • •✳• • • •

Keravath, on Port, Balfour

THE CHANGE FROM SHIPBOARD ISOLATION to port reality was always interesting, but Jethri usually took that transition quickly. Long ago he'd heard from Paitor, "Don't stop and stare around you when you come to port, even if everything is odd. It marks you a target for the grifters and shysters."

So Jethri hurried, the Scout ship's loan of "weather gear" useful immediately since the ship's connection to the port terminal was not a tight air-locked tube connection but a casually linked semi-see-through curtain and roof that held gusty wind and well-blown rain only partially at bay. He ended up with water on his face and in his eyes and his attempt to wipe it away was less effective than he liked. He'd prefer to pay some *attention* to who was watching, feeling oddly out of place dressed as he was in trade clothes rather than crew.

Jethri paused with the wind battering another clear section of sheeting to the point that rain bounced under the bottom edge, and puddled in small lakes.

The Scout ship's appearance on a Terran port was not unprecedented, the Scout had assured him, though he couldn't recall ever hearing of such an event when he was still Terran crew—but after his father died, he'd often been denied even the flight deck's bulletins, half hearing concerns only from unguarded crew talk.

Scout ter'Astin's assurances weighed heavy with him, there being so many, and all of them important, else the Scout would not be cramming them into his brain so ruthlessly. The Scout's own mission on world had to do with meeting several "specialists"—*which* specialty was carefully not shared with Jethri—and these meetings were described as lasting "no later than late evening, local."

He almost turned back, then hunkered against the second seam, and felt water going down his collar as he kept his face down and looking away from the wind side. The actual terminal was just ahead, but the buffeting was reminiscent of his run-in with a wind-twist in the middle of a vineyard, and he blinked against the water and the memory before pushing forward and gaining the autodoor just ahead.

He didn't at first see the person standing in shadows a few meters deep in the terminal as he shook the water out of his lashes and blinked, finally out of the supposed protection of the rain curtains. The sounds of the terminal were what he might expect, but there was another, that of someone close to hand, calling his name.

"Hey, Jeth—that's you, right? Jethri Gobelyn?"

The voice was hurried, female, Terran, low, and both the accent and the inflection familiar. There were others around, including a guard with a peacemaker club and an anonymous sheath, as well as three pilots deep in conversation strolling away from a hall at right angles to the gate he'd just come through.

Jethri paused, alert, Paitor's warnings not entirely overshadowed by his awareness that he was armed with both a pistol and a backup, and had a Liaden Scout on call at the touch of an emergency button.

She approached rapidly, with a spacer's pacing, which was no surprise here, and without hesitation, which must be unusual in someone perhaps unsure of who they were speaking to.

Jethri saw no immediate sign of menace in the pace, nor in the bag slung tight under one arm. The other hand swung free, with a ship's bracelet and several rings clear on the surprisingly pale skin.

Her face was wrapped in a dampish hooded rain cloak, and she was taller than he'd gotten used to females being; her eyes were nearly level with his, and intently interested rather than distant and bland or doubting as an unknown Liaden's would be.

The face in the hood was made up, lips overfull and sparkled red with silver, skin pale-toned and edging blue toward the eyes, eyes that were lined with blue that faded into the face color in artful streaks.

Her ears, too, were tinged with the blue, which matched blue rim-runners curving up the side, decorated with tiny glow jewels . . .

No proper Liaden would have such on her face, of course—not even a Festival dress-up could permit it!

He bowed promptly, out of habit, a bow of civil welcome his protocol master would have been ecstatic to see mere months ago, but one Jethri now knew to be lacking the graces it should have because of his uncertainty—

"It's me," she said diffidently, and he knew the voice and felt a pang beyond that of mere recognition before the next phoneme formed, seeing the face beyond the makeup.

The smile took his face from Liaden prince to Terran spacer even before he rushed her, arms and hands wide, to give her a hug she didn't avoid. "Freza!"

"Freza, from the *Balrog*!" she managed, even as he squeezed her.

"Perfect!" she said close into his ear and he thought for a moment she was going to bite it, but then she stepped lightly away, shook back the hood, and laughed.

"But what are you doing here? You look set for a shivaree!"

She smiled, and held out a hand, nodding herself into a delightful small laugh.

"A shivaree, Jeth? No, not yet." She shook her head, smiles and color and—"But tell you what, you are looking *so* good that you'll be on the next invite list!"

He was overwhelmed by the wealth of information there, the joy and the concern and the tension in the corner of the eyes. He felt his face letting the smile come through and perhaps a bit of warmth too. He took a half step sideways to avoid the hug trying to build again.

She moved, keeping opposite, excitement in her step.

"Just saw that you were on your way in, and thought I'd say hello. Could have spun me out of orbit with a hand-jet when I saw a genuine Liaden Scout ship come in, posting Jethri Gobelyn ven'Deelin as sitting second board! Had to be you, but didn't think you were going for pilot, but there, none of us never really thought you'd be able to get out from under Iza. We ought to talk, if you've got the time—we've got to talk! I already got a day lounge reserved!"

A day lounge?

He caught a beseeching look and a hand motion that urged quick decision.

His wrist chronometer suggested he had time, if the port was not too complex, and . . .and it was Freza.

He bowed, which made her laugh, but she reached out her hand, which was warm and strong, and he rushed away with her, as if he always did.

She said, "Shhhh" when he tried to to talk, and on they went."

· · · ✳ · · ·

The rush lasted longer than Jethri expected. As Freza took him at a rapid pace away from the check-through gate, he saw in the distance a wide hall that turned into a sort of mall, and through that, briefly across a roofed but open-sided way into another building, marked in clear Terran: Top Quarter Temp Units.

Inside, worn hush-step carpeting greeted them, and she pulled more firmly as they rounded a corner where an armed and uniformed Terran guard with her sidekick dog was paying more attention to the lovely lady behind the counter than to the room she might have been guarding.

The numbers looked funny to him: he wasn't used to seeing doors marked in Terran now, and he almost ran over Freza when she stopped and waved a passkey at a door, pushing him ahead of her.

He stopped just inside the room, seeing that things were larger here than he was used to, not just the day couch, but the table heights, the location of switches . . .

"Phawao . . ." she said once the door was closed, and sealed, and he could hear her breathing was rapid. His was not.

"Not used to full-G," she admitted, "'cause we've been keeping to—"

They were close enough together that Jethri caught the scent she wore again. There was no *vya* to it, which was perhaps a good thing, for her smile was quirking and she laughed, spun away, and held her hand up as a stop sign.

Flinging the rain hood back and then removing the cloak entirely, she tossed the outer gear causally toward a chair of uncertain hue, and ran her hand over close-cropped hair, gently touching hands to face

He'd remained silent, and waited, willing to watch. She wore day clothes one might see on almost any station—good light-soled gray boots, with soft slacks close enough the same color as the boots and then *Balrog*'s brown double-pocketed uniform shirt with her name in yellow script. Everything fit together pleasingly—

He opened his mouth to speak, took a step toward her—

"No shivaree today, Jeth—we gotta talk. Get in, take the coat off, dry a little. Sit somewhere, so I know where I should sit."

• • • ✴ • • •

It was safer to be sitting. He still had the urge—apparently shared by Freza—to rush into a hug. Also, since she was sitting, he wasn't as obviously taking her in as he might have been if she was standing. He resisted, not entirely successfully, his urge to break into a grin.

"I'm thinking to be out of here pretty quick, Jeth—how long do you have?"

Brought back to the present, he admitted to the appointment at *Elthoria*'s local trade advisor's office and the time of it, which argued for enough time to talk . . .

"Then, let me start, because meter's working from my account. Is that good?"

He short-circuited his bow in favor of a nod and a "Yes." This made sense *melant'i* wise as well as from Terran manners, after all.

"First, I've seen you, and you look well. Don't look starved, or slaved, or nothing. That's a start—they are treating you good, right?"

She waved vaguely at the port, and he took the "they" to mean his ship—

"*Elthoria* has been wonderful to me," he said, "and also, they are my new ship, owned by my new clan. I have nothing but praise for Trader ven'Deelin."

"So your ship is good to you? But you're flying a Scout ship. You aren't a prisoner or—"

He laughed, and caught his tongue before he spoke, holding back the urge to rush out with the whole story, for indeed, the whole story would be worth nights at a traders' bar if he was so inclined, and besides, time was short.

The smile came anyway as he started in. "Closer the Scout is my prisoner than I his. This is not my regular berth, I assure you! We are attempting to right an error, to permit the Scout to make good on a promise he made and which has been broken by others. My ship— my new mother and Master Trader—agrees with me, and with the

Scout, that this error ought to be corrected. It is . . . a technical matter of *melant'i*, let us say."

She shook her head. "Never thought I'd be hearing that from a Gobelyn, I guess, that they had a *melant'i* problem to take care of!"

He shrugged, laughed, reheard his sentences and could hear the Liaden and Terran phrases warring, the careful timing of one language feeling odd in the other. "Life goes as it does."

"You know the rumors, I guess? That Paitor or Iza sold you to the Liadens."

He nodded and kept from shrugging this time.

"Khat sent a message telling me as much. They may say it, but I say not true. What happened—and you can tell anyone asking, because it *is* true—is that the *Market* was getting crowded and wasn't no one really comfortable with getting out. I was low on the lists, and old enough. Iza'd made some arrangements, I guess, with *Gold Digger*, but I . . . argued with the captain and said no to that, and she told me to find my own ship. Happened I did, in the next port. Happened it was *Elthoria*."

Freza'd been watching him intently, which he liked, and let a wry smile cross her face. "Yeah, a bunch of folks have heard stuff from *Digger* alright. Seems like Mac Gold can't get to port and talk ten sentences before he's blamed you twice and three times for the *Digger* being late on the route because they were waiting for you and you'd been sold out to a tradeship . . ."

He bowed, hearing the words only after they were out of his lips: "I will recall this as it becomes appropriate. Your information is noted."

She leaned back some, taken aback.

"I don't mean to be starting trouble, Jeth, it's just that Mac . . ."

He raised both his hands significantly, "Slow, Freza, please. Mac Gold has never been on my good side, but any quarrel I have with him is his and not yours. If he is a friend, be not concerned . . ."

She laughed lightly. "Geesh, now I got you up into the high decks. I don't see Mac often and when I do see him it's because I got to walk past him to get somewhere. I think he's figured it out and he don't buy me a beer no more. He still stares like he does, but I think that runs across the whole crew there and is just worst on him. He's got bad eyes and a bad mouth."

Jethri nodded. "Always to both," he agreed, "but he'll need to be careful with such talk if he's around Liadens. If someone from my clan or my ship were to hear it, they might take it badly. I'll see if I can figure out how to get word to him to stop such tales else if Clan Ixin or a crew mate hears it, they may take his tongue for it."

Freza closed her eyes and he laughed gently.

"Figure of speech, I believe it, but Mac's not good social with Terrans, so he's probably really bad social with Liadens, and things could get out of hand double-quick. That's how I ended up with a new mother!"

"It's confusing, Jethri, it is. We hear you called a trader, we hear you called son of a trader . . ."

He looked to the chronometer, sighed as he tapped at it. "When we have our shivaree we'll save some time for that stuff." He said it jestingly, he thought, but it came out sounding like an invite to him, too.

She looked at him, calculation in her eyes and a smile on the corners of her mouth.

"Well, here's the thing—I'm not against it in the general way of things. But you got to know that if you come around ships—our ships, the central and north central loops, even the west central loops—there's some other stuff that Mac Gold's been pushing at people, and being this close to you, and you dressed up to take the shine off a hull, I can see his point."

He held out his hand, showed the apprentice ring—

"I'm a trader. Really." He caught her eye then by spreading the collar of his tunic, reaching for a pair of chains. On one was his Terran trade key—and on the other was his clan sigil, rabbit-and-moon.

"And this, he said, holding the key, says I'm a trader, too. This"—he leaned in her direction—"calls me a son of the house, Clan Ixin."

Now Freza shook her head, ear jewels not distracting him from watching her face.

"Not what I mean. Not the issue, really, not concerned about that stuff, Jeth. Mac Gold's claiming that you wasn't true crew on the *Market*—that you was a side accident from one of Arin's Commission runs . . ."

Jethri sighed and she held her hand up.

"Jeth, it don't matter to me, but it might to shipfolk. It's true though, it doesn't look like there's drop one of Iza's blood in you. You look so much of Arin—"

He overrode her then, his voice gaining tension with each word.

"I . . . look so much like Arin I could be his twin!" He closed his eyes as part of his pause, opened them to find Freza's attention riveted. "And since I only knew him after I was born, I can't tell you how it happened!"

Startled by his vehemence Freza sat back, her face serious. It took a moment for her to find words, and then they were uncertain.

"Yeah, Jethri, you could. I didn't really *know* Arin, but I'd seen him. And now, with you all dressed up, you could pass for him when he was doing the official bit. Hair's different, and that's good, but . . ."

"But rumors I'm a copy are exactly the kind of thing Mac Gold would go for, aren't they? Mad at everyone so not anyone, anywhere, can be as pure a looper as he is."

Freza smiled, nodded, and said lightly, carefully, "You know, you even sound more like Arin when you're mad. I *was* there, toting drinks for the common room, when he had to bust up the Glenleg shivaree. You even got a flashy ring on your hand!"

He glanced at the ring again, nodded. "Guess it does look flashy if you don't know it's a starter ring . . ." He paused, looked to her face, saw a lot to like there, went on "I keep finding stuff out about Arin that everyone thinks I know. Kind of hard sometimes. It's almost worse than learning what I need to do to get by with my new crew, since they know I'm outside the culture. But there's a lot I didn't know, and don't. I keep trying to learn it all . . ."

"But, like you say, there's schedules to do things, and learning to do, and we can't get all done at once."

He hadn't exactly said that, but she went on before he could correct her.

"Several things are happening, Jethri Arin's son; one is that someone's watching out for the *Market*. It's been on port a couple places that if anyone knows where the *Market*'s been or where it's going, it might be worth some big money. And then there's your name, same thing, and then some folks are after the *Envidaria*, too . . ."

His bow became a nod—he fought against the shrug, but once that happened, he let the grimace come to his face too.

"*Envidaria*?"

She laughed, "Well, yeah, I mean they've been after that for years so it doesn't make any difference, does it? If someone needs it, we carry a copy, but it's not just handed around . . . and the Golds don't have it from us, so they can't sell it, that's for sure!"

Too much at once—

"Who is buying what?" he finally managed.

"That's the thing. Mostly it seems to be regular ship trackers, like finance folk might put out, I guess. Seems to me the questions are thicker closer we are to Liaden ports, and closer to where we hear the *Market*'s already been, but I haven't put analysis to that."

A gentle buzzing noise then: "Gotta go, Jethri. I swear I'm watching for you. We'll catch you up on everything! Here's our schedule—you got one?"

He stood, pulled a card from his public pocket, his trader's card, handed that across and sighed: "*Elthoria*'s got a long-posted route—you can drop messages along there and I'll get 'em. I have to set up some personal boxes, I guess. And your route, I'll watch for news and send it. I don't know how long this business with the Scout's going to take . . . "

They hugged again as they parted at the door, his ear still smarting from the nip she'd given it and his grin not well-hidden as he played her parting words over in his mind.

"More where that came from, Trader, and that's a contract!"

"Done!" he'd managed, but then she was away, and the world around him was dimmer.

He sighed, and folded the borrowed rain cloak into his carry case before searching out his appointment with the law-jaw.

• • • ✳ • • •

The first time he'd come through here he'd still been in the wind-blown rain slicks, his hair and face as damp as the cloak. Now, though, he'd had time to recover not only from the rain but from the combing and shaping for his ID photoshots and vidclip made for his meeting. He had his collars right, some of his Ixin jewelry showing around his neck and his ring was showing color.

He felt good, having gotten work done, and he walked like he felt good and in charge. Thus, he was visible.

His new visibility meant there were a couple of bows, two salutes, some quiet near-whispered conversation after he passed—yes, it was obvious that Balfour wasn't really used to Liaden traders in full dress-up walking their corridors, no matter that they might see and handle an occasional Liaden ship.

The sides of the rain tunnel were furled now, with the edges of the passage just ended glittering with rain drips.

The drips showed that the rain had not long been gone, and the breeze still whistled through the covered way, the puddles not as deep as they'd been.

Deep in thought over the day's work—and with an early morning appointment facing him on the morrow—Jethri hardly noticed the cooling temperatures nor the glow on the horizon where the local star was rapidly falling below sight level. There were sounds of work nearby, and voices, and he caught the flash of port landing lights. In the lowering light he sensed a wide glow that domed the rest of the city.

Since he'd not been beyond the customs zone he had no idea of its size by sight or by numbers: ter'Astin had been far too canny to have Jethri doing more than covering incoming radio transmission during the inclement landing. What the Scout ship gave way in size to even a compact family trader like *Gobelyn's Market* meant local weather could make landings unstable.

He operated the entry with quick touches, casually turning to be sure that no one was close enough to see his codes or be sure if he'd used a card or keypads—of such things was security built!

Once in, *Keravath* was fairly quiet, only the comforting whisper of air circulation now, along with the occasional tick of one or another piece of equipment comparing the state of Board One against that of Board Two. Maybe the ship was a little noisier than usual—when the Scout was on sleep shift it often seemed as though there were more sounds and not fewer.

The ship's interior was more comfortable than the breezy world outside and Jethri tucked the dry raingear away. Out of new habit he dropped into the second's seat. Curious, touching controls that brought up the ship's outside eyes, he saw the city as *Keravath* could: glows of air currents in one screen, energy levels of the clouds and distant storm in another, and nearby—

And nearby, well within the ship's stay-away zone, were two

figures in workers' gear moving slowly away, a hip-height tractor following obediently behind.

Inexpertly he sought the camera controls, triggering an external light as well as the video control he wanted. The workers sped up slightly, leaving the ship's zone empty, and by the time he'd figured out the image zoom and follow, the zone was clear. And boring.

He stared at the screens absently, leaning into his seat as the fingers of his right hand twiddled idly with his right ear halfway up the rim. He laughed then—that was where Freza had nipped him to promise a contract for shivaree . . .

He allowed his fingers to continue their ruminative exploration a few moments longer, far happier to consider *that* bit of contract than the maze of notions and motions laid out for him this day by Jay Rivenkid Dorster, Esquire. He stared into the screen, seeing nothing but his post-Freza meeting.

. . . . ✣ . . . .

Despite the obvious police in other sections of the complex, Jethri hadn't seen any once he stepped down the two shallow steps to the section marked as "Upper Old Gate Mall" on the wall maps.

The people were many, sitting at tables or standing at small food and beverage booths, dressed Terran, or local Terran, with a fair number in kilts or skirts. Most of the others, in bland bluish or grayish trousers and mixed color shirts could have been from other back-ports Jethri'd been on, and the clothes of day workers. If Jethri's underbrain knew anything about it, many of them weren't all that well-off, though there was no air of desperation about the place.

There was an undercurrent of sound, which he took to be the rain, which he could see through sheeting the upper windows, elsewise the sounds were low voices calmly shared, either tired, indolent, or both.

He was watched with minor interest, and watched back, glad at least that his hair was no longer ship-smooth, for many of these wore their hair long and bordering on the unkempt, a mix of hats, scarves, and visors not hiding the prevalence of reddish-brown heads; a few watched harder and were dressed in a more forward and provocative fashion with shorter kilts or skirts and more open shirts, but none approached asking for his custom and he didn't slow, since time was coming closer.

His walk was short, and down three more steps in another section, this with a roof that leaked in several spots. He shivered, a touch of his world-side phobia returning to imagine a place where leaks weren't plugged and gases were free to escape hither and yon . . . but the directions were good even if the door he came to at Fifty-Six Gate Court Lower looked to be made out of polished wood set into a raw stone wall instead of something properly airtight.

He passed through that swinging door, taking the ENTER sign at its word, and discovered the door was indeed wood, not even as thick as his fist—and if the wall on the other side was not of the same raw stone, it was instead a matching tone of gray bricks.

The other walls of the room were a treasure. His trader's eye went to work cataloging the shelf space of books—hardcopy books!—the sidewalls full, the back wall full except for two doors, a hip-high shelf wall of books split the room. He closed the door, saw that the front wall held a treasure of paintings on cloth, and . . .

"Yes?"

Startled, Jethri turned, caught sight of a quizzically smiling face peering over the wall—from a seat on the other side of it. He bowed to the woman: by her lined face and near colorless hair, an elder . . .

"I regret I failed to see you. I am Jethri Gobelyn. An appointment made for Ixin and Gobelyn—"

"Why, yes, your name is here in the book. You are several moments early. Please, make yourself at home and I'll let Jay know you are arrived."

Making himself at home took the form of approaching the closer left wall and peering at the titles at easy eye height. The books stopped just short of the ceiling . . . and the shelves were wood, too!

He caught a motion out of the corner of his eyes—the elder had risen and was walking toward the back, from where presently arose some mumbles. She was dressed in trousers and top much like those in the courtyard outside, though not as strained with wear, and her shoes were simple sandals.

The sound continued, but Jethri's eyes were drawn to the wall again, which he moved along slowly, trying to absorb exactly what it was he was looking at. Some of the books matched in series, and each had the name of a planet, or a system, or a ship manufacturer or—

"Sir, Jay will see you now."

Jethri blushed beneath his bow, the lady's nice smile from just an arm's length away taking away part of the sting of his being quite so inadvertent in his attention. She turned and walked away, and he smelled something flowery—likely one of the scents the world-bound use to disguise themselves.

"Come on in and find a seat, Trader Gobelyn, and welcome!" The words were in ship-deck Terran, broad and loud, with a depth and smoothness so easy it was almost sung.

Jethri stood, transfixed. The man behind the huge desk stood, bushy red hair brushing the room's ceiling and cascading down to his shoulders, merging as it fell into an impossible mask of gray-red that left his face, temple to nose, open to view and the rest covered in a roiling mass of self-grown hair.

"Say what?" asked the man, laughing, lips and mouth showing as he spoke. "Do you say that my new friend the trader has never seen a real beard?" He offered a huge hand, and it took Jethri a moment to recall his Terran duties, and reach to clasp it.

"I'm Jay Dorster. Got a card here for you, so you won't forget me."

The joke was in the words, for how could any who met him forget such a man?

Jethri took the finely made card, saw the *Jay Rivenkid Dorster, Esquire* in bold type and even bolder the words *Trade Law Specialist*.

"Thank you sir," he managed, I'm Jethri Gobelyn ven'Deelin . . ."

The big man waved his hands. "Sit. You make me tired standing there!"

Jethri managed a bow and a thank you and found the center seat by touch as the big man sat. The beard stretched almost to his belly and Jethri needed to look up to see him clearly for all that they were sitting across from one another.

"So, possession problems, eh? Often the way things happen when you loan things out to a third party, so I guess you'll learn that from this little situation."

The big man hummed to himself as he went though a stack of paper notes, face bobbing in time to his own tune.

"So, we got some info from *Elthoria* and Ixin. Makes it complicated, this Liaden side of things. Your man ter'Astin, I have his note as well, and he's clear that there's a mess, but before I go any further, tell me it's true that you're a Gobelyn because you're Commissioner Arin Gobelyn's git."

Still the same question! Could he never get beyond his father? Jethri gathered himself, the attribution of ter'Astin as his "man" unsettling as it was both misleading and appropriate.

"Yes, it is true, sir." He manfully put aside the Liaden protocols, thought of his father being official, tried to sit firmly and honorably in front of this force of nature. "I . . ."

"Of course it's true! Couldn't be anyone but him stamp that face on a kid, but you musta heard that a million times squared. Sorry he left us so soon—had a good head on his shoulders." The shaggy head shook sadly a moment, then said, piercing gray eyes suddenly bright beneath bushy brows, "Do you?"

Against training, Jethri smiled, and then shrugged, formality shattered by the man across the desk top.

"The proof's not in on that, sir," he admitted, which drew a laugh and a snap of the fingers.

"Now I see, couldn't place your accent, but that's ship Liaden I'm hearing playing with the looper, yes it is. Guess eventually there'll be more young traders talking with that . . ."

Jethri suppressed the shrug this time, managed, "I'm the experiment, I guess. If it works . . ."

The big head nodded, ringlets shaking their way out of the hair momentarily and disappearing.

"One more question before we really start—how'd you pick up a Liaden berth, you coming from the *Market*? Was that a . . ."

"I was looking for a ship," Jethri said with some asperity, "because I was a redundant. 'Just taking up oxygen', the captain told one of the crew, and me. *I* did a turndown when the captain pointed me to an opening with one of her age-friends. Did some business that got the attention of Master Trader ven'Deelin and since I was looking for off-ship, and she had a trader berth to fill, it worked out."

"Redundant, eh? Well don't I know about that? That's what happened to me," Dorster said reminiscently, leaning back and letting his head touch the wall while the seat he pushed back groaned, just a little. "I was on the *Floydada* out of Trustee, with my mother being nav officer and backup pilot, but we could all see it coming—I was getting to be too much to feed, and wasn't a berth on board that would take me unless I folded up—I was sleeping in a chair. We got here, in fact, to Balfour, and they made it plain—fourteen or forty, I wasn't flying with them no more."

He laughed then, booming voice shaking the books on the wall. "They figured Vania would set me off to school and she'd fly, but they hadn't checked with her, and she left them on the tarmac, started a nav tutoring service. Served them right, I say. They picked up someone that Olaf-crashed them on Bumsted very next trip. Them Gorins—that'd been when your ship was still doing the north center I think . . ."

A shake of the head—"Well after that, I got schooling and a specialty 'cause I knew about ships and stuff. What happened *after* you got left off?"

"After? I . . ."

Jethri paused, looking for the right phrase to cover the rather awkward fact of his having two mothers these days. "After that, turned out there were protocol issues and extra training being needed—on account of culture differences. I got myself in some *melant'i* trouble that might have been fatal, and that got solved by bringing me in-clan, to Ixin. The only way they could make it stick was to make me a son of the clan."

Dorster listened intently. A rolling hand motion encouraged Jethri to go on . . .

"Likely next time there's a Terran riding trader for Liadens, if there is one, it ought to be a swap—even up—with a bit more experience all the way around, and a few more rules established."

The beard shivered as Dorster nodded quickly.

"Yes, yes, by damn! Someone should have done that a bunch of Standards ago. Ought to be a protocol, not just for trade, but for mixing traders! Well now, that gives me a—hold on!"

He raised his head, shouted out the door: "Vania, I need a new folder made up, dated today. Two of them. One's got this fellow's name on it. The other, call it—umm . . . wait."

A large hand disappeared beneath the beard and the bright eyes closed for several seconds, opening about the time the mouth did to say, "Here it is Van, other new file, dated today, is Mixed Trader Swap Protocol Proposals; I'll need that crossed to . . . whatever it gets crossed to plus I'll have notes later, remind me!

"Now, what happened that's got one of these scouts playing taxi driver for a Gobelyn? Why's there property rights in it? I'll be clear with you: this is confidential, but I may need room to work. Just asking some questions is enough to—well, you know how it works, right? Once you ask someone where you are, they start to want to know where you're going or where you come from. Asking a question is a wave with ripples. But before you start on the property, the rest of the questions I have up front are . . ."

· · · ✳ · · ·

Most of the up-front questions were simple, made harder by Dorster's intent eyes. The man watched as if everything Jethri said was in doubt, and demanded to see all the ID he had on him.

"My name will go on documents for you, my signature, and me and my good name is what may stand between you and being in jail someday. So tell me and show me what I ask and we may be able to solve problems so they won't happen, heh?

"And so, my friend, for the record, there is something not clear here—we need a date for your birth!"

Jethri felt an odd dread. "A date?"

"Yes, you know, one day you were connected to your mother's support systems and then, spank-a-whop! Out you were launched into the cold and dangerous universe, untethered, to eat and breathe and make noises on your own. That day—we must add it to some documents."

Jethri gave him the ship-year.

"A day. The single day, if you will!"

Jethri sighed, repeated the ship-year, finally recalling the most uncelebrated day on his so-called birth ship.

"Ship day two hundred and twelve," Jethri said, adding as carefully as he could, "That's day two hundred and twelve, ship cycle one seventeen, that's what my father specified, and that's what we celebrated, until he died."

Dorster blinked. "But when you were added to the rolls—at what port? They should have got you on the roster . . ."

"I think, you see, they didn't add me to roster immediately—I found out after . . ."

Dorster smiled. "I guess so. I do guess so."

Jethri suppressed his grimace and let the blush go . . . "Ship habit, sir. Not until I got my name . . . so it was sometime before I went on roster."

"Ah—right, I forget. Are you crew or are you passenger, eh? Well I know that, too!"

The big man tapped his fingers on the desk, Jethri's IDs in front of him.

"I see, well, then. A lifetime of ship-time, and not on planet long enough to get a homeworld? And there's space-time, Jump—they make things a little harder for us, my friend, and on some worlds it matters by day count, on others by date count to some silly local event. So we must be able to provide if you are sixteen Standards or sixty. Somewhere there should be a cross-reference for you—was your name announced in a bulletin somewhere? When were you first listed on a crew manifest, with birth info?"

"Not sure we did really, the birth date thing. They just listed me as adult crew a few years ago when I started doing out-ship assists—gave me a crew card and that was it."

"Do you have that card?"

"You hold the ID I carry."

"Ah, so *Elthoria*, which is not on port, will admit of you? Well, that is useful, not very! You will always need to remember, spacer, that you ought to have ID with current relationship to a planet or a port of power!"

Jethri considered. "*Keravath*'s key—do you suppose that's enough of an ID?"

"Well, here, here in this office, it is enough ID—I know who you are for I was expecting you, and it matches *Elthoria*'s information. We must get you a permanent card, and we must do it before you leave. You can't be out and about on worlds without a ship to back you up unless you have good ID. As it happens, I'm certified."

In the end, with cross-checking trade lists, they came up with what Dorster allowed was an acceptable haibinja, a date they could call his own start date without math-and-calc reference all the way back to his zero-day.

Then, the hard part, explaining the promises the Scout had made, and the thing with the fractins . . .

"Here, of course, right here on Balfour, you can find yourself your body weight and times ten, too, in fractins if you want 'em—you can't recycle the things and you can't just dump 'em in a pile because they'll still be there in a hundred years if you dig them back up. There's still the whispers that somehow some way, they might do something!"

"Yessir, I know that. The one I had, it was my lucky piece. The other thing, that was in a pile of stuff I inherited. Arin might have been able to teach me how to use it, but the Scouts were sure of themselves and—by Liaden rules, anyhow—the Befores were in their custody, and so they went to them. The book, though, that was mine—I wrote in it, and so did Arin, and that was to come back and be returned, no question."

"Sure," the big man said. "There's lots to work with, I think. Just got to find the right orbits . . ."

Dorster stretched in his overworked chair, making it creak once more, his hand disappearing under his beard and reappearing fingers first as he ruminated, then slowly moving his head until it covered his ear. The eyes still looking elsewhere, the hand moved across the busy mustache, came to rest over the nose and half across the eyes as he made a slow humming noise.

This went on until Dorster stood without warning—

"Come on. You're shipfolk—let me get you some 'mite while I do a bit of research. Won't be long at all, I think. Not too long, anyway. And Vania, she'll get your docs together so we can get you out of here straight as Pythagoras when the time comes."

Chapter Thirteen

· · · ·✳· · · ·

***Keravath*, on Port, Balfour**

JETHRI WAS STILL LOOKING AT THE SCREENS, the datastick in his inner pocket something he ought probably to share with the Scout. He had some points to make, and some questions to ask. Some of the questions were easy, and some were not.

Too, he'd had to make a decision and sign his name, and hand over live coin from his own pocket. There'd been a *melant'i* play in his head over that—the question of was he Terran now, or Liaden, and he'd made his choice that he was Jethri and needed to be covered wherever he was, like Dorster said.

The being covered wasn't as easy as it should have been though, on account that Iza never had done all that she should have when Arin died. She had neglected it on purpose, possibly, or just overlooked it. It was simple, really—with Arin gone, Jethri should have had a vouch-home, but Iza hadn't really done that, had not put him on the ship's roster as full crew even after he was trading, had not certified him on New Carpathia—where the ship was registered like most of the loop ships—had not even certified him as Terran, hadn't set up a proper chain of succession for his goods and rights in case he died, hadn't . . .

So now, besides being Jethri Gobelyn ven'Deelin doing business as Jethri Gobelyn, he was back-certified a Terran, on account of his father'd been certified and had Commission records so Jethri had a history that didn't depend entirely on the good will of Khat and Paitor, him counting no will at all in Iza's direction.

Paitor'd bought him a ten-year trade key based on his good work on the trade that got the refit going for *Gobelyn's Market*, but the key was for Jethri Gobelyn—so he had to keep that straight. On the other hand, to be able to face Liadens in court—even a Terran court— he'd have to be on record as being a clan member. That status was easy enough to prove, because it had been published in *The Gazette* at Solcintra, Liad, a kind of combination gossip sheet and newspaper of record for Liaden clans. All of this was now certified here on Balfour.

Certified records were trackable and being certified Terran, as he'd done first, meant he could buy a fall-back, which he'd also done. Worse came to worst, he could now stick Homeport, Waymart, on any record that needed it and *that* gave him law-jawing rights based on Waymart laws if he needed them—wherever he needed them— which he did, if there was any hope of getting the Balance they were working on fixed.

The trick was, he'd retained Dorster for himself. So he had, now, seven different tracks of what to do if and when they came face-to-face with the miscreants, and four of those tracks up for settling in the morning with his meeting—well, their meeting, since he'd need the Scout to be witness and do some swearing, too, at the hearing.

Now he just needed to explain all of that to ter'Astin, who still wasn't back. Sitting in the second chair he felt the circulation kick up a notch. Right, the storms coming through often meant temperature changes. He knew something about weather from his time on Irikwae so if it was getting warmer outside, then the ship was doing right by itself. It was nosier than usual, too, which probably meant that, despite closed airlocks, it was "breathing" and filtering local air—for all he knew it might be good enough air to fill some extra tanks.

He thought about dinner—ter'Astin had told him to expect fresh food coming in, but he was getting short in the stomach fuse department—and sighed gustily as he stretched, glancing over the board, seeing familiar lights in the right spots, switches where they belonged, screens large and small.

He stood, planning on changing out of the trade clothes he'd worn to the mall, his eyes drifting back over some anomaly in front of him.

He'd almost figured it out when he heard ter'Astin's tone ring, indicating that he'd started the airlock cycling. The Scout wasn't one to run with both sides of an airlock open at the same time, like some family ships might on world; the interlocks were not to be messed with—one door open at a time was the rule. The outer lock closed and pressure equalized—that's when the boards knew ter'Astin was back and the onboard line on the oxy use chart lit up.

There it was.

There on the housekeeping section there were three lines on the day's oxy chart. His, the Scout's, and crewman number three. Crew number three's record stopped not more than five minutes ago.

• • • ✳ • • •

"Have you moved beyond this area since you reboarded?"

The food smelled delicious, but the containers remained unopened on the counter as the Scout brought his boards live and scanned Jethri's captured video images. He grimaced and brought up a sub-board Jethri hadn't seen before, and his hands blurred as he ran routines . . .

"Not at all. I was sitting here . . ."

"Excellent," the Scout allowed, "Please take your board again; we have a lot of work to do."

There were twin *thunks* behind them then, and the young trader realized the pressure doors separating the tiny flight deck from the tiny berths had been activated, effectively locking those. Could there be a stowaway?

As Jethri sat, the Scout called the tower, requesting a feed of recent area scans, asking if there were comm feeds pending, if it was the habit of Maintenance to wander through ship-zone without being asked and offering to supply a copy . . .

"You, Jethri," the Scout said, barely glancing at him as he was now balancing three ship-to-shore conversations, "will run a check of the airlock records for the last ship-day, and match open and closing records against your own movements and against those of mine you know. Compare them with the pressure and usage charts you'll find for the cabin, as well, and if you select these controls—" Here Jethri's main screen lit up file areas he'd never thought to investigate.

"It is well of you to inquire if we have added crew, and admire that you noticed the added crew mark. *Keravath* rarely travels with three aboard, and if you will bring those usage records forward when you have them—we can check the sealing and unsealing of the berths as well, in the drop-downs.

"Yes, thank you. It is very wise of you to have the operating cameras on rotation, if I may say so, and would appreciate that as hardcopy as soon as possible. As well, perhaps you will be able to identify this person from our records, then, which I transmit."

Jethri matched the timelines on the outer lock, saw his own exit and return reflected clearly, and assumed the second exit of the day was ter'Astin, and knew, too which one was the Scout's return. Within very few moments of ter'Astin's exit there was another outer lock usage . . .

"Why does it say crew member number three?" Jethri asked. "You haven't added anyone to the roster, have you?" He hadn't meant to make the question sound suspicious, but wasn't sure he'd achieved neutrality.

"Ah. Indeed, why? Particularly since none has been added to the roster since the flight began but yourself."

The Scout excused himself momentarily, spoke to ground control, returned his attention to Jethri. "May I assume you did not lend out your key to the ship?"

"Always in my inner pocket, until I returned."

"As it should be. I then assure you, for good measure as you sit Second here, that I did not lend out my key to the ship, or offer a spare to another. In effect, my key was in an inner pocket the while I was on port."

The Scout sighed then, threw a long-distance scan of their small corner of the landing lot onto the screen. Jethri saw himself leave, judging by time—the rain and walls of the little tunnel made it difficult to see detail. He saw ter'Astin leave, recognizable in part by his pilot's jacket, and in part by hair color. Then there was a motion coming up the tunnel, someone wearing green, and then the image went muzzy and that portion stopped, to be replaced with a view of a distant gray ship in distant gray rain on a distant launch spot

"Crewman number three arrived on *Keravath* and utilized a key to the ship."

Jethri let that sink in—

"But how?"

"I suspect I know how, my friend. The answer is more than a little disturbing. The very first question now is *why*? So, let us compare notes on the opening and closing of various doors and entrances, and

we'll do a keystroke analysis, if we need to, on the rest of the ship.
Once we're positive we have no large-scale visitors on board, we'll
eat."

· · · ·✦· · · ·

As they ate, they pieced together a stealthy and knowing intruder,
the ship's normal routine a strange counterpoint to the mystery. The
normal things: some screens showing ship movements as their own
instruments received them, others showing trade relays and ordinary
traffic, with the muted sounds of distant discussions in Terran.

But the Scout ignored such things as Jethri tried to, the Scout
leading the way in describing the invasion.

The visitor had been on board for a very few moments, and had
entered Jethri's sleeping cubby, but not ter'Astin's. If theft was the
motive, there was no proof of it, for Jethri could find nothing missing,
nor was anything obviously disturbed. The Scout's handheld discovered
no sign of a telltale, and the ship itself reported no odd transmissions.
The course boards *had* been accessed and likely copied as they might
from Jethri's board, with access again noted to crewman number three.

"Not into my sleeping area, for of course mine are Scout's habits.
If I have secrets they'll be difficult to locate, or in well-guarded safe
spots, and not to be discovered for the turning over of clothes or
perusal of reading sticks. Since the safe spots are pilot-programmable
it would be unwise to attempt them if secrecy was important, and if
not we'd have overt evidence of damage or search in the ship."

The thought train waited while they both bit into some of the oil
breads and then the Scout made an emphatic hand gesture, which
encompassed himself, Jethri, and the ship at once.

"You will remind me, as Second, that on every port we shall set
full safeguards on arrival and we will check those safeguards, each, for
every exit."

"Understood." Jethri bowed a deep bow since it was a very emphatic
hand motion he was agreeing to.

"Good. And what other information might be of note, I wonder?"

Jethri shrugged, then ventured an oddity. "The oxy and other gas
uses. They're not yours, according to the charts, and not mine, but they're
different somehow. Does it mean the intruder's acclimated here?"

"Ah, what an interesting question and observation. We shall both
study on this as time permits."

Now, a sip of tea, and the tale continued.

"And so, the ship was looked at, and neither my station nor my areas disturbed, a sign that the intruder, for we can see by the usage rates that there was only one, is a pilot—a Scout pilot."

Another sip of tea interrupted. "And since the key was to hand, it was either a Scout pilot who has flown aboard *Keravath* in the past who copied or kept a key, or one who had access to the key locker usually controlled by the Master of Keys.

"As second seat you must know that an invasion of a pilot's ship is forgivable only under extreme circumstances. That the visitor did not care to explain such circumstances indicates that, in fact, such were not in force. In your case, they have intruded on your space; they have violated your privacy, and they have disturbed your goods. There is Balance owing to me, to you, and to *Keravath* herself.

"Additionally, there is Balance owing to the Scouts—but you see, we continue to cause you difficulty; so first, that is mine to solve, and the ship entry, that is ours to solve." Here he bowed, comrade mode, to Jethri, adding "There is nuance here you may not have learned yet, but I will not let the nuance be lost, I swear it!"

"The question is still why! Why did they steal my book in the first place? Why rummage through my clothes?" Jethri insisted.

"It is that you are known to have used Old Tech with much effect, and only recently. You are of a family of traders thought to have long traded Old Tech. Indeed, the trail now runs through the very items you inherited, through the very pocket piece you played with as a child. And your face is very much the face of Arin Gobelyn, who died with secrets someone wants.

"Understand, Second, that Arin Gobelyn was part of something larger than your ship, or your ship family: he'd been a commissioner of the Combine, and then, he was not a commissioner but he was not done with being part of something larger, because he had a plan or a vision, and he made a report on it that is now circulating."

"Circulating report? He's gone!"

The pilot's face gave away exasperation.

"Of course his report is circulating—else I'd not have heard of it. I would like to see a copy for myself, but it remains yet an object of interest for my agency."

An expression ghosted over the Scout's face, turned to a smile, and then the bow of one making a request perhaps not quite covered by existing *melant'i*.

"Perhaps the best path is for me to ask you outright—is it possible you own a copy of the manifesto called '*Arin's Envidaria of the Seventeen Worlds*'?"

Jethri sighed, shook his head Terran style, and finally said, "No. In fact I haven't a copy, and what's more, I haven't heard of this thing before today. You call it a 'manifesto'—is that a plan for all men to live by?"

The Scout's face went blank, as if he'd given something away, and he bowed, contrition being the lead note.

"If I'd seen a copy," the scout said, "I might tell you what it is, but what we know is that there have been some few—transmissions— gathered as Scouts travel. Where this information, this report, is mentioned, it appears guarded and secret, which seems odd of something related to trade. It has been growing of late, but only among certain ships. Oddly,"—here the Scout looked away for a few moments before looking back and continuing—"I say *oddly*, some of these ships are also often ships thought to be trading in the Old Tech or otherwise pushing the edge of permissible trading. If there were traders more like you, of course, we need not be concerned about messages that we cannot decipher . . ."

The day had suddenly become very long.

"I see." Jethri made his comment and his face was as bland as it could get, but he was afraid his voice betrayed annoyance, given the Scout's immediate reinforced bow of contrition.

"I'm puzzled," Jethri managed, "to say the least. If you'd like to know what I know about my father, perhaps we can talk on that. Do feel free to ask directly, so that we may both know how ignorant I am."

That sounded like pouting to Jethri, but he honestly continued in the same vein, feeling the force of ire behind his words.

"I will tell you that of secret plans spread by Terran tradeships, I do not know. Iza kept me away from such news, if she knew of it herself, and now, Scout, I must ask what kind of conspiracy is being built here? Is it being built against me?"

Jethri looked away this time, his heart skipping a beat as he heard "*Balrog* on final exit leg" from the low mutters of local traffic, his eyes scanning to locate—ah, exiting local orbit, not yet nearing Jump, Freza riding away with a copy of whatever the *Envidaria* was . . . His sigh was real, and informed his growing vehemence.

"Your ship—our ship, if you will— is invaded because I am here. You tell me that Scouts are chasing my father's words, and at the same time I must trust a Scout to act for me after Scouts have stolen from me, the word of Scouts not being universal . . ."

Jethri's ring flashed as he struck fist to palm in emphasis: "We have—I have—guidance from the lawjaw I spoke to. I don't know who you consulted, but there's plans I have here, depending on which world we go to, and which way *your people* want to act. A couple of the places—that's the blue option—I'm just supposed to have them arrested for theft, if we can get them off-ship, 'cause Liadens don't have particular notice there and I will, that is, *I do*. That Combine key, it marks me a trader, you see, on all of these seventeen worlds, Terran-based worlds every one."

"The red list, I need to go to the proctors on port, declare my name and my intent, and have the ships blocked to port and searched for my goods . . . and if I must, claim their ships forfeit."

Jethri laughed without mirth at that, shaking his head and staring down the Scout's gaze.

The Scout stiffened, and bowed permission to continue.

"It seemed extreme to me, too." Jethri shook his head, closed his eyes, opened them with determination, gathering energy.

"I thought that was too much," he said, "but now I'm not sure. We'd use something they call a Writ of Replevin, demanding my stuff back and holding theirs hostage for it. And since you're here, or will be there, with me, you're my witness against them. We'll need your card and signature tomorrow, so we can get this in order and have it with us. That's what you've got to do, if it comes to that."

Jethri waited, saw the scout waiting, wondered if he'd overstated something—

The Scout nodded a small bow of assent, and then it turned into a bigger, more formal bow.

"I have put myself in a position of being sworn to multiple masters. It is an exquisite *melant'i* play which my old delm—dead before I was first sent to the Scouts for training, alas—would have found amusing. And so I have told you, and I have told your clan, that having erred, I will support all efforts to return your lost items to you, though in the larger universe they might have little value.

"Having said that," he went on, "I must still do as much of my duty as possible to *all of my masters*; not only to my delm, but to those who do me the honor of calling me a Scout and giving me this ship to fly, and to those who have entrusted me with the will of their clan, and to you. Let us both speak to the point: we have a common goal and as for that common goal, we pursue it vigorously, and to some extent with the support of the Scouts."

The Scout stared vaguely into the screens, probably not seeing what Jethri was seeing—the tagged *Balrog* leaving the crowded close-control zone for the outer-limit free maneuvering zone—and then turned his dark eyes back to Jethri, his hands motioning an emphasis Jethri could not read.

"Count me on your side, if you must have a side, to the point of returning you to *Elthoria*, whole. That is *our* conspiracy. The rest of it goes as necessity requires. As an honorable man, grant me that. And let us continue with our quest. I will go with you to this court tomorrow, and then we shall go forth."

Turmoil in his head, the trader in him wished to accept the offer at face value, while the Terran crewman, still discovering his father and his heritage, was not so sure. He stared at the scan of the system, the retreating *Balrog* reduced to small font and numbers, wishing he'd known to ask after his father's paper when Freza mentioned it. The thing was deep, after all, layers of might know, could know, can't know, should know and shouldn't know. In truth, he couldn't tell who was at the center of all that—Jethri or Arin? Arin being unavailable, and Grig and Paitor too far away to ask, the solving must be up to him.

The solving was his.

After several moments, Jethri bowed. He'd come on this mission, after all, so his throw had been made.

"Yes," he said. "We need to talk, then—I really do have information on how to proceed, as long as we can locate the . . . thieves . . . solidly in Terran space—on one of those places with these Joint Commercial Chancery Courts."

The Scout bowed now, with a hint of a smile.

"I, too, have information to share. We have a destination! There is a message to the pair of us—I'll shunt it to your board shortly—from your mother the trader, who advises us that it would be useful to Clan Ixin and to *Elthoria* if you were able to take advantage of an invitation to a trade meeting. It happens to be at a station around a Terran world already on our list. It is a Combine world, and has much to recommend it to us for our search. I'll arrange for a lift-off after our morning duties!"

* * * ⚜ * * *

My son, said the letter, *within a short while of your departure from* Elthoria *we had the honor of receipt of an invitation for myself and for yourself, as* Elthoria, *as* Elthoria's *representatives or for yourself—that is for you in particular as the certified bearer of a ten-year Combine key—to take part in a regional trade meeting at Tradedesk Trade Platform, near Vincza, a new Terran trade center. The invitation is from the Carresens Coordinating Committee, and is signed by one D. Omron, of CEA. I know of this event—the meeting rotates among several worlds and venues over time and is shown in a number of trade publications; in general it is a meeting open to Terran traders of some repute. I have here as well a similar message requesting the attendance of Trader Jethri ven'Deelin's associate Tan Sim, as well. These invitations are all enclosed within the accompanying files. In good faith, though I doubt the utility, I have forwarded to Tan Sim his own invitation in the hope that he might be able, by replying, to make at least useful contacts for himself and your own independent efforts form this.*

Having Vincza on the list of potential destinations left me by Scout ter'Astin, I ask that you make the best of the invitation if at all possible, and if not, that you certainly acknowledge it and that the contact and honor are not lost to yourself and to Elthoria. *We shall all prosper by such expanded trade, I am sure.*

* * * ⚜ * * *

The lift prep, when it came, was not as happy a time as Jethri had imagined. Not only was he out a good bit of cash—promised to be reimbursed by the Scout!—but the writ and the piece of paper and sealed order wand was paid for and in force here on Balfour. He'd never done anything quite so official in his life, and it had left him a little tight in the gut for making such a fuss. What they'd created, was called a Certified Templatable Action for a Writ of Replevin. With it, they could make a ship stick to port, or even take a whole ship if they had to!

The writ was "propagating across cooperating political and social entities" right now. That meant a correspondent court could use their action here as an example and have proof that the order'd been paid for and seen before a law clerk twice and spoke over by a judge (even if by video from the other side of the world . . .) and that the witness was acceptable to the jurisdiction.

So, after all the wait and fuss, it just meant unless they walked out the door and caught the man with the notebook right here, all they'd paid for with their time and delay was guidelines for someone else to follow if they wanted to.

"In principle, Trader, you've got a four-step pattern to follow, and it ought to be good across all the signatory worlds. The thing is, though, that agreement is for all Terran worlds and for Terran-based ships and pilots. Come three Standards or so we'll have the rules firmly propagated so it should mean any ships and people doing business across the jurisdiction, so it wouldn't matter if someone's Terran or Liaden—we caught that idea from the Liadens, you know!" Dorster said, nodding through the vidscreen toward the Scout standing beside Jethri. "But if you're not sure where you'll pin these thieves down, then I'm not going to promise you more than 'ought to work.'"

They'd arrived back at the ship after a silent walk: who wanted to talk legal stuff in the hallways? More, he needed to do research and history checking on the Combine, and on Arin's business—what exactly had he done as commissioner, anyway?

One more definition, Jethri promised himself, waiting for a new lift time since they'd been held for an incoming emergency.

He'd started off looking for *Arin's Envidaria of the Seventeen Worlds* in *Keravath*'s general information files to no avail, and he decided it was probably just as well, since the files he could easily access, aside piloting information and the like which the Scout was only too willing to share, were files generally available on Liad's public infostreams. The Scout-specific reference lists—other than piloting— were not piped to his board.

Still, the general files might have something, he'd thought, and plowed along. Since the Scout claimed that he was unsure, research showed . . . nothing clear.

Envidaria by itself was available as a series of definitions, showing the word in related sentences . . . and in so many senses that it confused mightily. It appeared in general to refer to "things that work" or to more closely to the statement "this functions properly" or . . . well, it was confusing. He'd also tried the "Seventeen Worlds" and was offered screen after screen of information on a peculiar knot of worlds along the galactic arm that were mostly Terran, and constrained by the physics of dust clouds, particle jets, and gaseous remnants of a string of supernovas. The Jumps into and out of the region were extra long, and for the next few centuries, the easiest Jump locations would be fraught with hot magnetic bubbles, essentially doubling and tripling travel time into and out of the arm.

Seventeen Worlds is not a coincidence, he thought. His father had been a far-seeing man . . .

"Second, if you please, we'll need your attention here for lift in a short while. The mysteries of atmospheric flight are about to unfold for you—find the weather reports and let me know which of them you think we'll need to attend to—our projected orbit is already on the top screen!"

As he stored his searches and kicked in the weather call, something tickled at his backbrain, something his father had said to him, or that someone had said to his father within his hearing. There he was, sitting with the fractin frame in front of him and . . .

The blue light flashed, showing a weather advisory on the self-same weather system that had brought in the incoming emergency landing. He shoved the fractin frame back into memory. For the moment, thunderstorms and wind shear were going to be on his mind.

· · · ✳ · · ·

The trip from Balfour to Vincza was a Jump of a little over nine days. Jethri'd tried for four hours to make it into two short Jumps, but the math wouldn't make it work despite his surety that there were places that two Jumps could actually cut time. The Scout told him it merely proved he'd had access to old charts at some point and asked him to proceed with the rest of his duties.

"What I discover at Balfour is that your name is worth more among Terrans than mine, young Jethri—which is not entirely a surprise. By being both of *Elthoria* and having the heritage of

Gobelyn's Market on your resume, even my connections believe you are already a force to be reckoned with."

Jethri spent nearly a full Terran day in calculation on their way to the Jump point, avoiding a headache but managing to put such tension into his wrists that they popped noisily several times. He finally stood behind his seat, switching hands as he held onto the seat with one and stepped in place in the low G, getting his exercise despite the work needing to be done.

"You're sure that will work, Captain?"

The Scout let a smile escape: "One of the joys of such things is that the majority of miscalculated Jumps will result in nothing more than the ship continuing in the current trajectory—which is to say orbit—for we're within a very complex system and even under way, at some power, we're in orbit around all of these local stars. Although we may look silly to outsiders if we exhibit the full run up and then fail to go more extravagantly elsewhere, I'm not concerned of a failure, nor should you be. It has happened to the best of pilots, I assure you."

"This is what I have, and this is where it says we can make the Jump. The ship is powered, the stat fields are powered, the Struven Units are live, and we have eight more hours, ten minutes, and counting, since I have locked everything in on my board. The main board is not engaged."

The Scout made a hand-sign Jethri was learning to mean *no difficulty*. "I have been shadowing your work, which has been very straightforward. An excellent way to approach this."

"All I'm doing is plugging in values. There's not much to it. I'll probably have us in the outer halo for all I know about . . ."

The Scout laughed out loud. "You are showing true progress. Indeed, all I ask is that we meet the basics on this part of the run. We do have some time constraints on arrival—it appears we'll have less than five days of local transit before we're due in port, after all. This is something we'll work on then, however. I suggest you take a meal and rest; we'll have you at the board for the Jump itself."

Jethri stood, stretched, looking at the numbers and charts and maps and feeling an odd sense of understanding of what he was looking at, and what he'd done.

Something changed there, and he got a sense of dread: lights went from red to blue, from yellow to green, from—

The Scout bowed. "Your board is currently live and working; mine is shadowing. Thank you for your efforts in our behalf, young sir. Please announce yourself as Pilot in Charge and that we're set for Jump. After we Jump I'll set up a proper training schedule for you; we must arrive at Vincza in good order!"

Chapter Fourteen

. . . . ✳ . . . .

Coyander Kenso at Finifter

TAN SIM'S RETURN TO *COYANDER KENSO* waited on another round or two of white wine, or maybe it was the music that kept him, odd as it was, or maybe it was the *Coyander* itself. He had no other profitable place to go now, though he might see if there was an active entertainment section—

And he'd made money easily here, which was a surprise, his spec cargo moving with far more alacrity than he'd supposed possible.

He swirled his glass in meditation, recalling, too, that he ought to report in to the trade hall offices, if only to register his appreciation of the rapid transfers, and drop coin or offer a favor as best fit the office, so that when next he was here he'd be higher on the welcome trader list.

The musicians broke unexpectedly into song, the three of them, the first sound they'd made aside from their instruments since he'd arrived. Two of the instruments were stringed, and one was beaten with an amazing variety of implements. He'd enjoyed the change from his own keyboarding while understanding that he could easily adapt some of this to . . .

The singing was in a local dialect he could barely understand, but it was clear that his attention didn't matter to the group, whose energy was rising—well, the song was about a night well spent.

At least his day had been well spent. He did wish Jethri might have been with him to see the transactions—he would have been quite

165

pleased to see the last of those pod items moved for profit, and much of the pod cleared for incoming paid freight.

The so-called expansion pod remained one third full—that being the captain's speculation cargo, remaining unmoved after three ports. Since dea'Blanco insisted on representing it himself it might easily remain as if in stasis for the entire route, the captain seeking to sell it at bars more often than trade halls.

For himself, he'd made the rounds of three minor exchanges and divested himself of the old goods, asking far too much to begin with— and retaining far too much profit.

An odd thought that, the "too much prifit" but he'd seen it happen before and knew when it was true—either he'd misplayed the market and could have done much better, or the traders he'd dealt with had been in a generous mode, willing to bow to future gains by encouraging the new-on-port trader to return soon. Seeing the *Coyander Kenso* doing more than carrying freight for delivery might have shocked them. Certainly the name of Tan Sim pen'Akla had little enough to do with it, though Tan Sim pen'Akla Clan Rinork—

Ah yes, there might be a truth there. He'd always thought Rinork was a card to be shared carefully, but then Rinork had not always been good to him. Yet when Rinork's famed card was waved forcefully in an off-world trader's face the way Bar Jan was wont to do, why then . . .

Yes, he'd heard it said that Bar Jan traded more on his clan than his goods—said carefully, it was when Bar Jan and his mother were elsewhere, and not when the speaker knew that the last pen'Akla was about. And he'd wondered, too, what the *melant'i* and Balance was between Rinork and *Kenso*'s people to make such a bargain as the one that had captured him on a moribund route with a ship with crew and captain so depressed that it was a marvel it had the energy to come out of Jump.

He'd seen the contracts Rinork's man of business built, and if they had more behind them than any other High Clan's contracts, he'd not seen it—yet the strength Rinork showed, that strength showed more off-world than on, and more in the low places than the high.

Rinork had odd *melant'i* in some ports, as if there were connections Tan Sim was unaware of. He hoped, of course, he could discover these connections if there were some, or else avoid them if they produced unequal results . . .

The musicians, having finished their set, placed instruments down after perfunctory bows, fell together in a hug more properly a grope and rushed their bows and their goodbyes, leaving the barwoman with a bad expression and the few customers with little else to stare at but their hands.

Glass being empty and paid for, and music done for now, he charted a course to *Coyander Kenso* that ran through the trade office and perhaps by the trade bar as well. Sometimes the trade bar was good for company, and he'd likely not be having much of that anytime else in the near future.

• • • ✳ • • •

"Captain, I have copied all three of your test-mail locations with this request, and yet I still wait. This is a matter you've laid directly to my duties, you've informed me multiple times that I must not be behindhand in bringing exceptional trade opportunities to your attention, and that you value my experience. With all honor to your sleep, my *melant'i* as the ship's trader requires this interruption of your schedule!"

Tan Sim repeated the gist of the message once more into the voice-recall box, and when there was not a direct response, he one by one sent the text messages to the remainder of his shipmates, for all that they might never see the captain to speak to him but at lunch once a relumma . . .

And that message was a request that they repeat his need to talk to the captain on short notice . . .

For effect, he resealed the hardcopy of *Elthoria*'s request into the message capsule he'd been handed so hastily—if tardily—at the trade office.

"So, *Coyander Kenso* recalls our existence," had said the older of the women on duty. "Why, in the five trips on record, I doubt we've seen the *Kenso* nearly so up close as you, sir! And imagine to find you so active at nightside!"

"Why, Trade Mistress bel'Verand, I have had every intention of stopping in person to the office: *Coyander Kenso* having an expanding route how could I do anything else? In fact, I come to inquire after the proper expressions of gratitude here on Finifter, there being trade halls preferring immediate and personal attention"—here he'd bowed extravagantly to all present—"and others interested in odds and ends only a trader in search of a commission by a hall might know would be welcome."

His bows grew more profuse as he gave his complete introduction, and eventually, with the telling of tales and thanks for the superb treatment *Coyander* was enjoying, from first Jump recognition to the very moment—not to mention the careful preparations already under way for their departure, he also managed to give away a reasonable amount of his extra profit to buy the ship's *melant'i* back from the brink . . .

He was nearly down to measuring the success of his mission by the backache even he would admit when the assistant trade mistress made a sign to the trade mistress herself and . . .

"Why, there are messages and mail on file for your ship, Trader, and only a few go back more than two trips, if I recall correctly!"

He'd carried an office hamper of junk with him, grunting at the weight of it, for many of the items were local messages printed on actual paper and brought up from the world below to entice ships— and they'd been billed for the storage of it!

He'd watched them drop the paper and file cubes into the hamper with abandon, sighing, and bowing at their efforts. Finally, he'd picked it up—

"And one last, Trader. This one arrived early this shift, and we immediately messaged to your ship that it was here—for yourself!"

She'd dropped the message capsule into the hamper where it swam down into the morass—and so he'd tugged the lot to the so-called lounge, dumping it on the empty table in search of what was surely a message from Jethri, after all this time . . .

From the captain's suite, the sound of the pressure door finding equality—yes, he'd already known the captain overdid his oxygen along with his alcohol when the ship was at port—and the door slid to reveal the bleak-faced man.

"Trader, you have concerned the technical crew with your incessant messages and your . . ." He paused then, the papers, cubes, and out-of-date message capsule scattered across the table and onto his chair coming to his attention.

"We have mail, Captain," he managed. "We have mail going back seven Standards or more, I gather. Some of it is for you, some for the technical crew, and some for the ship. Also, this, for me!" Tan Sim held the capsule up. "Mail which arrived today and of which I was uninformed—"

The captain was unabashed. "The receipt message is in a queue, to be sure. It would have been discovered before we left the docks, Trader."

With no little irony Tan Sim began clearing the captain's seat.

"I'm sure you're right. It was only a matter of time before it was brought to my attention. And it is a good thing that it is found, for messages to traders like myself often have time value. Please, be seated, and we shall discuss this message, Pilot, and the possibility that we might change our route, with a view to an early departure, if it may be done at all."

"You would have me change the route?" The Captain sat heavily, rubbing his chin grimly. "To what end, Trader?"

"*I am invited,*" he said with some emphasis, "and as a consequence so is this ship, to a preview tour and inspection of a multiplanet trade station being built in the Spwao System. And there is a trade show, expanding this time as a show-off. Those who preview it before it is in the final orbit will have first preference for slots, cargo, and routing. *Elthoria* passes on this news, Captain, being unable to attend. But I am no pilot, and only vaguely understand the timing of such things . . ."

The pilot, having left the captain aside momentarily, closed his yes and said "Spwao. They've two planets and some belts as well; not hard in-system travel, just careful. That'd be why the station, so traders don't have to worry about the dust and junk, but can . . ."

His words trailed off, and when he opened his eyes he managed a smile. Then his eyes focused on a piece of mail with an ancient time stamp, and he swept it away with a grimace, coming more awake.

"I'll get the technical crew up here to help with this sorting. You have exact information? The invitation, it is not just for you, Trader?"

"Let me show you, Captain. We shall look at it together to be sure we're on the same wavelength about the potentials."

Chapter Fifteen

· · · ·✳· · · ·

Aboard *Keravath* in Jump to Vincza

JETHRI TOOK IT QUICKLY that a Scout's view of proper training schedule and Norn ven'Deelin's were related—except that the Scout expected much longer attention and prompter and more accurate recall—call it an order of magnitude more intense.

Everything they did was practice of some kind: meals included a description of cooking methods, a discussion of nutritive values and alternatives, warning of missing vitamins and minerals, and expectable allergic reactions from particular frontier populations.

The Scout played music in the background—Jethri was to be able to describe type and mode if not artist and creator of the last three pieces at any time. They spoke Liaden, except when they didn't—the Scout switched languages in midsentence, often demanding Jethri explain Terran in such detail and history that the trainee felt truly ignorant of his own heritage, and stupid to boot. Given options of modes in Liaden he often was challenged as to choice and then asked to describe it in Terran or Trade, whichever was least able to handle the question.

It was a little like being with Grig when he was in a mood—Grig also expected one to know what one knew at all times, and he'd ask strange questions sometimes that didn't make sense until days later. The Scout, it turned out, would drop in questions about space flight in a discussion of tea and spices; he'd ask about textiles during a simulated test of the thrusters . . .

There was quite a bit of that simulated thruster stuff, for once the actual gut-wrenching part of pushing the Jump activate button and watching everything on the screens go miraculously blank at the appropriate moment, much of what he did at the boards was ship training. Where it might vary from another ship the Scout was clear, and when what Jethri was learning was generic, ter'Astin was clear on that too.

By day five of Jump, Jethri was into his twenty-eighth cumulative hour of what the Scout was prone to calling "the station connect quick-drill" with the mode in the comrade side of things—Jethri played with translations and got "easy-style station attachment" from the Trade version and "playing at station-lock" from the Terran.

The *playing* part felt right part of the time: it was fun to see the problems coming up and avoid them, more like a puzzle than work.

They'd gone fairly quickly from easy mode to hard as far as Jethri was concerned—his board was locked to the sim and all the screens on the bridge were synced to the same thing. He had played at what the ship could do at first, finding that *Keravath* was nothing if not responsive—at least in drill—and seeing that as far as he could recall, it had about three times the fine control he'd seen displayed on *Gobelyn's Market*.

Once he was familiar with the basic controls, he'd started out at what the Scout promised him was "one-twelfth speed" and a zero-zero-zero-zero-one status—the ship being one ship length away from the simulated docking tube with no relative motion and all axes in perfect alignment, and latching equipment perfect.

They'd worked with perfection the first two days, then lurched into a bad latch, the while upping the volume and incidence of radio chatter and outside infofeeds; by the start of shift on day five they were pursuing a docking collar with a slow roll and uncertain latch that would require Jethri to hold station while a supposed manual connection was locked from within the airlock.

The work wasn't play this time. The Scout pushed him, the sounds were annoying, the ship gave him prompts about thrust variations in two units, forcing him to find an alternative for his preferred heel-and-toe approach to nodding the final hands' widths to connection.

Trying to balance the close with the two opposite end thrusters made the lock a fulcrum; *Keravath* warned him of potential torsional problems if they locked successfully at the change rates he was applying, creating either a trunnion wave in the hull plate or a gudgeon split in the lock itself.

Hands sweated: he lowered the incoming message rate, assigned priorities, turned some channels off entirely. Then the Scout repeated his name, instead of saying, "Pilot," making him take his eyes off the board and turn his head to look across to the piloting station.

"Jethri, you understand that once we dock we'll be under local relationship and marriage rules. We need not open the hatch; just docking will do it. Some of these rules are in explicit conflict with the Liaden Code. As I'm not privy to Ixin's plans for you, you shall wish to be extremely careful—"

"Hold that," Jethri told him with no uncertainty, turning back to his boards with a shrug. "If it is important you'll tell me later. Are my prime interior forward and aft thrusters to be considered unreliable for the duration? Do they have a self-heal I'm not informed of?"

"The test cycle can't be performed in this kind of proximity to a docking target."

"Lock them out then. I'll go with these others."

"Yes, Pilot. Pilot's choice noted."

The closing visuals showed three target surfaces—

"If this is manual lock we'll need you in place. I assume the program is fully functional and I'll be able to monitor the results here. If that's the case, do it."

"Pilot," said the scout, unsnapping his belts and moving rapidly to the portal to the outer ring, the speaker and function lights bringing news until: "In place, Pilot."

"Contact should be in twenty-five seconds from my mark. I'll tell you to act when we've maintained position for three seconds."

"Yes, Pilot. Three-second rule."

Jethri eyed the main screen until the ship was within ten seconds of contact, then had three screens, each with their own circle and pointer until they disappeared into a blue center—contact!

"Contact. Three count. Lock now!"

"Hold contact! We've obstruction. Moment. Hold contact!"

It felt like forever, but the upcount only said eleven seconds when the lights on the board showed good.

"Confirm lock, please?"

"Yes. Locked. Congratulations."

Jethri smothered the "Yeah, right" he almost said into a loud sniff, quickly pulling the rest of the board into balance for a docked situation, powering down, checking the links to see if outboard power or . . .

"Seriously, Jethri Gobelyn ven'Deelin, congratulations. You have done very well."

Jethri nodded, pointed the Scout to his seat.

"If you are second board here you will now take the con and finish the shutdown for me to check when I come back. I seriously need to leave this seat!"

The Scout laughed.

"Understood, Pilot. Do relax and get a snack, or tea. Tomorrow we will a have a well-earned day of rest!"

· · · ❋ · · ·

Jethri was not exactly blindsided by the news that he was to guide the ship to rendezvous. After all, he'd already been led to the board after a fine breakfast prepared by the Scout once before—breakfast a courtesy to the shift pilot!

That was yesterday and he'd been tucked into the second seat with First Board status half a shift before the Jump ended, waiting, cross-checking, three of the screens filled with information on what to expect on arrival at the Spwao System, Vincza the planetary goal, with Tradedesk in orbit, the true goal.

They went over emergency procedures, then into call-signs and—

"If I'm on deck when we arrive," Jethri asked, "what do I call myself? I'm not a pilot—"

The Scout made several hand-signs, one meaning *stop* and another meaning something like *This again*? before wandering over and standing near Jethri's station and silently staring away into the screens for some moments. Then he rounded fully on Jethri, bending closer.

"What is it, I wonder, that you feel we should call you? What is it that you feel we are doing with these lessons, with this training? Do you feel it a waste?"

Jethri looked into the same screens the Scout had stared at, briefly wondering if he'd met the same lack of answer in those images of space and planets.

Finally, he shook his head Terran-style, and started in.

"No, I don't think it a waste, if the idea is to—acclimate me. As I hear you, you wish to be sure that someone traveling with you is capable of handling the ship in an emergency. So you—"

"*No,*" insisted ter'Astin. "Not me. You. Yourself. What is it you are doing? What is it you are accomplishing? What are you experiencing?"

"I'm learning, is what I'm doing. I'm familiarizing myself with the ship. I'm training, so I'm a trainee. I have no status at this though. I have no idea why I'm training except it is your habit, your whim! I'm a stop-gap or a backup or a—"

The Scout made that shake of the hands which indicated dissatisfaction with a result.

"Look you, young sir. What we have been doing here is training you in what I know and can share the while I have been learning from you. I have been practicing my Terran and my Trade as well as learning of the culture of the loopers. I have been hearing and understanding accents. I have had my Terran histories corrected or adjusted dozens of times. And so far you offer me 'Trainee.' Trader, please, I'm sure you can do much better than that!"

The Scout looked once more into the screens. "It is true," he admitted at last, "that we are working with a lack of formal nomenclature here. We might say, I guess, that we are working you as an apprentice might be worked. Or that you are a pilot-intern. 'Backup pilot' lacks both dignity and accuracy, I fear.

"In effect we are to be making a presentation as a team here, Trader, and we need each the other's countenance."

Jethri saw a light change on the board, noted the manual countdown check, agreed with the status light with a quick touch to the control pad to confirm it, stared ahead into the screens.

He thought back over the training, thought over breakfast. Here he was, doing what he'd imagined himself doing as a child, sitting at the board of a starship in Jump—the same board he'd technically been sitting in when the ship went into Jump.

"Today, sir, today I feel as if I've won something, or that I'm a guest, fed by the house and treated properly as one of the house might be treated, a truly honored guest."

"So, then," the Scout offered with a touch of a smile, "we should have you name yourself 'Honored Pilot'?"

Jethri snarfed at that, letting the laugh go.

"That's a bit much. Still, it is true in a way, it is how I feel, but it could be misconstrued to show me as having a higher level than yourself, which is absurd to any observer. More, *melant'i* may suffer wounds from within and well as without, may it not? I'd rather not push in that way."

The scout's hands made a response Jethri thought of as *more or less even* which led him into more thought.

"Yet to say I am a guest pilot, then that makes no *melant'i* inferences as to my level or my ability, nor does it overstate my importance to the ship or your reliance on me. What traffic control might make of it—we should understand that they'll need to have confidence in my rating!"

The Scout stood and stretched, made one of those all-purpose dancing moves that showed him ready to move, to fight, to think, to act.

"Ah, Ixin's genius shows through. Norn clearly has not lent me a silly son seeking to burnish his name. So, you may have solved this. And the more accurate we make this, the more we believe it and the more impact we may get from it."

The Scout took a formal step back, and bowed.

"Hail to Jethri Gobelyn ven'Deelin, Guest Pilot. You will identify yourself as Pilot in Charge when appropriate, and if asked or pressed you may well say you are on the familiarization stage of a learning survey."

Jethri bowed . . .

"I will wager, Guest Pilot Jethri, that no one will ask very much about your training levels!"

• • • ✳ • • •

In fact, they had not asked after his proficiency levels the day before. The news that Liaden Scout ship *Keravath*—commanded by Scout ter'Astin, with Guest Pilot Jethri Gobelyn ven'Deelin acting as Pilot in Charge—had arrived, was good enough. The news in fact was received with good cheer and with confirmation of nearby ships and plotted routes, updated communication channels, and quite a bit of background chatter on the off-channels about Scout ships showing up here and Gobelyn not being any Liaden name they'd ever heard of. Scattered replies named half a dozen Terran ships flown by or carrying Gobelyns and chatter went on until three more ships arrived in-system and then two more and another as the trade show took shape.

And today, they also never treated Pilot Jethri as anything other than a complete professional, assigning *Keravath* a station berth at the still being built Tradedesk Station according to the invitation number and names they had now in hand.

For his part, Jethri managed calm despite the thudding of his heart and the occasional flash of sweat or flush of cheek; as Pilot in Charge he asked his Second to reduce extraneous comm chatter, and take care of minor housekeeping while the ship measured distance to their goal and checked the orbital changes he requested—and the scout provided backup there, out of his head, while Jethri calculated and double-calculated to be sure.

In the meanwhile he observed the system, surprised enough to mention to ter'Astin: "That's a pretty big station for one planet, isn't it?"

A chuckle drifted over from the Scout—

"Ah yes, for one small planet it is. But their intention is for it to be the *system*'s station, since the planets offer such interesting weather, and indeed it is seen as a regional trade hub. That the system also is well-connected as a direct Jumplink to five others makes it an excellent candidate for such investment! And it is rare for such a station to be built from scratch—this one's modules are still coming together—but what you see has been in progress with a single vision since your father's era as a commissioner, if I am not mistaken. Built in orbit here, tested here, and to be moved to the intermediate orbit over time, starting very soon. The reading is quite interesting, but I'll hold it for when you are not flying PIC!"

Finally, Jethri called through to the station, offering a flight plan to Traffic Control and receiving a noncommittal, "We'll get to you there, Scout, we'll get to you . . ."

"For clarity, Control, I am a guest pilot. Only Captain ter'Astin is a Scout here!"

"We'll make a note of that, Pilot Jethri. We've also got a bunch of incoming not quite as nimble as you, so we'll get back to you. We'll expect you to yell if it looks like someone's pushing you!"

The screens looked clean enough and their basic orbit and path hadn't been argued with, but Jethri mounted a tight scan, continuing to broadcast the basic *Keravath* ID without an assigned flight number.

Finally came a double call—"Here's your new flight ID number there, *Keravath*, repeat it to me and broadcast if you will, and I'll be switching you over to someone with courier chops to be sure we're all working with the same parameters. We don't often get to play like you do, you know! If there's a Scout sitting beside you, I'm guessing you're double-checked. Here's your new contact!"

Off comm Jethri looked to ter'Astin, unsure.

"Is my flight plan flawed, Scout?"

Jethri'd seen enough docking vids to know how clutter-free most large trading zones were, but this one had showed up as a busy and crowded place, with orbiting bundles and ships as well as odd bits and pieces of . . . stuff. He'd tried to think ahead . . .

"This course you suggest, Jethri, is a good way to enter into an extremely active construction zone. *Keravath* is completely at ease with such maneuvers, which would be inappropriate to a larger vessel. Going over your plans—correct me if I am wrong—you have cited and avoided the areas with the largest amount of free-motion equipment. You have decided that by minimizing time spent in these several orbit-trees we will be exposed to fewer correction necessities. You have correctly checked all of our inertial flywheels as well as the jets and have seen that with 'a little hurry' as I heard you speak to yourself, we can avoid as well that incoming crowd of heavy tradeships. I have seen you check against the posted planned routes of local commuting vessels. This is an adequate use of *Keravath*."

Jethri nodded, avoiding the telltale of wiping sweat off of his brows. Then he bowed as properly as he could from his seat, student to mentor, thankful of advice.

Permissions granted, Jethri started in, eyes busy, barely knowing he'd spent two hours while waiting for one last touch of business.

"*Keravath* here, Pilot in Charge Jethri Gobelyn ven'Deelin preparing to enter duty-free Tradedesk docking zone. Vincza Control, my marks have matched yours this last three hours, will you confirm."

"Guest Pilot, we have you moving in good order to Zone Three; can't miss your spot because it'll be the only one open on the arm. We confirm your vector, time marks, and velocity have all matched within acceptable limits; your calibrations continue to echo good. You'll see blue is your guide here in Zone Three, repeat please? And I'll need your choice of Trade or Terran on the final approach."

"Blue is my guide in Zone Three, *Keravath*'s calibrations echo positive. We will be working with Terran units and with Terran language, Liaden as backup but Trade's usable."

A chuckle there—"Can't cuss nearly as good in Trade, Pilot, agreed. We've got you set Terran, Liaden, Trade. Come to relative zero zero zero twenty five center line on your marker and we'll go from there, working centimeters per second on all fronts from there. Get your zero zero zero twenty-five center line."

Jethri shook his head with the irony—he'd spent more than twenty hours learning and fussing to be ready to take the full load of docking and now Vincza Control was nicely talking him in to dock past a row of unmatched ships, all marked with flashing lights and radio beacons, on a quiet channel; the video feed from Control matched nicely with their own docking guides.

"Thirty seconds, *Keravath*. Very clean . . ."

"Port, this is *Wynhael*, will we be docking this day? We have—"

"Wrong channel, *Wynhael*, please cease transmission on this link, we've got docking in progress."

Keravath was in motion, the guides lined up, the target straight ahead, clock tick showing twenty-two seconds—

"This is a docking channel is it not? My information—"

"Off channel *Wynhael!*—"

Jethri gathered in all the information, blues and greens as should be, docking probes centered—he had no time to get words in edgewise!

"Control please acknowledge, *Keravath* docking commit."

"These frequencies are nonstandard—" declared *Wynhael*.

"Commit marked *Keravath*, go!"

There was talk around him but Jethri stuck with it, compared the video images felt the slightest of vibrations, saw zero zero zero zero, heard the *clunk* as the lead link locked, called "Outboards?"

"Outboard stabilizers are good, we'll lock you all the way around. Thank you, Pilot, for putting up with that nonsense!"

Control went on for a few confused words about uppity Liadens, and laughed, and then went silent a moment, flustered.

"Sorry, *Keravath*. I didn't mean to . . ."

"This is Scout ter'Astin," came the voice from the actual Board One, "and you have our agreement on this issue, I assure you!"

From somewhere on the other side of the connection came laughter and what sounded like cheering, then the familiar Control voice.

"*Keravath*—Guest Pilot, when you have a chance please come on by our office on Deck Six at your earliest opportunity. I owe you a thanks for a smooth docking on your side, and thanks to both of you, I won the office pool for the day. Welcome to Vincza!"

Chapter Sixteen

• • • ✳ • • • •

Tradedesk, Dockside and More

"SAMAY PIN'AKER CLAN MIDYS, trade assistant on *Barskalee*," said the ship-dressed young woman before him. She performed a complex and well-nuanced bow of welcome and greeting, with overtones of respect well-earned and a hint of approval and appreciation. There was a smile at the corners of her mouth and eyes and a flawless grace about her.

This artful welcome was more than gracious, considering that she had the drop on him. He's come *this close* to heedlessly, and vigorously, backing into her, as he gestured to Scout ter'Astin to give over his chiding ways. She might as easily—and with perfect justice—given him a setdown.

Gone from Jethri's lips and his mind was the retort he'd been preparing in answer to ter'Astin's most recent gibe, urging him to act as if the day had length and the universe not entirely breathless for his arrival as the beauty of the season. True, he had stopped one more time to use the ship's inner vid system to look over his clothes, attempting to consider both the Terran and the Liaden necessities of being a properly dressed trader on his way to a business meeting of unknown import.

Such was the power of the lady's art, not to mention her lurking smile, that he immediately knew himself appropriately attired for the work in hand, even if all he did was return the lady's bow and flee to *Keravath*'s safe interior. He chose not to flee; a retreat would surely damage his *melant'i*.

The lady had managed to bow to him, and to the Scout, without pausing and without overtly changing mode—yet it was obvious that this member of Clan Midys was in fact more pleased to meet the young trader than the Scout.

She beat him to the now necessary, "Forgive me," part of the exchange as well, her voice quiet and musical, nearly lost in the echoes, hums, and air-moving noise of the passageway.

Jethri managed to pronounce his name and home ship, as did Scout ter'Astin, but they needed to repeat them a moment later, because the woman continued her "Forgive me" rather breathlessly. In the repeat, Jethri remembered to report that he was Guest Pilot on *Keravath*, but wasn't sure she gathered that, her flow of eloquence being rather lengthier than expected.

"Do forgive me. I did stop rather suddenly when I heard your lock operating, and I should have given you far more room, but I am unused to the protocols and dimensions on this station and I did not intend to interrupt either your passage or your conversation."

Jethri beat back the urge to redden, recalling that he had not, in fact, answered ter'Astin's last gibe, nor had ter'Astin been speaking loudly for all that the lock's own sounds had a certain depth to them.

"*Galandaria* need not ask forgiveness for a greeting properly given on a strange port," ter'Astin assured her prettily. He received a nice bow of acknowledgment in return.

Jethri tucked that phrase away, it sounding to be one very useful in the long run for someone whose very living depended on meeting others. Especially, he noted the mode, in which "strange port" carried, not only unfamiliarity, but the implication of alienness; of on-dock behavior even wild or unruly—which of course this place had small resemblance to, outside *Wynhael*'s minor pettishness.

"Indeed, Scout," Samay pin'Aker said. "I had not considered the matter in those terms, for surely those with *melant'i* must be considered equals when they stand among those without."

Her brief concentration on the scout gave Jethri the opportunity for a longer look.

Though her shirt with the *Barskalee* ship logo and her three-digit crew number would have her simply ship-born, as would her haircut—ship-short, but long enough to see that her hair was brown, and had a tendency to curl—she had what he'd come to think of as the High House nose. This was short and long at once, the face being long and the projection of the nose short—less pronounced than on the mythical average Terran face. In all, hers was a pleasant face, particularly when she favored him with a smile. Her phrasing and accent—obviously, he had study ahead of him in the House books, for Tan Sim would have by now known who her close kin and her cousins were, and the amount of her quarter-share.

"We should explore that idea, of the distribution of *melant'i*," the Scout said thoughtfully, "as time permits. I fear that the Code's strictures may not fully address the necessities of wider commerce."

He bowed then, briskly, reminding them all of press of business, and in short order they parted, invitations to visit as time permitted having been dutifully exchanged as well.

Jethri wondered if the station gravity ran light, as easy as his steps were as they marched off to the control room—

"I believe, young sir, that you ought sometimes to review recent portvids as much as you stare for dust on your boots as you prepare to exit the ship."

The Scout was smiling, his hands making a motion Jethri lacked the reading of.

"Yes, do look quizzical, my charge. That artfully accidental meeting took Samay pin'Aker a triple tour of the passageway if not more to arrange. It was all our luck that she didn't have to chase after us to ask directions!"

It was a Terran shrug he offered first, followed by a Liaden bow requesting elucidation. "I'm in orbit without referents," Jethri admitted.

"I mean that the trade assistant walked the passage before our lock at least three times in each direction, slowing as she came closer and speeding away once she was distant."

"But why should she? If she's a trader why should she not merely address the ship—but she's not a trader!"

"Exactly. Her duty may well not be in the trade hall but on the ship itself. It is my thought that she was sent—or she sent herself—to catch sight of you and make your acquaintance."

They reached the end of the passage, and turned left. A small group of Terrans was clustered mid-hall, and Jethri held his reply in reserve, even as he slowed his pace.

"Midcentral Crystal Logistics, that's who!" a woman's voice said excitedly. "I saw the ship! Saw it last time, at the dock here, waiting for the Uncle. Sure, it had a different name, and a different company but that's easy. And you know who's listed as PIC? Senior Pilot Dulsey Omron! Can't be anyone else but him!"

There were five of them, three apparently pilots and the other two perhaps locals, and one with her back turned said, "Give me time to count the times Dulsey is a name first or last on a galactic census!"

"You say it—but the ship's the deal. Have you seen it? Halfway between a courier and a family trader, got a couple pod points and a couple blisters just big enough to hint they're able to defend themselves. I'll see if I can find some images out of our files . . . That ship, *with* Dulsey, and it can't . . ."

The three pilots looked up; Jethri sighed silently, blaming himself for a boot-scuffle on the deck plate when they switched grav sections for interrupting his eavesdropping.

Their arrival at the group merited several nods, two bows, and—

"Damme if you ain't the pretty proof of a Gobelyn on port, boy! Been years. Bet you don't remember me! But I seen you on the same deck with your Da, more than once."

Jethri was inclined to agree with her on that not remembering: dyed black-and-pink streaked hair, fluorescent green short boots, legs barer than bare as they were captured in distracting yellow shorts that showed a touch of skin above as it led to a formfitting shirt worn under an overtight pilot's jacket. She had his attention as she turned, and then he heard her say "Damme" in his head again, and smelled the brew on her—and memory stirred.

The hair, that was a change, but the voice and even the pose reminded him of someone standing too close to him on *Gobelyn's Market*'s kitchen deck, leaning over him, that was it, so she could stroke Dyk's shoulder.

He extended a hand, and gave her a cordial shake, remembering to "smile Terran" broadly.

"You're Blinda Bushey, as close as I know. Don't 'member your ship, sorry. Must've been the kitchen . . . 'cause I wasn't much on the trade deck those days. Dyk gave you his wine limejel recipe for your pasta log with cheese. I got the extra three maize buttons because . . ."

"You better not remember that particular 'because' out loud!" She sounded jolly enough, but she looked serious, and her face showed a touch of color, while her hand was tucked into the protective arm of a pilot not much older than he was. She was half-turned now to block the pilot's view of Jethri, or to make her urgent lean toward him less obvious.

"Yes'm," he mumbled, recalling that the *because* was her and Dyk leaving him in charge of the galley while they did some private back-room work when Iza was off on port. Dyk hadn't often run off for fun, but if it came to him he seemed to like it well enough.

"So there," she said, waving her unencumbered arm at her fellows, "I told you I heard a familiar name there coming in. You flying a Scout ship, Jethri? Wow, like your dad you are, just do exactly what you want to, and show up at the big shindigs like any plus-side pilot will!"

Jethri had schooled himself on the *melant'i* of the situation he was entering, even as he'd dressed. It was almost guaranteed that as he went among Terran traders, someone would bring up his status on the rosters, and his father. He had vowed to answer these questions, impertinent as they doubtless would be, as if they were the merest commonplaces—which they were rapidly becoming.

He therefore managed a credible light bow of acknowledgment and a hand wave presenting ter'Astin: "The good Scout, Captain ter'Astin, allows me as guest pilot this trip. I am learning much!"

Blinda laughed, gave the Scout a well-practiced lookover and a half bow that started as a nod.

"I didn't mean to interrupt your walk, Scout, but I've known Jethri since he first learned to wear shoes, and some of his old shipmates and—"

"I'd have it no other way." The Scout gave back a rather exact copy of Blinda's salute, and one to each of the other's in the party, and a hinting hand motion to Jethri. "One always must affirm networks!"

"We have been asked personally to the control room," Jethri explained, "but if we're on station, we'll find each other again . . ."

"We will, we will. Bet you'll get a call for all the party suites, anyway, once the show's really under way, and we'll get all caught up. And you, you'll have to tell me what lucky ladies've been . . ."

The pilot in possession of her hand gently tugged Blinda out of the way, and the bemused pair from *Keravath* moved on.

The Scout spoke, gently. "I am lacking a book of Terran clans, my friend. I therefore beg that you will enlighten me, when we are back on ship, about your sudden new tension."

Jerthri shrugged and picked up his pace. Blinda wasn't a relative any closer than ninth or tenth cousins lawfully removed, of that he was sure, and he could play that tune.

"Not really a clan matter, but ship-friend stuff. Some ladies," he managed, "some ladies treat a guy they knew before they became adult . . . just like they're still just kids!"

He made the explanation in Terran, and it was a real complaint.

Ter'Astin chuckled. "There's a *melant'i* order of such things, my friend—age having consequence, after all. Though I admit that some who overexert charm may tend to overexert connection and consequence far beyond fact!"

• • • ⸭ • • •

The control room was not on the level marked for it: Jethri's push of the button opened a pressure door leading to an elevator. Once in the car they were queried by remote and could feel the device start moving only after they answered. There were numbers and letters showing on the read gauge—but what was floor A7B and why did the car pass floor 33C and Z16 to get there?

The scout laughed softly as Jethri felt the car go through a gravity field, so truly he had little idea of which end was up, or where, exactly, they were.

"Excellent security," the scout said when they had passed through one more change of gravity and decelerated to a stop.

The door opened, not into the control room itself but to an antechamber occupied by a smiling guard sitting behind a commanding console.

"Welcome to Tradedesk Control," she said. "Please, your names?"

They gave them; she repeated them to open space, and nodded toward a side panel which opened by splitting half to the floor and half toward the ceiling.

Inside was a corridor with a waiting guide who ushered them past two of the largest control rooms Jethri had ever seen, both dark and unused, and into one just as large which was lit, active, and filled with the sounds of low-key voices.

"Pilots! So good to see you!"

While the room had dozens of occupied workstations on one level,

their guide directed them up four steps to a dais overlooking the rest
of the room, a see-through shield between its single occupant and the
rest of the action.

"I'm Director ViChels Carresens; please join me."

They did, exchanging hand grips Terran-fashion, and then sitting
in the quiet around his console, behind what was probably more than
just a sound screen. The area was rather homey for a control room—
clearly this was the director's office as well as workstation. Several
screens showed images of children and oddities, and bins held papers
and notes galore.

"I witnessed your approach, Pilots, and commend you. Pilot
ven'Deelin, a very precise understanding of the situation with our
commit. Our assistant flight ops has won a bet by suggesting that a
first-time-in Scout ship would link within sixty seconds of the best
link time yet—and you did."

He turned a screen toward them, pointed at the graph.

"Here's the average time for all links so far, here's the average time
for first-time links, and here's yours. Only two first-time links have
been achieved in better time. Congratulations!"

Jethri felt himself reddening, suppressed the urge to say, "But I'm
not a pilot." He glanced at ter'Astin, who looked back at him with
bland interest.

"Thank you, sir," he said to the director.

"Don't thank me—I intend to mention this at every occasion.
Please understand the other speedy links were performed with no
other ships attached to the arm, and by pilots trained in our
simulators."

Jethri pressed his mouth straight. Out of the corner of his eye, he
saw ter'Astin give him a gentle, seated bow.

The director went on, "It would be interesting to see what you do
while we're in transfer—*Nubella Run* is set to dock in just a few days."

Jethri looked to the Scout and the director laughed.

"Yes, I forget, not everyone is as wrapped in my schedule as we
are in this office. My family—the Carresens—donated *Nubella Run* to
the effort—she will be docked and bound to the station, and will be the
motive force for our move. A brave task for any ship!"

The smile faded, and he looked suddenly more businesslike.

"But I bring you here for another topic—and that is this writ."

The saying of the word "writ" was punctuated by a slap of hardcopy pulled from a bin.

"The link-news squeezed into your log-in included several bits of legal stuff—including this writ. And I'm concerned about it, actually, in terms of effect on trade. I haven't the full access without you invoking it—all I know is that you *can* invoke it.—and as a signatory to . . . an agreement . . . well, it wouldn't look good if we start arresting people for you."

The Scout beat Jethri to the holding out of a hand by a moment, and he took the flimsies silently when given, flipping through, and handing them over to Jethri.

Jethri read *Plea for on-demand invocation of Writ of Replevin* and he blanched.

"I hadn't understood entirely the means by which this was to be disseminated," the Scout admitted, "and perhaps neither did my companion."

"Didn't," Jethri whispered it. "And I didn't think of it. They've built it into the autonews feed?"

Carresens nodded. "Right in with confirmations of arrival and all that. It started printing out before you were on the docks."

Jethri went back over the page . . .

"If you've come here on some kind of a hunt, I hope you'll understand that we need confidentiality and quiet. It wouldn't be neighborly to start cuffing folks, if you know what I mean."

"That's not why we're here," Jethri said, "At least not *here* here. We're here because I got the invite, and this . . ."

"What the guest pilot is saying," the Scout took over, "is that we have a destination farther on at which this . . . writ . . . may be required. We ask that you, too, keep it in confidence. Here, we are on a trade mission for my associate and we have no expectation that anyone connected with this writ's necessity will cross our path."

The director looked down at the papers and pushed them back into Jethri's hands.

"You hold these. Properly they are yours, in any case. If it becomes necessary to invoke them, you will talk to me first. Is that clear? I will see to follow-up, if required. Do not, I ask, make a fuss."

Out of the midst of the console came a buzzing noise, and Carresens said: "Go Blue."

"Trainee Molunkus on the module mover's got an anomaly in the power unit again. Only happens to him. If I send . . ."

"Hold, Blue!"

The director turned to them with a shrug. "So that's it. You're here for trade and networks and that's fine and we're glad to have you. I'll smile at you when I see you, righto? And I wish you luck down the road catching up with whoever's a problem. In fact, if you catch them, let us know—we're really just getting started in the trade center business and we need to know how these things work. Just not right now.

"Oh, and check in at the guard desk on your way out of Control. There'll be some tickets and such for you there. Thanks for coming by!"

The Scout stood a second behind Jethri, both knowing a dismissal when it was delivered.

Chapter Seventeen

· · · ·✳· · · ·

Tradedesk

AFTER THE DAY OF TOURS AND LECTURES—the first official day of the event—Jethri returned to *Keravath* to shower and change clothes for the evening reception in the Hall of Festivals. Ter'Astin came in while he was primping—the Scout's word, *not* Jethri's—and did some primping of his own. It seemed a little unfair, Jethri thought, that a pilot's jacket was considered to be the equivalent of formal trade wear, though the Scout did take the trouble to upgrade his standard dark sweater to a creamy shirt with a collar banded in green, and to set an earring to dangle seductively from one ear.

Toilettes complete, they left the ship together in amity, Jethri giving a brief overview of a day filled with discussions of trade volume and preleased warehousing, as well as tours of transfer docks and demonstrations of the internal pod-breaking room.

For his part of the conversation, the Scout offered the information that *Wynhael* had managed a docking in the end, being relegated to a zero-G low pressure sub-corridor where the next module of the not-quite-finished auxiliary hotel would eventually be attached.

"No more than they bargained for," Jethri said.

"Indeed, it did seem that they would be rid of the coin, no matter the market."

Between them as they traveled toward the Hall of Festivals, they managed to bow, nod, or shake hands with over a dozen fellow attendees. Eventually, Jethri had learned only that morning, Tradedesk

191

would encompass a number of smaller halls, as well as the great hall, but for this night only the large hall was public, the others being reserved for official needs and food preparation or else still skeletal.

Jethri was aimed foremost at dinner, and while the scout promised to eventually come to the repast, using the ticket given him by Control, the errands that had occupied his day had spilled over into station evening hours.

"A few people I must yet speak with, here or rumored to be here," he murmured. "When I am done, I will find you, doubtless surrounded by admirers, and the trade assistant on your arm."

"Doubtless," Jethri said, dryly and so they parted at the hall's end, the Scout going right toward the pilot's lounge, and Jethri, left, joining a goodly crowd of people on route for the great hall.

Jethri's tickets—two, one for him and one for "Guest of Trader ven'Deelin," which had immediately gone to ter'Astin— had come to him in a fine paper envelope marked with his name, and bearing a shiny red embossed message: "The Carresens Welcome You." A note had been tucked in with the tickets: *Trade dress is recommended for our quiet after-dinner reception and the Sternako Memorial Trade-off, in Gallery 770.*

Jethri's last few steps toward the hall were given over to comprehending the size of the place he was to eat in. The passageway had split into an atrium with levels towering above him; he'd seen starships small enough to cruise through the doorway he was entering!

There was an awning over the massive door, which puzzled him until he understood that it was part of an emergency sealing system. He'd nearly forgotten that he wasn't on planet, so vast was this place.

Dinner was a badged walk-in party two hundred paces long with serving tables and booths on both sides and grab-plates everywhere, occupying only one side of the hall. His ID and ticket netted him yet another ID at the door, where smartly dressed door dragons of both sexes smiled and asked permission before attaching the name bars.

"Honored Trader, the adhesive evaporates entirely in twenty-four hours; if you need it removed before then, please stop by and we'll use the sonic to clear it.

"Also," the server said, diffidently, "with your badge you may sit anywhere you like: you'll see the overhead color-coding if you prefer to sit with your own!"

Jethri's badge said JETHRI G. VEN'DEELIN in Trade lettering, and beneath that, a fairly accurate rendering of the same, in Liaden script. Three faintly glowing color bars depended from it, which was something not everybody had— for example the young man dealing with him had a badge saying FOLLY SMELKIN, that supported a single deep purple bar, the same color he saw flashing on the others handling door duty.

Jethri's bar colors were green, bright blue, and a red reminding him very much of Gaenor's *drai'vaina*. Looking around he saw a good sprinkling of people with the green bar—green bars must be the color for traders, he decided, recognizing fellow lecture attendees from the day's work. There were a few folks with the bright blue and there was one he recognized—the pilot he'd seen with Blinda! He had that bar and no other. So either blue was for loopers or for pilots, which made him shake his head. Not likely for loopers, so must be pilots. Well, who was he to deny the organizers one more pilot for their shindig?

The red bar . . . that wasn't so obvious as to meaning, and rather than holding up progress at the door he moved on, prepared to ask in case he couldn't figure it out.

The noise was louder than Jethri'd expected, but part of that was the music permeating the future trade hall. Careful spot speakers aimed hymns, dance music, classics, tonal stuff—each booth offering their own choice of volume, with the music fading away and replaced by a new tune or rhythm as he entered the next zone. It felt fine—and then it didn't.

A touch of dread worked itself on him, and he felt as if he were here under false pretenses—Master Trader Norn ven'Deelin should be here, not he, he who was not a pilot, and not really able to support the "Honored Trader" he'd been given at the door. Too, a glance around showed him a room filling with individuals dressed not quite at the height of fashion, ordinary folks wearing what might be the best of their day clothes instead of being dressed *and* polished and ready to trade, as he was.

Jethri jerked where he stood, as if run into, stiffened so hard he could hear the snap of his shoulder. He backed away from the table carefully, aware that he'd need to start again, but needing focus. The sound, the people all around, the motion. He caught a ragged breath, offered a half bow to someone he'd come too close to, took another half breath. He glanced down, trying to focus on something, and saw his boots with their multiple inlays of colored leather forming patterns that a careful observer might note as variations on Ixin's own moon-and-rabbit. He glanced down at his hands. Yes, he was overdressed, with his trade ring on one hand and the challenge of the firegem wonder on the other. Why did he think he, lowly beginning trader Jethri, could pull off wearing such a monstrosity in public?

The firegem said nothing, flashing the myriad of overhead lights back to him in a way the trade ring never could. Someone in a kilt wandered by, humming loud enough that Jethri could hear him, a reminder that he was not alone—

He swept a quick look around, taking a quieting breath, and another. If anyone had noticed him standing as still as an extra support pillar, they weren't staring at him now. *Air is good, Jethri*, he told himself. *Breathe!*

Standing in the very center of the aisle he let the echo from the half-dozen booths wash over him, the aural competition momentarily eclipsing the other assault on his senses: the smells.

Yes, that was it, the dislocating touch of panic had come not only from the scale of the place, but from the sensory overload. The hall vibrated with voices, music, and just plain noise, and the air was redolent with the powerful, enchanting, and puzzling scents of too much food!

He was, he knew, extra-sensitive to smells. His years on nonstop stinks duty made him all too conscious of the difficulty of overcoming even pleasant odors in a closed environment, and here was the kind of thing he might have expected at an extravagant outdoor affair on Irikwae. So much food and so much of it cooking, now, was . . . unexpected.

Eyes momentarily closed, he sniffed as he might have on *Gobelyn's Market*. Yes, his nose was well trained, and he got his breathing back into rhythm as he opened his eyes, concentrating, knowing he couldn't decode the whole place at once, which he'd figured was the problem with his world-side panics. To concentrate he might as well start with his trained olfactory, so he sniffed again.

The aroma of bread and baked goods was all around him, and the scent of fruits and flowers. Under it all and magnifying it, were the oil and greases. Vincza prided itself on the vegetable oils it produced, and in this place they were being used extravagantly. He wondered how the filters and stinks crews would be able to clear the place . . ..

Professional interest kicked in—which stinks *would* be hardest to deal with? Did they need special filters? What about cleanup?

He'd come to eat and to mingle and to consider how *Elthoria*—and truth told, how *Gobelyn*'s *Market*—might best make use of Tradedesk when it went full open the next couple of Standards. A little concentration now—starting with the food choices once again—would be a good beginning. Then he'd find someplace to sit. He really needn't be concerned that he was an imposter. He carried with him the ID he had from Dorster, he wore the badge he'd been given, he . . . why yes, patting the appropriate pocket for reassurance, he even had a printed copy of the file Norn ven'Deelin had sent, with his invitation information from the Casehardens Coordinating Committee. It had been signed by someone, who he guessed he should be on the lookout for. The name tickled at his brain without result. He could check if need be, but . . .

"It's *quite* too much to eat, isn't it, young man? I'm having a difficult time choosing where to start! Do you know all of the dishes or could you use pointers? I know the layout by heart!"

• • • ⚜ • • •

Grandma Doricky Gellman DeNobli *did* know the layout by heart—she'd designed the original, as she was more than glad to tell him, forty-two local years before. In the interval she'd helped with the "food suite" at the Carresens trade fair fourteen times . . . that was each of the previous times it had been held.

"Consultant," she said with a snark, "that's what they made me this time, on account of they're making the big push to bring Tradedesk online and I"—she pinched her eyes shut for a second—"managed to get myself crushed by an icefall at a cheese plant just after the last one."

"Crushed?" While she was tiny, and had moved slowly among the dishes, Jethri had ascribed her pace to her age, for surely she was the oldest functional human he'd ever met. Her eyes were as strong as her voice, but her hair was so gray it was bordering on transparent, and her skin was fine-wrinkled. She was as small as the smallest adult Liaden he'd ever met.

"Oh, I know, and don't you think I'm exaggerating. Crushed.

Took me a long while to get all these parts working, and I'm only good for a twenty-hour day if I have a nap or two any more, when used-to-was I'd work forty straight if I needed to. Thing is, I used to be a lot bigger.

"That dish," she said, pointing with wrinkled fingers, "is for purists. Can't suggest it to anyone not raised on-world. You need triple fermented vinegar to make it proper, and even then you need to be right comfortable with your crawling yeast, 'cause if it isn't able to crawl some while you swallow it then it's off and can make you sick for a two-day. There's some that're just plain allergic, anyhow."

"DeNobli," he'd managed as he walked by the dish—and in fact it did seem to be . . . wriggly.

He averted his eyes, and continued, ". . . are you cousins to . . ."

"Seven," she said, "right now seven lines of loopers and then us on planetside that don't make lines the same way, but we're a bunch. So if you know a DeNobli, likely is a cousin or was . . ."

"*Balrog* . . ."

"Yah, all of 'em. Cousins they'd be, but I think I only met Brabham—he married in, you know!—the rest of 'em are strange to me."

She paused, delicately placing two small dark-brown balls on a plate before wheeling on him.

"You're big enough for five or six of these. Gobelyn, eh? What was that, *Gobelyn's Market?*"

He waited for the inevitable . . .

"Is that smart-mouth Iza still about?"

Not what he'd expected.

He nodded, managed, "Yes, she is. Still captain there. What are these—it looks like candy and I don't much . . ."

"Captain? Hah, well, that'd be why a smart one like you is wearing *Elthoria's* flag, I have to say. I got stuck in a transfer room with her when she was just getting her rating and I'm glad I never met her again."

He waited, still expecting Arin's name to come running into the equation . . .

"Bloosharie," she said then, "that's what they are. I used to think it must be a waste, but it sure isn't—got darkcho around a filling made mostly of bloosharie."

She looked up at him, popped one of the two from the plate into her mouth. She sighed in what looked to be pure pleasure, then looked up at him.

"I'm not kin, but here, eat this . . ."

She reached up, the candy in her hand, and he allowed her to put it in his mouth . . .

It was startling, with a shell of thin darkcho giving way to a soft filling that was indeed . . .

"Bloosharie!"

She laughed, nodded. "Been brought up right, I see."

She took another for herself.

"Really fine with a good cheese. Suggest it, cheese and these and you're good for a day. Cheese about did me in—but one of the reasons I'm still around after the crushing, you know—we have ourselves some really potent cavern cheese.

"There," she said, "you're still growing; take a bowl of that soup there with the red-striped shrooms. Another planet trick. Daysoup."

Jethri did as instructed, and eventually arrived under the red banner with names of a dozen new foods and more plates and bowls than he thought he could empty in a three-day.

"If it looks interesting, try it. Need more of something go back and get it. That'll give you more reason to come back next time. And I hope I didn't mess up any orbits back there about Iza—I mean she's not a favorite of yours, I hope. I'm old enough to share my opinions but sometimes I forget folks have got to live together. So—not a favorite?"

He sighed, very gently, found a Liaden blandness suddenly in his face, and bowed.

"I enjoy being a trader on *Elthoria*," he admitted, "an opportunity arising from the natural aging and growth of the crew. The captain, of course, was alert to the necessities of the ship, ma'am."

She snorted as she sat down, motioning him to sit across from her.

"That's clear as a thundercloud. Looks like you've come away fine, though, and so we'll talk about other stuff, and eat. After that, if nobody joins us, I'll walk you to the Gallery where I can talk to some of my used-to-was friends while you get to the good stuff."

Jethri was settling; he had spork to mouth when his meal-mate spoke again, sharply enough to make him jump in his seat.

"One more thing!"

"Ma'am?"

"You can call me Doricky or Ricky, or you can call me Grandma. Don't need the rest of my names here—everyone will know who you mean. Now eat!"

He bowed to wisdom, and ate.

Chapter Eighteen

* * * ✳ * * * *

Tradedesk, Gallery 770

GALLERY 770 WAS A LOW-CEILINGED, comfortable cave, offering the intimate feel of a guild club, with carpeting on the floor, low-key lighting, paneling that might have been real wood, and off to one side, even a stone mantle framing a wood-fed fireplace.

Fire was something he'd had to get used to on Irikwae since he'd stayed in a house with lots of windows and working fireplaces in many of the bedrooms.

The idea that you'd *want* a fire for anything beside combusting rocket fuels had rocked him when he first faced it. It had taken a cat's calm assurance that tame fire was a good idea for him to begin to come to terms with.

He approached the fireplace immediately he saw it, to assure himself that it was in fact *not* burning real wood and producing extravagant heat. It was, he was pleased to find, artifice. Still, it gave off quiet sounds and, with the rugs, and the groupings of leather-looking chairs about it, did impart a sense of calm and comfort.

Doricky had escorted him to the door, down a casually marked hallway at the end of the main hall, where she'd left him in favor of three very mature women dressed nearly identically in ship livery.

"Just through there, Jethri. I'll introduce you around later, but go in and make yourself at home. Act like you live here—you have my permission! Now get!"

He'd taken her "permission" to heart, to the point of not seeking to determine who might be in charge of seating, nor even of immediately taking a seat.

He wandered the room a bit. There was art casually available—statues and sculpture, paintings, ceramics—and several discreet 3D touramas of plays he didn't recognize. He might watch a play, then, if the reception got slow, though maybe the plays were just to entertain until the reception really got under way. He'd seen a small stage on the other side of the fireplace, so there might be music later; and he'd glimpsed what he thought might be a bar.

He moved in the direction of his glimpse, finding not one bar, but two. The first was staffed by a pair of attentive servers about his own age, done up in fancy vests and three-cornered hats, each with purple flags on their badges.

The second bar was only an open table; there seemed to be no one in charge of the various open bottles, jars and dishes of what might be candy or something stronger, and lots of little trays of edemups.

Informed as to the precise location of refreshments, Jethri moved on, working the room as he'd seen Norn do. He had nothing like her easy skill in starting conversations with little-to-unknown colleagues, but she assured him that it would come with practice.

So—practice.

Here, he felt his dress was unexceptional, maybe even a little too conservative. In this group, the essence of trade and its sometimes attendant showmanship were seen: rings, jewelry, quality textiles. Almost everyone had something distinctive about their dress, even if it were only subtle refinement or outrageous extravagance. His boots were fine, but not outlandish, his rings merely what the trader had chosen to wear.

He kept up his slow stroll as the room filled, exchanging nods, bows, and greetings with traders he'd seen in the tours and seminars. He smiled, shook hands when required, repeating names—his and theirs as appropriate—

"Be here at the launch, will you? Only two Standards once the move starts! I for one want to be here for the start of the final orbit!"

Jethri started to answer this pronouncement, only to find the trader from which it had issued turn somewhat unsteadily to another, asking the same question with the same inflection. It dawned on Jethri then that the trader was likely drunk—which seemed a bad plan so early in an evening.

Yet there was something to the idea of a drink—Norn ven'Deelin's teaching there had been exquisite: always carry your own drink, and if possible, make it something unlikely to be easily refreshed by an overeager host or a sly competitor.

Thus, to the staffed bar he went, canny enough to avoid the bloosharie that came to mind after his earlier sweet, and canny enough to request good Liaden wine, like those from Tarnia's own vines . . .

He requested three of the premier wines, each in turn, and was greatly disappointed that they had none, though Ranny Suki—the female of the serving pair—made careful note of the label names and promised to see if there were any onworld which might be brought for the next day. In particular he had wished for a glass of the exquisite Felinada . . .

Lacking Tarnia's wines, and seeking still something that was neither an unknown beer or an unknown local vintage, he asked, "Would you have anything Altanian?"

She bit her lip in thought, shook her head.

"I don't know all the wines by source, Trader. A brand or style?"

"Yes, of course. Misravon, it might be labeled, or possibly the finer, which is Misravot."

Her eyes widened, and the smile returned.

"Indeed, sir, we do! A moment though, since it is kept properly stored out of light. Please stay."

He did stay, leaning lightly on the counter top, listening to the room. The banter was friendly but charged with challenge, and there was a decided feel of anticipation, as the questions "Have you seen . . . ? Did you meet . . . ? Who is new . . . ? What's the news?" were asked and answered in variations.

Once he had his wine in hand, he would, he knew, need to tour the room some more. He did hope that someone would talk with him, rather than simply offering or acknowledging his greeting. An exchange of names was very well, but *deals* were done in conversation.

Bartender Suki must be having trouble finding the Misravon, he thought. But he waited for her still, not only because he had said he would, but because while he waited he had leisure to assess the group here. He was among the youngest—perhaps he *was* the youngest—a handicap, because that meant he was an unknown. He wondered exactly how the attendees were chosen; he had assumed he would be among traders of his own grade, else the invitation committee would surely have asked Master Trader ven'Deelin to represent *Elthoria* here. . .

He scanned the growing crowd in earnest, specifically looking for people he knew, who might in turn introduce him to people they knew. . .

There was Doricky, surrounded by a group of elder traders. He didn't see Blinda, but then he didn't *want* to see Blinda . . .

Rinork's Infreya chel'Gaiban stood in a corner near the door, talking cordially with Chally Delacorte—he'd been one of the main speakers on the topic of scheduling and turnaround early in the day. Standing beside her was a Liaden-seeming woman he didn't know, her dress very modest, her badge bearing a pilot's blue bar, and a slightly askew red bar. Though she was merely listening to the conversation, there was something . . . arresting in her stance. Jethri resisted the temptation to study her at length, and deliberately continued his sweep of the room—no staring like a long-lost looper in this company!

The pilot's presence at Rinork's side, though, brought to mind one person he hadn't seen yet in this more exclusive setting. Where was Bar Jan? And wasn't it. . .interesting that his mother was here, appropriately badged, the proper position of heir at her side filled by someone who did *not* wear, as far as Jethri could judge, the Rinork face?

Thinking back . . . hadn't he seen Bar Jan earlier, in the Hall of Festivals? Jethri squinted his eyes thoughtfully . . .

Yes! He remembered. Grandma Ricky had asked him to achieve a small third round of bloosharie candies for her. And on his way across the now-crowded space, he'd seen Samay pin'Aker, though her face had been turned slightly away from him. Then he had seen Bar Jan chel'Gaibin stalking toward the door, his badge conspicuously lacking the red bar.

Samay's badge, Jethri remembered, had been colored red and green, which meant he should find her among the company gathering in Gallery 770. That cheered him—and gave him a goal. He straightened, gazing round the room in good earnest.

A nearby rattle interrupted his search, and there was Ranny Suki, guiding a small cart filled with bottles and objects . . .

Her face lit up at seeing him, as if he were a long-time friend instead of a passing trader, and she parked the cart, efficiently pulling free several bottles to show them off.

"Here, sir, the Misravon. I have several dozens of bottles in stock, I find, and here too, is the Misravot. We have one case of a dozen, at proper temperature . . ."

"One dozen shall do," he said with a slight smile, and she laughed.

"Well, yes, unless you set the fashion, in which case the Misravon will go to anyone asking for Altanian and I'll reserve the Misravot for you or your party, since you have requested it!"

He bowed, but she was stacking bottles into the cooler, seeming to have one too many for easy disposition.

"Odd numbers, I guess—oh, shipped through a Korval distributor says the label, so they'd be counted by Liaden figures. I'll have them all ready, for when you wish to share them with your party. Shall I pour one now, so that you may be sure of it?"

He bowed.

"Indeed, please do," he said, wishing he *had* a party. Well, perhaps the Scout would show up, or Samay. . .

He received his glass from Ranny Suki, her anxious eyes recalling him to his obligations. Solemnly, he raised the glass and sniffed, finding the bouquet appropriately hinting of spice. A little wine on the tongue then; finding it smooth in the mouth, and the flavor—as he recalled it—tart, with an overnote of sweet-blooming flowers packing behind it a complex secondary set of notes and flavors.

He smiled at her. "Excellent."

She beamed. "Thank you, Trader ven'Deelin. I'll pass the word that you requested the beverage and pronounced it of the first quality."

He almost told her what his opinion of the wine was worth, having tasted Misravot precisely three times before. Then, he recalled Norn ven'Deelin, and merely smiled, with a small inclination of the head, as if they understood each other very well.

"The trader has given the room the benefit of his experience and his opinion," Norn had said, after they had witnessed one such do precisely that. "This is not lightly given, nor offered to the unworthy.

If there are others more experienced present, let them bring their opinions forward, also. This is how we learn."

Of course, he being what seemed to the most junior trader in the room, there could be plenty to offer a more experienced opinion, but until then, his stood.

Still half-smiling, he carried his drink into the crowd that was rapidly becoming a crush.

His was a twisty course, following the least crowded portions of the floor. The gleam of a Master Trader's ring caught his eye more than once; he had stopped counting 'prentice and working trader rings for nearly all present wore one of those.

Eventually, his casual wandering brought him again to the fireplace, and the comfortable groupings there. One large, leather-looking chair almost directly catty-cornered from the door, was facing it. The person in the chair would be able to see everyone who came in, and be seen. It reminded him of images he'd seen of cruise liners where the captains apparently were seated in such chairs in order to impress the passengers. While it looked comfortable, and the view of the door interesting, it seemed, Jethri thought, a little *too* impressive for a young trader who knew his own *melant'i* to choose for himself.

He chose instead another leather-look seat, central of a small group of five, as far to the big chair's right as he could get. There was passage space behind the grouping, and to the sides, and the view of the room was very nearly the same view as might be had from the big chair, without being . . . obvious.

He settled comfortably, the glass in his hand attracting his attention. While bloosharie tended toward the reddish-purple side of things to his eyes, Misravot—at least *this* glass of the same, in lighting adjusted to local seeing and star colors—was pure, unadulterated blue. There were gemstones of the first water that boasted a blue so pure, and he'd been told that there were planets with skies that looked pure blue from the ground, though he often saw leanings to green and purple.

He twirled the glass, watching the surface where the reflections of the subtle ceiling lighting picked up the shifting colors. He recalled the room where he and Gaenor had played, and wondered if there was a secret aural mood trick going on in this room as well. He strained his ears, but if there was something to hear under the sound of voices, his ears weren't sharp enough to catch it. He did notice, however, a slow wave in the lighting, a change he hadn't noticed until he came to rest, nearly hypnotic if one paid . . .

"And so much for the party of the century—I say, *so much* for it that a prized guest stares at his drink all alone while the festivities go on around him!" There followed a sharp snap, as if someone had deliberately broken a glass pipette.

Startled, Jethri brought his attention to the room, where Doricky stood close to the large chair, leaning somewhat uncertainly on a walking stick.

He rose instantly to bow, careful of his drink. Master tel'Ondor would have been proud of his smooth combination of *honor to an elder, respect to the position, thanks for the quiet correction of a social infelicity* and *welcome to an event equal* that he managed.

"Would you like the chair, ma'am?" he offered with a Terran's wave at the seat he'd been in . . .

"Happens I would like a chair, as it seems that no one's quite sure what to do with me now that I'm not in charge of anything more than saying hello to others no longer in charge—well, and to those too new to know."

She nodded toward the chair in the corner.

"I will regard that chair as reserved, and I applaud your choice, which you should sit back down in as soon as you adjust this one to your left so I enjoy the same view that you have. *And* don't sit down until you fetch me the very twin of your drink. We will begin to set this place to talking, you and I!"

• • • ✳ • • •

The effect wasn't as immediate as Doricky had intimated it might be; Jethri had a short wait retrieving a glass for the lady, and took a little longer to return, due to increased traffic in the room. He did again see Samay, which he thought was good, and Infreya, which was perhaps not so good. That Samay and another person of Liaden bearing were speaking with Infreya was not to be wondered at, given Rinork's status.

"There you are, Trader!" Doricky greeted him upon his return. She took her glass and leaned back in her chair with a sigh and a grin. "This is becoming a crush, as we all knew it would. How do you regard it? And yes, let us at least sip your choice . . ."

They nodded a common trader's toast to success.

"*Ah,*" was Doricky's reaction, though Jethri wasn't sure if it was for the wine or for the busy group of six entering the room in high conversation, all personages he recognized as having given presentations or led tours. The group headed to the bar en masse, speaking all in Terran, some of it so heavy with accents that even Jethri was hard put to follow it.

"That's timing for you," Doricky said comfortably, adding, "An excellent choice in wines—someone's been showing you the good stuff!"

Taking another sip, she nodded again appreciatively, then made a hand motion—

"Not being in charge this time around, I haven't paid as much attention as I should to things. Didn't notice who sent you the invite."

Jethri felt a twinge of panic—but this wasn't a security test, it looked like.

"I was away from the ship, but it went to *Elthoria,* Grandma. The note tells me a name from the committee . . ."

She laughed briefly.

"I suppose the note does," she admitted. "But ships generally don't get notes or invites, traders do. Guess that's how we got those Rinork folks—they've got some exclusive runs and that kind of puts a bind on people. But you're right new to the halls, aren't you?"

"That's so, ma'am. But wait"—he fiddled in the middle pocket, pulled out the hardcopy—"here it is . . ."

He handed her the folded sheet as the volume of noise in the room picked up. Laughter was all over, and if there was soothing sound underneath, there'd be no way of knowing it now.

She paused, waiting for the light to change enough for a good view, and said a long drawn out, "Ohhh . . . oh."

Looking him hard in the face, she raised the hand with the note in it and waved it in his direction with quiet emphasis.

"You don't have to tell anyone else who invited you, right, Jethri? Just say you got your invite from the committee. Spare you a lot of interfering questions—and sometimes the committee don't sign these things, anyway."

That touch of disquiet came again.

"Is there a problem, ma'am?"

She shook her head, emphatically this time.

"No problem, none. See, the committee agrees on most of the folks who've come before—so that we keep things friendly. First-timers are usually run by everybody, but not always, and anyone who's bought in before can just run an invite in if they really want to."

She handed the note back.

"You know 'em, do you?" She blinked, and suddenly laughed, putting her wine in danger. "What am I asking? 'Course you know 'em! Now I see why you looked so familiar to me—and that Iza! Right, right. Your father was the Gobelyn who wasn't—he married onto the ship. People wondered at the time, but—well. No use reheating yesterday's 'mite."

Jethri looked from her to the signature on the letter—Dulsey Omron. He was perfectly certain that he'd never dealt with anyone— individual or trade group—going by the name Dulsey Omron.

He raised his eyes to Ricky's face, and said, quietly, "You have the advantage of me, ma'am."

She frowned, eyes narrowing, then nodded.

"I see that I do that, too. Second time I run foul of Gobelyn family politics tonight! Sorry, Jethri; guess getting crushed wasn't good for my thinking apparatus, either."

"As far as I can tell, you're thinking rings around me," Jethri said. "Please, ma'am, I'd like to know why I'm supposed to know this"—he fluttered the letter in frustration—"person."

She had a leisurely sip of wine, studying him over the rim. He met her eyes straightly.

"Well," she said, at last, "Dulsey Omron's the pilot who companions Uncle—I reckon he's got as good a name as any of the rest of us somewhere about, but that's what everybody calls him, just Uncle. None of us have kin-claim on him; just, he's been around forever— and her, too—always busy, always open to helping; scheming and hatching, like traders do.

"We wouldn't be hosting this party, like we've done all these times now, without the Uncle helping out. He's got hands in other projects, too; some go bust; some do right nice for the investors. His company's Midcentral Crystal Logistics—and what all this has to do with you is that he's Arin Gobelyn's for-real brother, and Arin was the spit of him. Which means now I can say I've met two somebodies who Uncle was blood-kin to."

Jethri took a careful sip of his wine. So, he'd gotten the invitation not because he was a notable young trader, but because his father's brother was doing him . . . a favor? *There* was a blow to his ego, but what did it mean for his *melant'i*, he wondered—and let the wonder go, because Doricky was still talking.

"Shoulda realized it, first thing. You're the spit of Arin, and Arin was the spit of Uncle."

That, Jethri thought, was something he could have happily lived a long lifetime without hearing. Unbidden, and much too clear, rose the memory of Grig the last time he'd seen him, on Irikwae, with his sister, Raisy.

Who had been the spit of him—or him of her, since Raisy had admitted to eldest.

He took another sip of wine and, seated as he was, bowed in Doricky's direction.

"Thank you, Grandma. It's always good to have news of kin."

"Isn't it?" she answered, and abruptly came to her feet, with only minimal help from her stick. Her smile was directed over his head, and she bent as much as the stick would allow, producing an entirely credible bow of welcome to a favored acquaintance.

Jethri slipped his letter away into an inner pocket.

"Trader pin'Aker," said Doricky, "good greeting! I'm so pleased to see you here. It's been many years since I've been able to enjoy your company. I wonder, have you yet met *Elthoria*'s newest trader?"

Chapter Nineteen

· · · ·※· · · ·

Tradedesk, Gallery 770

BARSKALEE'S MASTER TRADER Rantel pin'Aker Clan Midys, sat poised and polite beside Doricky, the small talk between the elders having quickly devolved into brief comments and questions from him and extended descriptions, histories, opinions, and genealogies from her. Samay, introduced briefly as his niece, sat beside Jethri with somewhat more equality in their discussion.

Since neither had previously traveled to Tradedesk, and neither had experienced a Sternako Memorial Trade-off, they fell from these similarities easily into conversation, bouncing between the Trade tongue and Liaden, with Samay showing traditional High House skill in one and a reasonable proficiency with the other. From time to time she ventured into Terran; her accent suggesting that she could use a tutor if she meant to continue.

As juniors, they'd been dispatched to the bar to retrieve drinks for their party. Jethri noticed that Samay was shorter than Gaenor, tending toward the slender. A chance remark of how long she'd be traveling on this trip revealed two things to Jethri at once: first, that she was, possibly, as much as a Standard his elder; and two, that Gaenor had never quite told him how old *she* might be. He'd never thought to look it up.

Their return with refreshment had brought a pause in the conversation between the elders, while the wine was duly tasted.

Master Trader pin'Aker was seen to smile very slightly—a Terran might have missed it entirely. He raised his eyes to Jethri.

"Your choice, Trader?" he murmured.

"Yes, sir," Jethri replied, and manfully did not add, *If you wish, I will gladly bring a more pleasing beverage.*

"Most enjoyable," the Master Trader continued, and this time raised the glass to Jethri. "Come, let us all bestow proper attention." He drank again, inclined his head, and turned once more to Doricky.

"This . . . *trade-off*, Host Doricky—will you do me the honor of explaining the history? I find myself underinformed."

"It's a history not many have, sir, but those of us who do, treasure it."

Doricky sipped her wine, and straightened somewhat in her chair, her glance drawing Samay and Jethri into the circle of those about to be shown a treasure.

"Emdy Sternako, of tradeship *Energia* had a reputation," she began, "of being willing to go anywhere to trade anything. He studied trade reports, news feeds, history, advertising—always, he had books and reading to hand; always, he was studying. His studying, his easy ways, and—even his friends admit it!—his silver tongue gained him the reputation not only as a trader of skill and merit, but as a man who could sell anything to anyone."

Doricky paused for another sip of wine, before leaning toward Samay, and beckoning her closer. Samay bent in, as did Jethri; even Master Trader pin'Aker leaned a little toward the storyteller.

"It was said," Doricky continued at the necessary volume to be heard over the noise of the room, her posture giving the impression that she whispered into their ears. "It was said, Master Trader, that Emdy Sternako once sold sawdust to a lumberyard—and at a handsome profit!" She leaned back, with a small smile.

"He was clever, and talented, too. More, he taught; he put together co-op deals that would benefit traders who were maybe not so clever, or a little less talented. He went out of his way to introduce other traders to profitable connections; he made himself available for consultation." She paused as if in silent reflection upon the virtues of Trader Sternako.

"A trader of rare *melant'i*," Master Trader pin'Aker murmured. "These are the qualities the Liaden guild looks for in candidates for Master."

"Oh, he was Master class, all right. If he'd been Liaden, he'd've had himself a purple ring, no question. Thing was, you might've thought he was Trollian—or even Liaden—except for one thing . . . ."

She waited. Samay being too patient to see the cue, Doricky finally gave in, waggling prompting fingers in Jethri's direction.

"And why wouldn't this Emdy Sternako be confused with a Liaden, Grandma?" Jethri asked with a little emphasis.

She smiled knowingly, her palms forward directly beneath her chin, allowing the stretched thumbs to frame the bottom of her face.

"Sternako came from an old family, and said he got into trading because he was poor as a child. He said he financed himself on his first trip by not buying razors or depilatories. Since his first trip was a success, he decided it was because he didn't take off his beard, and he didn't want to jinx his luck. So, he never took that beard off, and I swear, it went out to his shoulders!"

Samay took a deep breath, perhaps shocked at the idea. Clearly, going on a trade mission was widening her horizons.

"Ah," said the more experienced pin'Aker solemnly, "so he looked a bush with a face in it, which never you will find among Liadens!"

Doricky shook her head in agreement. "Bush is correct. First time I saw him it was so dark a brown it was almost black. Next time it was so gray it was just about white, shoulder to shoulder.

"Well, Emdy, he was one of the traders who early supported the building of this station, and the notion that all traders, no matter their language or their homeworld, ought to come together and do business as equals. For the first six of our trade shows, he made it a point to come to a party at the show—let's call it *this* party!—and offer to outtrade anybody . . . and he did, most every time."

She sighed then, long and hard.

"Then, we sent an invitation, but he didn't come. *Energia* was listed as late. Over a Standard they listed her as late, then they listed her as missing—not only here, but at all of his regular ports. He never exactly made firm commitments, you see—but we always expected him to show up. That empty chair there—that's his chair. Only two or three folks I know would dare sit in it!"

She nodded to Master Trader pin'Aker. "There's your history, right there."

"I am grateful," he said. "I concur, the history of such a man is a treasure, reminding Masters of our obligations, and providing a standard to which all may aspire."

"That's right," Doricky said. "Something to aspire to, is Emdy Sternako. And there's the bell! The trade-off's about to start."

· · · ✳ · · ·

The laughter had died down from the start of the challenge, which apparently was a joke of long standing between two friends, each offering to trade fair-value items they'd brought in ancient transport sacks.

"I have here," the first offered, sipping loudly from a very large mug of ale and displaying the object at the same time, "a used mechanical grease gun, as favored on Ynsolt'i. You may inquire after the age of the grease in it if you like or have an expert on hand verify that it is still usable. I paid a great sum for it, and I challenge you to make it worth my while to trade with you!"

He showed the grease gun to all and sundry, offered side challenges, quaffed his beer.

"You hardly have better than this, I believe," the second trader said haughtily, "so you'll wish to offer me cash plus if you want me to take your . . ." Here she looked to the ceiling and the far walls with exaggerated expression while she puffed on her lectrostim pipe, and held a seal-pak high. "*This* is a genuine top-of-the-line antique cake-art multispatula! Hard to find in many systems, since some folks don't appreciate proper cake. Do know, rascal, that this is a new and never-used item, still hygienically sealed."

"You've taken up cake-baking, have you, Trader?" The first trader, Donpa Auely, looked startled, and took a large sip from his mug while eying his opponent suspiciously.

"Much more likely," she offered with a sniff, "than you'd take up the care and greasing of anything but a beer keg!"

The banter worked, drawing a crowd to the stage. The audience now joined in as the traders sparred prices, throw-ins, add-ons, delivery fees, and celebrated the taxless free-trade status of Gallery 770. Side bids and side bets rained down upon the pair as they showed off their silly goods until, practically nose to nose, they traded a mix of friendly insults.

"Antique, but brand new, never used!"

The telling points, according to many whistles from the audience.

"Used and we know it works!"

There were not nearly as many supporters for this view, but they were very loud with their cheers. Oddly, Master Trader pin'Aker seemed to take the used-and-proven view, while Jethri'd been willing to make noise in support of the spatula. He'd seen such tools properly employed by Dyk and tried them himself, and knew a little, at least, of its worth.

He shifted in his seat, and very nearly brushed cheeks with Samay, who had leaned in his direction, perhaps for a better view of the action . . .

Jethri staved off the startle in favor of enjoying the view, a light bow and slight smile presenting themselves as the proper form for the moment; his blush a momentary and comfortable warmth.

Her smile was as wry as his, and they shared a near silent chuckle, each retreating from their lean. Jethri sighed and felt warmth in his cheek again, but Samay's smile became a passing grin as they both turned again to the trading, which was by now getting very energetic, if not decisive.

From the direction of the bar came a distinct and musical female voice, speaking Trade.

"This calls for an arbitrator!"

Doricky laughed out loud. "Yes, excellent . . . I say do it!"

The sentiment moved in a wave then, Doricky's approval having been a fulcrum; names were thrown out as possibilities.

"Arbitration needs someone neutral!" suggested another voice. "Who here can be neutral—those two scoundrels have bested us all at one time or another!"

"A first timer!" called someone from near the bar, and Jethri felt a thrill. Was Grig here?

"Here is someone unknown!" called Donpa Auely, using his chin to point at the first row . . .

At, Jethri saw, Samay.

Suddenly, the *whole room* was looking at Samay.

Her cheek darkened, and it seemed that her command of language failed, for only a moment. Then she took a breath, much like one would take a centering breath before beginning a *menfri'at* pattern, and rose. She bowed acceptance of a necessity, and spoke in Trade. "What needs done? I am unfamiliar with these protocols!"

Into the cheers of Samay's bows came another sound—Doricky's voice, getting louder and louder, saying the same words over and over.

"Hold launch, hold launch, hold launch!"

She repeated that phrase a dozen times by Jethri's count, standing and waving the walking stick over her head until the two traders stopped motioning for Samay to come up on the stage.

"Problem, Grandma?" asked the trader of the multiuse spatula.

"Could be. You two—you been busting through space for almost a hundred Standards, between you—and this person here is on her first trip to space, and never signed off on her own trade in her life."

The crowd hushed and Doricky took that as a sign to keep talking.

"You want neutral? Two of you up there to cook up trouble and tell jokes, and you can't even close the deal? You ought to have *two* arbitrators maybe—one for each!"

With this Doricky brought her stick down, leaned on it, and whispered at Jethri, her voice full of either meaning or menace, "Stand up like you want to and let me talk!"

Perforce, he stood, and there were cheers, apparently just because something had happened and they'd had enough to drink to make that good.

Doricky turned back to the pair on stage. "Have either of you traded with this man?"

They signaled *no*, and she went on.

"This man has a trade ring, *and* he's got a ten-year key—show 'em, Jethri!"

Glancing at Samay, he managed a quick, slight bow of joint endeavor. He then raised the hand adorned by his trade ring over his head, and pulled the ten-year key up on its chain and waved it energetically.

More cheers. Samay looked up at him expectantly and he dared to offer her a small smile.

"So he ain't a Master Trader, but he's lived ships his whole life I bet, and he's done something only a couple people in this room have ever done—been a trader on a ship out of Liad!"

There was a smattering of applause, but Doricky wasn't finished yet.

"Then, he bested that by being the first *Terran* trading off of a

Liaden ship! Folks, this trader here is the walking ideal of the whole Tradedesk project!"

That grabbed people's attention well enough, and really started them buzzing.

"So, let's have these fine folks identify themselves. After they do it'll be this: Cheers, and they'll do the deal. No cheers, well then, we'll let these guys talk your ears off through another brew or two!"

She turned, and waved at Samay.

"Sing out, and make an intro! And remember, this is fun!"

Jethri saw the confusion cross Samay's face and he leaned in close, whispering, "'Sing out' is theater talk, show-off talk for speak up or speak out."

She bowed to him, and to the crowd she bowed an embellished, deliberately exotic bow of welcome and introduction, twined 'round an amplified version of her first bow, accepting necessity and challenge. When she spoke, it was with authority and with her head held high. Yes, Jethri thought, High House indeed!

"Samay pin'Aker Clan Midys, A'thodelm pin'Aker. I am an assistant trade accountant on *Barskalee*. After I finish my training, in two Standards, I will become head of my line, of pin'Aker, and fourth to the head of my clan, Clan Midys. Thank you for this honor."

Some talk and respectful cheering—good. Jethri gathered himself, following her excellent example with a bow, and then trying as best he could to emulate her unconcerned assurance.

"Jethri Gobelyn ven'Deelin Clan Ixin." He didn't have a position in *his* clan's line of succession, except least likely to succeed, but he continued with what had impressed Blinda—and probably Samay, too, for that matter—"I learned to trade on *Gobelyn's Market*, I'm guest pilot on *Keravath*, and second trader on *Elthoria*." For emphasis he raised his trade ring again, then bowed.

"Thank you for this honor."

. . . ✳ . . .

"Donpa Auely," the trader touched his left hand thrice to forehead in the direction of Samay and then at Jethri, trader and pilot. While his badge told the same story, it couldn't tell the tale of his smile up close, nor that it was obvious that his apparent steady drinking had left no impression at all on his full beer mug. "I really appreciate you taking this dare, the both of you!"

"Jadith Sabemis, Trader-at-Large, sir and ma'am," bowed the other—with her stim-stick giving off the very lightest scent of an herb that wasn't *vya*. "Thanks. Just so you know, since you're new and might not have the plan, anything we make out of this goes right into the Distressed Travelers Fund—mostly used for spacers and pilots who get stranded without resource. We both donate what we get!"

Samay bowed, first to the contestants, then to Jethri. "A contest worthy of a *melant'i* play, is it not? The one who wins loses the most!"

Her Trade was clear, her amusement plain.

"You good with that, Trader?" Estimable Trader Donpa Auely held his brew high in hands as steady as his eyes. "We'll take your consultations in the spirit that we're all giving something to pay forward since we can't pay it backward."

Jethri's nod came quickly, and lurched into an awkward bow of joint endeavor as startling noise erupted beside him.

"Someone bring their drinks up here!" Sabemis shouted out over the crowd. "In fact, bring me a drink, too! D'you think we're all gonna work dry?"

There were cheers, and after the drinks arrived, more.

· · · ✦ · · ·

They'd managed to cheer the bidding and the crowd on to a total of two thousand Terran bits by dint of letting the groups form confederations, each promising aid to one side or the other, while the "arbiters" enthusiastically backed up the claims for the unlikely virtues assigned this particular used grease gun or that special unused spatula, surely the very last of its class as yet unused, think of the history!

When the joke was wrung dry, and the bidding come to an end, Samay leaned to Jethri, her face bright.

"So much enjoyment! And for you?"

He assured her that he had also enjoyed the show, and was about to ask her if she'd care to have a private drink with him, away from her uncle and Grandma Doricky, but—

"Samay! C'mon help an old woman collect money from these rascals!"

"Duty," she whispered, and left Jethri's side for Doricky's, who was standing in front of the stage, facing the audience, her stick held high.

"All right, folks, we're gonna do our final formal trade for tonight, now. Trader Sternako used to have this spot in the program, but he's not been with us for a while, so we take turns, in his memory. Since we already got Trader ven'Deelin up on his feet, we'll see if he can get us back to real-time trading. So, Trader, you got the whole floor in front of you. What do you have to trade?"

With that, she left, on course for the counting table, donors trailing her. Some of the remaining crowd moved away to the bar, but a disturbing number, in Jethri's opinion, were willing to watch this next act, in which the new trader made a perfect fool of himself.

What was Doricky thinking? He hadn't brought anything to trade. Who would bring—to dinner and a reception—who would bring *trade items*?

"Traders trade, young Jethri," Norn ven'Deelin murmured in his memory. "Is that surprising?"

He took a breath. No; it wasn't surprising. He was a trader; *of course* he would trade.

But, *what* would he trade?

News? But they'd been trading news all day among themselves, informally—or had the more experienced been keeping count, even there?

Cold panic in the pit of his stomach. He took a sip of Misravot to warm it.

His uncle Paitor'd told a story more than once about how, given someone with money and a need, a trader had sold his own socks to make the deal.

And he'd better do *something*, now, or he'd lose the tempo.

A breath, to center himself—and a broad look out over the audience, both hands raised in surprise, one palm out, the other wrapped around his wine glass.

The crowd laughed, understanding his consternation. Surely, he might have been better prepared?

He had their attention, and he needed to keep it. He also needed to think, so he talked.

Instinctively, he bowed. "Thank you for this honor!" he said, with a little too much sincerity—which got another rumble of laughter— the while his mind raced.

"I must admit, Traders, that I have left my pods on *Elthoria* in order to hurry here to be among you!"

Grins and nods from those gathered, as some more, drinks refreshed, came back to see what the kid was doing.

"I have no bulk deals as you might imagine, and I'm too fond of my socks to offer them up!"

Laughter and nods there—more laughter than he'd expected—so apparently Paitor'd not been the first to tell that tale. He saw Samay look toward him as she passed a handful of trade coins over to Doricky, felt the blush rising, as half the crowd must have seen him look in that direction as well.

It struck him then that he'd hit the right note, and he went on, in a slightly softer tone.

"In fact, I'm fond of everything I have with me this evening . . ."

That brought guffaws and titters—and Samay smiled.

He shook his head, raised the free hand—and called out: "As traders you all know that we're fond of the things we trade. We believe in them. Like tubes of grease or special spatulas, they are all important and useful. After all, someone somewhere always needs something!"

He got agreement, and the crowd was still willing to listen.

"And so, with this opportunity come unexpectedly upon me, I am happy to recall that I have a special item with me this evening, and a knowledgeable audience, an audience willing to understand that I offer real value."

He moved his free hand, not quite randomly, so that the stone in his ring glittered and flashed in the stage lights. Taking a quick sip of Misravot, he carefully brought the glass in front of his hand, and slipped the ring free.

"I have here," he said, "a rare item of fine make and properties. I will entertain bids, but if I find the prevailing bid not high enough, I reserve the right to match it. If no one is interested, I will understand, and even find it fortunate—for this item will show best on the hand of one with a true affinity for uniquity!"

He'd carefully enclosed the gem within his fist, showing only the high-shine band peeking out from between his fingers, and recalling the seller's words. That was another trick he'd picked up from Paitor: *If the words are good enough to sell something to you, those could be the right words to sell it to someone else!*

"Come down close if you wish to trade, and look you on an ancient ring, made of multibanded flash-formed Triluxian!"

It was true that not every trader is interested in every trade, that some preferred soft finery and some preferred multi-Standard lots of supplies of staples, or even things that were profitably unchallenging like bulk ore. Still, Triluxian . . . had adherents.

Some moved nearer to the stage, and Samay had come back to her seat, so she was close enough to smile to him rather than to the room.

"Triluxian, with an old inscription I've not definitively interpreted!"

It was true, as far it went—he'd not researched the ring after he'd bought it—the plan, insofar as he had formed one, was to eventually show it to Grig . . . but . . .

"Who will bid?" he called, raising his hand over his head.

There was a movement from the front. He glanced down—and into a face he had never hoped to see again. His father stood before him, in clothing so plain it might have been ship togs, just loose pants and a light sweater, with a stylized crystal on the right breast.

He opened his mouth, but he had no breath to speak. He met his father's eyes—no, *not* his father's eyes, for there was no welcome, no joy at their reunion, only . . . curiosity. The man—the stranger—shook his head slightly, and Jethri closed his mouth.

He looked away with an effort: merely a trader measuring the audience. His glance again swept over the man who was not his father, this time taking in his companion.

The woman was dark, spare, with a touch of exotic mixed genes about her face that could have been Liaden and Trollian and looper all rolled into one. There was perhaps something familiar about the set of her chin, the angle of her jaw.

"Dulsey Omron," he remembered Doricky telling him, "the pilot who companions Uncle . . . Arin Gobelyn's for-real brother, and Arin was the spit of him."

He smiled over the audience—and with a flourish opened his hand to reveal the whole ring.

The firegem caught in the light, multiplied it and sent it blaring back. Brilliant scattered dots and rainbow flashes like sudden meteors dashed around the room. The ring, band and gem spread delight and consternation as it glittered and gathered attention.

Some laughed, some gasped, some stared.

"Who will make me an offer on this item? Shall we have an

auction?" Jethri challenged the room, keeping his own gaze on the ring as more moved toward the front.

Some with a drink or two in them yelled out, "Firegem? I'll give a half-bit, if you polish it up and swear it'll catch me a virgin!"

Against the laughter and chatter rising from that noise, Jethri held steady, seeing in the back of the room Scout ter'Astin, and beside him the woman who had been standing heir-side to Rinork earlier.

Down front, Jethri went on with the business of trade.

"I have one bid, well below reserve. Who will give me a proper bid? I will prefer bids in hundreds of bits, or in cantra!"

That declaration drew gasps and complaints, sending a few away and drawing a few more in.

From closer to the front, Donpa Auely astutely asked, "What's it inscribed?"

Jethri looked, the lighting not being best for seeing it whole, but he remembered the shabby trader sitting across the table from him, and the tiny, ornate legend . . .

"Cobol 426 . . ."

"One hundred bits," Auely said, leaning forward, his hands resting on the back of Doricky's chair.

The man with the crystal on his chest made the sign for inspection, and Jethri moved toward him, but then slowed as the man spoke low to his companion.

Jethri tried to display the inscription, but the hand motion was clear—the man wanted to see the firegem!

Jethri showed it close, spilling brilliant refractions over Master Trader pin'Aker's face; Samay's and Doricky's as well.

"Two hundred bits," said Uncle.

There was a large soft noise as if the whole room had sighed at once.

"Yep," said Auely, and, "three hundred."

"Four hundred bits," countered Uncle.

Auely laughed lightly, looked to Sabemis, who leaned on his shoulder, whispering and nodding.

"Twelfth cantra," he said with a note of triumph.

"One-quarter cantra." The bid was given mildly, even carelessly.

"One-half cantra!" That was Sabemis, glaring . . . and she looked about, making hand signs asking for spot loans from friends . . .

The room stared at these bidders, back and forth.

The man in the plain apparel sighed, and bowed toward Jethri—obviously a capitulation . . .

"One cantra, plus four hundred bits. Also, I will buy your breakfast and an hour Standard of your time for a consult. I can pay you now."

Jethri looked up, where Sabemis and Auely were shaking heads and shrugging while the shocked silence became a buzz.

"Out here, Trader," he admitted, nodding to the opposition and then to Jethri.

"Offers?" Jethri asked politely.

No sound but clinks from the bar.

Doricky surprised him by slowly rising, using her cane to support her at first and then pointing to the empty chair, Sternako's chair.

"Sit there, Trader ven'Deelin. Sit there, I say, and let the man pay you. Someone bring us all a glass!"

Then there was applause. Uncle and Dulsey nodded at him distantly, eyes still on the ring.

Chapter Twenty

· · · · ·❄· · · · ·

Tradedesk, Gallery 770

THE WINE ARRIVED—Misravot, of course. Jethri wondered if the bar had run out of their supply yet, then decided that wasn't his problem. He accepted his glass from Samay, with an inclination of the head and a smile.

"You were magnificent, Jethri," she murmured.

That gave him a warm glow, which increased somewhat when Trader Auely raised his glass and announced, "Profit to the trader; pleasure to the buyer!"

"Profit and pleasure," those gathered by the chair murmured together, and all drank.

Jethri scarcely wet his lips, and smiled all around before putting his glass aside and nodding to Uncle.

"It remains to exchange profit and pleasure," he said. "If we may be excused, Gentles?"

That hint peeled off the casual observers, which left Uncle and Dulsey Omron—the victors—Traders Sabemis and Auely—the losers—Doricky, Samay, and a slim trader standing just at the edge of his eye . . .

"Trader ven'Deelin." Uncle gave his glass to his companion and came up to the chair. He extended his hand, opening the fingers to display the cantra piece, and the four hundred-bit coins.

Jethri inclined his head.

"Fair price," he acknowledged. "Please, Grandma Ricky; accept this gentleman's coin for the Distressed Travelers Fund."

"Right you are, Trader, thank you for the gift of your skill."

Uncle turned and offered the coins with a flourish; she accepted them solemnly.

"Enjoy your purchase, sir; it was fairly won."

Uncle turned back to Jethri, who rose and offered the ring on his palm. The firegem flared and flickered, outshining the artificial flame in the fireplace.

"Sir. I will tell you that I am sorry, a little. The ring pleased me. My hope is that it will please you, as well."

Uncle smiled, which altered his face, making him seem a little more like his own man, and considerably less like Arin.

"Trader, I cannot adequately express my pleasure in owning this ring. Never fear; I will honor it appropriately, and I will also honor you, who put me in the way of it."

With that, Uncle raised the ring and slid it immediately onto his own finger. The gem seemed to flash even brighter, for an instant, as if it knew the hand, and was pleased to adorn it.

There came a collective sigh from those around, who, one by one, bowed to the trader and the buyer, and moved away, quietly, to other pursuits.

When they were alone, Uncle reached into another pocket, and produced a quarter-cantra, which he again offered on his palm.

Jethri folded his hands together. "We are in Balance, sir; each fairly compensated for this night's efforts."

"You mistake me, sir. This"—he raised his hand slightly, to show the offered coin—"is your consulting fee, for one Standard hour of your time, tomorrow morning, at breakfast."

"Surely it is customary to pay such a fee after the consultation?"

"Surely it is not," Dulsey Omron said, entering the conversation with a laugh. "Take my advice, Trader ven'Deelin, and always collect for a consult ahead. Then you are certain of being paid, even if the client dislikes your advice!"

He bowed to her. "That's good advice, Pilot; thank you."

"You're welcome, Trader. We leave you now to enjoy the rest of your evening. We breakfast tomorrow at ninth hour, at the Framinham Cafe!"

· · · ✳ · · ·

Jethri watched his . . . clients? . . . relatives? walk away toward the bar. He should, he thought, be exhausted after the various exigencies of the evening, but instead he felt. . . energized. Even overenergized. Maybe there would be dancing, after all . . .

He took a breath, half-turned—

And there was the figure from the corner of his eye, considering him with an expression of perplexity, amazement, and . . . was it pique?

"It is an honor to observe the level of your art, sweet Jeth Ree, but tell me what I must do to persuade you to answer your mail!"

"Tan Sim!"

Jethri went two quick steps forward, arms outstretched for a hug.

Grinning, Tan Sim grabbed his forearms, a public touch permitted between close associates, Jethri recalled.

He hastily altered course, and gripped Tan Sim's arms, and the two of them stood gripping and holding, a riot of emotion for Liaden eyes, and the picture of restraint to Terran.

"Your pardon," Jethri muttered. "Misravot."

"What? Hasn't that head hardened yet?"

"Oh, it's hard enough, but in all the wrong ways—as you well know! As for my mail—I answered your last! Unless there's been one since I've been traveling . . ."

"Of a certainty you answered! You have every faith in my abilities. I own—it's well that one of us does so, but when one writes for advice, one does not wish for reassurance, one wishes for . . . advice."

"But, what could I have advised?"

"Had I known that, tumultuous youth, I might have advised myself!"

Jethri laughed. "I think I see the problem, here—*you* want a glass of Misravot."

After a moment, Tan Sim smiled.

"Do you know, I think I might."

"Well, then, here . . ." Jethri offered his arm, which Tan Sim took, and they moved in the direction of the bar.

"Now, give over scolding," Jethri said, "and tell me how you have come here."

"As for that—Captain sea'Kera was persuaded to put *Genchi* to the test after it was most carefully explained to him by his trader how wonderful an opportunity this gathering is, so wonderful that it must on no account be missed. Alas, *Genchi* is not a courier ship, and we have only just arrived. I see that there are seminars scheduled for tomorrow and the next day, Standard, so I still hope to make good connections."

"I have no doubt," Jethri said, as they moved forward in line toward the bar. "Also, I might introduce you to some of the honoreds I have met—and to Doricky, who will introduce you to a hundred more, I warrant."

"If you will introduce me to the trader with very deep pockets, who bought your pretty little ring, I would be most obliged. At least you must tell me who he is."

Jethri bit his lip. Tan Sim was his partner, and he needed to know this. Probably.

"The trader is known to everyone as *Uncle*," he said. "As it comes about, he is, in truth, my own uncle—the brother of my father. Tonight was my first meeting with him; I had only learned of his existence an hour before." They arrived at the bar, and Ranny Suki smiled to see him.

"Trader ven'Deelin! Another of your party?" She turned the smile on Tan Sim.

"My partner, in fact: Trader pen'Akla. He's only just arrived and is very much in need of a glass of the Misravot, should there be any more available."

"Indeed, I have the last bottle of your case here, sir! Allow me to pour. Also, there is a cold nuncheon laid at the back of the room, Trader pen'Akla. Please refresh yourself."

"I thank you." Tan Sim gave her one of his more charming smiles and a bow.

"Thank you," Jethri said, also, and they received their glasses and moved away.

"Do you wish to eat?"

"Do you know, a cold nuncheon sounds delightful. Tell me more about—"

"Trader ven'Deelin," a lately familiar voice spoke at his elbow.

Jethri turned carefully. "Master Trader pin'Aker," he murmured.

"Forgive me for intruding, Trader, I merely wished to express my congratulations on an excellent piece of trading and a very fine recover. A trader must sometimes think quickly to preserve the tempo and rescue the trade. These skills require practice. It was good of Host Doricky to arrange so neat a lesson for you."

Jethri blinked. Had he or had he not seen a *twinkle* in the Master Trader's eye? Best to answer modestly, in any wise.

He inclined his head respectfully. "Indeed, sir. I must remember to thank her for her care of me."

"You must, Trader; I strongly advise it. Perhaps, too, a small gift, if something appropriate comes to your hand."

"Thank you, Master Trader, for your advice. It will be my very great pleasure to choose a present for Grandma Ricky." He took a breath and laid his hand on Tan Sim's sleeve. "By your leave, sir, may I present to you my partner, Tan Sim pen'Akla Clan—"

"Pen'Akla!" the Master Trader interrupted. "Exactly the trader I had wished to find! Have you a moment to give me, sir? That is, if I do not interrupt business . . ."

Tan Sim blinked, and bowed prettily—but it was Tan Sim, with pretty bows something of a specialty. In spite of which, Jethri thought he saw a tremor along the carefully curved fingers, and remembered, darkly, that *Genchi*'s rations tended toward the low end of recommended daily caloric intake.

"My pressing business," he said, "is to find Tan Sim something to eat, as he has only just arrived among us."

Master Trader pin'Aker was seen to smile gently upon Jethri.

"Allow me, please, Trader, to take that pleasant duty from you. I promise that I will take most excellent care of him and return him to you in good order."

"Truly, Jeth Ree," Tan Sim added, sounded slightly panicked, "my meal can easily wait upon the Master Trader's business."

"No, no, Trader ven'Deelin and I are quite agreed!" said pin'Aker with a slight, indulgent bow. "I will see you properly fed, and we shall pursue our mutual business over what I am told are 'handwiches made of fresh-bake bread, local cheese, and the finest soy meats'!" He offered his arm, and dropped back into Liaden. "Come, Trader, who can resist such a treat?"

"Jeth Ree . . ."

"Go, please, eat! Master Trader, my thanks to you again, for your care. Tan Sim—I'm on *Keravath*!"

"Yes," Tan Sim said, and allowed himself to be borne off by the Master Trader.

Jethri turned away, sipping his wine absently, his mind occupied with the problem of a "small gift" for Doricky. Properly, such a gift, commemorating a service acknowledged, was small and personal. The more personal the gift, the greater the service.

He raised his hand to tug at his earlobe—and suddenly grinned.

Chapter Twenty-One

· · · ·✳· · · ·

Tradedesk, Gallery 770

"GRANDMA RICKY." He stopped before her chair and bowed, as a child to a favored elder.

She looked up at him with a tired smile.

"Now, Trader, you're not looking to me for bed-games, I'm thinking."

"I would be honored, if you think you might find me of use," he said, which was the proper response, and he *would* be honored, if she decided so.

She laughed, right out loud.

"Forty Standards! Hell, twenty Standards! But now? And having been crushed? Find somebody who can keep up with you!"

"But I came," he said earnestly, "to thank you."

She eyed him shrewdly. "Thank me for what?"

"For the opportunity to succeed," he said seriously, which was almost exactly what he would have said in Liaden. He dropped to one knee beside her chair.

"May I give a gift?"

"I'm never one to turn down a present. Is it a nice one?"

"You must be the judge," he said, and reached up to detach the modest gold ring that adorned his ear. Leaning forward, he affixed it to hers, and leaned back smiling.

"Like it was made for you," he said.

She lifted her fingers, felt the adornment gently, and shook her head at him.

"You're a fool, boy," she said, precisely as if her eyes hadn't become just a little damp. "A fool, but a pretty-mannered one. You can come find me again at tomorrow's banquet. 'Til then, go away and let an old woman rest!"

"Yes, ma'am. Rest well."

He rose, and took himself off, heading vaguely toward the door, though he was still feeling energy twitching in his fingers and toes. Common sense suggested that it was late, the first seminar on the morrow was early, and a trader might be best served by going back to his cramped berth on *Keravath* and trying to exchange energy for sleep. It did seem as if Gallery 770 had lost a number of partiers, so perhaps he wouldn't be alone in—

"You are very condescending, sir!" he heard Samay say, from very close at hand. She was speaking High Liaden and her voice was even colder than that aloof dialect demanded.

Jethri turned—and found her at once, not half a dozen steps to his right, her back rigid and her head up. He could only see the side of her face, but her expression appeared to be perfectly, politely bland. She was addressing Bar Jan chel'Gaiban, whose face Jethri could see all too clearly: also politely bland, though showing a little color along the cheekbones, his stance suggesting that he was amused by something, as an adult might be amused at a child's tantrum.

"How should I be condescending?" he said, spreading his hands. "I merely speak the truth as we both know it. We two are well-matched in clan and in *melant'i*, and there is then no question but that we may pleasure each other more satisfactorily than any other pairing available to either. Come, I offer bed-sport with a well-trained and well-regarded companion in luxury surely not available in any room on this . . . *station*. Let us go, before the evening becomes too short for pleasure."

He offered his arm.

Jethri hadn't thought Samay could get any stiffer.

"You misunderstand me," she said, her voice steady, and her tone cold enough it was a wonder Bar Jan's hair didn't show icicles. "I mean to say that I have already arranged for company this evening!"

She turned suddenly, and held out her hand to Jethri, her smile rather . . . forced.

"Trader, you find me at last! I hope your business has gone well?"

Clear at once was that Samay wasn't tolerating Bar Jan's advances, and wanted to be rid of him. Well, Jethri thought, he could certainly help her extricate herself from his attentions. He did feel a little pang, that it was a subterfuge, but still—Samay had been a pleasant and gracious companion all evening. She had submitted with good humor to the role of "arbiter" for the ridiculous auction, and had gracefully acted as Doricky's assistant. If she needed his help now to avoid an unwelcome connection, he would be churlish to refuse her.

So, he stepped forward with a slight, intimate bow, and a smile that deliberately excluded Bar Jan chel'Gaibin, offering his arm with a will.

"My business is well concluded," he told her. "Will you forgive me, that it took me from your side?"

She tipped her head, as if considering her options, then slipped her arm through his.

"I think that I might, since it ended well. But, come, shall we retire, before more business finds you?"

"I think that is the course of wisdom," he said. "Let us go, and quickly."

He allowed Samay to turn him toward the door, glancing over his shoulder to afford the jilted lover a cordial nod. "Trader. Good fortune to you."

Bar Jan chel'Gaibin turned away without a word and stalked off toward the bar.

· · · ✳ · · ·

Samay and her uncle had rooms on the station, an honor reserved for few, since there were, as Jethri understood, not very many hotel rooms yet ready for occupancy. They were still comfortably arm in arm, when they found the proper door. Jethri was pleased to see that Samay had become noticeably less stiff, as they put hallways between her and the Rinork heir, and by the time of their arrival at that door, they were chatting together comfortably, once more on the easy terms they had established in Gallery 770.

"Here," she said, pulling a key card from her sleeve.

Jethri stepped back, releasing her arm with a bow.

"I will leave you to your rest, and seek . . ." he began, but got no further.

She turned to look at him, her eyes. wide.

"But what is this? Come inside, Trader . . . Oh!" Her eyes widened. "Have you made arrangements?"

"No arrangements, but I thought—"

A door closed somewhat down the hall. Samay looked over her shoulder, then caught his hand.

"Come in, Trader, please, where we can discuss this in comfort."

She pushed the door open and bowed him in ahead of her. He could understand that she might not wish to air her business in a public hall, so he inclined his head and stepped inside.

• • • ⁂ • • •

"Comfort" was perhaps not the correct word for the room in which he found himself.

It was a nice room, and would one day be elegant, but for the moment it was filled with a temporary mix of furniture and fixtures brought together to permit the half-finished station to present itself at all.

Too, the room was set up for entertaining a crowd—cheeses and *chernubia*, wine and other drinks, and a dozen-plus chairs—

The single couch . . . was large enough that they could have reclined, their booted feet sole to sole at the center, and neither head would have quite touched the armrests. The lighting was also very bright—startling so, after the comfortable low lights of Gallery 770.

Jethri paused and looked around him.

"This will be a room for large events, I believe," Samay said, stepping in behind him and locking the door, "and I believe that the spaces are used differently . . ."

"Not," he agreed, "a place meant for quiet times. And large, if I may say, for one person . . ."

The merest trace of a blush whispered across Samay's face and she bowed lightly, acknowledging a hit. Jethri found much to favor in her forthrightness.

"My delm insisted I was to be treated as her representative here, which is absurd though I'm not to say so. This worked well in the Gallery, at least! So my uncle travels with his two favorites, as he always does, achieving a suite half as large . . . and I have been gifted with a suite sized for a Festival gathering! It is perplexing. By myself, I have not even a stuffed toy to speak to!"

She looked to him earnestly then, and offered lightly, "There are

options for us, Trader. We have, off of this room, aside from the usual
amenities, not less than three bedchambers, though one is rather
small, and—"

"Wait." He raised a hand, and she stopped speaking, her head
tipped slightly to one side, and her eyes very wide.

"You must forgive me," he said, "if I offend, but I must be clear
regarding the intention of the evening. My understanding was that I
assisted a comrade in evading a potentially distasteful situation. I gave
that assistance with no expectation of . . . of . . . usurping your
company for myself."

Samay's blush this time was more noticeable.

"It is I who must ask forgiveness. Indeed, it had been in my mind
to ask if you might be available to celebrate mutual pleasure this
evening, but the opportunity . . . then here comes Bar Jan chel'Gaibin,
who informs me that I needn't worry that I will be importuned by
Wynhael's associates; he has already lain his claim, for clearly of all
the station, only he and I are a worthy night match!"

Jethri felt his jaw drop, which he ought by this point in his training
be proof against, and manfully pressed his lips together. At least, he
comforted himself, he hadn't let the gasp loose. The effrontery was,
well, breathtaking! Chel'Gaibin was High House; he must have had
lessons: in protocol, in bed-sport, in—he *must have* meant the insult!

"I thank you," Samay said, "for your very complete understanding.
Please, allow me to offer you refreshment—perhaps some fruit
juice?—and we will discuss this matter properly between us."

· · · ✳ · · ·

Both of them deeming the formal parlor too . . . big, they had
carried a tray of light snacks and another, with pitcher and glasses, to
the room Samay described as the "small parlor." Though there was a
bunk bed in the room, it was easily ignored in favor of the grouping
at the front of the space. Here was adjustable lighting, and a couch
piled with pillows, and two comfortable chairs that friends might
arrange to accommodate soft voice and subtle gesture.

The chairs placed, then, and the lights softened, they each settled,
fruit juice in hand, smiled, and lifted their glasses in a toast.

"To enjoyable connections," Samay murmured, and Jethri did not
demur.

"Now, Trader, I must tell you—it would please me very much if you will stay. I know too well that the manner of your coming here is not, entirely, to Code. I say now that it was not my intent to . . . to coerce you. Please, you must not feel compelled to stay here, and I will beg you to inform me, if we have become . . . out of Balance."

She stopped, her eyes bright, leaning slightly forward in her chair.

Seated as he was, Jethri bowed slightly. "As I count, we are in perfect Balance. If my arrival was irregular, I am still happy to be here."

Tension left her shoulders; she leaned back in her chair, her slight, enchanting smile on display.

"Good, that is good." She sipped her juice, then gave him one of her clear, straight looks.

"You must understand that I am not yet . . . fully in the habit of— which is to say . . . I have not previously invited a night friend into my own bedchamber! Doubtless had I more experience, I might have found opportunity to speak earlier in the evening, and thus prevented . . . the slight disorder which we have together overcome. However, you need not be concerned that I have no skills. Certainly, I have been properly, and thoroughly, tutored in the art. More, I have been to several Festivals. Surely, I should say that, if it pleases you, you may call me this evening by my small name, my friend name of Maya, or even, if you like—I offer you this for quietest moments, which my nanny and my aunt both called me—Nera, after the small birds. I find it soothing, but it is not a public name!"

Jethri felt his throat catch, for he knew that such a name was indeed a gift.

Carefully, he smiled. "I hope I shall earn such good names for my tongue," he murmured. "I do hope you will call me Jethri, and the short form is simply 'Jeth' if you like. I am not so lucky as to be short-named for a bird or a cloud or a jewel!"

He sipped his juice, recalling the rest of what he ought, in respect of shared pleasure, to likewise reveal to his partner.

"I fear that I bring rather less to the evening than might be assumed. Indeed, at the time you were being tutored in the arts and graces, I would scarcely have been bundling. My own *I'gaina Prenada* has given me what is said to be a thorough introduction, and was kind enough to pronounce me an apt and energetic scholar. However, this was well within the *relumma*. I have no Festival gleanings to increase our delight, nor even, I fear, very much skill."

"Appreciation and energy are very welcome in a bed-friend," Samay said firmly. "I expect that we will deal well; certainly, we must between us produce a unique pleasure. But you must tell me, Jeth, what is this *bundling*? A Terran art?"

He laughed.

"Say, rather, a Terran work-around." He said the last word in Terran, saw her puzzled glance, and held up his hand for a moment while he made a translation, "A circumvention," he achieved, in Liaden.

"I understand the word," she said after a moment, "but what would the problem be, that bundling . . . *works-around*?"

"That . . ." He discovered that his glass was empty, and reached for the pitcher. "May I refresh your glass?"

"Please."

That done, he sat back again, and looked to her face, seeing interest.

"You must understand, that I grew up on a Terran family ship. Such ships are not to compare with Liaden tradeships. They are typically very small, and privacy is . . . not very easy to achieve.

"That being so, when two ships or more came together, and bed-friends were chosen, the adults—those experienced in the arts—were given rooms and formal privacy. Those of us who were not yet experienced, but who knew the pangs. . .we bundled.

"We would find a corner in the kitchen, or back in a storeroom, or down in 'ponics, make it all nice and soft with shipping cushions all around, drape blankets over all, make the lights dim, and . . . cuddle. There is, you will appreciate, not much room in such an arrangement, though it is, I will say, comfortable, and comforting. Typically, there was insufficient room to undress and, as the bundle was within public space, there was the possibility of being interrupted at any moment, so clothes . . . may have become disordered, but were rarely discarded."

Compared to the lessons Samay must have had—assuming that Gaenor's tutoring had been typical—his experience sounded . . . somewhat cramped and limited in joy. And yet, he remembered certain encounters, even now, with breathless—

"We shall do this!" Samay announced, rising to her feet.

He blinked up at her. "Your pardon?"

"Teach me this art, of your goodness, Jeth. My own tutors taught that there is infinite variation upon delight. I would learn this variation, if you would teach."

She was serious; he could read it in the lines of her body. For a moment, he thought to demur, then recalled that Gaenor, too, had told him that delight had many faces. Who was he to deny a previously unknown joy to a night friend?

Jethri laughed, and rose.

"If you will learn, then I will teach. First, we shift the pillows."

• • • ✳ • • •

They'd left one small light on, but blocked it to get good shadow, and he'd allowed the taking off of boots sufficient preparation.

Samay entered the tent first, as he held the cover back courteously. He followed, tucking the entrance snug around them. The bottom bunk made a slightly softer, and larger, bundling space than had been standard on-ship, but since he was was slightly larger than he'd been, back then, he considered it authentic enough.

"This is . . . cozy," Samay murmured. "And now, do we . . . ?"

He stretched out on his side, and patted the mattress beside him. "Lie down, Maya, with your back against my chest."

She did so, making a warm, seductive, and nicely fragrant armful. He raised a hand and stroked her hair where it began to curl—where it would curl again, once she was back to Liad and had returned to the fashions of dirtside society.

She sighed, and nestled her cheek into his shoulder; then, taking the initiative, she stroked tempting fingers along the inside of his wrist. He gasped at the unexpected pleasure, and she laughed, soft and wicked.

• • • ✳ • • •

A little later, he shocked her—not by using her softest and most private name, Nera, for, after all she had given him free use of it, for this time of shared pleasure. No, she had asked, as he nuzzled the back of her neck, what they might—had this been a bundling on his own ship—do next.

He had kissed and nibbled her ear, whispering that they might stroke each other's faces. Her gasp had been very noticeable, her demur gentle. It was, after all, nothing more than he had expected. He wouldn't have mentioned it—or dared it—if she hadn't asked. And really it was more than fine, since just then she'd executed a stretch like a dance move, offering the hollow of her throat to his lips.

A small while later, she had shocked him, holding his head to her breast, and murmuring. "Jeth, this will be a fine thing to recall when I am married, for my delm is aiming me at old"—here she barely managed to suppress the name of the lucky groom—"*a qe'andra* of extreme *melant'i* and form. He is unhappy with his heirs, one hears, and thus wishes more of them to confound expectations. I think if that is the marriage she makes for me I shall request to travel on *Elthoria* to and from it so you may tell me of things not covered by the Code!"

Alas, that thought had sobered them both, with Jethri trying not to think of Maya in a boring old man's arms—well, really, in any boring man's arms!—or himself locked a year away in a contract marriage allowing no sound of Terran or Trade . . .

Despite such shocks and thoughts, they found comfort together, play at last ceding place to drowsiness, as she tucked herself into the curve of his chest and settled her cheek on his arm, he with his cheek on her hair under the doubled bedspreads.

"Sleep well, my friend," Nera murmured, and he answered, mistily, "I thank you for the honor."

Chapter Twenty-Two

· · · ·✳· · · ·

Tradedesk, Framinham Cafe

HE LEFT NERA STILL DROWSING beneath their tent, and returned at all speed to *Keravath*, there to shower and to don fresh clothes, remembering to shift cards and other pocket items, and also to replace the earring he had given to Doricky with a simple topaz stud, which pleasantly echoed the stones in his trade ring, and was therefore appropriate for a modest young trader's day wear.

Scout ter'Astin was not in evidence, nor did the ship report his return since he had exited the ship with Jethri, last evening. Jethri hesitated, wondering if he ought to be concerned, then he remembered spying the Scout and his companion last night, and half-smiled. Very possibly, the Scout had found something to occupy him elsewhere.

Jethri finished his braid, and left the ship a-pace, arriving in the doorway of the Framinham Cafe on the note of ninth hour.

He cast about him, but neither Uncle nor his companion was immediately present.

"Good morning, Trader," said a lyrical female voice from behind him, speaking Terran.

He turned, as Dulsey Omron stepped through the door, closely followed by Uncle. Both were dressed as they had been last evening; both looked well rested, though Jethri somehow caught a sense of hurry from Uncle—was that how *his* face looked, when he was working with short time?

239

"You are prompt, and that is excellent," Uncle said with a nod. "We suddenly find ourselves needed elsewhere, but our consultation—that, we must have! Come, we've reserved our usual booth."

Scarcely had they seated themselves than the tray arrived, slotting into, and sealing, the booth's door. They were now private—and, Jethri saw, as Dulsey pulled a small box from her belt, they were about to go off the grid entirely. She touched the box's face, placed it in the center of the table, and nodded, while sliding a plate of steamed rolls off the tray.

"I hope you'll forgive our little eccentricities," Uncle murmured, pouring tea into three mugs. "We like our private business to remain private." He glanced up. "I am, by the way, your Uncle Yuri, Arin's brother. And this lady is Dulsey Omron."

Uncle Yuri was wearing the firegem ring on the third finger of his left hand, where it fit like it had been made for him.

Jethri smiled, a little wistfully, and nodded. "It becomes you, sir."

"Thank you; it is remarkably satisfying to have it back. Where did you say you found it?"

Dulsey had taken two rolls and passed the plate to Jethri, who also helped himself to two and sent the plate on to Uncle.

"I didn't say," he murmured.

"But will you?"

Jethri bit into his roll, which was stuffed with savory vegetables, and deserved his appreciation, which he gave, for several heartbeats.

"I believe that I will," he said eventually, raising his head to meet his uncle's considering gaze. "You trade Terran side, and the trader in question is Liaden. He's retired, never really had access to outspace, and he's stuck, stuck bad, with some Old Tech toys that're enough to ruin him, if the Scouts find him out."

"You interest me. Do you care to say who this trader is and where he might be found?"

"His name," Jethri said promptly, "is tel'Linden. I met him at the trade fair in Cherdyan City, on Verstal."

"And he has more stock, of the quality of this ring?"

Jethri moved his shoulders, accepting a plate of fruit from Dulsey, choosing a few pieces and passing it on to Uncle Yuri.

"He had fractins—real ones and fake. More real ones than fake. Frames, broken down, so it's not obvious what they are. Old Tech kahjets . . . Nothing I could buy, being a Liaden trader, so-called, on a Liaden tradeship, trading for the next while mostly in Liaden space."

Uncle nodded thoughtfully, and looked to his companion.

"He may be worth our while, this Trader tel'Linden. It may be that we can assist the trader in his stocking difficulties and also assist him in returning worth to his clan." He paused to savor a roll, and nodded to Jethri.

"We will of course pay a finder's fee for those items which are found to be of use."

"You needn't—"

"No, Trader, we need," Dulsey interrupted. "It is how business is done, and we would not be behindhand."

There was, Jethri thought, really no arguing with that. He inclined his head.

"Any such fees may be directed to my attention, on *Elthoria*."

"I may say," Uncle commented, "that it is satisfying to note that our work on your gene mix was well done. Your brother had thought that we might increase the sensitivity to fractin- and other timonium-derived activities. I confess, I had not considered it a trait that could be manipulated to good effect. But Arin often saw further than I."

Jethri put his cup down, quietly his mouth a little dry, despite the tea he had just swallowed.

"Arin is . . . was . . . my father."

"Yes, that is how it is said among those who are not of our particular . . . family. In fact, at the level that matters—the level of genes and DNA—you are Arin's brother. Not a clone, for as I say, we did work, seeking to enhance certain specific traits, which have matured well. We shall so note it, in the files."

"I'm . . . manufactured?"

Dulsey extended a hand and touched him on the sleeve. Uncle looked . . . thoughtful.

"Yours was a more deliberate mixing of genes than is provided by the random universe, yes. Manufactured . . . is a valid comparison. I will note that the process we used to capture the individual now known as Jethri Gobelyn ven'Deelin is *only* distinguished by deliberation. You are unique, and you are yourself. Nor were Arin and I exactly the same. When we have more time together at leisure, Dulsey can enumerate many examples illustrating that point."

Jethri considered that, and decided that he still wasn't clear—and now that this particular box of sticky string had been opened, he needed to *get* clear, if for no other reason than honor demanded it.

"Clones are even more illegal on the Liaden side of things than they are on the Terran," he said, looking his uncle straight in the eye and holding the gaze. "I owe my mother, my Master Trader, my ship, and my crew mates the truth. If my presence is going to cause them trouble, then . . . I shouldn't be present."

"You are not," Dulsey said from beside him, "a clone." Her voice rang with a truth so absolute that Jethri fully believed her at once.

"You do, however, bring to mind a topic which we must address, now that we are together. You were, as I said, intended to fill a certain purpose. Now that I see the investment of time and resources has borne profit, I would see you at work more fitting to your nature."

Jethri shook his head, wryly.

"If I stay on the Liaden side, being able to find fractins, and telling the difference between the good ones and the imitations, isn't exactly a feature," he said.

"Ah," said his Uncle Yuri, looking at him with interest. "And do you intend to stay on the Liaden side? I can offer you a very lucrative contract with our family company, as a fractin and Old Tech hunter. You will be utilizing your natural skills for the good of your family, and you will remain *on the Terran side.*"

That last, that sounded right stern, but Jethri only shook his head.

"Thank you, sir, but I'll stay on *Elthoria.*"

He met Uncle Yuri's eyes. Uncle Yuri frowned.

Beside him, Jethri heard Dulsey laugh.

Slowly, then, Uncle's frown melted into a smile.

"Good," he said. "Excellent. You are important to the process. I congratulate you."

"Process, sir?"

Uncle waved his hand.

"The same process that involves Tradedesk. The process of building ports and markets that do not have a Liaden side *or* a Terran side. The process of preventing a war that will be—according to my calculations and, independently, Arin's calculations—inevitable. Following usual trends in such matters the war would split both the

Liaden side and the Terran side into camps hostile to each other and to splintered noncompliant subgroups.

"This would not only be bad for trade, it would be bad for humankind in space. Far better to build Tradedesk, and begin a Liaden-Terran trader exchange program. Cooperative action. Notice that I do not say easy action, or perfect results."

"The galaxy not plunging into war seems like a good outcome to me," Jethri said.

Dulsey laughed again, and Uncle actually chuckled.

"So it does. Now . . ." He glanced at Dulsey, who nodded softly.

"Now, Jethri ven'Deelin, we must away on business of our own. Thank you for a very enjoyable and informative hour. Doubtless, we'll meet again. But even if we do not—continue as you've begun: live well, and profit."

Chapter Twenty-Three

. . . . .✳. . . . .

Tradedesk

THE FIRST SEMINAR BEGAN SOON, but not so soon that Jethri felt it necessary to rush down Tradedesk's wide halls. His conversation with his uncle had given him food for thought, and he was deep inside those thoughts when he heard someone say his name.

He stopped, blinking, and gazed about.

"Trader ven'Deelin," Master Trader pin'Aker said again. "Well met, Trader. I wonder if I might walk with you?"

"Yes, of course, sir. Forgive me for my inattention . . ."

"No need, no need! Who among us here does not have much to think upon? The possibilities exist for the increase and betterment of trade across many fronts! And yet, we are so different—Liaden and Terran. Are the cultural accommodations even possible?"

"I think they are very possible, sir," Jethri said. "I own myself but an indifferent scholar, but surely, if I can make a beginning . . ."

"Which you have done, admirably, if by beginning we mean to say that a Terran can be taught the language, the Code, and all the myriad tiny details that make up a society. Certainly, I make no doubt that the *next* exchange—a Liaden trader to a Terran ship—will be equal to learning the language, the Terran Code, and so many details. But what we want, young sir—what we *want*, is not a Terran trader who may learn to be a Liaden trader, nor yet a Liaden trader who may learn to be a Terran trader.

"No! I say that what we want is a trader who, standing as himself,

245

with only his skill to hand, can trade from that position equally—to Liadens, to Terrans, to whomever else we may find, as exploration expands."

"You argue for a trader-scout, then, sir?"

"Do I?" Master Trader pin'Aker frowned in thought. "That is an interesting notion; I will think upon it. I confess my initial belief is that Scouts succeed by doing just as you do—blending into the society they wish to study. But, yes, there may be something in your idea, Trader. My thanks."

Here he moved his hand, as if brushing something lightly away from him.

"Fascinating as these topics are, there is one, closer, I believe, to your interests—and mine. I am indebted to you, Trader, for the opportunity to speak with Trader pen'Akla last evening. He had much to say which interested me. A most personable young trader who may, I feel, with careful nurturing, one day achieve the purple.

"I will tell you, as his partner, that the trader did confide some of the details of his current situation to me—no dishonor to him! I had asked him to clarify some few things his mother had spoken of to me, earlier in the evening. I understand from these discussions that I may be in a position to do Trader pen'Akla and yourself a good turn. With this in my mind, I will be contacting Master Trader ven'Deelin. If there is a reason why I should not, I beg you will tell me."

A good turn? Could Master Trader pin'Aker be willing to act as ven'Deelin's cat's-paw, and buy out Tan Sim's contract with *Genchi*? Jethri felt a flutter of hope so strong that it was a moment before he could speak.

"In-indeed, sir, I can think of no reason why you should not speak with my mother on your topic. I think, if I may say so, that you will find her . . . receptive."

"Norn ven'Deelin is a remarkable trader; she has long been a friend to those younger in trade, and a willing mentor to those who aspire. We have had several comfortable talks on the topic, so I may confidently say that she, as much as I, believe that, as Master Traders, one of our many duties is the nurturing of traders, and the widening of trade. We do not achieve excellence, nor do we serve the trade, when we allow young traders of potential—or, indeed, any trader!— to be abused and his vocation used as a whip to break him."

He paused then, his lips pressed together firmly.

"Well," he said, "no more on that head. I will do myself the pleasure of calling upon your mother soon, I think. When I see her, I shall report that I left you aglow with your successes, and in the very best of health."

They had come to a cross-hall. Jethri bore to the right, but Master Trader pin'Aker halted, and bowed.

"Good-day to you, Trader ven'Deelin; I leave you here. My thanks for a most thought-provoking conversation."

* * * ✢ * * *

He looked for Tan Sim at the first seminar, but didn't find him.

But he did find his long-lost host, and First Board Scout ter'Astin.

"Trader, I have news of your property and a time and location from which it can be retrieved."

Jethri stepped quickly to his side.

"Where is it? Who has it? What—"

"Peace," the Scout said shortly. "Let us to *Keravath*; this is not something you will wish bandied about in the halls."

Ter'Astin's face was impassive: a good Liaden public face. But there was something about it, or perhaps his stance, that convinced Jethri that the Scout was weary. And truly, his book! News of his book held more urgency for him than the next seminar.

"Certainly," he said. "Let us repair to *Keravath*. Have you eaten?"

"I have ordered in a nuncheon; it should be on dock when we arrive," ter'Astin said, walking rapidly down the hall.

Jethri stretched his legs to catch up.

"Had you an enjoyable evening?" he asked, when it seemed that the Scout would simply stalk along, silently.

A black glance sparkled under dark lashes.

"My evening was pleasant, and fulfilling, thank you. I hear various tales of your own prowess, as a trader of great skill, an arbiter of reasonable resource, and a connoisseur of wine and bedmates." The glance this time was accompanied by a slight smile. "Truly, you amaze. I blush to think what I will say to Norn."

"You need say nothing. Master Trader pin'Aker assures me that he will share all. And, as he has it as his intention to go to her soon . . ."

"My blushes are saved. On a similar topic, I feel I should tell you that *Wynhael* left station while we most of us slept. My good comrade

Roe of the control team relates a horrific tale of an emergency departure filed, and a captain in a dangerous hurry. He tells me—in the strictest confidence!—that there was a moment when he feared the station would be holed." He moved a hand, perhaps describing *Wynhael*'s departure.

"However, as you see, we are unharmed, and *Wynhael* is no longer with us, so—a good beginning to a new day. Would you agree?"

"I agree that a lack of Rinork and chel'Gaibin is welcome," Jethri said.

Their conversation became interrupted then, by their individual and joint necessities to acknowledge greetings from acquaintances, and so they reached *Keravath*'s dock.

Jethri picked up the caterer's box as the Scout worked the lock, and they entered, lock sealed behind them, and privacy insured.

· · · ✳ · · ·

"The crux of the matter," the Scout said, as they unfolded the box in the galley, "is that I have found who holds your birthright."

Jethri, who had been contemplating a stack of handwiches that might easily have fed the crew of the *Market*, looked up, excitement cramping his stomach.

"Who is it? Do you have it?"

"I have this"—ter'Astin reached inside his jacket and withdrew a single sheet of folded hardcopy, which he offered—"given to prove that the article is, indeed, in the possession of this person."

Jethri snatched the paper, unfolded it. . .

"It's a page from my book," he said. He recognized it—one of the pages where he had sketched a figure, his father had refined it, and he had refined his father's iteration . . .

He looked up.

"Tell me."

"'Tell me' the child says." Ter'Astin leaned in to pick up half a handwich. "Well, the short of it is that this item—your book—is not in the hands of the Scouts, but in other hands, even less tender of the promises of field agents. These hands are somewhat unscrupulous. Certainly, they have stolen the book—or had it stolen. They are, however, willing to return it to you, its rightful owner, and they are so gracious to give us a day and a planet upon which you and they will meet in order to accomplish this. But . . ."

Jethri looked up from the page he'd been studying.

"But?"

Ter'Astin smiled thinly. "But they wish payment. As it happens, they want payment in kind. Your book"—he jutted his chin at the page Jethri held—"for the *Envidaria*."

"I don't have the *Envidaria*," Jethri snapped. The Scout met his eyes blandly, and Jethri turned away first.

"I need to use long-comm," he said, and sighed, suddenly seeing the elegant, subtle curve of Samay's neck. "I will also need to leave messages here. We will, I think, wish to depart soon."

"I think so, too," said the Scout, and went to wake *Keravath's* board.

Chapter Twenty-Four

• • • •˚֍˚ • • • •

Gobelyn's Market

SERCONIA'S LESSONS were still on their minds when they jumped into the Franticle True system, there being four stars all dancing in a complicated set of orbits within easy reach and all moving with a lazy general relative velocity and together they were Great Franticle, the parts being bright little Franticle Blue, Franticle Hon, Franticle Core and Franticle True. Down the road there'd be trouble, according to some of the calculations, with Franticle Hon and Franticle Blue having a hot date that could just cause some problems with the other two . . . in not all so many hundred thousand Standards. Near term it meant there was plenty of mass to go around and Great Franticle one of the neighborhoods where odd stuff could happen to incoming ships.

Of the eleven planets and forty-seven notable moons in all this mess only one moon and one planet were comfortably habitable, Franticle Blue having a clutch of gas giants, Franticle Hon a bunch of rocks, Franticle Core more comets than any one system ought—and Franticle True, of course having the livable planet and moon.

Khat didn't mean to yawn at it all sitting there with screens up and all the sensor ears open; the arrival had been enough to rouse Iza to be in first chair. But Cris had been on an alternate shift last ship night, stopping by all wide awake on the topic of Iza slowing down and the ship chemistry being odd and loose after seeing some big ships run; then they'd talked about her trips and then it was time for Khat to take the boards a quarter shift before Jump end, Iza letting Grig's watch be short. Seemed to Khat like that was happening a fair amount, Grig getting a short shift, start or finish, and Khat wasn't sure if that was humanitarian Iza sending a man to help his wife with the kid or Iza sending a message to Grig.

Iza called out, "Got that tumble again, Khat, catch the numbers for us—tumble's not useful!"

Iza'd killed the tumble in a few seconds of shifting floors and sidewalls, and then cross-haired the destination, minor curses—not unusual in the captain—for the fact that they'd actually overshot and would have to kill the outward-bound vector before they'd be able to start in, adding at least a half-day to the front end of things.

Given a stable orbit *Gobelyn's Market* found the orients, and with them began picking up the comm feeds. With two inhabited worlds and a large-scale station, there was a fair amount of comm traffic, and as much or more because of the mining operations among the rock belt.

Iza called out, "In and safe" to the crew, something she remembered to do every three or four Jumps despite the all-clear call being right there on the checklist, and Khat relaxed since she hated being the one to have to follow up on Iza's misses. Actually checking checklists was what subordinates were for, that seemed Iza's idea.

Khat pulled herself into the flow of routine by main willpower, and all too quickly suppressed some bad words of her own before kicking the news over to Iza, who might as well know it now as later, because it had to be told.

"*Therinfel* is on close-docking orbit around Franticle Orbital Center, Captain. That's one of the Liaden ships was at Banth when I had the run in on Banthport. The one that tried to ding me for money 'cause of Jethri."

Iza grunted: "Jethri. Boy's always been more trouble than he was worth."

Khat waited—ship's immediate security was her concern. The search patterns she'd talked to Paitor about looked to be taking on an unexpected urgency but . . .

Having no immediate challenge to her declaration, Iza ordered, "Check all the damn home ports, then, of everything we got out there and whatever comes in—get Cris or Grig on it—and let me know if there's more of them show up, or if this one takes leave. No direct contact with any Liaden ship without you talk to me. In fact—"

Iza went to all-call then, with, "Hear this, official for the duration of Franticle visit, all crew acknowledge in staff order by the tick, on my mark. No one is to contact or respond to contact with any Liaden vessel or personnel unless sitting in First or Second Board or covering for First or Second. If there's an emergency, then use sense. Acknowledge, and questions as you see me before we hit port."

That meant Khat first, with the others answering every sixty seconds—not time enough for questions, but time enough to admit of a question . . .

"Captain, acknowledged," she said, hands busy matching ship's warn aways with home ports where it wasn't plain. "Just the one ship so far, and looking."

Iza grunted again, said "Thanks for the heads-up, Second," and took her calls while they waited for the local traffic control to get their signals and offer a course.

Khat nodded, knowing Iza's shifting gaze would catch it, and added—"I'm noting that we have the tumble—I'll check with Cris to see if there's a look-up for that in the new Struven Units."

It was Iza's turn to nod. "We best both be keeping track of stuff— log it, won't you? And keep your own log, that's a plan, in case Cris isn't anymore."

· · · ✦ · · ·

"Grig Tomas, I'm running with a known troublemaker on orbit, and there's four other Liaden ships in-system . . ."

Grig was who Khat saw first as she leaned in with a smile, the door being open, the sounds clear.

Grig and Seeli were at kid-feeding, in what had been Jethri's tiny cabin. Without Jeth it was more rather than less crowded, since the baby tank was bulky and both the crew members were close enough to Jethri's size to make no matter.

He glanced up, face letting the smile go a little wary with the topic.

"You talked to Paitor on this yet? He's got the records. . . ."

"He's still digging some records for me, but he's got those deliveries to schedule out, too; what he told me was to ask your opinion about it."

In the midst of adjusting her grip on Travit, the kid having a mind of his own about the arrangements, Seeli looked up, smiling at the smile but taking in Grig's tone and sighing.

"Hi, Khat," she said, half-bowing to keep the boy at his work while she spoke. "I expect we're not having quite as many opinions as we used to, for a while."

Grig's chuckle was immediate. "Guess I got my orders, Khat."

Khat shook her head, and shrugged. "Can't do much about it right now, but maybe before the run gets started we can have us a better crew meeting and get some of this 'crew and passenger' stuff cleared down. . . ."

"She's right you know," Seeli allowed, dabbing at a drip on Travit's wrinkled face. "Travit's in Jethri's space in more ways than one. Won't be a big issue for a few roundabouts, but in the long haul we could see some friction. 'Course, always the chance Iza'll get a look at just the right place and retire from the seat . . ."

Khat's reaction was almost a snort, and Travit's face turned to hers with the sudden recognition that someone else was present.

Khat smiled and Travit did, and then Grig spoke, low and serious, turning all the other faces in the room toward his.

"As to your question, Khat, I think it's very likely that there are Liaden ships on port much of the time. Doesn't surprise me—the mines do some business with Liadens, and so do the farms. Besides, you know the equations. Franticle's a spot where it makes sense to break long Jumps in the sector, what with the MIF factor so high on trying to go double or more around here."

Khat nodded, noncommittally admitting, "True."

Missing in Flight happened more in some regions than others, and this was one with a higher chance than others. Some pilots claimed there were ghost ships in the dark clouds of gas, waiting to unveil themselves to unsuspecting crews before adding one more to the MIF roster. Others pointed to the oddities of energy flow and density in that dark wall. Since part of what pilots depended on Jump was precise mass and energy duplication, the possibility of lumps in the undercurrents and underpinnings was not to be denied.

Travit sneezed milk and Khat looked at Grig.

"So you're not concerned?"

He shrugged. "Not enough input, Khat. Let's see how many of those ships are close when we peel the pods out, or when we check in at the port. That's where we'll know if we've got issues, I'd guess. And you can probably get the trade shop to pull up ships, history by home port—calling Solcintra will get you seventy or eighty percent of Liaden ships. Just go in with Paitor's key or your pilot's card . . ."

Khat nodded.

"Watching it," she agreed. "We're watching it."

• • • ✳ • • •

Crew stood by not quite calm while the docking was being lined up, Iza and Khat snug in the control room with Cris and everyone else on wait-and-hold.

With the ship having to match multiple connects on this dock, and the walk-in lock-to-lock arrangements a little too snug for comfort but the station only offering lock-to-lock or station-owned tube, the sometimes tedious hard-lock was the best, the three pilots had agreed, with the tube being more trouble than it was worth once the stability bars and pressure joints were considered. It would have been different if they'd take a flex tube from the *Gobelyn's Market* side, but Franticle True's lookout was that they didn't risk tube blowout on the main structure, that being what was available today and for the next port-week.

Crew, being spacers, took on a bit of extra tension with lock-to-lock, and that was magnified by more than a trifle since they needed real people for certification and account set-up before anyone else could even take off for a joy walk on the station, much less have the ship land on Franticle True itself.

The fact was, sending two on the first groundside run made more sense security-wise than sending one, and if they were sending two, it made more sense not to send two pilot Gobelyns, nor two of the top four in the command chain, nor two with neither a trader nor a top Gobelyn, nor did it make sense to send the chief pilot . . .

Iza'd not been entirely pleased with the arrangements Cris and Seeli'd brought her, complete with decision tree and walkout schedule.

Her druthers would have been doing everything that needed done by 'lectronics and trade office serial numbers and invoices, or up here stationside, but the need for full legal witnessed signature with scans meant there wasn't much choice about sending Paitor and if they sent Paitor then there wasn't any sense in sending Khat, currently pilot two, and then the choice got thin quick: Cris was fast enough to play security but didn't have the experience, Iza had the experience to be security but was already out of the match for being top pilot and top

Gobelyn and, besides, Iza was a little too ready to step up for that fight, as anyone who'd seen her in nose-close confrontation could say.

Iza's only actual administrative quibble with the walkouts was that it seemed a shame that if they got down to the last possible walk-arounds that Grig couldn't go with the kid and Seeli instead of Khat, but true being true, that could look like Grig was getting preferential treatment with a double leave, but the only one she shared that with was Khat. Since Khat was also the one taking lead on the docking, Iza wanting to test Khat's new-earned range of experience, there wasn't a lot of talk.

Khat, being on the spot, kept the crew up to date, with time-to-latch estimates every several minutes while the locals gave her guidance. Once they gave over final control to her she kept a running commentary going, knowing that Grig and Paitor were waiting to welcome customs and then be off for certification.

* * * ✳ * * *

The station was noisy enough, the so-called main deck encompassing five levels and a variety of ships and traffic from local commuters off to the moons and outer stations to direct-flight pod ships too big or too specialized to land anywhere with an appreciable atmosphere. Paitor, in his trader role, had led the three-man customs crew on a brief tour of the ship, the bored agents making it plain that they didn't much care what was on the ship as long as what was on the ship didn't come off.

To land groundside Franticle True, yes, they'd need a customs check. As long as the *Market*'s basic plan resembled what they'd filed—after all they had the recent rebuild records to hand!—customs was pleased to have them there, paying attachment fees by the second while waiting for the pods to be switched out by local operators, which ought to be starting any minute now.

The hard-docked airlock meant that every trip in or out could be watched and recorded by the lock's built-in video cameras, sniffers, and sensors. . . .

Two of the customs team took the lead and allowed introductions to flow over them, the third customs guy taking up a spot behind them as they moved out.

"Pleasant," was what Grig said to Paitor once their escort set off at a pace, Grig pointing vaguely to the green-and-purple vines climbing gridwork not far over their heads.

"Makes it feel just like home, don't you think?" suggested Paitor.

Here their guide, Lead Agent Henrik, fell for the conversational bait: "Ah, I see you appreciate our ongoing program to welcome travelers to a homelike environment! These plants are a project voluntarily funded by our merchants and appreciative visitors— eventually, all of this deck will have a canopy of green, with flowers as appropriate for the season. I am so glad you noticed!"

The loopers exchanged glances warily, having heard the phrase given in Terran rather than Trade. "Voluntarily funded . . ."

Grig's hands moved slightly, which Paitor took to be another comment, seeing as how the hands said *Careful double watch set* and then Grig added in his best amazed-by-the-city voice "And look, why they even have Liadens here!"

The Liadens *were* there allright, six of them, with three in piloting jackets over ship's livery and three more, without the jackets, all conspicuously looking at something else; conveniently here was a wall and false ceiling, among the green-twined yellow flowers . . .

"I guess they're impressed, too," Grig said, varying his walk so that Paitor could be ahead of them as they needed to go single file behind their escorts momentarily as they entered a crowded food court.

"There is a lot going on," Paitor admitted, allowing the more collegial of the customs chaps in front of them to wax poetic about the station, the history of the Franticle stellar group, the superiority of the current administrators over those just thrown out of office a few months ago, the . . .

Paitor's hand wave of *a lot going on* encompassed an alcove Grig had already spotted, his nod acknowledging that he, too, had seen two more Liadens in livery there, watching them walk by.

"Indeed there is!" the custom man replied.

Coming at them, another set of persons, these a solemn mixed lot of Terrans and Liadens, three of each, none liveried but one in full trader regalia from bright-work boots to begemmed rings on fingers and multiple wristlets of precious metals.

The tour-minded customs agent saw the oncoming trader and committed an abominable bow on the run which had Paitor and Grig suppressing laughter . . .

"We have of late been expanding trade opportunity for our sector and the outreach has been quite successful as you see. Why, from far Solcintra itself come some of the galaxy's most important traders, eager to make sure that Franticle takes its proper place in the pantheon of major trade routes."

"Why, in that case, your honor," offered Grig suddenly, "I'd suppose you'll have available a recent almanac or gazetteer for our edification, perhaps even a dozen-year history of arrivals and departures. Surely your Liaden traders would expect such?"

Paitor caught up the tone then, his questions inspiring their host. The short remainder of their walk was an encomium to the founders of Franticle, who'd themselves brought other worlds out of the darkness of the early days, and even been part of the establishment of Standard Years and time back when Liadens had encountered remnants of the intra-Terran wars.

Full of attention, the pair from *Gobelyn's Market* absorbed the history with good grace, hearing the last of it in an inner office with ugly plastic furniture, walls full of the portraits of new leaders, and before each portrait, vases of flowers in an astonishing range of colors.

Just as they tended to the formalities of account setting, the pair tended to slipping of appropriate bribes ostensibly to assist with the general greening project, the careful avoidance of local political connivance, the slipping of another set of bribes to assist with the "coloration project," with Grig preferring to support some subtle blue flowers as sampled in front of the gray-headed and bearded Vice Chair of Environmental Improvement while Paitor made sure to like the very bright reds as shown before the largest portrait, that of the Mentor of Youth.

Henrik guided them to the office door, the joint bribes securely in his control.

"There," said Paitor, "we're to leave now—but wait, did we find the access codes for those gazettes or almanacs? We're here, after all, about setting up new routes and perhaps making a hub. Those codes . . ."

Henrik looked perplexed by this direct question, and then shook his head.

"Traders, I cannot give codes and angles to someone who has not been accepted to the Franticle Navigation Guild. I think though—since you're already scheduled to drop pods here, and get what you need from the local feeds—I think that I may be able to . . . Hold, please!"

The pilots watched outside traffic on the overhead screen as they waited, Paitor offering Grig small bets on the pedestrians and their destinations and professions.

Henrik returned, smiling.

"I believe we are where we wish to be, Pilots." He nodded to himself more than to them, smiling again.

"From here, you'll need no escort to your ship, for I am sure experienced traders such as yourself have taken note of the way—and as for deck passage, my signature assures! If have any challenges, you have complete authorizations, certifications, and recognitions! Do not fail to use them! And understand, my name carries weight onworld as well as off!

"So here, "my name, Gentles, and information! Feel free to call upon me at your least need—I am sure I can cure any issue."

He shook hands first with "Trader Paitor" and then with "Chief Hand Grig" and to each offered as a parting gift a thick stack of cards. The outer cards were simple business cards of high rag content, but within each stack were stiffer cards, thinner, as might be used to swipe a terminal.

"I've included also some odds and ends of traffic notes for you, to help you make your routings easier."

He ushered them out, adding carefully, "And also, Traders, my friend and fellow classmate Yassir Bluestone often leads the full customs team—do let him know you've spoken to me and I approve of your coloration choices, which you made respectfully!"

The door slid closed behind them, as the hall traffic swirled busily by.

"And so," said Paitor, "now we know who to pay on customs."

Grig nodded, moving ahead, scanning for space in the flow of traffic and then using a quick even-up hand wiggle to show his reservations about the arrangements as well as to point out an opening.

"That means we're not going to be making all that much on this run. . . ."

"Running with cargo is better than running without, and we'll do reasonable. We'll call it a shake-out. Needed something not too complicated and once we're in place we'll probably find us a few somethings on spec—"

"Shift change!" Paitor's observed as locals clad in colors matching the flowers they'd voluntarily supported filled the deck, making headway difficult and conversation impossible. It wasn't until they were at *Gobelyn's Market's* own gate that Grig stopped in the lee of the entry ramp, using his height to advantage as he scanned the throng.

Grig unsealed the lock and frowned as the inner cycle worked. Neither had touched their stacks of cards as yet, and neither mentioned it now, with Grig making the quick swipe of *alert on* hand-sign.

"We were followed," he said in low tones as they waited for the lock to cycle. "One woman—a pilot by dress—was waiting for us and followed well behind; she's walked past and was pretty intent on us in a 'not looking at you' kind of way."

"I know pilots, and so do you. Maybe looking for a berth, might just be looking for a tumble!"

The lock sniff-puffed as it opened, the *Market's* cooler, drier air welcoming them as they left the din behind.

"Don't know that many Liaden pilots, Paitor. How about you?"

Paitor shook his head, "Not that many, huh? I do wonder what we got ourselves by pushing Jeth out!"

"It'll calm, I expect, it'll calm."

"Mention it all-crew before we touch down," Paitor suggested, and then the inner lock opened.

Chapter Twenty-Five

• • • • ❈ • • • •

Gobelyn's Market, Franticle

THE SHIP WAS QUIET NOW in the unnatural way it always was when worldside on a full-pressure and full-size planet, where the sheer weight of the atmosphere and pull of the gravity made everyone—and the ship too— a smidge too heavy.

The cheerful Franticle air control tower'd been talking about how nice a day it was, and when they were off talking to someone else, the radio brought them sucker ads and propaganda in local dialects as well as Trade and Terran, a noisy mix-up that grated on everyone, especially Iza, who merely amplified the noise to complain of it.

Khat's preparations had let her leave the flight deck to Iza and Cris, with Paitor as backup, the *Market* echoing with the piped-through sounds of the landing. They were set for one Standard Day, and in that time needed to do the official stuff and let the rest of the ship get a walk. Paitor . . . well, he'd surprised Khat . . .

"Really, Iza, you'd think we were planning a frontal assault instead of a visit with the licensors. You've got you and Cris, and I have work . . ."

"We all have work to do, and since you're listed as a pilot on the lists, you can let that history go until we're down," Iza insisted. "Might as well all get with the program here, since Cris is going to be looking at oddities while I bring her in. You get to back us both up and pull in your precious trade scans at the same time!"

In between the sucker ads and mixed in with the propaganda was a reminder that they ought not to stray off course in landing, on account of once they were under customs-zone lock deviation from course, landing outside the zones could mean complete ship strip search and all kinds of other bad things. It was a more or less common warning from planets that did it this way, but it sounded ugly. Paitor and Iza being careful on this head, and Khat too, following their example, hadn't ever had to deal with this kind of a problem personally. The noise had to be heard . . . but once down, the speaker'd been quieted to local news . . .

Ship sound, too, was quiet now that the door was sealed. Khat leaned into the lock's sidewall, patting her pockets, hideaways, and wallets one last time before pushing the cycle button. Franticle was more a practical world than a safe world, so security was up to her—but then that was always the case, the way she saw it, even more so since her run-in on Banth.

Grig, beside her, was less active, standing with his eyes closed and waiting patient and silent, for their first sight of Franticle True. Maybe he'd been here before, after all. There was a lot more to Grig than met the eye, she'd gathered from Paitor, a lot more than just a big guy older than a kid and not to full grayhead yet. He'd been on the first-out crew dozens of times for *Gobelyn's Market*, that was sure, and maybe hundreds of times altogether, depending on where that age gauge of his actually settled.

Waiting, carry check done, her hand automatically checked the ID card hung round her neck and she made sure Grig's was on and showing, which was a waste of time since he'd hardly make *that* mistake. She pushed CYCLE to let Franticle True's nice day in.

• • • ※ • • •

The nice day was too hot and wet and smelly for Khat's taste, and oddly noisy too as she stepped into a barrage of screeches, caws, tweets, and flutters. Birds, upset birds even—hundreds of them or more, wheeling overhead or walking dazedly on the ground. Feathers lay scattered about, littering the bleached gray of the port's hard apron, with some few more wafting down from the sky in arcs.

There was more noise beyond that of the birds. An underlying rumble of powerful engines working somewhere close, with distant horns and warn-aways added to the din.

Grig waved away a swirl of mottled green-gray with a mumbled

"Damn!" and then pointed toward the side of the ship away from the lock.

"Third landing ring, spot forty-four. They gave us a swamp and didn't tell the owners ahead of time."

Khat was swatting at the air now too, grimacing at bits of fuzz that floated and fell, but the feather fall seemed mostly over so she brushed her formerly crisp and clean officer's outfit.

"Should have worn a hat!" She offered this to the world at large but only Grig was in range to hear, and he answered with a grunt.

By then Khat was oriented and could see the swamp in question, barely three ship lengths behind them. A breeze blew straight at them from the swamp. In the other direction, all was flat as far as she could see, with buildings and ships that popped up onto the landscape at random intervals. Closer and not interrupting that panorama, a knee-high orange fence skirted a section of the same gray pavement they stood on, and on the other side of that a scooter-cab was arriving, striped diagonally in red and white, bearing a yellow crest on the door.

"Official lift?" Khat asked, but then several more vehicles came, decked out in other stripe combinations, all crowding, with several of the drivers exiting the vehicles and vying for their attention with waving scarves.

"Orderly place," was what Grig said, picking his pace up. "The red-and-white was first, so I'm good for going with them, if there's room for the pair of us."

The walk was longer than it seemed, and at the end of it there were half a dozen of the vehicles, with drivers standing near, offering hands for their bags, which instead they both tucked carefully under arms.

"Here sir! Pilot, here!" one driver yelled, blue scarf waving like a flag, and another, with green and purple insisted, "Fastest driver, cleanest taxi," and another, "Rebates for round trip; rebates!"

A ruddy-faced woman, with no scarf but a jacket and helmet matching her scooter's orange and white, cut artfully in front of the others, inching toward them with an exaggerated grin, saying in mixed Trade and Terran, "First in line, I have most honors to travel you to trade offices!"

Complaints then, from the other drivers, led by the woman with the blue scarf—they were all women Khat saw, wondering if she should have read the planet guide to see if only women could drive—but there'd been a change of regime, according to the cross talk from other ships, so the planet guides might not have helped.

With a flick of the wrist and a gentle twist, Grig danced a step, allowing Khat ahead and past the interloper, while the others raised their voices in a thick and indistinguishable dialect not meant for outsiders. Drivers from the back of the line closed on the orange-and-white quickly, with much waving of hands.

The pilots took the opportunity to drop into the original red-and-white, sitting side by side on the bench seat. The driver managed a "Thank you for your care" and then turned her back on them as the near-silent machine sped away from her competitors and the noisy birds. It wasn't the pleasantest world Khat had been on, but it beat cold mud.

· · · ✻ · · ·

"First come, first served," Khat read out loud from the "Procedures of This Office" chart posted at the front of the room. It was an important room on the top floor of an important and ugly square building deep in the heart of Franticle's important government section. Why they put it here, where the denizens and the citizens had to compete for lift space, she couldn't divine, but that was like so much about planetary affairs to her: just how it was, might as well accept it.

Still, for the third time in the last hour, she read the second line of the procedures out loud, the one just after "Good order will be maintained at all times."

They'd been there four hours before she started, and each time she read it, she was louder, and closer to the target, even if timed to go under the overloud PA announcement of the next person or group to be handed in to an examiner.

There were two targets, actually: the clerk in front who apportioned the people in the sitting line to either of the two closed offices being the one she was most interested in expressing herself to, while the guard at the back who brought people forward was obviously under her direction, and hence forgettable.

Barney, a local pilot working on a license upgrade, looked worried at Khat's third iteration. He didn't move away from her—he'd managed to post himself to her right side shortly after he'd arrived—but he was clearly not wanting to hear a fourth time. They'd been moving, after all, and now were in the first row, about where they should have been two hours before if a series of passes, flashes of cash, and secret words hadn't managed to drop others into spots between them and the access clerk. The cashflash was way too expensive for the *Gobelyn's Market* crew to handle . . .

"So, Revo Nine?" He'd been grilling her carefully and was amusing enough for Khat to allow it to go on. She wasn't likely to get tumble-time anytime soon, but a good flirt was a good flirt, and practice didn't hurt even if she had a bed warmer on ship.

"Sure," she allowed, "two of them. One was damn ugly rigged for asteroids and small-body work so I wouldn't call it normal—I wouldn't have certified it to land in atmosphere but I could have if they didn't need it to lift again."

"You got to know your ship," he allowed. "You can take a decent ship outside of them limits but you gotta know yours, too!"

Nothing for it but to agree with this wisdom, so Khat nodded, cut a couple hands full of *true course true course* in hand-sign, and went on.

"The other one was a sweet little thing," she reminisced, ignoring the guy's previous mention that a Revo Nine was a middling big ship to handle, "and I had the same one three trips, not back to back. As pure on the last trip as the first. I had a good second each time—different second each time, you know! If I had a good second I could fly one of them all year and not feel I was wasting my time. Damnedest thing was that I had the junk buggy in between. So I went from a Ver 3B to a 1-C Alter back to my Ver 3B." Khat poured the sad on, and his face got sad, too.

"Get your hands mushed up if you have to do that too often," he said and she nodded.

He'd already handed a card to the patient Grig, who was working on pilot catnaps as they waited, and two to Khat—one "with my direct lines, you see," and he was leaning a bit in her direction when there was yet another multibody stir at the back of the room. Khat sighed, but he stiffened where he sat, turning to glare at the newcomers, who were speaking a little loud, like they didn't trust people could hear them.

"*Therinfel!* Tradeship *Therinfel*, here's your call."

The ship's name was said as if *Therinfel's* folks had been sitting in line the whole time, Khat saw, and wondered if they'd somehow inserted that ship's name ahead of others in the sign-in record. She'd closed her eyes briefly when she'd heard the name. Knowing the ship was in-system was not the same as being in close proximity to crew members.

· · · ⁑ · · ·

"Liadens!" Barney said it quietly, but loud enough that several others in their row and the row behind heard, and the sounds they made, low though they were, were not pleasant.

Grig, Khat saw, was no longer catnapping, but like her he was not turning to glare. After the others turned and grumbled, Khat permitted herself a glance and allowed her elbow to touch Grig's, her fingers forming a quick *prior pilot sighting* and then slower, spelled out, *Banth.*

He nodded as the rustle of cloth and boots moved toward the front of the room, turning slightly with bored eyes and a yawn.

Three Liadens, it was, Khat's *witness fight third one* getting to Grig and maybe to Barney, too, before she turned her face toward the local, saying, "But you know a Revo Nine just does not have the go-on of a Kavin. Any of them."

The third one in line was a pilot—she'd seen him in the bar at Banth—who took her measure when she'd come up armed after flooring the chel'Gaiban, and seen him tactfully not go for his gun or hideaway. She didn't know how to read the Liaden insignia, didn't know if he was just a pilot, or if he was head pilot. Didn't much matter; if he got a good look at her, he'd remember.

"You've flown a Kavin? We don't get too many out this way—I think I've only seen one."

For his side, Grig twisted in his seat so that Khat's back was against his and her face turned away from the new arrivals.

"They're great. Not a real high-volume yard. Someone told me they're a knockoff of a Liaden design, but all I have to say is that everything on them is sweet. Never saw a ship where everything was balanced quite so nice. I've flown two and I can tell you I'd have taken it anywhere they wanted me to go with either of them. The one was practically a courier—five minipods was all!—and the other was a double rack with two internal minipods."

Khat extolled the Kavins until Grig touched her elbow; when she dared look two locals were coming out of the second examination room all in smiles while the clerk escorted the Liadens into the same room with a flourish, ducking in behind them and pulling the door to. The inmates of the waiting area mumbled among themselves, Khat not the only one to shake her head.

"So you don't like Liadens either?"

Khat sighed slightly, studied her nails, looked across the small distance to Barney's hopeful face. "Can't say that—haven't met all that many of them myself."

"You've met some? They actually talked with you?" His face showed he doubted this very much.

"They're people, that's all. Grew up different. But yeah, met a couple, and I know a trader—loop born he is—who got himself a trader's spot on a Liaden ship called *Elthoria*."

Barney's lips unsneered, went bland, tried a smile.

He looked away. "Never did meet any. Passed a couple up to Franticle Orbital, had more rings on than my grandmother and just stopped where they were like they had no idea how traffic works on a deck." He paused, and his face hardened, showing more lines on it than Khat would have guessed he could muster. "It was more like there wasn't anyone else around who was worth thinking about!"

Khat thought about that even as she nodded. "Could feel that way—I think that's the *melant'i* stuff. If they don't know where they stand with you they have got to assume they're the big jets and you're not." She smiled across, expanded the thought train—

"Figure it like walking into a bar at the end of a route. If you're in the big room, you grab a seat, look around, see if you know anyone, or if you want to know someone. Mostly everything's even."

He shrugged, nodded.

"But if you walk into that same bar and walk right on into that back room, the select lounge, the premium zone—whatever they call it there—then, you walk right in, you'd better know someone or they better know you, 'cause else everyone needs proof you belong there."

He nodded, agreeable.

"That's how Liadens live mostly, like they're all in a premium room all the time, always ready to come out and be biggest jet or sitting back counting how far they gotta go to get there, or how careful they've got to be of who. Always on the pose for 'I'm more dangerous than you are' I guess. Where they come from, one mistake, one snub to the wrong clan, and you could be in for a decaying orbit!"

"Sounds like too much trouble to me," the local replied with a sniff.

"Not easy, is my guess."

"But hey, tell me who you know on a Liaden ship? A trader even, that's got to be a first. Talk about not easy!"

They nodded together over the ease, ignoring the sound of someone well behind them in the queue giving up and walking out. As if on cue, Grig reached to a leg pouch and offered Khat and Barney each a pilot's fruit bar, pulling them back in a seamless motion when the clerk finally emerged from the meeting room she'd taken Therinfel's representatives to.

Khat felt Grig do as she did—look away from the room, toward Barney. Barney did not look away, instead moving his head to peer around Khat with avid interest, as did half the room. The clerk closed the door quickly, avoiding looking into the meeting room or at the larger assembly, finding a path to her desk by dead reckoning or habit, whichever was stronger.

Grig handed out the rations again, taking his thanks from Barney, who was quiet while he ate, giving Khat a break. They'd barely finished when the other room opened and in short order the people in front of them rose, only to have the clerk wave them aside with a curt, "No confirmation on that bond your agent was to post. You can wait, but I have a crowd and must call the next."

"*Gobelyn's Market*? Tradeship *Gobelyn's Market*."

Khat winced at the volume of the announcement, and perhaps misreading that expression, Barney patted her on the knee before she rose, whispering, "Good luck, Pilots!" as they rose to enter enter the inner sanctum.

· · · ✳ · · ·

"*Gobelyn's Market*? Is *Gobelyn's Market* crew here?" The words came in an awkward Trade, as if they'd learned from someone who barely knew Trade.

It was unexpected, and Khat already at the ragged edge of polite after what Route Administrator Clowfar had called an "expedited" hearing on the ability of the *Market* to operate within Franticle's space as need be. They'd all the ship's public technical details with them, and an abbreviated discussion of the piloting depth on the ship, and of course the go-ahead sign from officials on the station. She'd thought herself exhausted—and this was not what she needed.

Grig's sign was subtle but Khat caught it, taking the right side, so she could cross-draw if need be. The express lift was half full, with two Liadens unknown to Khat focusing their attention on her as they dropped fifty-seven floors at a pace unsettling to the seven or eight citizens if not to the pilots. She'd seen them too late, but really, they'd been good about using the taller and bulkier locals as cover, and stepped in just as the doors slid shut.

"*Gobelyn's Market*?" inquired the tall one again, he a good hand shorter than Khat and a head and half or more shorter than Grig. He bowed with a flourish to her corner, taking in Grig's presence a half a heartbeat after he'd started his bow and trying to include all who might qualify.

They were posing Liaden: both competent-looking, both with hands close enough to pull points that they might be trouble if that was their goal.

Grig bowed to both of them, a bow that meant something more to them than to Khat because they both stiffened and gave him more attention. Khat used their discomfiture to adjust herself.

"Yes, consider us of the *Market* if you will, Gentles. It is good of you to have noticed."

Khat inwardly chuckled, for to her eye Grig's stance was exactly what was needed in close quarters. He'd looked to have gained twenty percent in volume and ten percent in height and he'd managed to speak both softly and at volume at once. He spoke a well-accented Trade, and then in Liaden said something Khat only caught part of, the part that was *Therinfel*.

A different bow from the tall one; a pause of the machine brought them with a press of gravity to an intermediate floor where none entered and five exited, squeezing between the Liadens gingerly. The lift dropped again, the Liadens ignoring the locals.

Grig chuckled, saying quietly to Khat, "Yes, our friends are of *Therinfel*, as we'd surmised." He switched then to *sotto voce* loop lingo, adding, "Stinks shifties can't sneeze no-perm, brain slogs mudtrap."

Right. These were flunkies, boss must be waiting at the main exit, mudtrap clearly being ground level.

She nodded agreeably to Grig, smiled at the Liadens, said nothing, shifted slightly, saw one of the Liadens shift, too. Was there a point to this or had the Liadens accidentally taken the same lift? Perhaps they were merely recognizing fellow traders, after all. Or perhaps being two on two she'd just determined which Liaden was supposed to cover her.

Another intermediate floor brought an exchange of locals, three off and three on, and Khat used that change of circumstance to put a squarely built citizen between her and her cover. She also shook her shoulder out, likely giving her cover concern about her handedness. She was ambidextrous, for what it was worth, but feeling rusty of her weapons training. She'd been so busy in the supposed off year that some things had been let to slip.

The stop at the bottom was smooth, and Khat leveraged the square fellow's lack of speed with her own quickness, taking eye motions from Grig to mean she'd go left and he right.

"Talk with us," the taller Liaden was saying as the passengers all proceeded forward at once, and Khat took her left, turned, saw that both of *Therinfel*'s crew were following her, went to slip around a pedestrian snarl and found herself face to face with the pilot she'd seen on Banth, and then today, heading into the meeting room. Beside him was a silent and cold-eyed Liaden woman wearing unmarked pilot leathers and an open sidearm.

He offered, politely and in Trade, "I see you and you see me, how good a thing this is to be recognized, Pilot. Recognized, if not met, perhaps we have some shared *melant'i*. We should talk of *Gobelyn*'s *Market,* yes, Khatelane Gobelyn? Yes. And of this Jethri and his errors. And perhaps of Balance. And of this Arin who is dead. There is a beverage shop nearby, where we have arranged a table seating. You should come."

· · · ✳ · · ·

They did come, Grig looking first to her for direction—she higher on the family charts than he, she second pilot overall to his reserve, damn the luck. But she asked his opinion with a raised eyebrow and got his reply in the form of a half-tick nod, a relief.

The beverage shop served local teas, coffee toot, and brews, with Khat's choice quick toward the high-power root tea and Grig's the same, spiced.

"You have the advantage: you know I am Khatelane Gobelyn, and this is Grig Tomas, our clan being our ship *Gobelyn's Market*. You and you—I do not know."

The woman gave a short bow and said nothing, while a larger bow came from the man, who admitted to being Ved bel'Mora Clan Traybin, a pilot of *Therinfel*. "You'll perhaps not be familiar with my clan, as we are not currently housed on Liad."

Khat nodded, repeated his name and thanked him for the share, knowing it would take a deep check for her to be sure of any clan's existence much less prove a homeworld. She turned to the female pilot beside him, who bowed again lightly, making as well a vague motion perhaps indicating lack of language.

Khat looked to Grig, who bowed to the silent woman, said a few words Khat didn't know, adding, "Grig Ric Tomas, sustaining pilot, tradeship *Gobelyn's Market*."

His head motion was a clear follow-on and the bow she made became deeper, again unreadable by Khat, followed by a few words or names.

"Cousin, we have here, I'm told, Pilot Trainee tol'Vera Clan Croyn, apprentice applicant to *Therinfel*. She has not had training of the tongues as yet, her clan not affording that necessity until proof of competence in her trade."

Khat repeated that information as best she could, despite a great deal of surety that this was no trainee pilot, nor one of any clan she'd be likely to locate in a reference source. Her language ability? Why bring one with no understanding to the table?

The others were not acknowledged, though there were five of them scattered around the room like guards. She'd dealt with retrieving Iza often enough to consider them as such. . . .

"And so," Khat said as the drinks arrived and the waitress dismissed after being sure that they'd each gotten their own order, the waitress having an accent best described as thick, "we have come to speak with you, as you are sure we have much to talk about and so much in common."

The others got what they got, with Khat remembering to offer a pseudo bow indicating thay were all able to sip now. It was as much ceremony as she had on the topic.

There was a hint of a smile on bel'Mora's face.

He bowed, saying in a slow if clear Trade, "It is clear we deal now pilot to pilot, as pilots are as direct as traders are long-winded." He made a hand motion full of emphasis, encompassing the lot of them.

"It is as I suggested, Pilot. We share a certain *melant'i*, all of us here, the *melant'i* of the practical who must reach a destination necessary for others though the others have no understanding of how the course is laid or calculated.

"Thus, directly, I shall acknowledge I am requested by the head of my trade mission, for *Therinfel* is not here alone, nor by accident, to determine if your presence here is due to ours? When traveling far from common routes, one must know and be concerned of complications—are you in fact tracking *Therinfel* on an account of a perceived incomplete Balance?"

Khat shook her head briefly, suppressing the urge to laugh and weighing the information offered. So, *Therinfel* was once again part of a mission? And this pilot not the one in charge, but following orders.

"And how would we know *Therinfel*'s destination? When last I saw your ship and yourself you were at a backworld I barely recall."

That brought bright eyes, and perhaps a glance from the woman who spoke neither Trade nor Terran.

"We do trade, Pilot, and so often traders tell other traders, just as crew tell other crew."

Khat nodded acknowledgment.

"This coincidence is that—my home ship is just now finished refits and starting on our new route, and I back to it after my hire contracts are done. Since our ship's travels are determined by the captain after the trader makes his deals, indeed, we go where the trade moves us and how the captain takes us. My job is to make it happen safely, backup to the captain. That is why I am here today, representing the ship as the captain properly stays with the ship in a system and on a world new to us."

An awkward pause, then, "You must understand that the young chel'Gaiban took much of a fall to his *melant'i* there on Banth. He was rigorously schooled on his errors by those of us senior to him in travel and port etiquette, and I doubt will ever make such an error again. Yet your proper response to his mistake becomes less sure in following after the error of your kin. That young chel'Gaibin also erred in attempting to directly deal with you on a Balance price is not in question—he should have arranged for a meeting of *qe'andra* and men of business to determine such a Balance price in an orderly fashion, don't you think?"

At this Grig bowed his way into the conversation, oddly enough speaking quick sentences to the apprentice rather than the supposed master. She briefly opened her mouth as if to reply.

Grig turned quickly to Khat—"Pardon, Khat Gobelyn, but I felt that the apprentice was being left out, and ought to know that her over pilot, who says he is not a trader, is merely pressing my pilot to admit a falsity as truth under cover of polite discourse. Since she acts backup to him, it was clear that she should know, as a matter of courtesy."

Khat blinked: yes, it would have been possible for her to have conceded a wrong point, pressed in such a fashion. Liadens, even speaking Trade, were famous for their complex contracts and hidden meanings.

An interesting bow then from the shipmaster.

"Your point is taken, sir; one must not permit a dependent to remain uninformed in a complex situation. The question of fault is always one meriting extreme attention, since badly attributed it may lead to confused action . . ."

Khat saw the hand motion of the apprentice and thought she saw a response as she continued speaking with Grig.

"And tell me, if I do not trespass on secret, how is it that you have such a clear understanding of our tongue when it is so rarely of interest among Terran spacers? An odd accent to it, perhaps an old-fashioned one."

Here Grig spread his hands wide and smiled, gently, going on in Trade. "Spacers are of many molds, Pilot, and oft have much time to spend between stars doing other than polishing brightwork. My family and my cousins have had this interest of languages—you have spoken of my cousins Jethri and Arin, and thus of my own line as well. While not proficient in all things Liaden, I believe Jethri's interest was sparked by Arin, his father."

Grig spoke a quick word to the apprentice, then turned back to Trade:

"Cousin Arin came from a family ship long involved in active study during Jump, and he'd been apprenticed to a ship where learning was prized as much as piloting. Indeed, I became Arin's pilot because of those habits of his, for he needed to study and be prepared as a commissioner. Arin refreshed his languages with me, as well as his piloting and his math and his chemistry.

"Thus Jethri's mistake—his error, if you will—might have come from his father Arin, or perhaps from before that, from our Uncle, who had the teaching of both of us. My accent surely was from him."

Grig paused with a pilot's hand flourish, indicating *operation in progress continues.*

"Now of my Uncle, what can I say? His learning? I wish I'd have the time to tell you of the things he thinks of and talks about! History is a playroom to him, culture and art his familiars! Last I saw him he was an aging man with a large library and a younger mate who challenged him not to let his mind rest, not to feel old. His travels and sources were not much shared, only the results of them.

"That is what I can tell you, Pilot, if my Liaden is old-fashioned or out dialect."

Therinfel's pilot bowed. "Ah, but see, you already have it that you are among those who are not of Liad's Highest Houses, unlike Infreya chel'Gaibin and her heir. We need not quibble over who has a better accent—as you are a learned man and I a native, we each must admit the other's facility with words adequate."

It was that pilot's turn to wave hands as if in thought.

"Still, sir, we find ourselves at odds and I wonder if we may act for a moment more as traders and less as pilots to bring our *melant'i* more in tune with one another. For my part I will begin with the assertion that your cousins are very interesting people, this Arin and this Jethri. Both holders of the Liaden tongue. Both, I gather, traders of some ability. Both, in fact, involved not only with trade usually falling within the basic—do you call them 'loops,' I think?—of Terran trade interest, but moving beyond to the larger trade spheres and routes of Liaden interests."

Grig looked to Khat, shrugged, offered to bel'Mora a nod.

"All true. As I mentioned, the family studies."

"Agreed," said the Liaden with a slight bow, "you have said. And like a good scholar, your cousin Arin, he has published, is that so?"

"He was an active man, often quoted."

"Then let me offer this, if I may. It is my belief that while young chel'Gaiban is overcareful of his *melant'i* among Liadens and undercareful of it among Terrans, his mother Infreya, as Delm Rinork, will be at pains not to involve her clan in more"—here he fell to a rolling, tumbling hand wave—"disorderly events. It is my belief that Infreya would, as a trader of some worth and cunning, be interested in the study your cousin Arin Gobelyn performed for his duties before quitting his position as commissioner. It is a document, this *Envidaria,* which is exceeding difficult to come by. In return for a copy of this study, which would of course be kept in extreme confidence, I feel Infreya might invoke a homeworld existence for her heir, since he becomes troublesome away from Liad. His means of achieving Balance, direct or indirect, against your Jethri—or against you personally, Khatelane Gobelyn—would be much reduced!"

He'd looked right at Khat with that, and so had the apprentice.

"I am not a trader," Khat allowed after a moment. "I'm a pilot, and second in command of a ship. You offer to intercede in a matter of a potential threat I'm aware of in exchange for a document I've never seen. This becomes a difficult moment for me, Pilot bel'Mora."

She sipped tea.

Grig shifted slightly, ostensibly also to have another sip of his tea. The apprentice shifted, as did Pilot bel'Mora. Eyes were careful, hands even more so.

Cup in her off hand, Khat continued with some heat and careful volume, "You must understand that the boy did wrong to grab me, but I've knocked him down and bloodied his nose in front of a bunch of people, and that's what he deserved. That's Balance, and I count that done."

She sipped more tea, weighing the cup, light angles, Grig's position . . . looked up and continued.

"Not only is there a hint of threat to me, but more to Jethri, and as far as I can see, that's done, too. It ought to be done, anyhow, the way we do things, since he's not here to agree or disagree to it. So here's what I see. You've made me a hypothetical offer to fix something that's not broken anymore, if it ever was."

Khat looked the apprentice in the eye this time, shaking her head, jetting on, "Under this hypothetical offer from someone not present is the insinuation that a failure to agree—a failure to produce what I don't have—will both continue and extend the threat. I can only program so many alternative courses, Pilot, and I'm seeing the best one for me is for my shipmate to finish our tea and then to continue our day, with thanks for your time and hospitality, and let you continue yours."

She set the empty cup down, firmly. The hand moved from the cup, clearly making the hand-sign *time,* and the follow-up movement indicating *we go.*

Grig nodded to her, placed his cup down soundlessly.

Pilot bel'Mora looked between them dispassionately, a bow which meant something she didn't know tilted toward Khat. He said something in Liaden which brought the apprentice a little straighter in the chair . . .

"Not a mistake, Pilot," Grig suggested. "Khat here, she's First in my view. Her *melant'i* must be served. We have been patient, we drank your tea, and we have heard you. If you tell us that the offer is not theoretical, but . . . but you have not done that."

"Also, Pilot," Khat broke in, "you misunderstand my view of the situation. I said I'd finished with my Balance. It was stupid of him. But I'm a spacer. I was born in space and I live in space. Shouldn't be anything that gives *me* a right to lock a man on a planet for his whole life, just on my say-so. Offering me that is like offering me a chance to stab him in the back for free—and that's not how Khat Gobelyn works. You can take *your melant'i* and walk through the mud with it!"

That brought both of the Liadens straight in their chairs but by then Grig was standing, half in front of Khat as he helped her pull her chair out, gun hand free, for all of a sudden, the stakes had risen.

"*My melant'i* need not be part of this discussion, Pilot, if you will simply admit your error. Else *Therinfel*'s bad will toward you accumulates with chel'Gaibin's. Have you no understanding . . ."

"You're not even good enough to pay for my tea," Khat said, throwing a coin on the table to cover their due, and then to Grig, "we're gone."

· · · ✳ · · ·

Gone was easier said than done, what with the uncertainty of the tearoom's staff over their hurried departure and the rush of the other Liadens to attempt to block their exit. A few seconds were wasted going around wait staff and they were out the door.

"Called off the help," Grig said as they hurried down the

still-crowded large hall. The sound of loud voices rose behind them, and a clanging, scraping noise. He signaled and they took a quick right down a service stairway, and then into a larger room with an exit onto a busy loading dock. Ignoring protests they dropped a few feet to the pavement and strode out into the hazy-bright afternoon.

"Yes," she said. "But back to the ship anyway unless you have a better plan."

He didn't. "Taxi stands are on the main routes, I'm sure."

Finding a main route that wasn't the one leading to the building they'd just left wasn't easy, but they crested a small hill and saw a corner populated with the little cars.

"Do we have one?" Khat asked as they jogged that way, their plain garb marking them against the colorful dress of the local citizens. Ahead, the taxi stand . . .

"One of what?"Grig sounded slightly winded.

"A copy of Arin's study."

"If Paitor hasn't told you, you're not supposed to know."

She said something quite impolite under her breath. "I've been told something now by someone, haven't I?"

They hurried around the pedestrians, sweat breaking out on both of them.

"Until we can talk to Paitor, quiet on it. He should have said something."

"Other way?" Khat said, pointing to one of the Liadens from the tea shop arriving at the taxi stand—

"Transit this way," Grig suggested, pointing to a sign Khat couldn't decipher.

"No, wait. We might as well just get a taxi," Khat insisted. "There's only one of them!"

. . . ⁜ . . .

In retrospect, they might as well have broken up the beverage shop. That was Khat's first take on it, but Paitor sensibly pointed out they'd have had local damages to pay, and local injuries, too, within the city's jurisdiction. That might not only have been expensive, but fatal.

"They're coming off a coup, Khat—any excuse to show how well they keep order and discipline. They could have sent in a squad and shot the lot of you, claiming you were fomenting revolution."

"What you should have done was not talk to them at all," Iza said bluntly. "Is that what I've raised? Is this how I run my ship? Not enough sense to see a trap on the way? You, Grig? We sent you because you're supposed to have sense!"

"My call, Iza," Khat insisted. "It was my call from the first word they gave us. We needed to hear . . ."

"Jethri. Jethri! Damned if that's not what you heard, isn't it? They said *Jethri* and the both of you were all ears!"

Khat took a deep breath and dove into the argument. "What we heard was a couple of things. To start off, we heard *Gobelyn's Market.* Sound familiar? *Gob-e-lyn's Mar-ket*! They'd announced us in the exam room, so anyone there could have heard of us. So yes, that got our attention. Then they said another name you might have heard of. They said *Khat-e-lane Gob-e-lyn.* You know, the name on all my licenses and certifications. Same last name as your brother has. Same one you have, right? *Go-ba-lin* one said, but the other got it right."

Paitor tried to break in, but Khat wasn't giving up the floor, and Iza started and Khat still didn't give way.

"So yes, then they said Jethri's name. They did, and we both heard it, right, Grig?"

Grig nodded and signed *yes*, but in the flow of things Khat kept going, not giving an edgewise for anyone else's words quite yet.

"They also said another name you might have heard of, right after. Tell me if you remember this name, will you, because sometimes I think you don't. They told us they wanted to talk to us about 'dead Arin.'"

Into the ensuing silence came Grig's voice, very low. "They told us they wanted to talk about Balance and Arin, too. The exact phrase they used was 'This Arin who is dead.'"

Iza glared at them all, the piloting crew, Paitor and Khat up front, with Grig half behind, and Cris too. The kids had been left out, and Seeli and Dyk. They'd get a report later, but for the moment the ship was on port lockdown, sitting at a perpetual ten minutes to lift on a hotpad they were paying premium rates for, all the pilots on the flight deck.

"Arin has nothing to do with this ship," she finally said, "and hasn't for more than a decade. Arin's nothing to this ship. What does dead Arin have to do with *Gobelyn's Market,* do they think? What could they . . ."

Iza raised her hands to shoulder height and flung her arms out as if pushing a heavy weight away, turning away from the lot of them before grimacing behind a hand held over her mouth. Her gaze focused somewhere else—maybe through the deck itself and the planet and out into space—and then she closed her eyes and raised them again, open to the group.

"Can't let this get in the way of the ship, can we?" she said.

Khat agreed with a quick, "Right," nodding and gently adding, "but that's why we had to see what they were on about. Liadens have these feuds and Balances they do. We all know it, and we needed to know if it was Jethri they were mad at, or me, or if Arin had crossed someone thirty years ago and left a Balance against the ship that was just coming forward. Liadens are like that."

Iza nodded at Khat, and then at Grig, and then spun back to Khat with an exasperated sigh.

"So, you were PIC on this trip and you had to do a pilot's choice. Grig was running second and backed up the Pilot in Charge, like he's supposed to. The fact is that once you were in that tea parlor, problems were going to happen. I'll accept that. Now explain how we got from a tea parlor in the middle of the city to a taxi battle in front of the damn ship?"

• • • ⋇ • • •

Khat went over the day again, glossing over the trip in and omitting this time the amount of general fees, service fees, taxes, route certification charges, and suggested facilitation payments required to get them into and out of the routing permit meeting.

"Once we were out of the building and got to the taxi stand, a Liaden was in a spot to get in our way—he had a comm, and was trying to raise someone when we got there. He didn't want a taxi, but I guess he was under orders to make sure we didn't take one, so he tried to block the door. Grig just went around to the other side, and then he tried to block Grig so I ducked in my side and he stood in Grig's way. Another taxi pulled up then—"

Here she shook her head. "And that's how it started, because then the rest of *Therinfel*'s crew was running up and I told the driver to launch, and Grig ducked into the second taxi—it was all orange stripes—and the guy with the comm tried to get in and Grig let him . . . and I lost track of his course.

"At the next light there was Grig right behind me grinning like a fool but in a red stripe and signing what looked like he was going the *long way home*, with the orange stripe right behind him. My driver asked me if there was a problem and I told her, since she knew I was going to the port, that the orange stripe was trying to beat me out of a deal and I needed to get to the ship first. So she looked at me in that mirror and asked, 'Lady own deal?'"

Grig laughed then. "So, what I see is that little blue stripe on afterburner and I asked my driver to lose the orange stripe. She'd seen me signal to Khat and laughed, and took a suicide turn at the next corner, and another—I shoulda had a brew!"

Khat shrugged. "Didn't do all that much good, I guess, because when I got out here the field customs crew were out, checking every single cab in line, in single file. I came in first—but my driver told me she saw Grig's cab down the queue, and while I paid her off there he was, but in front of him came this bel'Mora and the apprentice, with bel'Mora jumping out and yelling that I'd insulted their *melant'i* and sullied their name.

"That's where the taxi drove between them and me. And their driver tried to push her out of the way, and then Grig's driver . . . got him out and got out of the cab herself, I guess . . .

"And that's when the other Liaden showed up finally and he tried to wade in . . ."

Grig tried to say something but Iza held her hand up.

"Traffic violations. Inciting to violate public propriety. Evading building security." She threw the sheaf of hardcopy on the desk, shaking her head. "I admit it ain't assaulting an officer of the law, but the pair of you better never talk to me about world-side decorum again, if you get my drift? You better never talk to me too hard about keeping the ship's name clean."

Paitor broke in then, "Iza, you know the port's seen worse than this. Only a mark on the record, and we're not even—"

"Look, brother, did we see it or not? It wasn't until the proctors were standing 'bout right beside them that they really started throwing punches. And it isn't date night at the bar stuff. I mean look at this one!" Here she reached into the pile and pulled out a fluttery white sheet.

"Impersonation of an inebriate!" She waved her hands about, "Whoever heard of impersonation of a drunk?"

Paitor held up his hands then. "So far, that's what we have for our investment at the station, sister. Every violation they saw had to be answered. They were all dropped as far as they could. May I?"

Iza handed the paper over and he gathered the rest from the desk.

"Here, it is noted, our first time on port, unfamiliar with local custom; here it is reduced to six days' restraint reduced to cash fine; here it is—"

Iza waved him silent.

"So we got a break. A very expensive break. But what made you try to deck the guy, Khat, with the proctor right there?"

Khat looked to Grig, which Iza didn't miss. She didn't miss the direct line hand-signal, either.

Khat nodded at both of them.

"Needed to do something before he said something in Terran—he wasn't doing a good job with Trade, but I needed to interrupt, just in case. But we gotta be sure to tell Dyk and I guess the youngers, too, so they'll be wary."

Iza shook her head.

"So what he do? Call you a looper?"

Khat grimaced and gathered some breath in case she'd need to shout over Iza. When Iza just made a face, Khat went on.

"He threatened me. He threatened all of us, and the ship too. First he said we'd better be willing to deal with him or a go-between—actually that *you* better be willing to deal better than Grig and me—because even he was willing to share the rumors that were going round, the rumors that might get us banned from one end of the galaxy to the other. And he told me it wasn't even a tight rumor, so if he started, people could check up on the rumor and we'd be in trouble because some Terrans are saying the same thing about *Gobelyn's Market,*"

"What's he saying? If he's talking about Old Tech, I can let anyone come on board and search, right? Right, Grig?"

"I already promised Seeli I don't have any Old Tech, Iza, and I told you I don't. So unless you got something left over from Arin yourself—I bet Paitor don't!—there's no Old Tech here. I'm not happy, I'll tell you, that you had to ask me."

"Stand down, Grig!" Khat realized she'd said it, and had everyone's attention.

"Look—he said something in Liaden, and then he said it in Trade. He was getting louder, like he was going call it to the proctor. He said 'Clone,' dammit, he's going to call us all clones!"

Grig snorted, but it didn't override Iza's strained laughter.

"Clones, is it? Gonna get us locked out of ports 'cause we're all clones? Well we don't need to worry about that 'cause I got that problem outta here. And Grig, the way I figure, didn't give Seeli a clone, and ain't none of us is going to be matches. They can gene test me all they want."

Khat made a noise like a spit.

"I'm doing my best to get us thrown out, Iza. I expect to be captain on this ship one day and I don't want to have clone tests over my head all my life!"

. . . ·❖· . . .

The throwing-out part of Khat's plan worked well enough, with *Therinfel*'s crew already shuttled out to their orbiting ship before the *Market*'s final judgments were paid. The *Market*'s lift out was a vicious polar trajectory meant to fit them between ordinary traffic in a direct-to-Jump injection pattern that would have been fine if they were going to Liad but else wasn't a good solution for any of the destinations a working family ship of dedicated Terran loopers was likely to go. Grig cajoled Iza for a dispensation, getting Cris to sit backup to Khat on the lift, seeing that they were pressing the envelope on Travit's cradle's comfort levels and he had the medical certificates no one else had.

Khat reported in and as PIC did the lift itself, with Cris effectively Second Board while Iza kept busy with the problem of turning the polar orbit into a transfer orbit to a decent Jump point. That meant Cris and Khat side-monitored Seeli's ongoing readouts of Travit's condition as well as her ongoing and voluble discussion of Grig's lamentable lack of contrition for putting Travit, the ship, Dyk, Khat, Cris, "the kids," Grig, herself, and Iza—listed in that order of importance—into a collection of dangers ranging from targeted gunsights to polar auroral radiation belts to meteor collisions and G-stress, not to mention long-term flagging as malcontents and the likelihood that lunch would be late, too.

About the time ground control made Iza cuss when it ordered, "*Gobelyn's Market*, your orbit is confirmed, please maintain," they began to hear a good bit of local chatter, with Cris tuning through and pulling out a thread to highlight—a ship on nearly their own heading, closing enough to rendezvous if they wished.

"*Vernon*," Control said, "talk to *Gobelyn's Market* before you make any sudden delta-vee out there, you're almost in a yellow approach zone!"

Iza glanced up from her calculations. "Had a triple cousin born on *Vernon* when I was tie-down, if I remember right. Talk to them . . ."

"*Gobelyn's Market*, Khat Gobelyn at PIC," she said. "Might be cousins *Vernon*—who has what for a grandma?"

There was a pause then, and a laugh, "Think the cousins done married off-ship a half-dozen Standards ago, Pilot Khat, but thanks for asking on this, I'm Pilot One Geo Frenkl. I'm gonna have to get my landing figures final real quick. Pilot Khat, your cousin Tanny is off to *Grayspinner*. Elsewise I'm up to first recent, and Chi Frenkl's running second. Got news for me?"

"Pilot Geo, hi there, ship news here . . ."

Khat paused, looked toward Iza, who was studying her boards as hard as she might, head tilted just enough away that it was clear this conversation didn't have anything to do with her . . . "News here is that Grig Tomas and Seeli Gobelyn got themselves a boy named Travit Tomas, 'bout two months back and are settled; and also that Jethri Gobelyn's got himself a new ride, spun off to be a trader on *Elthoria* not two Standards gone."

There was a pause and a, "I got the Grig Tomas news clear, but can you repeat that berth on that cousin Jethri?"

Khat looked to Iza again, who still held head down at computation.

"Yah, Geo, that's Jethri—he went free-crew when we put the *Market* in for a major refit. He was that wandering age, you know, and he's got himself sub-trader on *Elthoria*—they did adoption as I hear it."

A pause longer than speed of light might be blamed for, and almost too long for chatter.

"Heck, that's news, I'd say. Only that's not *Elf Lord*, out of Caratunk, but *Elthoria*, out of Liad, is that correct?"

"Liad, that's the one, Geo."

"Pilot Khat, we'll pass this on to *Grayspinner* and around, if that's good."

"News is news," Khat said amiably, seeing Iza still staring elsewhere, "and thanks."

"Got you, and got your news too, Pilot Khat. If you got fuel and time, we can do a scan—we haven't had a shipside visual for a couple trips."

Khat held, seeing Cris pulling up the radar image of near space. Iza tapped the light indicating *seat empty* and leveraged herself to standing.

"I'm off to pull snacks. If *Vernon* needs pictures, you'll clear it with Control—my figures show us up to a two-hour link-up if she needs us to do a roundabout. Just give me hold-warning before you pull any power if they need something sooner."

Half looking at the floor and the other half more at Cris than Khat, she moved toward the hatch. In the doorway Iza turned and looked hard at Khat.

"Khat, you did good. New is news, and he's your cousin by name, so we'll give him his due. You got it right though—Seeli and Grig first, if we're asked, and Jethri next. We'll not bad-talk the kid—it'd make more talk than not. And good, for not mentioning Arin. Anyone nosy enough will ask, or they'll ask around."

With that she was gone, in time for Control to beg Khat for attention.

· · · ✳ · · ·

Control was a little abashed to be moving the *Market* into look-see, but the courtesy was for *Vernon* and the *Market* was closest to rendezvous by several shifts. Iza, back on the bridge, was all smiles on her call on the timing being within seconds.

For her part, *Vernon* was polite. Khat admired that and it made their time arranging the rendezvous go easier, in particular the part where Khat was working out exactly who was rolling first, since it was *Vernon*'s call. It wouldn't do to have a reaction jet test spin that ship into the *Market*. . . .

Khat looked to Iza as they closed—and all Iza said was "You're doing good there, so just go on, but I bet Seeli'd appreciate it if you kept them a bit more in the circuit on this."

Khat nodded, did an all-call to the ship on the upcoming movements, and plugged the video feeds into all available screens as well, getting thanks from all over for the challenge.

"We'll run all the sensors and a lot of eyes over you—tell me you're all stable!"

Iza turned up the meteor shielding and lowered the gravity, advising in quiet tones as they finally closed, while Cris and *Vernon*'s second in command did ranging calibrations and shared visuals. The left of the main screen showed *Vernon approaching,* the right side showing the *Market,* and the scan's color-coding of the mini dust-and-gas cloud explained why they could actually hear occasional pinging scrapes of ancient comet or shattered meteor almost anywhere in this system.

Vernon, in sight, turned out to be a light-haul ship smaller than the *Market,* and likely built in the system's local yard out of leftover parts—not pretty, and without an easy clue as to a maker. The markings were austere at best, but the visual symmetry was not quite right for a long-haul vessel.

"That's a good plan, there, Cris," Iza said quietly. "Can we get that across all the vids—you want as many eyes on this as you can. Grig?"

"Here, Iza," Grig replied.

"You take reports from the rest of the ship and send them up here if we need them. It'll keep us sharper up here if—" Iza said.

"Yes, Iza . . ."

"Thanks, Pilot, I didn't think—" Khat said.

"You're doing good, Khat. I just been doing this longer and have some tricks to pass on yet," replied Iza.

Khat laughed quietly, flipped a switch, and pointed to the open sound link while she signed *plan moving forward.*

"We're starting to record in sixty seconds. My plan is to do four slow passes and you can tell me then what you need us to get closer to, if anything. Confirm?"

"On your mark, Pilot Khat, thanks!"

· · · ※ · · ·

The ship had worked hard. Most obvious was the scored line on the underside of *Vernon*'s semi-airfoiled shape. Khat cringed—if that was a scrape, the little ship had been out of service for some fixes.

While the main vids were focusing there, Cris continued to mutter to *Vernon*'s second, every so often agreeing or not on some other point, with *Vernon* identifying dings by date or past pilot, or both.

Zam and Mel must have split their time between the feeds—Grig reported their observations in brief, condensed lumps. They'd managed to get a stereo effect and an estimated mass on the ship, just for fun. He even reported, "Zam and Mel suggest a more fashionable font and color for the *Market* nameplate and numbers, and I promised to pass that on," and later, "Zam thinks the shipyard left some graffiti behind!"

"Hey, *Vernon*," Khat eventually said to her counterpart, "I'm not seeing much from our side. Looks like all your rear and ventral reaction jets are clear. As close as we can get, I'd trust that you don't have bends in that old dinged section. My radar's not showing any holes you're not supposed to have, I think, and we're not seeing any signs of outgassing. Beyond that—"

"Pilot Khat, I'm seeing the same pictures you are. Let me poll the crew . . . we can likely call it good both ways."

While that was going on, Cris and Grig were on another channel, and Khat could hear Cris saying "Zam's got a good eye you know. Maybe a rescan . . . At close power?"

Khat looked in Cris's direction, about to ask what the discussion was about when Pilot Thuy came back on the link.

"Cris?"

She looked up at him to smile, but saw him grim-faced about something, and sounding grim-voiced. "Let's make sure we've swapped all the data both ways—highest data density. Then we stand by at a distance while they test, still swapping vids and sensors and then watch us," Thuy said.

Iza's, "The Captain concurs," was immediate, and, "Assigning observers now," came across the all-call from Grig.

Grig sounded as grim as Cris, and a glance at Cris showed him touching keys to send information somewhere—information that wasn't showing up on her screens.

Khat patched through to Grig, on a private connection, asking, "Assigning observers to what, Grig?"

"Zam's got good eyes, Khat, and so does Mel. There's an anomaly we're checking."

"And it is so worrisome that you can't tell their pilot about it?"

There was a pause, which Khat imagined was a sigh, or maybe it was a sigh because she heard Seeli talking quietly in the distance, something about spec sheets . . .

"Won't mean a thing to her, Khat. Just that it looks like something's odd about the externals of the Struven Unit on the right screen. *Our* Struven Unit."

Chapter Twenty-Six

• • • •✳• • • •

Port Chavvy

PORT CHAVVY WAS NOISY with the hum of people and equipment, the storefront videos full of improbable promises. There were people of many appetites and necessities, and potential trouble to make someone fresh off the flight deck of a two-man ship jumpy without the added burden of anticipation. He wanted to see Freza and he wanted to get what he needed to retrieve his book. . . .

The truth was, Terran ports feel different to a spacer than Liaden ports. Liaden ports are all business all the time, with the practical and utilitarian overriding the constant mercantile appetite of Terran ports, the Terran appetite including shopping stalls, walking vendors, and sensualists offering to do or to have done just what the working pilot had been dreaming of, cooped up in that lonely spaceship for all those days . . .

Jethri tried to take all that into account as he worked his way through passageways joining the crowded multilevel commercial port's shopping arcades with the working side, the real port. His credentials on dock were trader and pilot—on this side his credentials were a willingness to pay and an ability to keep what was his.

They'd come down to this side to check the dropboxes for incoming news from home, from Vincza, from wherever, and whatever news the Scout was running with was keeping him on high-frets, too.

From his left, then, a nearly bare chest and slim arms with tiny wrists, waving a package, the move tending to push him to the side, out of the flow of traffic . . .

"Genuine *vya*, in concentrate, good Pilots. The best, and only a quarter bit. Want to try it out, ten bits for the quick."

Truth told, Jethri'd seen less clothes on people, but rarely revealing quite that much nor even so close . . . and the mystic scent of *vya* was thick enough to override the generic smell of fried this-and-that hanging heavy in the air.

He moved a hand toward a potential hidden knife as Pen Rel had instructed and sure enough the seller backed away, with a huffy, "Don't get that short-fused with me, hon, I've been on this port for three whole years, and got all my papers!"

Jethri kept his mouth shut, aiming toward the actual docks, and toward *Balrog,* the Scout a half pace to his left and almost a half-pace behind, letting Jethri's newfound urgency take the lead, as *melant'i* would have it.

The Scout's "packages waiting" news had been messages eventually downloaded into hardcopy direct into a sealpack as they waited, the clerk being stone-faced about dealing with a Liaden, his third in as many days, as he'd let on. Jethri's Combine key had calmed the ether somewhat but the news that there were enough Liadens on port to make a storekeeper take note was disturbing at best.

It was during their rather lengthy wait for the Scout's info that Jethri's portable comm connections finally propagated through the local nets and a message from Freza was bounced to him—promising him an audience today, if he'd like, in fact the sooner the better since they did have a shipment for him—and they'd had inquiries from two different Liaden ships asking about the same item. He'd spent considerable thought on the reply, wishing not to overconcern her. . . .

"Two Liaden ships, asking outright on the availability of a book hardly known among Terrans," he said to the Scout, "and she's put them off, saying that it isn't on any of their invoices and she doubts there are any on ship."

The Scout's bow had shown his concern, and so Jethri's reply was succinct.

Arriving shortly in person, with backup pilot, for my shipment.

The day was already longer than they'd planned, for the mailbox forwarder used local hours, and they'd stopped in the trade bar while waiting for it to open, that being early in the local day, to find that they were noticed and somewhat artificially ignored, though Jethri's ordering two near beers in good Terran seemed to hearten the barkeep.

Crowds seemed the rule.

They'd seen only two exceptions to that rule—the low docks themselves and the contiguous warehouse zone which was but casually separated from those docks by intermittent fencing, painted lines, and message walls. These housed as well an impromptu open market where those not satisfied with retail bargains could barter, trade, or finagle.

Jethri longed to visit the market—he often did well in such places—but the pressure of his appointment weighed on him as they crossed into the dock zone itself.

Liaden docks—he was trying to concentrate on his environment and not his mission so he let his thought backtrack—Liaden docks tended to be sized smaller for Liadens and bigger for their ships and equipment, so that the walks on a Liaden dock might not be quite as wide, but the room for mechanisms and locks and connectors tended to be larger. The equipment itself might not be bigger—but Liadens left more room for it. By what Jethri'd seen, Terrans tended to overbuild some things, after all, as if they recognized that they were less delicate and more argumentative than Liadens.

Liaden docks tended, too, to be newer—but then he realized that might be a function of *Elthoria*'s routes as compared to the *Market*'s— in fact all of his impressions of Liaden docks were of the docks being capable of handling large ships and not just in-system and planetary ships.

This segment of dock might have handled *Elthoria* at either of the two far-end berths, where it would have taken up all three levels' worth of height and more, but in the section he strode through now, the ships were much smaller than *Elthoria*, and much less grand in many other ways. In fact, the crew members standing or sitting about in the marked areas just aside the gangways and hatches was something one saw more often on Terran docks and Terran worlds— Terrans were more gregarious than Liadens at dockside, more likely to act as if the dock was an extended shift room or a sun porch open to neighbors.

They'd had salutes and hand waves in passing, even with his focused stride, and he realized that he'd fallen back into that Terran habit easily. He doubted he'd ever spoken to any of these docksiders before in his life, but like most Terran docksides, the fact that one was seen twice meant he'd be recognized . . . there was a level of community there that Liadens reserved for allies, or clan, or even line.

Balrog's location he had from the bar's diagrams, and third level meant they'd have to take a lift, which he wasn't in favor of, or take the catwalk-and-stairs edifice to that level, which was probably a good idea, given his adrenaline spring.

He made no mention of his plan to the Scout, merely angling to the open-railed stairs that enclosed the lift stack for Section 3B, his stride barely changing as his footsteps rang out. He deplored the noise of these boots, but they'd been the fancies, as specified by Norn ven'Deelin at the start of this trip, which seemed at the moment like years ago. The Scout might as well be a cat as much sound as he made in Jethri's wake, and he was barely in Jethri's vision at each turn of the stairs.

Arriving on the third level, the light gravity having impeded him not at all in his rush, Jethri turned hard to the right, a slight and probably purposeful scuff behind him letting him know the Scout was with him. On this level there were a third more gangways since they served even smaller ships and the neighborly spotting of knots of crew was even more in evidence—except something was wrong.

Jethri saw the looks he was getting on this level, and the wary set of some of the standees as they sipped at beverages or leaned on tool carts. The buzz of conversation was lower even if the echoes were more insistent.

"Jethri, my Second," came the low voice suddenly close to his side, "may I suggest . . ."

Jethri slowed, paused, scanning the hanging signs for *Balrog*'s spot, looking now for people who really might know him by face and by name and by ship history and . . .

He turned to the Scout, who was being as inconspicuous as he could.

"I see they're expecting something and wondering if I'm it."

"Yes. I shall have to tell Pen Rel that you're able to do more than basic risk assessment . . ."

Despite his mood Jethri managed to laugh, which was a good thing for he'd realized he'd let the tension build in him, something Pen Rel would surely have been unpleased with. Probably, in fact, he'd been stalking these last few steps, which wouldn't do at all.

"No need to look immediately, but there is a woman approaching from our direction of travel, Terran, carrying, but not openly, and who must know you, for her tension is not for you. Behind her some distance, standing with a small group, there is a Terran crew member, acting backup for her, as I read it."

Jethri closed his eyes and opened them. "She wears a blue ear cuff, perhaps?"

"She does, in fact. Along with a blue face decoration or tattoo which matches it."

"Then we're closing into the alert zone, Pilot," he said. "You have your opportunity to step back and be aside of this problem of mine . . ."

"Surely," ter'Astin's bow was of the most elaborate, so elaborate that Jethri smiled, for it was a bow of extreme irony, reading the hand motions, a bow to one most wise . . .

A nod then, and Jethri turned in time to see the skip-step that took Freza's rapid walk into a trot.

In spite of it all, he was glad to see her, and reached his arms in her direction despite the distance until they nearly collided.

"Jeth, I have your note, and see you have mine," Freza said simply, leaning forward to take his hand in what started off as a shake and turned into a wrist hug and then a real hug, to brush her lips close toward his right ear, saying quickly and quietly, "Glad you're here."

She didn't have the makeup on this time, but now he saw that she had a misty blue tattoo, all fine lines and quiet shades—an image of a spiral galaxy it was, running from her hairline and even maybe into the hair in front of her ear, parallel to the ear—where her make-up had been heaviest when last he'd seen her—and the blue ear cuff shone out all the more against her pale skin and close-cropped hair. The make-up she'd worn made the cuff less obvious, he realized. She'd do that if it was a comm instead of decoration, he decided.

She moved close to his face, whispered in his other ear, saying, "Sorry we had to leave so soon last time," and finished her words with the self-same kind of nip and then she was nodding at the same time toward the little man in plain pilot clothes who walked behind with a smile. It was just polite social for her to take Jeth's hand and smile, but it was pointed social news for her to show a public tendre this way, saying to all witnesses that Freza DeNobli of *Balrog* knew and welcomed this dandy-dressed trader.

The witnesses were no less alert, Jethri could see that just by looking over Freza's shoulder, but some of the immediate tension had gone out of those closest to *Balrog*'s gangway sign, which meant something . . .

Freza waved the pair of them toward her ship's flag, hanging over the breezeless gangway, saying in a serious voice that belied her public smile, "There's been four passes, up here. Four that we noticed, in a group. They just walk on by, if you know what I mean, slow and comfortable. Except they're all carrying weapons and they're all on alert. Looks like a patrol, but they aren't authorized, and they don't talk—at least not to anyone but themselves."

"And the port proctors?" That was the Scout's question, in a somewhat accented Terran, as she'd not bothered with Trade. "What have they told you?"

"And how would we ask them without calling for trouble? They walk about like they do and the proctors can say it's just shipfolks walking about. Would you call proctors?" There was a proper indecision there, Jethri thought.

"A show of force," the scout allowed, "is still a show of force, no matter how small. Are they the same people in each walk? It may be that a call to the security office will—"

"Will be met with a yawn," suggested Jethri, breaking into the exchange. "According to the news sheets, this isn't always a calm port, and until there is trouble making noise somewhere, there's trouble enough that could be happening, and places enough, that local security glances at their cameras and eats with their guns on their belts."

Freza looked to Jethri, candidly asking, "Are you sure this is the best time for this? We can deliver, if we have to. We've still got a day plus on port—"

"No reason to risk any of *Balrog*'s people on this, Freza, if it is a risk. This is all on me, especially if the reason they're walking your door like this is me. Might as well do this now and—"

"This discussion will take place undercover, perhaps?" The Scout's voice was low but penetrating, and Jethri cast a quick glance to the already assenting Freza.

"Two minutes, then in," she said, hand leaving the ear cuff as if she'd untangled it. "Got to clear a spot."

"Thanks," he offered, pointing beyond *Balrog*'s flag. "What's in the neighborhood?"

"Not too much. Two empty slots, and then poor *Dulcimer,* trying to do some get-by work inside. Word is they had a couple bad supply canisters burst during a fifteen day Jump from Fort Cavanaugh. Whatever it was—fine food flour or something—got everywhere. They've been on round the clock since they got in but don't want to talk to no one or have help in, so they're likely a little out of true. About the only thing we know is that they rented that rack of tools and have been cleaning like mad people."

He could see tools, a portable wall full of them sitting on the walkside as far away from the occupied slots as could be, where some other ships had deck chairs and tables. A kid sat there on a stool, back to the walkway.

Out of true.

He nodded, sighed. A ship was out of true when it might not pass a customs inspection, or when it might have an extra, undeclared person or two on board, or when . . . yeah, and if recalled right, the *Dulcimer* never had been a rich ship, and always close. With them up here on top rack and away, it wasn't like they were looking for attention. So it might have been a crew problem they didn't want to share.

There you go, he thought, not my concern. He felt for the kid sitting out there by his lonesome, and hoped he hadn't caused the problem. Been times enough growing up that Jethri Gobelyn had been the one doing wait-work just because he didn't know enough, or do good enough, or was the problem himself, and was close enough to being out of true, too.

• • • ✳ • • •

Balrog was cramped, even more so than *Gobelyn*'s *Market*, and by the looks of it, older by at least a generation, too. Jethri couldn't recall having been in the ship more than once, and that had been in his strap-seat days well before he knew by looking the age of a ship, back when he, Freza, and a dozen other youngsters were unleashed in the care of an august older and very skinny crewman named Brabham, with three fingers on one hand and a set of glass goggles on his face, while the rest of the older adults went elsewhere to talk or do adult topics while they waited for some delay in pod transfers.

The always cheerful Brabham had let them talk and play, sometimes interjecting a song or helping with the drawing of a picture or the selection of a game, and sometimes telling stories that couldn't possibly be true about secret pirate ports and creatures who'd make you feel good sitting on your lap or even just being in the same room with you. He'd also overseen lunch on the big table and snacks for them all, and asked them to "keep the riot down to beat-cop level" when the room had reverberated with the energetic get-together of children used to near isolation.

Jethri'd still shared his cabin in the market with some of Arin's in-progress frames in those days and remembered distinctly being told by his father, "Don't talk about these with anyone else, Jeth—and if someone asks you about them, why, you think they got sold to the scavengers on Triplepoint."

That had been a strange thing for his father to suggest because getting them together had taken a lot of work and some of Jethri's suggestions as well—it seemed sometimes adults couldn't *see* the stuff that was right in front of them when it came to working with the bits and pieces of the Old Tech. He'd helped get the real frames together—in fact, he'd helped show that some of the frames, like some of the fractins, weren't real—they were just counterfeit look-alikes with nothing of power to them. Later, of course, he'd discovered that the working frames really were a secret, but he'd been older then, and anyway, no one asked.

They'd entered the airlock and Freza'd waited until it was closed and circulating to point to the slide lock on the sidewall. They weren't going to the formal little trade office, which might have been expected, but right into family quarters, even if ter'Astin was an unknown.

The Scout bowed the acceptance of the honor and if Freza saw it he couldn't tell since she led on so quickly, and drew the eye so well. They passed several hatches and doors, and then went left, and he recognized at once the room he and the other children had been loosed in—

And too, he recognized Brabham, sitting quiet in a well-padded chair, still with the goggles, the three-fingered hand lifting a mug in Freza's direction and then theirs, saying, "Welcome and be seated all. Beer and 'mite and coffee I got, but that tea isn't where it oughta been!"

Freza made a face. "We still got that problem? I'll fix it this time, I swear, even if I need to put in for new crew!"

Brabham shook his head sadly. "Isn't good, you're right, Frezzie. Tea, these days, it's only neighborly to have tea beside the coffee. And it can't take that long to sign the log on it, and can't cost that much from stipend—but tell me our company."

Jethri'd seen the Scout's face go very bland. Right he was, that ship problems ought not be discussed in front of others, and more surprising to Jethri was Brabham's smile of it. Perhaps it was just an old argument. . . .

"This is Jethri Gobelyn ven'Deelin. Arin's own son, and now son of Ixin, too. Trader like you see, and sits second on that *Keravath* parked on the oddball port. Behind him is Scout ter'Astin." Freza paused, and shrugged. "*Keravath*'s a Liaden Scout ship, and the Scout is Jethri's pilot."

"Pilots," she said with a motion that was a cross between a bow and a hand wave, "this is Brabham. He's our Past Pilot, Trade Consultant, Economist, and Library, too."

Past Pilot was something Jethri hadn't known, but it went along with not having reaction time down. There was a lot that was automatics with modern ships, but decision making and follow-through on a flight deck took more than a quick mind.

"Pardon I don't get up—my back's not so good, and it takes me awhile to move anywhere right now. Spent the hour's move looking for tea. Jethri I met you, when you was half as high. Scout, we never did meet before." He reached out his hand to shake theirs.

After Jethri took it he bowed—it seemed appropriate for someone with such titles and experience, even if his own recall was of a jolly kid-sitter with a keen eye for keeping spills and frets contained. "I remember, sir, it was at Farleydock."

"Yes it was, and you've got a good memory. I'd have known you from your father anyhow—but you know that, I'm guessing."

Jethri's nod gave way to the Scout, who also bowed deeply.

"Indeed, I think we've not previously had the opportunity of meeting. I am honored."

"Sure, we're all happy to be here," the skinny elder said with a hand motion acknowledging the introductions, "and you haven't said what you will drink, now that we all know we don't have tea for the pilot. Sit. You too, Frezzie, you're making my shoulder twitch lurking at the eye corner."

The table wasn't so big these days as he remembered it, and they ended up with Freza close enough with Jethri to knee-touch, which she did, and the Scout on the corner, closer to but not in the way of the elder's access to the drink fountain. The requests made the Past Pilot laugh—and he handed the beverages out in solid ceramic cups.

"Here I'd got beer so you could all relax and you all want to be sucking down the 'mite. You'll not mind if I don't switch engines in mid-lift, I hope?"

Three motions, all giving him permission to stay the course, and he nodded absently.

"Take a sip, all of you, and I'll see what I can say here." Pointing at Jethri with his mugged hand, and then toward ter'Astin, he nodded and said, "You brought him and Frezzie let him in, so I guess you're fine with this gentleman hearing a little bit about *Arin's Envidaria* if it happens?"

Jethri nodded above the mottled golden foam of 'mite, the thick flavor restoring his confidence in his mission.

"I am," he finally managed, good Liaden training suppressing his urge to wipe the mite from his lips with the back of his sleeve. "I am, since this gentleman brought me first real notice ever I had of the thing. Freza hinted, but . . ."

The beer stopped halfway on its way to Brabham's lips and he looked at all three of them as if waiting for a punchline to the joke. None coming, he shook his head briefly and took a hefty swig, raised his free hand to pardon himself and drew more to his mug before turning back.

His smile was grim and he looked into the foam, his mouth making a small half-whistle before he raised his eyes to them again.

"Well, that's the problems with secrets, isn't it? You can't get on the all-call and have a check-in very well, just asking 'Everyone that don't know the secret, please call in now!'"

Next, the elder let his weight onto his elbows, sipping thoughtfully and peering at Freza.

"Frezzie hinted, and the Scout told you. All this in the last thirty-eight days, I guess, and something you should have known before you got your first whisker!"

Jethri shook his head, began shrugging into an apology . . .

"No, that's what I said. Secrets will do that to you, and who knows what they're worth or when they're not worth it? Someone should have let you in years ago, and it isn't your fault you haven't seen it. Who's to guess that Iza and Paitor would be such a fool's crew on this? And Grig . . . ah, but Grig might have promised, and it would be just like him to keep a secret like that, old pharstbucket that he is!"

"Next question then, I guess, since I'm in the circle here." Brabham pointed Terran-style. "Have you read *Arin's Envidaria,* Pilot?"

His gaze stayed on the Scout, whose easy demeanor became a wider answer than it might have: "This *Envidaria* is only rumor for me, sir, and as far as I know, for any of the Scouts—we've heard it discussed in ship-to, but as far as I know it has not been seen."

"Discussed? So you have—" Brabham said.

"Existence only. Mentions of availability, promises of passing along, sometimes the news that there is a meeting. Circumspect. I think you may rest easy that it is not read out and shared on ship-to."

Jethri, meanwhile, had been running the phrase "old pharstbucket that he is" over in his mind—and with a pause in conversation he broke in with his own question, to Brabham. "You know Grig—did you know that him and Seeli have git?"

The elder laughed and grabbed another big sip of his beer.

"So old man Grig finally found himself a young one, did he? Good for him, 'cause that Seeli's steady and will be able to deal. Yes, that ought to work."

He sipped again, and despite his back he leaned toward them conspiratorially.

"So, here's the news, and, Pilot, I hope you'll keep it close—actually, both of you under pilot's seal, if you will."

His gaze had gone first to the Scout and now fell on Jethri, who bowed. Information not to be generally shared—and the question was, would such a "seal" hold for the Scout and the son of a Liaden trader?

"We're close in, some of us, to this idea Arin brought us—and, Jethri, he said he got it from you, talking away after some or 'nother game you played where you out-traded a bunch of older kids and a Combine Trader, too, stuck as you was with a bad board. That was the story, but the idea was complicated and got a lot of politics and then . . . and then . . . Arin took a hit."

"But the secret, that secret's been worked on, and . . ."

"The *secret*," Jethri muttered, "has been awful dangerous, hasn't it? If people are hunting it so hard they're threatening ships, and hurting people, and you say someone's working on it and I say it may be time to let it loose!"

Brabham sighed, very heavily, and took a sip of his beer. He looked to each of them, put the beer down with a *thunk*.

Jethri thought he'd speak, but Brabham shook his head like he was rejecting things to say, and kind of chuckled to himself.

"Some agree with you," he said finally. "Some say with Arin gone, the idea ought to be gone."

He looked down at his hands then, as if something was written there, and then when he read it, he wasn't happy with what he saw and looked up in a hurry. "But we have the outlines, and we've got a couple things moving, even without him. And we haven't given up.

"So you know, you're welcome to join in, Jethri. You are. You've got connections, here with us, I mean—and you've got other connections. We'll need other connections, reliable other connections, if you want to join . . ."

Jethri felt the trader in him working to the top and fighting with the son in him—the son wanted to say "I will!" and the trader wanted . . . something more. Trading he knew something about, and he could keep a trade secret. He wasn't sure he was up to full-scale conspiracies.

Jethri spread his hands wide, showing that he was open to discussion, open to thinking about it, welcoming information.

He started, letting most of his glance move between the Scout and the economist, feeling the presence of Freza's knee and leg against his, with her silhouette in his eye . . .

"I'm not at all sure what you offer, Pilot. You have the information and you say you have an organization. That may be, but I do have connections, and I have responsibilities, I have trade in process and a partner elsewhere and a Clan I acknowledge, and a bunch of family leftovers from a ship I was called an extra on and invited to leave. What offer can you make me? What exactly is there to *join*?"

From beside him came Freza's voice, low and light, with her leg pressing firmly against his.

"We're building something new, Jeth. You've even been to a key part of it, and talked with Doricky, and she's been a key part in it. What it looks like is just ordinary trading, and a lot will be like what we've all been doing.

"I can tell you some of it will be entirely new, because the routes will be new, and ports will have to be built and rebuilt, conditions coming on to what they're going to be. It ought to last awhile, too, because of the conditions, you know, and Arin saw that. Could be a couple hundred years and more where his system will work good, and by that time, it won't be system, it'll be habit and culture. So we're going to make us into a big family or two.

"Some other stuff, some other stuff might happen. Might have to build a couple ships, you know. Our other ship—DeNobli's, I mean—it's been refreshed so often it don't have anything original except the ice in the freezers. Some work being done, some crew training—but that's beside the point."

"The point is that change is here, and we're in it. You, you sir, you're change in person. So, since I'm the local keeper, I'm asking if you're looking to read the plan. I thunk you have to read the plan, and soon. I've got a copy for you—ought to have been one for you *before* you left the *Market,* but Iza hasn't communicated word one with us, nor let word through to anyone on board as far as I know, since the day Arin died. Didn't dare just send you one to ship address without knowing who might pick it up. Grig knew the outlines since he helped Arin do some test flying on this idea. Good man, that Grig, comes from a good family."

Freza's knee was still warm on his; he nodded to the Past Pilot and turned to her, found he couldn't help but smile a little, as hard as he'd reached for trader face.

"You've read it? You're with it?"

"Know it by heart. Guess we're all in on it," she said, not avoiding his gaze. "All of us here."

"I keep a study copy, because it's not like it's law, but it's ideas. Good ideas, backed by math and science both."

She looked away, biting her lip, and looked back with a half-laugh.

"I don't want to be mysterious, Jeth, but it isn't fair to talk about it to you without you read it first, I think. Telling you I'm with it wasn't even fair, in case that puts you off it before you do, or leans you without thinking about it."

He sighed, and only a little of it was because Freza let up the pressure of her leg as she adjusted her position, and more of it because duty seemed plain.

"I'll have to read it, because I can't see how my current orbit will get me there. I'm really pretty well set on *Elthoria*. I have work, I have a Clan, plans, and I have friends . . ."

At the mention of friends Freza nodded in agreement and broke in with a chuckle. "Looks clear from here, too. You'll read it. It's on a reader, Jeth, and we'll have to code it for you."

She glanced to and then nodded at the Scout.

"Officially, you can't read this. Practically, you can't read it too—it has to be handed to you and we haven't got permission to share it that far. Jethri—you said yes, right?"

He nodded, wondering how they'd proceed if there wasn't anything to trade.

"Pilot," she said, unwinding from beneath the table and nodding at the eldest. Here in the ship light the colors on her face seemed to grow right into her ear loops. Jethri let his glance linger, judging it was an effect he could come to like.

"I shoulda listened to you beforehand, Freza, but hold on, you knew what was best and I didn't . . ."

"Before I do read this—is there a master copy of this thing? One that's not on a reader? One that can just get sent out so people—traders and all—can know about it?"

The keepers of the secret looked between themselves several seconds before Brabham spoke. "Plan is to do that, when the time is right." Jethri looked at the pair of them, nodded. "What you've been saying here is that this whole thing's something that Arin Gobelyn came up with and that it's just as much my birthright as anything else he might have left me—commissioner rings or loose change or my name. So I'll read what he left me. Then I'll tell you what I think. I'll tell Freza straight up what I think. And you tell me if you'll keep a man from grabbing his birthright, won't you?"

Freza, standing, agreed. "You'll see why we've been keeping it secret, Jethri. You will!"

With a grimace Brabham half-rose, unsnapping a side pocket and handing her a multiridged mechanical key. She took it in her fist, nodded first to him and then to Jethri, the nod becoming a head shake indicating which way they'd go from here. As he followed, Jethri heard the ex-pilot changing the topic.

"Scout, you'll get your Second Board back in a few minutes. Meanwhile, I'd like to talk to you about that protocol you're using to snatch comm traffic. . . ."

· · · ✴ · · ·

A slide key admitted them to a small storage room with a ladder in it—in space it would be a zero-G area and the boxes and hardware lock-strapped in place over head would be easily accessible. Here it was less so, local gravity holding sway with as it did, which sent the pair of them clambering up the ladder and jumping across a gap to pick their way between sets of replacement pipes and mountings and thence to a large panel full of tools they had to walk between. Freza stationed herself at one end and gestured for Jethri to the other, and then she gestured again, which sent him to his knees as she went to hers, and she reached into a recess, pulling hard—

Snap!

Jethri found the corresponding recess, which wasn't easy at all, and pulled the handle he found there, to be rewarded with a similar *snap* and the sound of a small alert buzzer.

"Good. Lift your end . . ."

Jethri did as directed and the panel, hinged on the long side, opened to reveal a capacious well, fairly full of interesting bundles wrapped in radar-absorbing cloth and boxes marked with digit-and-letter combinations but nothing else.

"Come on in!"

She scrambled over the bundles, and he did the same, ending up in a half-crawl when he reached her as she was tugging one of the bundles loose.

"Here we go, Jeth," she said, kneeling within a couple hand spans of him—and placed a key into a cubby safe still lower into the well, a key which went in easily and turned with a quiet snick.

The lighting wasn't good, but within were a few small boxes. Freza pulled one out, and unfolded it wordlessly, displaying how to unfold it into—a personal reader to be worn on the face like minigoggles. He took it, and it was made so that it hung on the ears and nose. Low enough not to obstruct vision if he was looking straight ahead, but able to be glanced down into . . .

"Nothing in it!"

He felt the earslides for controls—

"Good," she said. "Not activated to you yet."

She pulled a similar device from her own pocket, then, and he saw it meshed somehow with her ear cuffs when she put it on. Her reader drifted on her face and then he realized it was matching itself to her face color, that the section over her filigree tattoo was taking on the blue beneath it.

"Fold it back up, Jeth, and hold it like so, between any two fingers you choose on the left hand and right hand. Don't have to be thumb and forefinger, but remember which ones they are. The little blue decoration goes toward the front, that ought to be on the right, and the red one on the left.

"Yes, good. I'm going to ask you to squeeze pretty hard at my count of three, and keep squeezing about the same strength without shifting things around for about ten seconds. Once you do that, you'll put it on immediately. Got it?"

Freza looked at him over the reader she was wearing and smiled. "Here's your count!"

Following directions meant he couldn't exactly see what she was doing, but the activation went just as she said, a glance down showing him a starfield image blooming until it filled his vision—and the glance away took it away. He recognized something of it—so he looked back.

Yes, it *was* the spiral arm where the seventeen planets were located, and as he watched, the image zoomed through and close-up, enticingly familiar.

"It'll feel odd the first few times you use it, if you haven't used one before, but you get used to it. Tap the left arm and your book goes on, tap the right and it pauses—hold them both in and you'll have a menu."

He glanced at the menu, saw a face very much like his own, only a little older, and with an air of competence he only wished he could feel.

"Hello."

A voice he knew was in his head then, and he startled where he knelt, nearly losing the reader as he looked about. "Oh!"

Yes, he did know that voice . . . and suddenly missed it amazingly. He'd never had a chance to say goodbye, never had the chance to—He realized he was staring at Arin Gobelyn's image.

"I'm Commissioner Arin Gobelyn. Welcome to a discussion of long-term trading potentials I hope you'll be interested in becoming part of."

"Oh!" he said it again, eyes wide in the dimness, the image becoming that of his father standing in front of exactly the image that hung on-screen. It was eerily like looking at a video of himself playing at fancy dress—

In the background someone was talking . . .

"Jeth? I'm sorry, I should have."

On the reader: "We're facing an unprecedented cloud of gas and dust, a cloud which must change trade routings and practices in this part of the spiral arm for centuries. An early simulation showed the potential to leverage this situation into a long-term trade policy of utility to all of us—and our descendants. I have prepared four short sessions on my proposal, including an introduction and overview of the basic concept, brief studies of several regions where the concept could be implemented within our lifetime and within current technical constraints, and a policy discussion of why even partial implementation might assist greatly in the inevitable, and I hope peaceful, merging of expanding trade streams which lies before us."

"Jethri! Just . . ."

He looked up at Freza through eyes brimming with tears. Iza had never shared anything like this, and he'd not thought about it, but his father had studied and traveled and worked and left records and he'd never seen them!

Looking up and away stopped the voice of his father, stopped the motion on-screen, let Freza's "Hold, Jethri!" come through.

Freza had moved closer to him by now and had her hand palm up, barely an arm's length away from him.

He took a deep breath, nodded, laughed, wiped away the tears.

"Surprised, that's all," he said, realizing that his chest was tight and that he really needed to center himself and get back to the Scout and go deal with the rest of the problems the universe had for him now and not stupidly muddle learning with . . .

"I have to tell you that most of what we have is written. No voice, and the pictures and images and graphs, you'll have to eyeball them. Those lectures, they were what he was doing when he went to meetings, and what he could share for people to take to discussion groups. I really do owe you—I should have told you!"

He shook his head, sniffed, pulled the reader off his face and folded it.

Freza reached out and squeezed his hand, then reached into the cubby and gave him a pouch.

"You can wear that, if you want. I carry mine—but even if you got mine you couldn't read it. My unit's set for me; your unit's been set for you—tuned for you is more like it—it won't even turn on for me now unless I do a bunch of stuff with my controls, and I have a master unit. Take it off your face and no one else can read it . . . and if your eyes aren't on it, it couldn't be removed. The sound—I don't know, that's not something others can hear, either. It goes right to the nerves, I think. I'm told that folks that're almost deaf can hear this well!"

"This isn't Old Tech though, I mean . . ."

"It isn't."

Jethri took the pouch, leaned back away from Freza with a start, too willing to lean into her.

"Jeth, we're fine. Tell me that—tell me you're not angry!"

He took his time sealing the reader into the pouch, threaded the pouch lead around his belt and slipped it down beside his hip, inside the fabric of his pants.

He took a very deep breath then and looked at her, seeing—Freza, taking off her reader, touching her ear, concern writ in the lines of her face that he didn't normally see.

"I'm angry," he told her, "but not at you. You—you I'm glad for. No matter what the book says, I'm glad to have it. I'm mad because so much of him was hidden from me for so long!"

Jethri saw her nod, and reach a hand to him again—but in the midst of the action she showed *stop* again, then signaled a *hurry*, hand at ear level.

"Chatter from down the row—one level down. Looks like there's a parade again, Jeth—we better go see what's up!"

Chapter Twenty-Seven

· · · · ·❋· · · · ·

Port Chavvy

"YOU SET, ARE YOU, PILOT?" Brabham asked when Jethri came back.

"He's infected you, has he?" Jethri heard himself say, realized he was still unsettled. Meanwhile, the Scout went bland, but Brabham laughed.

"Happens you carry a key to the door, I hear, and we've heard twicet that *Keravath* has this Jethri person sitting second. That's you. Take your honors where you get 'em, just like your punishments."

Jethri bowed, hitting the precise edge of honor to the wise, a touch of honor to the aged, and a full helping of acceptance of honor given.

The elder laughed again, and was echoed by the Scout. Brabham offered, "That'd be a tall orbit to fall from, I guess. I'll take it."

"Be seated and we'll see what we can all learn!"

Freza squeezed by him and they sat in the same places, with fresh mugs of 'mite passed to both of them. The storeroom had been cold, he realized, and the warmth of the 'mite and of Freza was much welcome.

In truth, there wasn't much to be seen from their crowded staff room, even with the viewscreen unlimbered. The feed they had were people's faces on other ships. They weren't taking a live video feed from *Cruikshank*'s crew since the dockside crew wasn't currently equipped. Instead they were getting voice reports as relayed and interpreted by the crew, and since the *Cruikshank* wasn't much more than a scheduled shuttle back and forth from here to Vincza, they weren't as used to Liadens to be able to tell what they were looking at. Short pilots—yeah, they could see that, dressed with their jackets and working clothes. They could see what must be crew clothes, and a couple wearing boss duds. Could be traders, could be tourists.

What was apparent though was that they were intent, once again, on being conspicuously present, walking three and sometimes four wide, taking to the center of things so that everyone passing had to take a skinny path, and people getting passed from behind found themselves squeezed to the outside and up against equipment boxes and benches.

"There—down the stairs again," came the report.

"It does look like a patrol, the way they are marching on the tick of the clock, doesn't it?" This from Brabham, who'd brought up a screen to show off the timing.

"Or an exercise program," suggested the Scout, "or even working off demerits, or testing boots, or making room while work on their ships goes forth. It might be anything. In fact, if you hadn't already had these unsolicited requests from them, I'd dismiss it."

The Scout bowed to Jethri, and then to Freza.

"I admire your interest in remaining below the notice of record keepers. At the same time I am a pilot with a ship here, and a mission, and both are potentially affected by this situation. Has the required transaction taken place?"

Though Freza said, "Yes," after glancing to him, Jethri bowed a more formal affirmation, adding in Terran, "We may go as soon as we wish. *Balrog* will do as it needs."

Freza leaned forward, patting Jethri's hand.

"*Balrog* will be fine. I'll walk you down—and once you're in and set, then I'll walk on by the security office and ask them to take a look at the situation—how's that?"

The Scout kept his face neutral, but bowed to Brabham, and rose as Jethri did.

"Local custom," he said. "I thank you for your time and the grace of your table."

"We know your faces, both of you," said the old pilot from his seat. "Wherever we meet, we'll be looking to have you visit!"

· · · ✦ · · ·

It had seemed like a good idea, getting on the way, with Paitor's "Best path to done is through begun" a guide for Jethri. They'd taken leave, Freza's quick weapons check not unnoticed by Jethri or the Scout, and headed out as soon as the pack from *Wynhael* was said to be moving away again.

"Better slow—we may want to wander back . . . they've turned at the stairs, left someone at the elevate."

That was Freza, voice low, listening to her comm set.

Jethri moved his hands in that *query action* motion he'd picked up from the Scout. There were voices ahead and the Scout signed *pause*.

By then, though, they'd been spotted.

Jethri heard the sentences; they were annoying, and loud enough at first to be just above polite conversation, spoken in awkward Trade, voices rising somewhat in pitch but more in volume as the group approached, effectively closing the walk to others with their meandering.

"But there, my friends, is an excellent example of what trade guided by proper traders and Master Traders might do for the galaxy." At least he didn't point with his finger, thought Jethri, though the chin jab was obviously meant for him. "Wearing clothes of a Liaden cut, why, that one there may be permitted into the company of traders and delms. I've heard reports that none other than Parvet sig'Flava was seen flitting about him, can you believe—but there, there's always rumor that offers much that might challenge even one so *insatiable* as sig'Flava."

The return banter of his troop was not all in Trade and the Liaden side of it carried.

"Lately, of course, he has been seen . . . frolicking in the company of Terrans, where he then cruelly bent the *melant'i* of a member of a minor clan who had not the sense to see opportunity when it was presented to her. So there, you see who he chooses now, returning to the glory of a wandering . . ."

Jethri's ears burned so hard he let the words go by and he was afraid the color of his anger might spread to his face. It was just such a thing a bully might use to start a port brawl anywhere, and here, where Freza'd shown him as favored to the docksiders it might serve, anyway. There were plenty of them about, and some of them not at all finicky about watching a fight, or even joining in, after months of a space route.

The group slowed even more, coming out to an even dozen of them to Jethri's quick scan, and he knew he was doing what the Scout had mentioned before: he was looking at the risks, knowing the while that the two most dangerous were those in the fanciest clothes—Rinork's son and his lieutenant. If Rinork had let him loose with this crew it was likely a sign her son's pushing had her permission to go forward.

"We needn't take them in a frontal assault, my Second," said the Scout with a trace of amusement in his tone. "The three of us may simply move to the side. We *can* move aside."

"Then we do that," said Jethri, "to the left."

Jethri'd already started in that direction but the bulk of the oncoming group was changing direction too, angling to that portion of the walk.

"Jeth, maybe now we call the proctors and get them to walk us through," suggested Freza. "We can just turn about . . ."

But that was becoming less possible because the docksiders were standing away from their chairs and beers now, whether to rally around Freza and her friends or just to watch a scuffle wasn't obvious. Perhaps the proctors were even now on their way, Jethri began to hope.

"It will be hard, my friends," went on Rinork's heir, "to ignore these three who approach, even though we all know that Rinork and Ixin do not meet, for come full on us now is the new son of the House, this man who relies on men met in back hallways to tutor him in his bows."

There was murmur from his backers and one as well from the forming crowd of onlookers.

"Perhaps he and his pilot will be kind enough to the remove himself from our path and return with their painted doxy to some place out of the way of . . ."

"I see and I hear the delm's heir," Jethri called out in Trade, his voice much firmer than he felt. "It is in the nature of spaceports that ways are tight, and we shall merely pass by, knowing each that the other was present and acted properly."

With a bow recognizing the import of Delm Rinork's heir, Jethri signaled that he would move aside, the while fuming that he shouldn't push on the affront to Freza, nor even on something as distantly in his *melant'i* as the description he had heard of sig'Flava, which in a Liaden port he might have. "Pass, please. In all honor, pass."

"So, artificial Ixin, do you mean to play as if you are civilized these days?"

Now stopped and with the weight of the wall behind him—he preferred that to the side that was railed and overlooking the interior atrium—Jethri bowed again.

Multiple challenges there, but Jethri was trying to let them pass, even as Freza was talking to someone who wasn't him in a quiet voice, saying, "Alert crew, *Balrog*, and pass the word. Jethri's trying to let 'em slide by though . . ."

"Please, pass, Bar Jan chel'Gaibin, you and all of your company. We shall report it as a calm passage to Ixin herself."

Bar Jan signaled stop to his group, and they did so, all but Bar Jan himself: he came closer.

"Oh, Ixin is the key, is it? I should be impressed that you'll say pleasant things about me to Ixin? And what about the *other* family you have? You seem to have far too many sides to cry to; does Ixin also adopt all of the Gobelyns from their House ship *Gobelyn's Market*?"

All of this was delivered in such an oratorical manner, with pauses and postures and flourishes, that Jethri wondered if it had been practiced in front of a mirror the way he'd practiced his own bows.

In Liaden, chel'Gaibin added a short phrase Jethri's ears caught, and so did the Scout's—none of the other Terran watchers knew the words but they got the venom of "*Hift osti skant!*"—which in Terran became, more or less, "Honor flees what touches you!"

"You must clarify all of this, Jeth Ree." He pronounced the name as if it were both Liaden and a cuss word, as far as Jethri could see— and no doubt so could the Scout and other Liadens as well. The errors were no errors; instead it was a pile of insult upon insult, establishing an almost unsupportable amount of Balance due.

"From what sides to gather your *melant'i*, Oh Trader? That you dare to be seen in public with a disfigured woman? That you travel to ports that don't recognize a Master Trader's ring? How can you defend your place when you have *blood kin*"—and that was not in Trade, but in Terran as if the insults were studied indeed!—"blood kin, willing to strike someone in the face—in the *face*, false Ixin—without warning or provocation? That Balance is worth more than the other one she did not pay, but worry not, it is not forgot and is writ in bold, and I keep close accounts. I will see my accounts Balanced."

"He wishes you to challenge him, Second. I would not advise you to do so . . ." The Scout's words went by barely noticed, with Jethri reviewing the number and depth of the insults inflicted so far, most of them egregious enough singly to require a major Balancing and together—

"Your catalog must surely be incomplete," Jethri started, his mouth working before his mind fully caught up, "for you have yet to discuss my clumsiness, my infelicity of language, and my ongoing partnership with a valued member of your own clan."

The barely permitted sneer on the man's face gave way to a flash of startlement. Could it be, thought Jethri, that Tan Sim's arrangements would be unremarked? Or was it merely considered trivial?

The Liaden trader gave a small laugh and a short bow of acknowledgment. "But I have already discussed that, have I not? The absolute failure of your joint puppy-plays at bowing were brought to your attention the last time we spoke, before Rinork as well as Ixin!"

Jethri plunged ahead—"We went beyond that, and so he has my name to call upon! I continue to favor him, to wish him well, as he was well the last time I saw him."

"What foolishness! Your efforts to influence the boy are of little moment. He can hardly own his own clothes much less a pod after the end of his current voyage—there's a penalty for nonperformance, and it will come first from his stipends and then from his private funds. He is broken, does he but know it, and if you have partnered, well may he draw you under too!"

Jethri sighed hard, almost too hard to his own mind, put his hand up to signal pause . . .

"But there, we have spoken of the one we have most in common, and find that he is alive to both of us yet. Now we might declare that we've noticed each other on port." Jethri made an encompassing motion with his arm, including the entire Liaden contingent.

"Your time and that of your companions is surely more valuable than mine, and I beg you to pass on that you need not be seen talking overlong with one you admire so little. Forgive me for keeping you."

His motion continued, and with a sweeping gesture he showed Bar Jan an open path, only somewhat littered by the curious Terran docksiders, who assisted by backing out the way themselves, emulating his sweeping arms.

Jethri heard Freza's suppressed laugh and her muttered, "Sorry, Jeth," but by then Bar Jan's face had gone past bland to jaw-throb as he saw the growing crowd exaggerating and repeating Jethri's gesture.

"You would do well to learn the rules of Balance, Trader, before dealing with a true Liaden. Your bloodkin follow your lead and overstep, and now you bring the thing to others who can have no clue as to what might befall . . ."

"Not their quarrel," Jethri said in colloquial Terran, then giving his closest translation in Trade before falling into a formal Liaden to say, "This is among those who have read the Code; the Code declares it!"

Bar Jan palpably stiffened and his color rose.

"You dare to declare yourself covered by the Code?"

"As well as I am able, I follow the Code," Jethri declared, still in Liaden. "That's what the Code is for—to help *me* act correctly at all times in an uncertain universe. If others act otherwise it is because they are not covered by the Code—that would be the people behind me, for example, and my cousin Khat and most of my bloodkin, who act from Terran learning—or because they are badly schooled and misapply or refuse the direction of the Code."

Jethri pulled what he could from his lessons with Master tel'Ondor, understanding that between them, he and chel'Gaibon had wandered very far into fight-now territory. There was an out of sorts, and he sought it, wishing not to have a fight here on the docks with hard-armed Liadens and a bunch of shipfolks dressed for no more than a neighborly chat or maybe a quick-fisted brangle.

He bowed, much lower than he should, and moved closer than he liked to his tormentor, using the most formal language and most careful tones in the quietest voice to keep the words as much as could be between the two of them.

"Thus, permit me to suggest that we can keep this to ourselves and you will pass by, with forbearance of friends and acquaintances permitting us both to move on and begin anew at another and more propitious time."

Jethri knew his reading of the Code was sketchy, but he was dealing with someone who claimed to be of a High House, someone who should recognize the offer as a way to avoid what could only be a chaotic mess if allowed to go to a portside brawl. The forbearance thing would let them both bow to their trains and suggest that something had been taken too strongly and should be set aside by all. It was one of the outs given to the very young, or the very inebriated, and each could use the *melant'i* of having been generous under pressure. . . .

There was, at first, no response.

"He still seeks your challenge, Second."

The Scout's quiet words came through Jethri's tunneled attention and failed to chill his narrowly controlled anger. He'd almost rather be bloodied in a fight than take any more of this bashing away at his family and his right to be left alone to just trade in peace. The more he thought about it, the more he wanted to strike out . . .

"We can take them," was Freza's take on the situation, right behind ter'Astin's and exactly what he didn't want to see happen. The low sounds from the docksiders made it clear that they, too, were expecting trouble. Would someone just call the proctors? An out-and-out, cross-culture fight wouldn't sit well on his record when it came time for a Master Trader test, nor would it sit well—he was certain—with Norn ven'Deelin, his Ixin mother on *Elthoria*.

Jethri's hopes rose as chel'Gaibin turned half away as if to direct his company to move on, but then he saw the gesture the trader made with both hands, a turned back, and a shuffled left foot, as if he'd brushed something repulsive off his cape, and then kicked it away in disgust with the very tip of his boot so as not to sully himself otherwise.

Taking a deep breath, Jethri tried once more, somewhat louder, pulling to mind the proper section numbers of the Code, and in Liaden voicing the phrase, "Honored chel'Gaiban, I beg your consideration—the Code clearly states that accidental face-to-face meetings or confrontations may be treated with forbearance in cases like this . . ." Here he named the lines and numbers, emphasizing the parts that might permit chel'Gaiban to be seen as being patient with a child, a drunk, someone of distressed or untrustworthy mind—

The trader whirled then, crossing most of the distance between them in three quick steps.

"I—I am incompetent you say? *I* am to be excused for my behavior by you, my supposed better?"

He turned to backers then, raising his voice even louder, his Liaden rolling in *melant'i* play cadences. "This man harbors dangerous secrets, secrets that will cost the lives and livelihood of Liadens! He permitted himself to be adopted by Ixin so that he could move among us, and now see what he does? He stands side by side with one of the conspirators who would insure that Liad fails! He is a danger to us all. He must be stopped before his condescension convinces."

On one side of him the Scout straightened and began to move forward, and on the other side, it was Freza, who he restrained only by putting his arm in front of her.

Before Jethri could reply, before even he'd recovered his surprise, chel'Gaiban looked about to be sure that all eyes were on him, and called out in laborious Trade:

"I spit on your condescension, you savage! I spit on your caution, I spit on your blood kin and I spit on your mothers and whatever port scum might have begotten you."

With that he *did* spit on Jethri, whose efforts to cover his face only made Bar Jan laugh, while the whole performance drew mixed jeers and mutters from the locals.

"There, you fool! You have the necessity of saving your honor. I shall meet you when and where you will, and I will watch you suffer with gladness! Name your second!"

"Jethri! You can't do this!" Freza held on to his upper arm while he wiped his face with a clean rag she'd dragged from her pocket. The Scout stood impassive guard at his back, having volunteered his services as his duel second with one quick bow.

Jethri looked over the eager crowd behind him, shaking his head at the size it had grown to.

"Certainly," he said in Trade as he tried to center himself, "I can't do this here . . ."

"Jeth, think!"

He nodded at her quietly, an odd calm on him now. Something needed to be done and he meant to have it solved before he supped— if ever he did again. Something needed to be solved—but they needed more room, that was certain.

"Jeth, wait. Proctors say they'll be here in force in ten minutes!"

"We've got to move quickly then, don't we?"

Jethri turned to the still-raging chel'Gaiban.

"The proctors are on their way. If you wish to do this, we'll do it now."

Chel'Gaibin turned—

"Come, there's more room at the end of the deck. My second has appointed himself and I accept. We'll do this at the end of the deck— it'll take the proctors longer to get to us there."

· · · ✦ · · ·

"Tell *Balrog* to spread the word to slow the proctors," Jethri told Freza as they marched toward the far end, as if he had the right to give such orders. She cussed up a storm about it, and complied, the while talking in undertones as if to herself as the crowd moved and swelled.

The destination was the long wall just beyond *Dulcimer,* where several impromptu vendors had set up, and where stacks of hand-carted goods and free-boxed goods awaited placement on the local break-load freighters, or maybe were open-stored from *Dulcimer*'s own holds since they weren't much beyond the rented rack of tools.

The Liaden contingent was outnumbered four or five to one as they started forward; Jethri took one look at them over his shoulder and thought it best to ignore them. They were not pursuing him— they were joining him.

"Have you dry-shot or sim-shot against a live opponent?" the Scout asked. "Drilled? Held a triple shot?"

"No," said Jethri, "only targets. Only pocket guns, only to be sure I knew how they worked if I need to work them."

"Do you intend to die or shall I seek his second and make amends if they are to be made?"

"His the fault—that is, his the challenge, is that right?"

The Scout, a quarter step back, "That is correct. He permits you to choose the field and the weapon—which is acceptable, as you see, else we'd not be in motion. As to the time, it is apparent that we agree on that, since he and his second shall be there promptly as well."

"All I have gunwise is a pocket pistol—are we supposed to supply our own? The rules . . ."

"Given the haste, I am assuming that neither side will have access to well-matched dueling equipment. We can only hope for equivalences in power, and will have to, I suppose, work with a back-to-back start and pace off."

Jethri hurried on, eyes not quite forward as he passed *Dulcimer* and its rented tool rack, the guardian child now joined by three adults, dusty and pale, all leaning against the rental rack, eyes on him with benign interest. A tall skinny woman barely beyond girl saluted him, and when she did, the even-taller young man beside her did the same. He'd love to be able to talk and chat, to admire the rentals which were always so pretty—and so expensive!

He could see the set of Coslet calipers, and a thankfully sealed set of contagion flamers. Less esoteric were the multiple matched sets, all properly handed, of hammers, punches, bars, and expansion sockets. Oh, to be back in the simple days when these were the things he worked with, safely out of the eyes and ken of other people!

He nodded to them all, the tools and the people, bowing a little to the child.

From his side, a harrumph . . .

"I must, according to Code, have a clear answer to my question, Jethri of Ixin. Shall you continue this, shall you beg forgiveness, or shall I work to achieve an understanding with his second?"

Jethri strode on, rounding the corner at the end of the walkway to stand on the end deck where, if there were a large ship docked, there'd be a pressure tube or other entrance. Instead the currently unassigned area's temp users moved toward the rush, and the words, "Fight, Liadens, duel, proctors, fight, spit, mess, duel, Liadens" came from the crowd, the din not banking Jethri's tension, but building it.

"I heard you, Pilot," Jethri admitted, and suppressing a gulp he went on as calmly as he could, "and I think where we're at is *it needs fixing now*. He can apologize, and offer a Balance amount, else we have to settle it. So talk at his second, and see if there's a reasonable offer."

They stopped, looked at each other, Jethri receiving the bow of will expressed and understood, which Jethri accepted with an assurance he hardly felt. Fights he knew about, and rarely to his own advantage. This stuff, these duels, full of dare and bravado and clan honor, they were not what he'd grown up to—

The Scout studied the ends of the area, waiting for *Wynhael*'s crew to catch up, studying the cases and boxes and vendor shanties, measuring something only he saw and moving them toward a section of blank wall, but for a single emergency door, behind them and leaving the same at the other end of the walk for the opposition.

Jethri paced, Freza nodding to herself and the saying "Jeth—if you're sure . . ."

He nodded at her bleakly, pleased that he'd at least seen her today and sorry if he was about to bring blood and anger into her day.

"Have to," he told her, "else they'll be after everyone, pushing and full of themselves. Got to stop some of it—show them there's ways around or we'll know why not!"

She reached for his hand, nodded, dropped his hand to touch her earpiece, nodding, and looked seriously into his face.

"*Balrog*'s let the other levels know, and they'll do something about being in the way if you need it to slow the proctors, in or out . . ."

He nodded, paced. The Liadens, for all their necessity, were taking their time. Freza paced beside him, wordless, soundless.

The scout came to him, pointing to the end walls and saying things Jethri didn't really want to hear; they seemed to come in bursts, but that was, "Clear line of fire."

The Scout's arms pointed to spaces, waving people out of them.

"He's some experienced," opined the Scout. "I have no information about his performance. He's likely more familiar with the weapons than you. He means to make you as nervous as possible with his paces . . . Your goal must be to massively disable or kill on the first shot. Do you hear me?"

Jethri bowed, felt himself almost bouncing on his feet, the energy growing in him . . .

"I do, Pilot," he managed, glaring at the slowly approaching figure who was smiling and chuckling with his mates as if this was a common occurrence, this going to kill someone.

"We'll pace, whatever you decide, I guess, and when I turn I keep as thin as I can toward him, showing him my shooting arm, and when I aim, I aim for the top quadrant. If he shows any chest I shoot left center line."

"Practical. And if you're new to it, I'll try to keep it close. Ten paces or maybe seven."

Jethri nodded. Something he'd hardly been accused of on the *Market*, this being practical.

Wynhael's contingent was finally in the area—Jethri briefly entertained the idea that they were hoping the proctors would arrive to interrupt the proceedings—and the Scout moved forward to talk with the opposite second, who now was wearing his holstered gun openly, as were others of the Liadens. Perhaps they were not happy with the odds if something went wrong.

"We have the felicity," said Bar Jan's second, "of being able to offer the opportunity of using first-rate dueling weapons, long in Clan Rinork's possession. Please feel free to inspect as we discuss distances . . ."

Jethri froze, and then he heard the words over in his mind, saw the pistols being unwrapped and displayed . . . a sealed matched set of prize pistols!

"We shall not!"

Jethri strode to his second, demanded of him, "You will not accept such coincidence in my name, Second! And you will follow first the Code!"

Bar Jan practically laughed, his smirk growing large, but Jethri ignored him.

"He is out of order, as you know! First, the terms!"

A bow of absolute obedience from the Scout, and he turned to his opposite, face serene and steady.

"Jethri ven'Deelin, Clan Ixin, sometimes known as Jethri Gobelyn, suggests that he is open to an apology from Clan Rinork, and will accept a thoughtful compensation from Rinork, after a reasonable and thoughtful apology is received. Otherwise, we reserve the right to choose weapons, as by the Code we are encouraged to do, and to prosecute this to the fullest extent, without reserve."

The Scout looked up into the opposing dozen, and said, "Those of you who swear to Rinork, you should know your nadelm is at extreme risk. Please advise him and his second to take our offer, else your House is at risk of losing him."

This pretty speech Jethri could not judge, but wondered was it out of hand to appeal to a group of clan members and crew to outrank the perpetrator?

Young Rinork's face was almost as bland as the Scout's. "Your offer infers a risk out of proportion to normal situations. Do you think we suffer that?"

"Ixin has a history of preparing children well, I believe. It is a history Rinork knows. In my role as second I must remind you of this. My primary is competent and secure in his abilities."

Bar Jan was smiling now, which by this point he should not be: the formal was the formal and not be trifled with. He shared glances with his followers, making light by gesture and expression of the offer.

Jethri seethed, and kept seething, the sheer effrontery and trickery of his foe at the fore. Who came out walking on the docks with matched dueling pistols?

"We shall not demur nor offer tribute," said the Liaden's second, taking his lead on slight motions from chel'Gaibin. It was properly done, though Jethri still vaguely hoped his man would cave.

· · · ※ · · ·

The Scout turned to Jethri, whose mind kept repeating the mantra he'd heard Paitor and his father say back and forth to each other when entering into a trade port, or talking of negotiations: "All I ask is an honest advantage."

Clearly, chel'Gaibin was not so fussy.

And what honest advantage did he have?

Oh, ay, he had the crowd advantage—he could see them pressing forward to watch, some with smiles and nods for him, though to many of them he was simply another fancy trader off a big ship, far away from their experience, just one who'd been wronged. Others knew he was Terran, some few knew he might be called a looper himself.

"Your kind offer has been refused. The opposition suggests dueling pistols—which they have to hand, I note—at twenty-five paces! I suggest personal arms rather than duelers, but otherwise I have little to offer if you will not consider a demur at this point."

Jethri glanced back toward the crowd, along the line of ships were comfortable *Balrog* set second to *Dulcimer*'s hardworking crew.

Personal arms.

He said it loudly, in Trade.

"Tell them their offer to use Rinork's weapons continues distasteful to me. Nor shall we use our personal weapons, which might give either of us an unfair or unlooked for advantage. We shall solicit neutral weapons, as may be found on any dockside. The good people here will offer what we need, I'm sure!"

The crowd buzzed, and some began unholstering guns, knives, and daggers, moving forward to display them . . .

"Again, give Rinork the opportunity to admit their error. They must have this, as their man is not capable of defeating me on this dock."

The Scout bowed without hesitation, and repeated the information as intended, in Liaden.

Scorn on the faces of *Wynhael*'s crew, and chel'Gaibin laughed—

"It does not matter whose random pistol I use, the man falls to me," he proclaimed in bad Trade, "Yes, borrowed weapons will do, neutral weapons will do, greasy weapons, I do not care! Please call for them so we might end this farce!"

Jethri looked about him and could hear the stories stirring, if he won or if he lost. This would travel even faster and further than his infamous leap.

He turned half to the crowd while looking at the trickster, and then more to the crowd, some small hope growing.

"My opponent, be not afraid of random weapons! We shall ask for matched sets, and you may choose left hand or right hand as you need, for I'm proficient with either."

To the crowd, and particularly to the dusty, tired crew of *Dulcimer*, he said, "Please, quickly!"

Turning to chel'Gaibin he said, "We shall duel to incapacity or death. Is that your understanding? You shall not withdraw?"

"I shall not withdraw, upstart. As I am of Rinork, incapacity or death shall be sufficient." There was no bow, not a courtesy.

"As you will, Rinork!"

Jethri was vibrating and near breathless with tension but he looked out toward the crowd, motioning them closer before turning and defiantly bowing a bow of sorrow before unleashing his plan.

"Stink hammers and starbars, seven paces and closing! We shall have a smash to remember!"

The crowd roared with approval, replacing guns and knives to their safe places, and eyes turning to *Dulcimer*'s rental rack of tools.

Wynhael's crew, from the least to Rinork, stood motionless.

The Scout managed a very credible bow of approval, and turned to explain.

· · · · ✳ · · · ·

Having it to hand, Jethri swung the starbar, feeling the balance of it and the grip. It was a number seven, extending his arm by half, and by the looks of it was nearly new, the pry edges lustrous, the tip sharp enough to peel hull steel, the closer end a counterweight larger than his fist.

It was the stinks hammer that was key, of course, for in a dock fight, one struck with the hammer and guarded and defended with the bar. A good stinks hammer had lots of mass in the head, and could—properly thrown—crush a skull or cave in a chest. Wielded in hand it might have the same results, but the tear edge could slice a face or a throat, the poll could be used as a grab to bring someone closer so that the starbar could be used to batter . . .

All this Jethri knew by repute and from the careful jousting he'd seen Grig and his father play at in the back hold several trips—so long ago that whatever close-in technique delivered was long gone, the examples in his head only in awed memory. Once Arin was dead and gone, the only fighting Jethri'd heard about was Iza's on-port fist-and-bottle work, and that only at a distance, since she'd been careful not to include him in any of her carousing, or for that matter, to let him carouse himself, though he'd hardly been of age for it.

"Brawling is not a duel!" This was chel'Gaiban's second, holding the items he'd chosen from the offerings, "how can you think so? The Code requires the first strike to be at a distance! Can you demonstrate this?"

The Scout turned to Jethri, eyebrows a query.

"He may have some point . . ."

"He has none!"

Jethri, hammer in hand, strode to the wine vendor in the corner, pointing to his wheeled bulk tank.

"I'll buy that—how much?"

The startled man stood back from him, eying the tools warily . . .

"Sir, I'd need to inventory . . ."

Jethri reached into his pocket, finding only the "luck" cantra Norn ven'Deelin had given him when first he'd joined the clan—

He threw it to the man, who recoiled and let it fall to the floor until he recognized it and then scooped it away.

"Will that do?"

Chel'Gaibin was yelling something but Jethri ignored him as the man nodded and retreated from Jethri, who strode to the tank with its

neat Decade label the size of his head and at eye height—and put his
back against it.

Then Jethri called out—"I demonstrate!"

"One, two, three . . ." He enumerated each footfall and stepped
out seven quick paces, whirling with confidence, the hammer flashing
over his head and leaving his hand cleanly, centered on the logo, the
tank's explosion into a shrapnel of plastic and metal and a cloud of
red wine booming across the otherwise silent deck. The hammer's
clang against the outer metal wall echoed close behind, all joined by
cheers from the boisterous audience.

"Action at a distance!" Jethri's voice carried over the din, and
raising the starbar he still carried, he cried, "defensible, and with
follow-up until the issue is decided!"

Chel'Gaibin was hidden from Jethri's view behind his tool-
carrying second and the knot of *Wynhael* crew, and from that side
there were voices, raised to each other in varying modes—including
a mode of command so high Jethri doubted he'd heard it outside the
training room—saying, "You will support me! We shall follow
through, at any cost!"

Chel'Gaibin's second fell back from his master, bowing almost to
the floor.

"Sir, your hammer, sir. And your cantra, sir, it was beautiful! I'll
deliver an invoice for true cost. . . ."

The vendor smelled a bit of his wares and was not entirely steady
on his feet, wiping the hammer, handing it to him with the toweling,
still rubbing it as if shining a precious object and the last moment,
stepping between Jethri and the action across the way.

Jethri absently took and pocketed the cantra, checking the
hammer and finding nothing amiss. He restrained the vendor, who
was Bah lo, according to his nametag, gently removing the still-
admiring hand from the hammer, stepping toward the seconds, who
were deep in an urgent conversation marked by the hand-signs they
flung between themselves.

The crowd parted before Jethri— who called out to the Scout, "The
proctors will be here momentarily!"

"There's doubts," said the Scout, "on the progress; were there
an arbiter of Code nearby we'd need refer to them. There is not,
and now . . ."

Rinork's heir appeared before them then, brushing the crew aside, glaring at all three of them, starbar and stink hammer clutched one to a hand.

"I am acclimating myself to the weapons. We will not, in fact, be needing an arbiter of Code as the case is that I have agreed with the fine points as presented. If one may suggest crowd control, I shall be ready in a moment. Second, I leave him to you."

That bow was a command—and the hands of the pilots flashed.

"I'll take the crowd, Jeth. You get ready!"

That was Freza, and she suited action to words, by raising her voice to an out-and-out shout.

"This is a private affair of honor, so you'll all have to stand away, get out of the way. Move back—you can watch, but you're in the way."

Someone started yelling—"And who are you, stranger . . ." but Freza'd already pulled a ring from her pocket and put it on, waving it over her head.

"I'm assistant sector commissioner for the Seventeen Worlds—anyone not involved will clear the space so we can continue, please."

Jethri saw a quick rush of hands and bodies then, while Freza named several names while pointing. "Right side, center, left, make a path! Clear the lane!"

Freza looked into his face from five paces away, giving him a look as inscrutable as a Liaden trader's before giving him a wry smile, saying more to him than anyone else "Brabham is the commissioner—took the job a ten-day ago. Now get this over!"

She turned her back then, ter'Astin saying in an underbreath as he hurried Jethri toward the area still flooded by the pooling wine. "Things happen. The second would retire were he able, but he feels he cannot. The boy—"

A clang and yell rang out—and there, Rinork's heir had thrown the starbar to the decking where it slid into a line of startled spectators, the hammer following with dangerous bounces and caroms, scattering all.

"Ixin! Ixin, you shall fight properly or die where you are! Pull your weapon!"

In one glance Jethri took in the charging chel'Gaibin, gun in hand, rushing away from his own pursuing second, saw that gun arm coming to point . . .

Jethri saw the Scout was turning, gun coming to hand, but he, sensing motion behind him, ducked . . .

Jethri's throw was desperate and full strength, his carry-through bending and turning him, knocking him off balance so that all he heard were shots and a thud and saw a flash of light and a strange whine while he rolled, grabbing for his pocket gun to—

A huddled pile of of clothes and blood lay on the deck, writhing, as someone dared to kick the fallen gun away. The yelling gave way to silence other than the crying, and then another kind of roar as the crowd rushed toward the fallen Jethri and he couldn't see—

"You're hit," said Freza as he pulled himself to his feet, while the Scout was snatching at pockets and pouch, pulling something out . . .

"Let me see," demanded Jethri. "Please, out of my way . . ."

The man lay, shivering, face blooded, arm at an impossible angle, huddled against himself as best he might, watching Jethri approach, a semicircle of observers standing away.

A Liaden it was who bowed, quite carefully, to Jethri, to the wronged, to the victor, presenting the hammer as if it were a precious gift, while the eyes of the downed man were wide and unblinking.

Jethri wiped the sweat away from his left eye, took the hammer, saw the man on the floor shiver, a spasm going through him as he tried to move his arm, blood and flesh tangled in the sleeve, bone splinter—

Jethri flinched, realized he was breathing hard, free of anger but full of tension . . .

"Jeth, you're bleeding!"

Freza, beside him, the Scout, too, tearing something, the while saying to Freza, "He must choose, he must choose!"

Jethri shook his head, Terran-style, hand to the side of his face again, feeling the sweat but unsurprised, now that throbbing had set in, to see that it was blood.

The still-shocked second stood away from chel'Gaiban and when Jethri's gaze fell on him he bowed submission, he bowed error, he bowed—

"It was not the plan, I swear—sir."

"Acceptance," Jethri said as he recalled that bow, *accepting the word of one of another clan.*

"I hear you, Pilot, and believe you. Call for medics, call for proctors. This man has had an *accident*, do you understand? He is incapacitated. Take him away!"

"An accident?"

"Yes, an accident!"

The second bowed fervently, ordered cleanup, ordered others around the fallen man—

Jethri's view was blocked now, and Freza was by his side, her work vest showing sudden pockets. For his part he stared as *Wynhael*'s crew did what first aid they might for Rinork's git. An alarm went off, signifying medical emergency.

From the crowd then, a woman called out, "I'm a medic, and have another coming, let me through!"

A ship medic that was and . . .

"Hold still!" A hand was on his cheek then, Freza's voice in his ear. He stood as rooted already, no need to order him . . .

"Sting coming. Close your eyes."

It did sting, and by the time the bleeding at his hairline had been wiped and spray-sealed, the first-aid efforts of *Wynhael*'s crew were taken over by uniformed professionals.

· · · ❋ · · ·

"And what happened—can you give me that again?"

Jethri sighed. "I knew the man—we've met before. He's traded on some of the same ports I have. He was showing me his gun and there was an accident."

The proctor got a distant look in his face—brushed the plate that said Detective but Jethri didn't know if that meant he'd turned the recorder on or off.

"Wonderful strong accident, wasn't it? Got you blooded? Got him smashed near to finders?"

"But that was it, you know, he was showing me that fancy pistol of his and he had that armor on, and when the gun discharged—why, I bet it was heard all over the port—that armor had to dump energy from a couple of shots. Fellow panicked . . ."

The proctor held the stinks hammer out to him. "And this?"

"Borrowed that from the *Dulcimer*, you know. I saw you talking with them and it isn't any of their fault, other than now you've got that listed as evidence about the time they'll be needing it. It's just a stinks hammer and . . ."

"I know what it *is*—and this?"

Here he pointed to the chipped face edge where the shot had grazed the hammer, sending shrapnel into Jethri and a couple other folks as well.

"Yeah, I'm not so good with those things anymore, I've been trading! When the gun started going off, it was the only thing I had, so I held it in front of me . . . I took the angle wrong and . . ."

"And that's how you got wine and blood on it?"

"No, the wine was because I was testing the hammer. The blood was from the accident . . ."

"*Ga hod*, boy, but you've got a silver tongue. A wrong answer for everything, and all of it possible."

Jethri shrugged.

"So you're ship-bred, are you? Terran ship-bred?"

"My mother's line is old, and my father's. Raised on *Gobelyn's Market* . . ."

"And was you? Now—I've seen that ship name recent, really recent . . ."

He turned to his associate, a stern-faced woman reminding Jethri a lot of Iza, from the hard smug look in her face to the clip of her hair.

"*Gobelyn's Market?*" the detective said again, and she pulled her comm unit from its hanger on her belt and threw fingertips at the screen, but even as she did she was saying, "Right, wasn't that the one was in face-off with a Liaden ship and got throwed off-port somewhere?"

Jethri kept his face Liaden bland at that news—thrown off-port was not something they'd been doing when he was with the *Market*, and must have made Paitor's trading heart bleed!

She looked up, grimly.

"*Therinfel*, it was, not *Wynhael*. *Wynhael* is the ship the hurt boy's from. We didn't have a warning for them, but for the *Gobelyn's Market*, Pilot Captain Iza Gobelyn, and First Mate Khat Gobelyn. Liadens laid charges of smuggling, of interfering with clan business— dunno that's a crime here, money-changing fraud—heck, that'd be hard to prove, too, wouldn't it?"

"I'm not on the *Market*, am I? Haven't been for over a Standard. Look at the old record and you're going to see pure as can be . . ." He was not so pleased to hear the *Market* named this way, but Khat's new spot was good. . . .

The woman with the comm scrunched her nose up. "A warning or two on that first pilot, but ship clean as can be for thirty Standards."

"Humph . . ." was the lead proctor's reaction.

"So you know, the boy with the bad arm, he's still to sickbay. Got his—what's that man called? His helper with him."

"A valet. Gentlemen have valets. That's what he says he is—"

The proctor shook his head, "Not any place for a gentleman here, right?" He looked up, coloring, toward Jethri.

"That Scout tells me you're accounted a Liaden gentleman these days. How you worked it I don't want to hear. He tried to tell me your *melant'i* is appreciable, whatever it means. He sets quite some store by it though, says you're substantial and appreciable . . ."

What to answer? Was his *melant'i* considerable? Yes, then, here it was, with his public victory . . .

"Everyone has *melant'i*," Jethri explained in as downport Terran as he could. "Part of who you are. Me, I'm adopted to a clan, so once the clan's important, I get some of that, and since I carry myself well, I get some of that. If I screw up, that falls to the clan too . . ."

The proctor looked long and hard at him.

"That means it won't help us if I go check all the cameras and see if any one of them was actually working, because what you did was right?"

Jethri bowed: "I have acted with as much honor as I might today. That anyone was injured was an accident of the day . . ."

The proctor leaned close and said, pulling out a small instrument, "Right. I need you to breathe into here, so we can tell you wasn't drinking that wine that's on the deck and you ought to just let me press this against the flesh of your palm . . ."

Jethri sighed, breathed into the tube, and then held his hand out as directed.

"Be it noted that the subject has complied with testing and that neither breath or blood shows signs of intoxicants or inebriants."

The associate played fingers over the face of the comm, and the proctor nodded.

"So now, since I'm told that the young man in sickbay isn't talking anything but Liaden right now, I'll need you to translate and help identify him, if you will. That guy that's with him has about half a word of Trade and nothing of Terran. I'll also need you to sign in the line for the rescue fees and for the crew we scrambled to stop a fight that never happened, since he's not talking. If someone else is at fault, they'll pay. You being a substantial fellow, we won't need to check the cameras. I think that's what you was trying for, Pilot. Always is better to keep things in the health system instead of the judicial system, don't you think?"

Chapter Twenty-Eight

· · · · ·✳· · · · ·

Port Chavvy

THE PATIENT WAS IN the portside infirmary, where the waiting room had a proctor flirting with a medic. The proctor that had come with Jethri and the Scout stopped with his uniform mates and wordlessly waved toward the room with the green light on outside it. The voices there were quiet, almost soothing.

"Been in space, not a spacer, is what I think I got so far. His muscle mass is a bit low, I'd say, but that could be . . ."

There were three medics, one checking straps and connections to a wall of lights and readouts, two others examining the stark white and wrong-looking arm of the man on the table.

Jethri knocked on the door as he walked in, took the simple Liaden "You!" from the examination table as an expletive.

"I'm Jethri ven'Deelin," he told the medics in Trade. "I speak Liaden, Terran, and Trade."

"A moment, champ," said one, "you're what we've been needing. We're going to need some permissions real soon, and this fellow's on relaxants."

Standing near Bar Jan's head was a man in Rinork's house livery. It sounded as if he'd been singing a low distracting song to Bar Jan. He looked up, serious eyes and grim face.

"Trader ven'Deelin?" The accent was heavy in Liad's homeworld breathlessness. He didn't wait for an answer, though, straightening to his full spare height and making his livery straight as well.

"Trader ven'Deelin. I am Khana vo'Daran Clan Baling," the man told Jethri over a simple bow to ranking authority. "I have stood as valet to this man Bar Jan chel'Gaibin since the day my uncle retired from that position fifteen Standards gone. I stand at his side still, as he'll have me and needs me."

That little speech gave Jethri time to weigh the nuance and see it as a canny play. Should he bow to acknowledge, *melant'i* would require Jethri to give direction to the valet, at least in this short-term situation. Should he *not* bow to accept, he'd be deferring responsibility to the Scout, who stood frozen and mostly unnoticed just inside the door. The station authorities were not being singled out as having any authority at all.

"Shanna, do you dare?" Bar Jan attempted to sit up, the quick restraining efforts by the medic reinforced by straps already holding him.

The valet ignored the mode of superior to low hire, replying in a soothing subtle mode used by family and servants in dealing with children.

"It is what we have learned to do, my lord, when an illness came upon you, or the migraines. We have both of us learned to permit things done which must be done. I have neither the language nor the *melant'i* this man does, my lord."

Bar Jan cursed quietly, then asked—"But where are the others?"

"Back to *Wynhael*, sir, which is how I was informed of your need. I came immediately."

"And is my delm informed of my situation?"

"Yes, lord, the delm is informed; I made my way as quickly as I might to see if I might aid before she arrives. Rinork was asleep, keeping to her day schedule as she does."

"Does she know I am . . . impounded here?"

"I am informed only that she has been informed, lord, and was determining action. My sources are adept, as you know. I felt it best to be here well ahead."

"And you, Ixin? Do you come to gloat?" A nuanced question that, asked in a severe mode. Perforce Jethri replied in as neutral a mode as he could manage.

"I come to translate. I have informed officials that an accident occurred, causing us both wounds, thus I am here to be sure your recovery goes forward."

"I have seen my hand, fool. Recovery . . ."

"Have you seen my head, then? I must have it checked in some hours to be sure there is not a concussion."

Chel'Gaibin lifted his head as he might and saw the dressings Freza had applied.

"You have the luck of a *dramliz*, have you? But why an accident?"

"If they decide otherwise, we are all at risk—they might hold you and your second as rioters, or my second and associate as such, and all the crews as witnesses. We shall contrive other arrangements among us than jail cells, if we can."

"Champ, your buddy here's going to get a quick scan, he is—we'll need quiet. He may have pain—we need to put a scan board under his arm and then it'll take about fifteen seconds each time I say 'go.' They'll give us some sound images to work with and some heat images, too, and between them we'll know something.

"He can't see it, but if you want, you'll be able to watch that image build up there on that wall plate. We'll decide if we can do the work here or send him down to a bigger med center civilside. His other friend there—might be he should hold that free hand and be ready to have it squeezed right hard."

Jethri translated, telling both the valet and the trader as the med techs shifted a gridded white board nearby. The valet leaned in and without ceremony took hold of the free hand as the gridded board slid under the damaged arm. A swing arm was popped up out of the bed unit and brought within a hand's breadth of the arm and a small sliding device on that hummed gently.

"Right then, go!"

Jethri translated, watching the image of bones and ghostly outline of skin and muscle as it built up. Bar Jan said something very low and got just as low a reply from the valet.

"And go," said the medic, having clicked the device at another angle, and this time Bar Jan's good hand visibly spasmed and it was the valet who made a small sound as his hand was clenched.

"And go!"

Jethri's anatomy lessons were long ago but he saw enough of shattered bone, broken skin, and muscles torn from their moorings to cringe. This damage was no simple wrap and wait . . .

"One more, if you please. On the count of *go*!"

The sounds were louder and more complex this time, overriding the ordinary sounds of the air vents and making the small scuffles of sound from the bigger room fade into the background.

The sliding scan made three trips up and down that arm and it was as if the man being scanned shrank; his face got hard and he shut his eyes while both arms shook.

The medic did something that turned the image from side to side, showed it upside down, from interesting angles. Bone splinters, fractures and fractured fractures.

Sounds from the machine went down and sounds in the hall got louder, but when the doctor touched a button and dozens of points were highlighted as problem areas, Jethri grimaced, concentrating on what to tell Bar Jan.

"Hospital. Tell your buddy there I'll give him a boost on the pain med and we will send him directly to the big hospital. I've already sent the images and we've got a bed on call; even once everything's closed up we'll want to keep it still as we can for several days . . ."

Jethri heard a noise then, turned, saw Infreya chel'Gaibin standing in the door with several retainers, glaring.

"Do not take him away!"

She entered the room, glaring at all, with venomous attention coming to rest on Jethri.

"I will deal with him if you do not have the grace to finish it and he has not the grace to suicide!"

Rinork pushed her way to the side of her son, drawing a gun, the valet suddenly in between mother and son. She pushed against him without recognition, peering around his shoulder to hurl invective at volume.

"Failure! Schemer! You—"

She brought the gun up against the efforts of the valet to stop her.

Bar Jan shifted but restraints held him. His wide eyes shut and—

"Stop!" Jethri swung a forearm, slamming gun hand away from the trapped man. Before she could recover, the Scout had the gun.

"How dare you," she started but Jethri overrode her Liaden outburst in louder Trade.

"If I'd have killed him, or if he died of it now, we'd call it a fair fight and it'd be over. If you shoot him in cold blood, they'll space you for murder!"

The Scout approached, bowing equal to equal. "We all witness. If you were to shoot him now, I'd put you in the airlock myself."

Rinork herself stiffened. The Scout returned the weapon, sans charge.

The valet closed in, putting himself between the mother and the son again. Two of *Wynhael's* crewmen stood in the door, indecisive.

Rinork closed her eyes, shoving the empty gun into her pocket, whirled on the hapless valet—

"Turn out his pockets, take his jewelry. His clothes are not worth stripping."

She stood over the still-shaking man, momentarily blocking the valet from doing this duty.

"Open your eyes to me. You will do this!"

The shaking subsided, and the eyes did open, slowly came to focus.

"Tell me who I am."

A voice, barely a gasp, said, "Rinork. You are Rinork."

"Yes, I am Rinork. And you are dead. Dead to me, dead to the clan."

He sobbed then, tried to pull himself together, closed his eyes, sobbed.

In strong clear tones then, to the medics and to Jethri, she said in Trade, "He is dead!" Then she switched to Liaden, eyes glaring into Jethri's.

"Bar Jan chel'Gaibin is dead, as I, Rinork proper, declare to all who may hear. So shall it appear in the Gazette, that he died of his own folly on a Terran port. There shall be no Balance for stupidity."

"Do as I said," she told the minions at the door. "Leave him his clothes and nothing more. And you," she said, pointing haughtily at the valet, "have made your choice. Be his man and burn him when he dies—he is dead and you have jumped ship, as all proper Liadens shall know!"

Jethri looked to the Scout, who turned a bland face to him, his hands showing the pilot's sign *hold steady, hold steady, hold steady.* The Scout spoke then, gently, to Jethri alone: "I am helpless against tradition, helpless against the Code. It is her right!"

She turned, and her minions did as they were bid, reaching through the man's feeble protests, ignoring the protests of the medics, taking rings and necklaces and secret pocket things, pulling his boots and emptying a hidden cache.

The crew of the *Wynhael* was gone, leaving only the breathing body of a dead former Liaden High House trader, and his valet among strangers and enemies.

Chapter Twenty-Nine

• • • ◦※◦ • • •

Arrival on Halatan

HE WOKE IN TIME to get himself some 'mite from *Keravath*'s kitchen and retired to his cabin to spend another round wearing his reader. It was just as well that he wanted to study as the ship was approaching docking, but the Scout was surely out of sorts with the whole of Jethri's troublesome birthright and seemed disinclined to require his attendance at the second seat, or even at table for meals.

This section started with Arin's face leading a lecture, and then into the main thread of things. The information that the filament of the spiral arm the Seventeen Worlds called home was facing incoming gas and dust clouds wasn't exactly news, but the results of *his* tests and scan was.

Jethri felt a thrill of realization about reported dates of Arin's computations, and the depth and range of them. It might be his book could tell him for sure, but even quick arithmetic showed him how likely it was that the fractins-and-frames building he and Arin had played at for hours at a time were likely the times when Arin had done the computations on the gas flow and compression so important to his *Envidaria*.

And those results? Arin calmly elucidated the problems: the shift in gravity potential would simply move some Jump points out and away from the current expectations, and those changes could be a simple second of two, or light-minutes or even up to light-days. In some other places the Jump points could paradoxically move in, close to the stars, dangerously close—test runs would need to be frequent and accurate. The same system could go through phases of these changes: compression along known dark matter filaments could induce waves and the chance was that some of the underlying filaments might also move, creating the conditions that could eventually sling-shoot gas giants out of borderline stable systems or move rocky planets in.

Here in this section Arin was explaining a technical equation Jethri realized came from the piloting math, and it was images recorded in *Gobelyn's Market's* tiny trade office.

"Watching this curve," he said, "we'd expect minor changes over decades. Yet, if we look at the simple compression function here, and here"—Arin picked up a book as a prop, his book!—"and go to some likely rotational rates that one might deduce from a simple calculation based on numbers easily derived from recalling that the incoming gas is going to be streaming and heating at the same time it is being compressed, we'll see that the density goes way up. It begins to rival stellar mass as it transits. Look at this: ships above a certain size and mass limit will simply not be able to match the numbers and will spend a lot of energy for a Jump that cannot be made to work. Beneath that limit, yes, trade can go forth."

Here Arin opened his book, referred to a page, and put a number from that page on his display board, holding the book to point at the numbers in emphasis. He solved the math manually, with a bit of theatrical stuff at the end where he showed that "which lets us derive this number: an infinite amount of energy is needed to make the translation at the mass of a supermodern twenty-pod-plus ship on the Liaden and recent Combine approved major ship design, but a finite and doable translation at the mass of oh, say a common Loop ship or even some of the minor ore carriers.

"I've solved these equations theoretically, of course, because they'll fluctuate." Here he held the book in front of him and waved it again. "This is doable, and a trade system based on what we'll have is necessary unless we wish to see this whole section cut off. Eventually this compression ring will pass. We're talking four to five hundred years of potential complete isolation or we can build systems that will allow our ships and regions to survive and even prosper. Consider the lead time on building major trade vessels: fifteen Standards or more from laying the first spine to launch. Consider the current backlog and commitment levels to that building. Let the Liadens and the Combine folks have their games—they are committed to the size of ships they have for at least seventy Standards and closer to one hundred twenty Standards. There are larger ships in design and procurement, and I must say, let them build!

"My proposal is to let them work and for us to use the routes we'll have with designs we have or will build and we'll connect with them at a few points and still be part of trade while we build our own resources and avoid costly direct competition."

"Thank you for your time."

One last flash of the book, used to underline the math between loop ships and major trade vessels . . . and the *Envidaria* cut back to text.

The text he read several times and, as much as economics impacted trading, he'd not been pleased to slog through those sections, where sums and assumptions went from exa to pico, all based on the idea that someone somewhere knew exactly what moved markets. The gravitic anomalies, the changing shape of allowable orbits, and even the idea that a well-nigh invisible wall of sub-space stress might affect a ship's ability to transport food, such facts he had little problem with.

The other issue, of course, was this courier pilot, one Rand yos'Belin. Jethri'd been amazed to hear that ter'Astin's time at Tradedesk had been even more fruitful than his, but that was settling out in a direction that looked good.

It was kind of a hard thing knowing they could trust the woman, who was the same pilot he'd seen at Infreya chel'Gaiban's side at the Hall of Festivals. He'd guessed from ter'Astin's less convoluted explanations that she'd likely been the pilot who'd rummaged Jethri's clothes on *Keravath*, and this made him think ter'Astin had known her longer than he knew.

If ter'Astin and she were old bedmates reacquainted on the station, it might mean that—

What it meant was that the Scout was a professional and needed to be trusted on this.

The question of trust, though, brought him around to Freza, and what he might do about her. They both had schedules, and they both had things they were sworn to . . . but . . . yeah, he trusted her, and knew she understood he had things to do, too. Here he sighed, wondering if he'd end up with callouses on his ears if he saw her often enough. She'd made it plain that a shivaree would be fine with her, but they'd left Port Chavvy in a hurry in order to make the meeting here and finish with the whole birthright and *Envidaria* thing—and besides, they'd not had much in the way of a decent location with the *Balrog* being as small as it was and *Keravath* worse.

"Just let me know, Jeth. Give the word and we'll get things going the very next place we can."

She'd kissed him then, they having a more or less in the shadows location, and added, "Remember, if we get started we'll probably want more than a day to do things right. I'm willing to see how things play out, if you are."

The plan was that *Keravath* would land ter'Astin and him on Hatalan, which was about as neutral a place as they could find. They'd meet Pilot yos'Belin, with the Scout for his side, and they'd switch the hostage book—with his fractin a promised throw-in—for the *Envidaria*. It being fresh from the source, he'd swear it the latest edition.

Then, since *Elthoria's* schedules looked to be set that way, *Keravath* would take him directly to her next port, Ynsolt'i. In some ways he dreaded returning there—but the ship needn't set down so he wouldn't have to visit the landing area where he'd seen a man suicide for fear of the treachery of Liadens.

A low tone sounded. Well there, he had much to think on, and a landing to observe. He stuffed the *Envidaria* in its holster, and headed to the flight deck. In a little over an hour, they'd be on the ground.

• • • ✳ • • •

Busy was good, yes, and the Scout had given him a few minutes at the controls, insisting he ought to learn something about the ship's handling as they fell out of orbit and toward atmosphere.

"Is this not all automatic?"

The Scout chuckled. "No fear, Pilot Jethri, it shall not be your hands on the controls as we touch down. Nor, it happens, will it be mine, though I will sit backup. Hatalan has now a more than adequate integrated air traffic system—if we wish we may watch mere airliners or distant blimps float by our glorious starship . . ."

The Scout laughed again, as if the approaching landing was allowing concern to slip away.

"I forget," the Scout said, "that unlike most of my contemporaries, and most of yours in trade, you are not a planet dweller nor have been willingly. Many young people see starships as a freedom they cannot have on their homeworlds, and often ascribe amazing power and riches to pilots and anyone who leaves the surface of planets regularly.

"This place is full of sand and grit, Sir Guest Pilot. The children often become farm overseers or cattle chasers. Some of them cut wood for a living. Since the place as a whole seeks some ancient magical condition—perhaps it is 'Resumption' in Terran?—they sometimes fail of attending properly to illness. We have Scouts on-world to study and assist certain of the sub-sects here, for some declare that all Terrans are lapsed from propriety and they suffer Liadens for us not being declared Terran. The place is a danger to travelers: many of the halflings and older with sense seek to escape and thus fall prey to, well, the glitter of firegems or offers of short flights. Yet they are so strict with those striving for elsewhere that a single unpermissioned liaison of joy may ruin a life.

"The governors of this place *are* Terran but whole territories of it are subject to only the vaguest of regulation, Terrans having no master code and the subgroups scrupulously denying any other group's rules. Land rights, ownership, those things count. Otherwise? Otherwise even Scouts are careful.

"And so, you and I, we will stick to the port here, where there are patrols and common sense. I've told several Scout encampments of our coming, but I doubt they'll visit us, since they are perforce in the hinterlands. And the hinterlands are wild places indeed!

"So what we shall do, Jethri, is that your board will go to training mode now, and mine to live-connect. You may follow our path in screen three, and the planet's view of it on screen four. You may follow as closely as you like, but I must be the contact so that I can in fact be backup!"

· · · ✳ · · ·

The landing was, in fact, faultless, but the final ten minutes of descent having taken place in silence, Jethri had encountered a surfeit of thought. His book would come back. His fractin would come back as well, for what worth it might have, and when the book was back, the Scout's mission would be all but done.

Arin's work—his *father*'s work—that really wasn't being stolen from him in this trade, though still it felt a bit wrong to give up the reader. Really though it was a trade. It wasn't *really* being stolen if Tradedesk was working. By now the ship *Nubella* would be in place, the long slow transition from orbiting Vincza to orbiting the star begun.

He'd be a trader again, all Balanced. Uncle would do whatever it was that he did, Khat would be doing what she was doing, Freza would do what she was doing, Samay would continue her training and eventually become head of her line. . .and so his thoughts went that way again.

Thus, while carefully observing the landing all the way to gearlock on hotpad, when the switch to pad power went blue he told ter'Astin, "If I may use the commlinks, Scout, I believe now would be a good time for me to send a note—to a lady of my acquaintance. You understand."

The Scout bowed.

"Indeed, Second, I am hardly surprised. One must, after all, keep memory fresh if one wishes to send flowers again soon."

· · · ✳ · · ·

Jethri accounted it one of his life's great accomplishments that he no longer wished to hide his face from the sky when on-world, but in this place he wished he might hide it from the wind. As well as he knew the world was round and circled by three seas, from this viewpoint it was flatter than a chopping deck and wider than a star system, with a glaring yellow-white primary making him wonder why they were without shields. The wind rushed his ears while it tickled and tugged at his hair, throwing against him stinging bits of dust and grit. The part of his face unprotected felt hot from radiation.

Hands protecting eyes, they'd gone to a taxi, and hands over eyes emerged from it, staring into a row of bright white buildings stretching into the distance. The driver, paid handsomely ahead, agreed to wait, the vehicle quivering in the gusts that seemed never to stop. The buildings showed two flat sides and one slanted into the wind—the grit flew up and over them, building drifts of sand behind.

"Land is cheap here, the saying is, and so the locals rarely build up. The world is barely tectonic, and staying low is important. Out there—you can see a wall of wind-gatherers stealing power!"

Jethri hurried, no urge to study the things that engaged the Scout's attention. Nonetheless the Scout pointed, "Over there government buildings, and up that street, the single brown building is a workhouse for dissenters."

The white building in front of them showed a flat side, and gently came down fluffy sand fallen out of the airstream. There were words in Terran, and some few in Liaden on the building. "Field Relief," it said in Terran, and in Liaden the closest was "Alien Assistance Lounge."

Into that flat side they went, Jethri's "Woof!" of relief at entering bounced from walls of the white rock. They walked across a sandgrid, through cool air, onto a dark and shiny stone floor, the scout pointing—"There, first door."

Jethri'd guessed that, for a faintly familiar presence was behind that door, he was sure.

Within the first door was a small anteroom with a miniature sandgrid and beyond that was a carpeted hallway leading to a marked conference room.

Ter'Astin smiled at him and knocked on the door, entering before the answering "Come" was fully enunciated.

How was one to treat a person who held your property for ransom? Surely not a familiar greeting even if one's name was known, surely not . . .

The woman who stood at one end of the table was a pilot dressed as a pilot, a former Scout, he'd been told, and thus, like ter'Astin in his day work, free of major jewelry or cosmetics. If she had a scent it was the scent of her warm skin and not of a perfume. Her hair was pilot-cropped and indeed, he'd seen her recently in the distance at the side of Infreya chel'Gaiban and could have picked her out of a roomful of pilots because of that.

The bow he'd started, one of acknowledging a reciprocal trade opportunity, was largely blocked by ter'Astin's surprising—nay, shocking—bow somewhere between that of joy of seeing a comrade to delight in seeing a paramour, by his close approach to her corner of the table.

"Rand, we have come, as I promised we would. And as pleased as

I am to see you, we must be gone soon, for the taxi is counting time and my expense bill for this effort becomes more extensive by the moment."

Jethri finished his bow, gave over the idea of repeating his name to one who knew well who he was, and said, "I am here to trade what is mine for what is mine, Pilot."

Her bow to him was an echo of his.

"Yes, a straightforward trade, is it not? In that case, let us see what we speak of."

With main force Jethri resisted bowing again, instead pulling the reader from its pouch and placing it on the table before her. She reached into her pilot's jacket and casually flipped a fractin there, where it slid perilously close to the edge. She reached for the reader and seemed surprised with Jethri's speedy retrieval of it.

"I am lacking my book and my fractin, Pilot. The fractin there will not suffice."

He replaced the reader in the holster, waiting, feeling now some reciprocity as he considered where the fractin might be.

The Scout and yos'Belin exchanged glances and some flick of hand-talk Jethri couldn't catch, but the Scout backed him up saying, "The boy is all but Master Trader, Rand. And he is kin to the Uncle. Who knows what he sees that we don't? The lack of the book might concern him, as well."

She pursed her lips then, and reached into her jacket, in fact bringing forth the book and gently shoving it to him while he felt the fractin being active, declaring itself.

Jethri caught the book to him, flipped pages—complete, as far as he could see. It felt vaguely like it was welcoming his touch, but perhaps that was simply the leather surface, or the texture of the pages.

The pilot reached for an inner jacket pocket again, but Jethri shook his head Terran-style.

"Ma'am, not to be obtuse about this, but it is either in your left belt pouch or in a pocket under it."

Having the book, Jethri detached the whole of the *Envidaria*'s holster and placed it on the table while she stared hard at ter'Astin's blandness, then put the book in his side pocket.

"You did not say we were dealing with *dramliz*, my Scout," she said, her hand efficiently opening the pouch and giving over several fractins.

"One does not underestimate the Uncle's kin!" There was annoyance in ter'Astin's reply.

Jethri took them in his left hand, rubbed his right palm on them both and bowed as he returned the one that was not his while the one that was his thrummed in his hand.

"This one belongs to someone else."

She looked it over and was tucking it away as ter'Astin was bowing to both of them, saying, "That's done then. We shall . . ."

"Not yet," snapped yos'Belin, reaching for yet another pocket.

Jethri, in the midst of rubbing his fractin as he had as a youth, saw her motion and began to shift into one of Pen Rel's defense positions. The Scout saw him reacting, and by then her gun was out, coming up—

One or another of them had tangled their legs under the table— what Jethri saw were two struggling figures wrestling over a gun, bouncing first on the table and then on a chair top before falling . . .

Jethri's knife was in his hand but then there was a piercing whistle and a rush of pilot jackets, with someone saying, "Please step back, Trader, you'll not need your blade . . ."

· · · ✳ · · ·

The gun had gone off in the struggle, doing no more damage than putting a hole in the table, and now the room was clear of any but the Scout he knew, and another, this one Commander Anthara ter'Gasta Clan Idvantis.

"Has no one heard the noise, Commander?"

The Scout lounged, looking none the worse for the wear. Jethri sat several seats away, his fractin soothing, while ter'Gasta paced, periodically looking at the damaged table.

"You have luck, ter'Astin! Any of you could have been killed, or all of you. Why not wait until . . ."

"Commander, that's not how the flow of event went. Yos'Belin had not much to say, I had not much to say, and the trader was not full of words. The issue was to make the trade, which we'd done, and thus you have your pilferer in custody. Did you also come up with her backups?"

Jethri looked up, seeing sudden levels. Not an accidental recovery, the Scout had been planning this—

"She was the one who violated *Keravath* then?"

"Oh yes, Guest Pilot, she was. She also violated Scout Headquarters security before her sudden retirement."

Commander ter'Gasta bowed. "Several other areas beside the key cabinet were involved; she had on her even today a key I think is to the pharmacy."

Ter'Astin bowed a quick acknowledgment.

"In that case, we shall proceed. You have the information and the people you can find, and likely leads to several more. I have a mission to complete, and young Jethri here wishes to make up lost time with an admirer."

Jethri barely felt his face warm—and yes, he had several admirers he'd like to see . . .

"Your ship is on port. You're free to go as soon as we have our items of evidence to give to the security detail."

The Scout looked askance at the pacing Commander.

"The room is here, please take measurements and, if you need, I will speak and write a full debrief as we travel to *Elthoria*."

"Captain, thank you. You will debrief en route—that is a sensible approach since we already have the incident reports you sketched on your way in. The other evidence is what we need—your associate here has them at the moment, as I understand it."

Ter'Astin risked a glance at Jethri and then back to the commander.

"Unless Trader ven'Deelin is even more subtle than I believe, he carries his own property and no other at the moment."

Jethri sat forward in his chair, considering his book, his fractin, his knife . . .

"Do not be absurd, Trader," said the commander. "You'd hardly be able to overcome a pair of Scouts. Please return the items yos'Belin took from us and we will all move forward."

"No, ma'am. The Scout is correct. I own all that I carry. The Scout has said so and he tells the truth."

"All I want are the things that were being traded. So that would be the reader, the book, and the fractin."

Jethri stirred, began to measure the room.

"The reader, ma'am, was transferred to me by a friend, and it is a birthright. The book was given to me by my father, and it is a birthright. The fractin I selected for myself from a pile of fractins given to my father by my uncle for me to play with. It is a birthright."

"Trader," she began, but ter'Astin stood.

"This man has told you the truth. The book you demand is his and always was—he lent it to me for our interest, so that it might be copied. It was copied and it is now returned to him. The other items . . ."

"The reader—"

"Is mine."

"Surely it is Old Tech and must be . . ."

"It is Terran Tech, I say, and it is mine."

"I'll call in the support, Trader. Please put the items on the table. Begin with the fractin and I—"

"No, ma'am, that won't work now. The fractin will not permit itself to be hidden away from me. It will answer my call. These are mine, and I shall walk out of here with them."

The Scout bowed to Jethri, and addressed himself to the scowling scout.

"Commander, the agreement was that we would return the book. The reader never was ours and never was in our custody. The fractin I cannot answer for other than to say the trader is an honest man. If he says we shall not keep it, we must recall that he is kin of the Uncle."

"Captain ter'Astin, you are risking your rank. The Scouts need these items and we shall have them . . ."

"I have a key to *Keravath*," Jethri said, standing slowly and bowing to them both. "It is as much mine as the items you claim are yours belong to you. In fact, the more that you insist on these items, the more likely I am to own *Keravath* for a pleasure yacht. It is a pleasant enough vessel. . . ."

"What nonsense do you spout, Trader, give—"

The Scout—*his* Scout, ter'Astin, had slumped into a chair, mirth written across his face. "I tell you, Commander, the trader is only an honest man. We should likely forget about the fractin . . ."

Jethri stood, offering the commander no immediate attack but recalling the method Grig used to look larger and more dangerous . . . He put on the aspect he might have had when faced with chel'Gaibin's gun, and then he gently reached into his pocket and unshipped his weapon.

There was a slap on the table as he threw it down.

"There, Commander. I invoke this. Concede my ownership of my goods or concede *Keravath* and whatever else your group owns on this planet."

"What is this?" She looked at it in bewilderment, hesitating to close with it.

"In piket, Commander, it is a Scout's Progress," said ter'Astin. "Here, it is a Writ of Replevin. I do believe this hand is his."

Chapter Thirty

• • • • ✳ • • • •

Gobelyn's Market, **Clawswitts**

DYK WAS IN HIS GLORY. They'd had seventeen visitors in the last two days, including several for dinner, and knowing they wouldn't be lifting again for at least two more meant that he'd shopped fresh and was baking like mad. He'd even got to bake several very delicate cakes and a frijohn.

The rest of the crew wasn't in the same mood. Travit seemed not to like his air quite so thick, so Seeli was spending time with the room door closed and the dehumidifier running.

Grig had been to the commissioner's office three times and never yet in the door, since he was running side-guard to everyone else who was going there. The news hadn't reached outside yet, but it was Paitor who'd gone in with Khat to do the official depositions, and Cris was sucking all the trip files into usable units with the help of Zam and Mel when they weren't running here and there for Dyk.

Iza'd taken to sitting on the bridge doing optical survey, getting relief or backup from Mel and Zam, and Cris between the files stuff.

Seeli sat with the kid, mostly reading the fine print and the legal behind it after Paitor and Khat brought stuff back with them.

Therinfel's little trick of calling them thieves and scoundrels had been the chaos point for them: they had to keep their reputation straight and make sure the harassment stopped. It had been the Gobelyn name that got them in to see a couple of commissioners at once, and it had been Khat's good flight records that helped boost the idea that she wasn't a danger to anyone who wasn't a danger to themselves. To that end, they'd had witnesses come by the ship and record statements, and some of those had walked on down to the Commission office with Grig to redo them under oath.

All of the commission work was going to the hard side of this: getting the official harassment complaint certified by the commissioners to Terran worlds and run to the Liaden Trade Guild and Liaden Pilots Guild, too.

Time being what it was, Dyk got permission from Iza to wave three cakes and Niglund Boilt dinners in front of the air processor so the whole ship smelled good, and after about ten minutes he declared lunch come early since Paitor and Khat and Grig had another trip all set—the Liaden Trade Guild was sending someone to receive paperwork if they cared to tell the story in person.

The other thing they'd finally done was—to the same guild—sent Khat's personal letter of complaint against Bar Jan chel'Gaibin. Khat wasn't sure if she'd have to give a deposition there again, but she was willing to.

The big news for Dyk was the food, and Dyk drafted Mel and Zam, and convinced Seeli to come out with Travit for a few minutes anyhow, and they took over the big room, even Iza willing to come down from the bridge as long as Zam and Mel would switch off.

They'd barely sat down when the formal note came in on channels, for Khat. She was back in a moment, sat down heavy.

"The Guild has disallowed me a complaint against chel'Gaibin," she said, shaking her head, with Dyk making a nasty noise and Grig pointing a heavy look at Zam who'd picked up a port term not best used in a family with a Liaden trader in it.

"No need for it," she got through the buzz, "'cause word is he's been published as dead."

The buzz got louder, with Khat frowning over it and Dyk trying to pass everyone a second serving of whatever they'd had. "Not the news I was expecting. He wasn't old, and if he'd been polite I guess he was a looker. Just. I dunno. Just 'published as dead.'"

Paitor nodded, thoughtfully. "No use complaining, unless you got an unpaid invoice or something . . ."

"They said they'll send me something official for my files, but Delm Rinork calls all Balances even."

Khat scrunched her face. "That's hard. Can't blame his mother, I guess, for calling it even. Not sure—well, fair don't count, does it? Dead is dead."

The news meant that Mel and Zam wanted to know more about what had happened in the first place and by then Grig had mentioned, real low, and just once, that "published as dead" was something that might happen to someone who'd stepped outside of lines.

That brought things around to *melant'i* and how much could it really mean, which wasn't something—as Grig pointed out—as useless to consider as it once was.

About the time Dyk was cutting and serving the frijohns came another beep from the comm—

Mel recognized it and sang out, "All-trade channel!" and rose before Paitor's dessert got set back on the plate.

In a moment he could be heard saying a bad word and then saying something under his breath before his voice boomed out from local speakers.

"*Balrog*'s got news out on the trade channel and this is tagged special for us, attention Gobelyns!" There was a pause of about three beats and he said, "Oh wow!" And then—"You want me to feed it in?"

Iza was eating and shaking her head so Khat jumped in:

"First mate says play it, and then get back here before someone snatches away your food!"

A voice fed in, starting before Mel got back.

"Freza DeNobli here, from the tradeship *Balrog*, with news representing the Seventeen Worlds, and of interest to Combine key carriers and all traders. With the permission and encouragement of next of kin we have begun transmitting to multiple bounce points, including the operations channel of station Tradedesk, now in transitional orbit near Vincza, the full and complete authorized version of *Arin's Envidaria*. This release is . . ."

"That's Arin's secret stuff! What are they thinking? How can they . . ." Paitor's shock was palpable and he shook his head, saying to Mel suddenly, "You're recording, right? Full encouragement of next of kin?"

Freza was talking in the background, but Grig's chuckle grew into a guffaw so loud Seeli made him be quiet so he wouldn't wake Travit. Didn't much matter, his grin was big still.

"Jethri!" Grig said the name like it was prize. "Had to be Jethri because Uncle Yuri never did agree with it. And it wasn't really supposed to be secret, it just was going to be refined. But it *is* time! The boy's right."

Iza was the only one still listening to Freza's talk in the background, and Grig caught her eye, quelling his wide smile to a slight grin, and nodding in her direction.

"Jethri Gobelyn's gonna make his mark. Boy's the very spit of Arin, ain't he, Iza?"

Freza's voice was promising a repeat transmission daily for a ten-day when Iza pulled together a wan smile with a shake of her head, which turned into a nod.

"The very spit of Arin, Grig. The very spit."

Epilogue

Elthoria
The Young Gentleman Returns

"MOTHER."

He bowed, affection to close kin, which he felt was true enough, especially since he'd teared up like a kid the instant he stepped from the lock into *Elthoria* proper.

The tech on duty, one Kar Sin bel'Witnin had bowed greeting to one long missed, and added, "Trader Jethri, welcome back to us. The Master Trader sends that you will find her in her office."

"My thanks," he'd answered, voice husky. "And for the welcome, also."

Now, he found his voice even more clogged with emotion, so that he stopped, hoping she would understand all that he meant to convey.

"My son, you return, and make us whole again."

She rose from her chair, for he had not found her behind her desk, but in her favorite chair, hands folded on her knee—idle, when Norn ven'Deelin was never idle.

Rising, she extended her arms, and he came into her embrace, bending so that he might put his cheek against hers.

Her hug was stronger than he might have expected, her fingers a little cool, where they pressed his cheek.

"There!" she said softly, and patted his cheek gently as she moved away. "Come now, sit down and allow me the pleasure of beholding you. Shall you wish for wine?"

"If you please, ma'am."

She poured, which ought to have been his duty, as son and as junior in trade. He reckoned that he'd be back there soon enough, and this hour, for his homecoming, the usual mode was suspended.

He received the glass from her hand, and held it between his palms. She seated herself with a soft sigh, and raised her glass.

"To the joys of coming home."

"To the joys of homecoming," he answered, and they sipped, and smiled at each other.

"I must thank you, first, for transmitting such fascinating reading. It will require more study yet, but I believe *Elthoria* may be well placed to assist in the goals put forth in this *Envidaria*. Allow me to praise your father to you, my child, as a bold and forward-looking man, of which we see too few among us. His death diminishes us all, and yet his work—his work enriches us."

He felt the stupid tears rise again—well, it had been a series of tight Jumps from Hatalan, Scout ter'Astin being unwilling to leave the business there overlong. He was exhausted, was what it was.

"Yes," his mother said softly, and then, more briskly, "Allow me to hold you a moment more from your bed to satisfy a mother's natural concerns. Are your affairs now in Balance? Have you recovered those things which were reft from you?"

"Indeed, Mother, my affairs are perfectly aligned. I am in Balance with the universe."

"Is it so, indeed? How long do you suppose this happy state will endure?"

"Possibly another five minutes, ma'am."

"So long as that? Well, let us see."

Jethri had a sip of wine.

"Well! I will also allow you to know, briefly, my child, as you indulge me with another sip of wine—I allow you to know that Rantel pin'Aker has contacted me, suggesting that we might deal together profitably in the matter of a certain young trader. We shall find ourselves on the same port in only two Standard Months, and will meet then on the matter."

Jethri smiled. "The Master Trader was extremely taken with Tan Sim, ma'am. He said that, with proper nurturing, Tan Sim might well achieve Master."

"And well he might. But first, he must survive. Rantel and I will make that our first priority, with your leave, my son."

He grinned at her. "By all means."

"Excellent." The corner of her mouth twitched. "You must also be made aware, my child, that Tan Sim was not the only young trader with whom Rantel was taken."

"We might have shown well in comparison to others who were present. I think, ma'am, that Infreya chel'Gaibin may have . . . insulted Master Trader pin'Aker, and I was present when Bar Jan made a serious misstep with A'thodelm pin'Aker."

"Well, here's worthy gossip! You will tell me more—you will tell me every detail of this grand adventure, after you have rested and refreshed yourself."

"I have one more piece of news that ought to be given, and then I will seek my bed." He took a deep breath and met her eyes.

"Bar Jan chel'Gaibin challenged me to a duel on Port Chavvy . . ."

She met his eyes calmly.

"Did you kill your man, my son?"

"Yes, ma'am, I did, but not in the way you mean. In the simplest telling, I shattered his arm. He was alive and on his way to reconstructive surgery at the planetside hospital. I was at his bedside, to translate, when his mother came in, and . . . declared him dead. She emptied his pockets and . . . left him there." He took a breath, keeping his eyes on hers. "He had his valet with him."

He hesitated.

His mother entered the small gap in the conversation.

"*The Gazette* reports the death of Bar Jan chel'Gaibin, upon an outworld. It is said that Infreya will raise the next younger to nadelm, but there has been no announcement. It might do well to find from your partner if he has expectations in that direction."

"Yes, ma'am. I wrote Tan Sim about Bar Jan's death, since I . . . and I asked if he had any new plans."

"That is well done. But there was something else you wished to say on this topic, I think."

He took a breath. The Scout had warned him that, culturally, Bar Jan, being *cast out*, was even deader, if that was possible, than he would have been if Jethri had killed him outright. No proper Liaden would attempt to aid such a dead man. Jethri's answer to that was, in this, he was Terran. He had done what he had done, and the Scout had said no more.

Norn ven'Deelin, though, was a proper Liaden, and though he didn't see how he could have acted in any other way, knowing what he knew, and bearing the responsibility that . . .

"Speak, my child."

"Yes, ma'am. I made—in Bar Jan's name—I made an application to the Distressed Travelers Fund."

She considered him for a long moment before she inclined her head.

"We of the clans, we embrace our customs, and hold them close. This one . . ."

She sighed.

"When I was your age, young Jethri, I had a favorite who styled herself a philosopher. Ah, the discussions we had on the loftiest topics imaginable! I can only think that such heights lent a certain savor to the wine. In any wise, she took the position that what dies, when one is cast out, is one's *melant'i*. It is of course possible to survive without *melant'i* though it is a difficult state, and those who do live so are to be pitied."

She sipped her wine, and raised the glass in a soft salute. "You have done well, my child; your *melant'i* increases.

"Now!" She rose, and he did.

"Seek your bed; rest. You are not yet on the schedule. Come to me when you are perfectly rested and we will review your necessities in balance with the ship's and consider how best to honor both."

"Yes, ma'am," he said, and put his glass down on the table. He bowed then, affection for close kin, combined with obedience to a master.

She laughed, and waved her hand, sending him away.

Obedient, he turned—and at the door, he turned again.

"Mother."

"My child?"

"It's good," he said, "to be home."

· · · END · · ·